"One of the best historicals that I have ever read... a truly moving story. Beginning with Anya Seton's KATHERINE years ago, I have preferred to get my history that way first and then go back and read the academic sources. Worth brings the characters to life. In some instances her description is sheer poetry. Months after reading TOMORROW, thinking about the story still evokes a strong emotional response."

—Professor Tamara Kaupp, San Jacinto College (ret.)

"TOMORROW WE WILL KNOW reveals a richly detailed but little-known history of Christian Constantinople in 1453 as its few defenders battle the mighty Ottoman invaders for their right to exist. Sandra Worth's best work yet will have the reader tearing through the pages to see what happens next—to Constantinople, to Emperor Constantine, to his valiant military commander, and to Zoe, the woman who is their inspiration and they both love."

—Cheryl Bolen, New York Times and USA TODAY bestselling author of *My Lord Protector*

"From her heartfelt historical characters embroiled in a moving love triangle, to the escalating suspense of the final battle that will determine the fate of the Eastern Roman Empire, the author — with impeccable research and inspired storytelling — captivated this reader, bringing new excitement to the historical fiction genre."

—Robin Maxwell, *Los Angeles Times* and Amazon #1 bestselling author of *The Secret Diary of Anne Boleyn and Jane: The Woman Who Loved Tarzan*

"TOMORROW WE WILL KNOW is an utterly compelling novel, rich in detail, meticulously researched, and beautifully crafted. Sandra Worth's skill as historian and storyteller is evident on every page. Not to be missed."

—Tasha Alexander, New York Times Bestselling author of *Secrets of the Nile*

"In TOMORROW WE WILL KNOW Sandra Worth gives us a sweeping saga of empire and love. Worth deftly portrays the battles that will eventually bring down Constantinople—but more importantly she makes us care about the fall of that city through her vivid, flawed, and deeply human characters. By the time a blood-red eclipse of the moon brings fear to both rulers—Christian and Ottoman—leaving each to wonder whether it portends loss or victory for his side of the battle, readers will be biting their nails and holding their breaths.

—Sophie Perinot, author of *Médicis Daughter* and *The Sister Queens*

PRAISE FOR

Sandra Worth

Awards include

National Best Books Award: Best Historical Fiction of the Year
Moxie Films/Ray Bradbury/Francis Ford Coppola sponsored
New Century Writer Book Award
Romantic Times Magazine Reviewers Choice Award:
Best Historical Biography of the Year

"[A] gifted literary talent." —*Midwest Book Review*

"Worth… whets the appetite for history." —*The Knoxville News Sentinel*

"[A]n impressive feat." —*Publishers Weekly*

"Worth is an extremely gifted writer with the ability to immerse her readers into the lives and world of her characters." —*In The Library Reviews*

TITLES BY SANDRA WORTH

The Rose of York: Love & War
The Rose of York: Crown of Destiny
The Rose of York: Fall From Grace
Lady of the Roses
The King's Daughter
Pale Rose of England

Tomorrow We Will Know

A Novel of Imperial Constantinople 1453

Sandra Worth

WALTER BOOKS
SEATTLE

Map of Constantinople by Sandra Worth
Cover design by Richard Turylo
Editing: Tamara Kaupp, Ph.D.
Formatting: Polgarus Studio

First Edition February 2023

Library of Congress Control Number: 2023901439

Worth, Sandra
Tomorrow We Will Know / Sandra Worth. —1st ed.
Includes bibliographical references
ISBN 979-8-98660778-8

1. Europe—History—Fall of Constantinople. 1453—Fiction 2. Constantine XI Dragas Palaeologus, last Christian Emperor of Rome, 1449-1453—Fiction

Printed in the United States of America

This book is dedicated to my husband,
who was the light of my life and my inspiration.
In remembrance, always and forever.

"The Moving Finger writes; and, having writ
Moves on. Nor all thy Piety nor Wit
Shall lure it back to cancel half a Line,
Nor all thy Tears wash out a Word of it."

—*Rubaiyat of Omar Khayam*

Acknowledgments

I wish to thank medieval scholar and author Jean Truax, Ph.D., for her stalwart support throughout the writing of this book. She not only gave freely of her time to read the full manuscript, but she provided generous assistance with research and hard to find documents and was always willing to discuss the manuscript over coffees and lunches. I am indebted to Professor Tamara Kaupp for her careful attention to the editing of the manuscript, and to my former agent, Jennifer Weltz of the Jean Naggar Literary Agency, for believing in me and this book. Her insights were invaluable. My friend, author Linda Shuler, a writer of exceptional talent, is another who gave generously of her time and assistance, as did author Cheryl Bolen who also read the manuscript and helped in every way possible. Last but never least, I wish to acknowledge the contributions of my beloved husband, Walter, who took me everywhere I needed to go, to see everything I needed to see, and who was always patiently at my side, giving unstintingly of his love and support. I could not have done it without him. I only wish he could have been here to read the book.

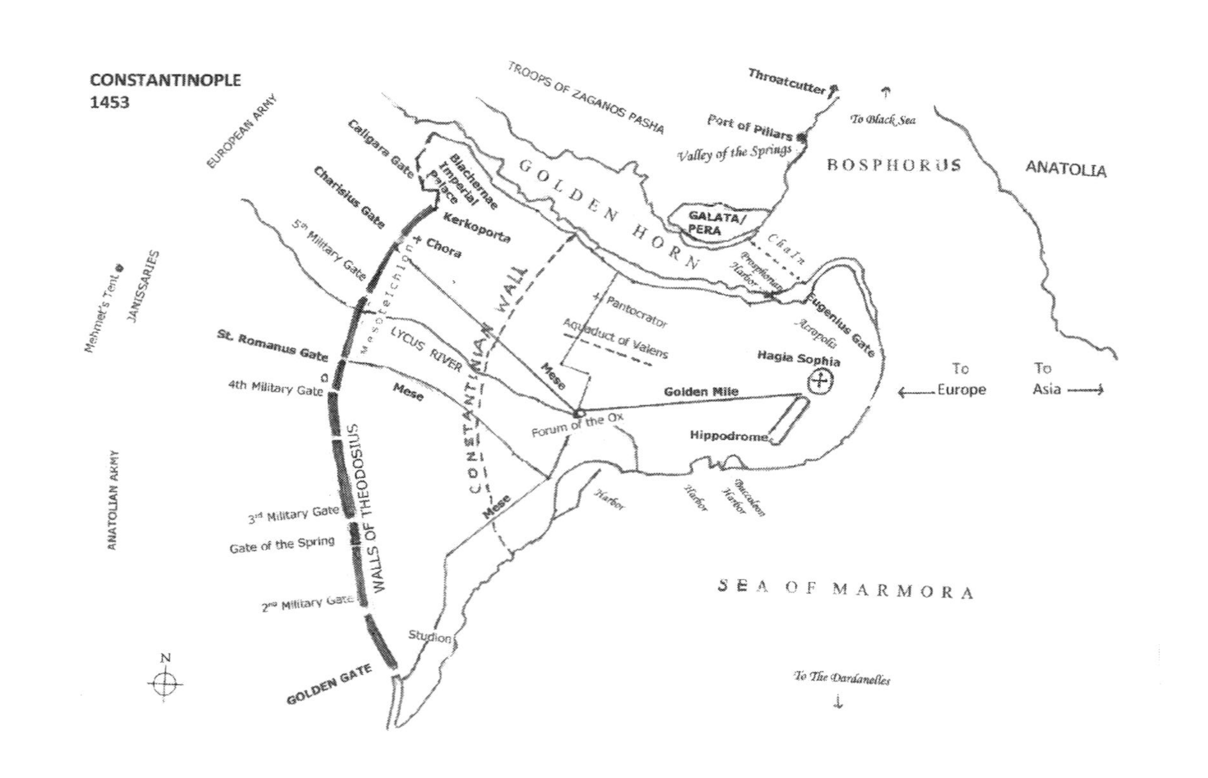

CONSTANTINOPLE
1453
EUROPEAN ARMY
TROOPS OF ZAGANOS PASHA
Throatcutter
Port of Pillars
Valley of the Springs
To Black Sea
BOSPHORUS
ANATOLIA
GOLDEN HORN
GALATA/
PERA
Chain
Prosphorian Harbor
Caligara Gate
Blachernae Imperial Palace
Charisius Gate
Kerkoporta
Chora
5th Military Gate
Mesoteichion
St. Romanus Gate
LYCUS RIVER
CONSTANTINIAN WALL
Pantocrator
Aqueduct of Valens
Eugenius Gate
Acropolis
Hagia Sophia
To Europe
To Asia
Mehmet's Tent
JANISSARIES
4th Military Gate
Mese
Golden Mile
Forum of the Ox
Hippodrome
WALLS OF THEODOSIUS
ANATOLIAN ARMY
3rd Military Gate
Gate of the Spring
Harbor
Harbor
Buccoleon Harbor
SEA OF MARMORA
2nd Military Gate
Studion
N
GOLDEN GATE
To The Dardanelles

Tomorrow We Will Know

Prologue

MISTRA, GREECE
JANUARY 1444

"Zoe, Zoe!"

The eleven-year-old girl tore down the hillside, ignoring her nurse's cries. The January wind blew strong, but it was warm and bore the scent of winter flowers.

"Zoe! You need to braid your hair!" her nurse pleaded. "It isn't seemly—" Her voice faded into the wind.

Zoe paid her no heed. Her mind, her heart, and her feet were focused on one thing and one thing only: *Prince Constantine was back from Thrace!*

She caught sight of his tall figure at the gate, illuminated by sunlight so sharp and bright that he seemed encased in shards of glass. "Constans, Constans!" she cried, calling him by his nickname. Prince Constantine of Mistra might be much older and the heir apparent to the throne of Eastern Rome, but there was no ceremony between them.

Amid the movement of men and the neighing of horses, Prince Constantine turned. A wide smile brightened his handsome face as he watched Zoe fly down the steep slope, sure-footed as a mountain goat, her auburn hair flowing behind her like a banner. It was a familiar sight upon his homecomings and one dear to his heart, for he had no children of his own and little chance of them. His first wife had died young of the plague, and his second in childbirth. He had never married again.

He opened his arms wide to her. A gangly child and scrawny as a waif, Zoe was not beautiful in the classical sense, but there was a magic about her. She was spirited, but sweet; her face was angular, but interesting; and her features, though irregular, held the eye. An artist might have preferred her nose a trifle shorter, but it was thin and well-shaped. Along with a generous mouth and disarming smile, she had the most beautiful eyes: huge, honey-brown, and thickly lashed, they sparkled like jewels in her little face. Such an arresting contrast did they make with her auburn hair that one could be forgiven for staring.

The first time Constantine had seen Zoe, she was a bewildered six-year-old child standing alone on the stone pier, watching her parents sail away to Constantinople without her. The Grand Duke and Duchess Lucas and Daphne Notaras had taken her two sisters with them but left Zoe behind. Bathed in the glow of sunrise, the poignant little figure, so forlorn and vulnerable, had tugged at his heart. At the same time, he was swept with admiration. While tears stood in her eyes and panic was written on her face, she held her head high and didn't vent her anguish. He recalled the thought that came to him: *I must protect her.* As he came to know the child, he realized she also had a fine mind, for many times she surprised him with observations strangely worldly in one so young.

At this moment there was no sadness about Zoe, and no out-of-place wisdom, only a child's bubbling joy that made him forget his troubles. She ran into his open arms, giggling with delight. "Constans, what took you so long? I thought you'd never come!" She looked up at him accusingly.

"I tried, Zoe, believe me, I did try—" he said, scooping her up into his powerful arms.

"Put me down!" she cried, kicking. "I'm not a child anymore. I'm a lady!"

Laughing, Constantine let her go. "You do not behave much like one, do you?"

"Indeed, she does not, my prince!" panted her old nurse, closing in on her charge, picking her steps carefully on the steep, stony path. Beads of perspiration glistened on her brow. "She is a naughty child, a handful! She ran off before I could braid her hair. You look like a milkmaid, Zoe," she scolded.

"A charming milkmaid," Prince Constantine laughed.

Zoe gave her nurse a triumphant smile. Turning to Prince Constantine, she extended her hand to the new hero of Eastern Rome who had recently driven out the Latin occupiers of Greece and rebuilt the crumbling Hexamilion Wall that protected the Peloponnese from their enemy, the mighty Ottomans. No one was as brave as Prince Constantine or as noble.

"Who says you are not a lady?" Prince Constantine grinned, obliging the child by kissing her hand. "You are the proudest lady in all Christendom, my little Zoe."

Zoe had no chance to savor Constantine's compliment, for a sudden scattering of dust and crunching of boots on the gravel path announced the arrival of Constantine's councilor, George Phrantzes, and his entourage. Tall, with intense brown eyes and a taciturn demeanor, he strode up to Constantine.

As always Zoe registered a vague sense of confusion in his presence. With his curly beard and high forehead, Phrantzes bore a startling resemblance to the broken bust of a stern Roman emperor in the palace hall that had always intimidated her. Nor did she know how to feel about him. He was one of Constantine's closest friends and her father's dedicated enemy.

"How go matters at Mistra in my absence?" Prince Constantine inquired, embracing his councilor warmly.

A hesitation. "Well enough, I suppose, my prince," Phrantzes said, "though the Duke of Athens has appealed to his former lord and master, Sultan Murad, for help to recover the duchy that you seized from him, and the Venetians have demanded the return of their colony of Vitrinitza." He stole a glance at the Prince of Mistra from beneath his grizzled eyebrows.

Constantine gave a hearty chuckle. "I know you do not approve of my campaign to evict our foreign invaders and take back our lands, Phrantzes, but behold, I return victorious yet again!" As his men cheered, Constantine rested a gentle hand on Phrantzes's shoulder. "Have no fear, my friend, all is—" He broke off, his attention diverted by a commotion at the city gates.

A rider galloped up the hill, horse's hooves clattering, helmet glinting, a hawk circling him as he rode. He dropped from his saddle, his scarlet cloak whipping around him, the two-headed Roman eagle on his breastplates flashing in the sun, one head looking East, the other West, even though western Rome was long gone.

A messenger. Shielding his eyes from the sun, Constantine watched him approach untroubled, for the day was sunny and unburdened by a sense of threat. But when he drew close enough for Constantine to take in his grim expression, realization came. His royal brother, Emperor John, had sent him, and when had good news ever come from Constantinople?

The messenger made his salutation in the Roman manner, with a sharp click of the heels and a fist thump to the breast. "My Prince," he said. "I bear tidings of great import from your gracious brother, His Serene Majesty Emperor John VIII, concerning events at the Ottoman court."

Urgently he related the shocking news. Constantine listened intently, unsure what to make of it. All at once shrieks filled the air, and the circling hawk swooped down so close over the man that the shadow of its serrated wingtips darkened his face. Constantine followed his fearful gaze to the city gates where the hawk had settled, gripping in its claws the emblem of the Roman eagle.

An omen?

He was less inclined to superstition than other men, yet a frown touched his brow, for he was keenly aware of the hand of fortune in human affairs. Recovering, he turned his attention to the messenger awaiting his response. The tidings were momentous, but what did they bode for Rome?

Maybe everything. Maybe nothing. Only time would tell.

The touch of a soft warm hand on his own scattered his gloomy thoughts. He looked down.

Young Zoe was gazing up at him with her doe eyes. "Have no fear, Constans," the child said. "God is on our side."

The Eastern Roman Empire 1448-1453

One

Mistra, Greece

"Zoe, stop twisting your neck!"

"Why do you think she has come, Eirene?" Zoe said, straining to see out the palace window where a litter with the imperial emblem of the black and gold double-headed eagle of Eastern Rome wound up the steep green slope of Mount Taygetos. "Something must have happened!"

As a gray hound watched in a corner, Eirene piled Zoe's rich red hair on top of her head. She pinned it out of the way and followed Zoe's gaze to the window where the picturesque town of Mistra nestled on the hillside. Orange tile roofs, olive groves, and cypresses sparkled in the August sun. "Perhaps the Empress Helena comes to visit her son. She hasn't seen him in a while. Now, be still."

Starting below Zoe's bosom, Eirene wound a golden cord around her midriff and smoothed the folds of the silk tunica that was styled in the fashion of ancient Rome. The only concession to modernity lay in the sleeves, which were long and sewn with jewels at the cuffs. She stepped back to assess her handiwork and smiled.

Tall, auburn-haired, and delicate as a woodland sprite, Zoe dazzled in coral. She herself was pretty enough with her chestnut hair and high cheekbones, but Zoe had a special allure. Eirene might have been resentful if she didn't love her like a sister. Wrong analogy, she amended inwardly, thinking of Zoe's sister, Maria, who resented her. Turning to the jewel casket, she withdrew a massive necklace worked in gold and set with turquoise pendants.

"The *maniakis* is heavy. Hold it while I secure the clasp."

With her eyes riveted on the litter, Zoe absently balanced the wide gold collar over the cowl neckline of her gown. "Constantinople is too far for the Empress Helena to come just to see her son," she said anxiously.

"Patience, Zoe. If she brings news, I daresay we'll know soon enough," Eirene replied. She unpinned Zoe's hair and fire shot down her back.

Zoe took a seat at her dressing table and examined her face in the mirror. Depending on the hour of day, her auburn hair took on highlights of flame or dark copper, but today it was lifeless, and she was pale. She reached for a vial of pomegranate dye and smoothed the ointment along her cheekbones. Leaning into the mirror, she darkened the brows that arched over her sparkling honey-brown eyes with a dab of charred apricot pit mixed with linseed oil. She laid down the brush. It was hopeless—and she had so wanted to look her best for the empress's welcome feast, and the dancing, sensuous music, and merriment. She sat listlessly as Eirene brushed her hair with a double set of boar brushes, but when she moved to sweep it up into curls, Zoe stayed her hand. "Leave it down."

Eirene met her eyes in the mirror. "I'm no fool, Zoe. That he admires your hair is no reason to flaunt yourself to him. He's going to be emperor one day. He needs to marry for an alliance against the Ottomans. Rich as you are, you can't give him ships and men." Eirene's position as kinswoman, friend, and lady-in-waiting gave her leave to speak freely, for she was a Notaras herself, albeit a poor Notaras, only distantly related to Zoe's illustrious branch.

"If he fell in love with me, it wouldn't matter. Emperor Justinian married Theodora, and she was a circus whore and brought him nothing," Zoe bristled. More gently, she said, "I won't give up, Eirene. Neither should you."

Zoe didn't miss the sudden hesitation in Eirene's nimble fingers as she braided her thick locks with silk ribbons. Her cousin was a widow at nineteen. Her father had died fighting the Ottomans at the Battle of the Hexamilion Wall, and his death had left her family penniless. At fifteen she had wed a man willing to take her without a dowry, but he was a drunkard who beat her mercilessly. If he hadn't lost his footing and fallen into the sea weaving his drunken way home one dark night, he would have killed her someday.

"One marriage is enough for me. All I need is a dog, Zoe," Eirene said. "I have neither the desire nor the dowry to—"

"Oh, a dowry is no problem!" Zoe broke in, ignoring her protest. "My father has enough money for both of us— When I'm empress, I'll see to it that you wed the man of your choice, whether he wants to, or not!"

Despite herself, Eirene laughed. She loved this irrepressible, generous-hearted girl who was so aptly named after a sprite in the Garden of Hesperides. Drawing Zoe's braid to the side, she pinned a jeweled cap of golden mesh on her head and arranged its dangling pearls over her brow, but as she looked up, her gaze fell on Prince Constantine's tall glittering figure awaiting his mother on the palace steps. Gravely, she said, "Be wary what you wish for, Zoe."

Zoe followed her gaze. Her prayers for Prince Constantine's love were always followed by a wish for his happiness. But tragedy shadowed him, and he seemed to Zoe a lonely figure. Maybe it was loneliness that had made him reach out to her when she was little. But whatever its source, she had responded by taking him into her heart with a love that grew deeper with every passing year.

Eirene spoke again. "There is only grief down this road."

"I know," Zoe sighed, moving to the window. "But he can't marry someone else, Eirene. I love him too much."

Eirene came to her side. "Then we should pray he is never emperor."

Zoe knew she meant the prophecy. Instinctively she opened her mouth to protest that prophecy was a useless art—that sometimes they came true, and sometimes they didn't—that only fools put their trust in them. But no words came, for this was no ordinary prophecy. This troubled even her. It had been around for centuries, as if waiting for Prince Constantine to be born.

As Prince Constantine stood before the palace steps watching his mother's gilded palanquin weave its way up the steep green slopes of Mount Taygetos, he was filled with unease. Even from the distance, her drooping black figure spoke of ill tidings. What had prompted her to undertake the dangerous journey across the sea from Constantinople to the Vale of Sparta? Was she ill? Had she come to bid him farewell? It had to happen one day, of course. She was old; almost seventy. It was natural that a mother die before her son, but he had always dreaded the day. She was his friend, his most cherished advisor, his wisest counselor, the one he could pour his heart to without shame or reprimand. How would he make his way without her?

The litter-bearers came to a halt. Forcing a smile, he approached.

His mother, a Slavic princess by birth, had taken vows after his father's death, but she was not clad in the nun's garb this day. She wore widow's weeds: a flowing black veil, a black silk tunica styled in the Roman fashion, and a black velvet cloak clasped at the throat by a diamond brooch. The black attire accentuated the white of her hair, the vivid blue of her eyes, and the marble paleness of her complexion. He kissed her hand and lifted his gaze to the lined face that still held vestiges of the beauty she had been in her youth.

"Welcome, *Mana mou,"* Constantine said, as the litter bearers lowered her palanquin.

Helena gazed at her son, relieved to find him looking better than when she last saw him. It was a year after the Battle of the Hexamilion Wall, and the toll that his defeat had exacted was still evident then. "My beloved son, Mistra suits you well."

Her voice held an unsteady note. Ever attuned to his mother, he was instantly alert. "What is it, *Mana mou*? What has happened?"

"I'll tell you when we are alone." She took the hand he offered and climbed out with effort.

In his privy chamber, Constantine helped his mother into a one-armed reclining couch that still had some of its mosaic inlay. She relaxed into it and dabbed at her eyes. "Your brother Theodore is dead."

Constantine let himself down heavily into a chair. "How?"

"Canker." She made the sign of the cross.

"Poor Theodore."

"He was confused and troublesome most of his life, but I blame myself," Empress Helena murmured. "There is much I shouldn't have said… And much I left unsaid."

"Loss and regret always go hand in hand," Constantine replied quietly. Both his brides, Theodora and Caterina, had died within two years of marriage. The double strokes of death following so close on one another had left him too scarred to wed again. His single life was mostly free from fear of loss, pain, and regret, and in the main he was content.

Helena watched him. Of the seven sons she had birthed for her husband Emperor Emmanuel, she had buried three. Constantine was her fourth-born in a brood that had proved ambitious and meddlesome. But he had been a joy to her from birth. He was not only the most loving and princely of her boys, but the most charming, with twinkling hazel eyes and a ready smile quick to show his dimples. Her gaze went to his sandy hair, now lightly dusted with silver at the temples. "How old are you, Constans? I forget."

He smiled. "Forty-three. I wish I could forget."

"You look younger."

A servant brought wine and sweetmeats. As they sipped the wine and nibbled the *apotki*, Helena's thoughts returned to her brood. Only with John and Constantine was she close, and it grieved her to know that destiny had not been kind to either one. Loss, failure, and disappointment had been their portion. Of the two, John had suffered most. Ever since he'd mounted the throne, he'd known naught but care, and it had left him a wounded man. His adored empress, Maria of Trebizond, had died of the plague, and he had no children. Except for Constantine, his brothers had spent their time quarrelling with one another in the Peloponnese or intriguing against him in Thrace. The people, too, grumbled against him. Now he was ailing. She saw him in her mind's eye as he had been in Constantinople: bed-ridden, exasperated, weary, mulling the news of his brother's death. "Theodore dreamed of the throne, but he died too soon. Before me," John had rasped. Struggling up in bed, he'd thrown aside the faded silken covers. "It was ambition that killed him, not canker. If he hadn't been so obsessed with schemes to be emperor, he would still live."

"All brothers fight when the prize is a throne," Empress Helena had sighed.

"I suppose I should be grateful Theodore didn't ally with Sultan Murad and march on Constantinople, like Demetri," he said in a wounded tone, referring to his youngest brother.

Empress Helena had handed John his cane and watched as he dragged himself to the window, wincing with every step. Servants ran to assist him, but he waved them away. Once he had been a golden-haired youth who'd dazzled all who beheld his handsome face. Now he was just another white-haired, frail, crochety old man.

For a long while, John had stood silently, looking out. Helena knew what held his gaze. The scene outside the palace of Blachernae was always the same. Men always repaired the land walls, moved stones, dug the ground and mixed mortar. Their donkeys always waited patiently.

"It is eight years since I returned from Italy, Mother," John said, making his way back to bed. "Eight long, thankless years."

His words swept Helena like a bleak wind. John had gone to Florence seeking Western help against the Ottoman Turks for the invasion all knew was coming. But the papacy had refused to support him unless the Orthodox church acknowledged full obedience to Rome. Desperate for the aid, John had signed the agreement. Two years later he'd returned to Constantinople with nothing but empty promises and an accord that had split his people into those who were pro- and against-union with Rome. Now the Latin church of the west kept attaching more conditions, and all John could do was repair the walls.

"At least you have one brother you can rely on. Constans has always supported you," she said.

"Constans is the one I would have succeed me as emperor. He is pragmatic. And a warrior if it comes to that. He will do the right thing… God knows, Mother, I have tried to keep the peace by forbearance and tact. I have tried to prepare for the future—" A sudden spasm of coughing knocked the breath from his body. Helena rushed to his side and held a cup of water to his lips.

"We are getting old, Mother," John had sputtered, spilling more than he swallowed.

She propped him up against the pillows and made him comfortable. Laboring for breath, he turned his gaze back toward the window. Helena sat down on the edge of the bed and took his hand with a troubled heart. His skin was wrinkled, almost as wrinkled as her own, and illness had enfeebled his grip, as age had done hers. She let her eyes follow the direction of his gaze. Aye, he had prudently spent every bezant he could spare on repairing the great walls of the city, that they might be ready for the inevitable onslaught. He had done what he could. But would it be enough?

Helena returned to the present with a jolt and blinked the memories gone. She put a hand out to Constantine, and he came and joined her on the couch. But when he slipped his arm around his mother's shoulders, he winced; it was as if he held a fragile little bird. "I know not how hard it is to bury a child, *Mana mou,* but I dread losing you." He took her hand to his lips and imparted a kiss.

"You always were my favorite son," she smiled.

"And you, my favorite mother."

Helena laughed. She rested her head on his shoulder and they sat quietly together for a time before she pulled away. "There is something I must tell you before it's too late, Constans. Something that weighs on me… about the news you received in Mistra after you rebuilt the Hexamilion Wall."

Constantine tensed. "The murders of Sultan Murad's son, Aladdin, and his babes that changed the Ottoman succession."

"Only one person stood to benefit from the crime," she said, her eyes meeting his.

"But *Mana mou,* Mehmet couldn't have done it. He was only eleven at the time."

Helena had wrestled with that question herself. But the royal sons of Ottoman sultans were half-brothers, born of different mothers. They viewed one another more as rivals for the Ottoman throne than family. Both Mehmet's father and grandfather had gained their throne by civil war, though Mehmet's father had always chosen peace over war, if given a choice. Helena thought of Mehmet's oldest brother, Ahmed, who had died suddenly under mysterious circumstances at nineteen. There had been talk of murder then, too. This, however, was different. Aladdin and his babes had died a bloody death as they'd slept in their beds. If it was Sultan Murad's youngest son, Mehmet, clearing his way to the throne, it showed a frightening ruthlessness. Helena felt a moment's grief for his poor father. Murad was a good man. He had been a friend to her husband.

"Mehmet has a prodigious intellect and is far older than his years …" she said thoughtfully. "Someone could have committed the murders at his behest. No doubt someone who would ascend with him…. We will never know the truth. What we do know is Mehmet has immense ambition and counted for nothing while his two brothers lived. Now he will be sultan."

She reached out and laid a gentle hand on his. "You would do well not to underestimate him, my son."

Constantine's celebratory banquet for his mother that evening was subdued. Black pennants were hoisted on the walls, and the palace windows were draped with mourning cloth. Two weeks later, on a rainy day in August after the three Feasts of the Savior, the Dowager Empress Helena bid him farewell at the city gate.

"I cannot bear to let you go, *Mana mou.* It seems to me that you have only just arrived," Constantine said anxiously.

"John is very ill, Constans. I must not leave him alone long."

Blue eyes met hazel. If Constantine knew why she really had to hurry back to Constantinople, he gave no indication. His brother Demetrios stood ready in Thrace with an army at his back, waiting for John to die so he could seize the throne. And only she could stop him.

Two

His mother's departure left the usual void in Constantine's heart, but he filled it with work. The months rolled by as they always did, burdened with running the principality. As ruler of the Peloponnese, all authority rested in him, and nothing could be done without his directive. He was the sole source of law and order, and every official document required his signature. As a result, from morning until late in the day, a stream of ministers, clergy, scholars and petitioners waited to put their concerns before him.

Zoe missed him.

In her bedchamber, unable to sleep, she rose and made her way to the window seat. It had been three months since the court went into mourning for Prince Theodore, and she scarcely saw Constantine anymore, even at a distance. She longed for his company. He had been both a father and a brother to her growing up—closer than her own three brothers whom she barely knew. His absence struck deep.

At least he was taking the news of his brother's death in stride. "God gives life, and takes it away in His own time, child," he'd replied when she had conveyed her condolences. He hadn't stopped calling her "child" though she would be sixteen in January. Somehow, she had to make him see her differently. Had to make him see that she had reached marriageable age...

If only she could ask her mother's advice about love, she thought. Hugging her knees, she gazed at the stars. But her mother would never help, even if she were in Mistra. Daphne Notaras was a great beauty of royal blood, but she'd been a cold, aloof presence as far back as Zoe could remember. She couldn't recall her mother ever taking her hand when she was a child, or giving her a kiss, or even answering any of her little questions. She had simply ignored her. Once, when she was four, she'd learned to spell a long and difficult word. Filled with pride, she had run to recite it to her mother, but her mother had never looked up from her embroidery. After standing awkwardly for what seemed an eternity awaiting an acknowledgment that never came, Zoe had left, dejected, silent tears rolling down her cheeks, convinced she had disappointed her mother in some unknowable, unforgiveable way and there was nothing she could do to win her love.

Assailed by a wave of loneliness, Zoe glanced at her cousin. Eirene's dark head was barely visible above the covers, and as always, she slept soundly. "What is your secret, Eirene?" Zoe had asked one day. "A tranquil heart," Eirene had replied. "How do you get that?" Zoe had inquired. "By not wanting what you can't have," Eirene had said pointedly.

Overcome with a need for the peace and beauty of her favorite church, the tiny Cathedral of St. Demetrios, Zoe tiptoed to her cloak and gauzy veil hanging on a peg on the wall. She always found comfort there, whether in the garden amid the twittering birds, or inside, surrounded by its mysterious murals and flickering candles.

A dog whined softly in greeting as she approached the chamber door. "If you wish to come with me, Pegasus, you must be very quiet," she whispered to the hound Eirene had rescued from the streets. As if he understood, Pegasus rose to his feet and followed her out silently.

The cathedral was an inky shadow on the hill below, its domed, red-tiled roofs a blur in the dimness. In a cobblestone alleyway, Zoe passed a servant bearing a jug of water on her head from her trek to the well and an Orthodox priest in a tall black hat who murmured a blessing. A rooster crowed, announcing dawn, and the streets in the lower city came alive with barking dogs and the whirring wheels of merchants carting wares to market. She creaked open the garden gate to St. Demetrios and was met with the lovely sound of trickling water. The wind rustled the leaves, and sheep bells tinkled in the distance. A nun watering a pot of pink nasturtiums threw her a smile.

Zoe followed the worn flagstone walkway past the fountain into the cloister, and a flock of doves flew off with a wild flapping of wings at the sight of Pegasus. When she sat down on the low stone wall that bordered the hillside, she could see out over a drop of a thousand feet and up to the glorious ring of seven snow-capped mountains that surrounded the Vale of Sparta. These living, unscalable walls of stone had guarded Sparta like centurions since the beginning of time, protecting them from invaders. A profusion of orange and lemon trees scented the air. She inhaled deeply. There was such beauty here, such serenity. Such peace—

"A sight for sore eyes," said a deep-timbered voice, interrupting her reverie.

Constantine. Her pulse thundering in her ears, she rose to her feet, not realizing she moved.

"Prince Constantine—" Her gaze swept his handsome face and his proud, familiar stance that emphasized the set of his powerful shoulders and the force of his thighs. Clad in a short black tunic and black boots, he wore no adornment except a golden sash at his waist, and though he was pale, she thought he had never looked more handsome.

"Stay as you are, I pray you," he said. "If I were a carver, Zoe, I would capture this moment in marble." Indeed, when he'd stepped through the archway, he had caught Zoe in profile, an expression of mysterious melancholy on her face. In her blue cloak, with her gray hound at her feet and her auburn hair flowing loose down her back beneath a sheer veil, she looked almost ethereal. So might the mythical Zoe have looked in the garden of Hesperides if the Grecian goddess had been brought back to life amid the orange trees of Mistra.

He took a seat beside her on the low wall. Zoe dropped her lids to hide her emotion. He had come without his usual entourage and they were alone except for the occasional priest moving about quietly. Such a thing had not happened in years. She stole a glance at him. He was still bronzed by the sun, though the days of summer were long past, and the dawn lent his sandy hair a golden halo, making him seem younger than in the palace halls. Her gaze moving over his brow touched on his strong jaw that was defined by a closely cropped strap of beard and rested on the scar across his cheek from the battle of the Hexamilion Wall. It held a special place in her heart; he had almost died there, and it meant God had spared him for her.

He turned and smiled at her. Her breath caught. She lowered her gaze in confusion and saw that their knees almost touched. She had never been so close to him before, except as a child when he used to sweep her up into his arms.

"The Vale of Sparta," he murmured, reverence in his tone, his dimples flashing as he spoke. "It was here in Mycenaean days that Helen, the loveliest of the queens of history, lived until she eloped to Troy with Paris. And here that Leonidas, King of the Spartans was born, who saved Greece from the Persians…"

As she listened to his melodious voice, memory rolled back the years, and she heard her old nurse calling to her as she ran to greet him at the city gate. Theirs had been a special relationship, filled with chatter and hugs. She would confide everything that had happened since she'd last seen him, and he would comfort her, laugh with her, and tell her about his ministers and the silly things they had done. But everything changed when she grew up and he became burdened by his duties.

"—when I come here, I think of them, the ancients," he was saying. "How brave they were. What we owe them… You are too young to look back, so I doubt you understand why the past should matter so much to me, child."

Zoe leapt to her feet. "I am not a child!" she cried before she could stop herself. "I am a grown woman old enough to wed!" A monk threw her a startled look as he passed.

For a moment, Constantine seemed at a loss. Then he took her hand and drew her gently down beside him. "So you are. Forgive me."

Zoe felt her cheeks flame. The touch of his hand scorched her and made her feel out of control. She forced herself to look up, and their eyes met.

Placing a hand under her chin, Constantine tilted her face up to him. "You have the most beautiful eyes, Zoe. They are an unusual shade of brown. Like topaz." He had always admired her eyes, but he had never looked closely before to see the gold and smoky flecks that lit their depths.

Zoe was flooded with joy though his tone was as casual as a dye maker selecting the hue he would mix for the day. She flashed him a radiant smile.

For a moment, Constantine lost his train of thought. Suddenly curious, he asked, "What brings you here, Zoe? What do you seek?"

Zoe looked around at the magnificence that surrounded them. "To me it seems the place where God Himself resides. I have long felt that He lives here and not in Constantinople, as the bishops claim."

Constantine chuckled. "The bishops might find heresy in your words."

"I will allow them their opinion, if they will allow me mine," she smiled.

Constantine threw his head back and pealed with laughter. Zoe watched him with soft eyes. For a time, they sat together in peaceful harmony.

"I regret you have grown up, Zoe," he said at length. "Youth is a blessing." He dropped her hand, and Zoe felt as if he'd splashed cold water on her. She looked at him, wishing he had not released it; hurt that he wouldn't want to hold it forever, as she did with his.

"Youth is also a curse," she bristled.

"You are right, Zoe. We make mistakes in youth that we regret in old age. But how to know what a mistake is and what is not… That requires wisdom." His voice drifted off and a faraway look came into his eyes. Zoe knew that he was thinking of the Hexamilion Wall. As soon as he'd rebuilt it, the enemy had demolished it. The carnage had been fierce. Thousands had died that day and tens of thousands taken into slavery. Worse, Rome lost the goodwill of Venice and Genoa who might have served as allies against the sultan.

"Nurse used to say that wisdom is learned by making mistakes," she offered, to allay his guilt.

He looked at her in surprise. "Nurse also said you were a handful," he said lightly. "But for me, you have always been a joy, chi—my young lady."

His words thrilled Zoe. Her eyes strayed to his lips. Time stood still and her entire being filled with waiting. *If only—*

"Prince Constantine!" came a man's urgent voice.

Zoe turned. George Phrantzes, Constantine's chancellor, was striding along the colonnaded walkway. Beneath his heavy brows, Phrantzes's dark eyes held a strange light. Something in his demeanor brought Constantine to his feet. From nowhere, a cluster of monks and priests appeared on the balcony.

"Your gracious cousin Theo Palaeologus has arrived from Constantinople, my prince—" Phrantzes stood aside to reveal a gray-eyed man in his forties. In his hands he held a velvet cushion bearing the imperial crown.

The air filled with gasps as he knelt before Constantine.

"I am sent by your lady mother, Dowager Empress Helena, with sorrowful tidings," Theo Palaeologus said. "His Imperial Majesty John VIII, by God's grace Emperor of the Romans, is dead." Murmurs and a rustle of movement went through the crowd as everyone made the sign of the cross.

"The dowager empress bids me inform you that as his regent, she carries out Emperor John's deathbed wish," he continued. "From among your brothers, she chooses you, her eldest surviving son, to rule the Roman Empire."

Constantine stared at the crown. For a bare instant he didn't know what he felt: numbness perhaps, and sorrow that his brother, John, was dead. Then all hesitation vanished, swept away by a tide of overwhelming, incredulous joy and an exultation that made the blood sing in his veins. All his life he had tirelessly prepared himself to be emperor. Now that day had come. Glory of glories, that day had come! He reached down and set the crown on his head.

Theo rose and clasped his fist to his breast in the ancient Roman salute. "Hail Constantine XI Dragas of the imperial house of Palaeologus, Emperor of the Romans!"

Everyone took up the cry. Here was the acclamation that had decided the emperors of Rome for over a thousand years. A sense of history assailed Constantine as men hoisted him up on their shoulders and the courtyard filled with the rustle of silk, clink of metal, and prayerful song of priests:

"God grant you many years!

God grant you many blessed years.

In health and happiness, God grant you many blessed years!"

Phrantzes spoke, "Empress Helena requests that you be invested as emperor by acclamation of the people of Mistra and anointed by the Bishop of Mistra."

Constantine understood his mother's message. It was the custom for the emperor to be crowned by the Patriarch of Constantinople at the famed Hagia Sophia, the great Church of Holy Wisdom. But the new Patriarch, Gregory III Mammas, was a staunch unionist. For him to anoint an emperor who was also pro-union could provoke the antiunionists to revolt. He would heed his mother's advice and forego the ancient rite. His first duty was to avert civil war.

Only then could he deal with the Ottoman threat.

Three

Zoe awaited Constantine's arrival in the throne room festooned with silk banners and evergreens and crowded with jeweled guests. In the light of the hall's eight fireplaces and hundreds of blazing candles, even the unsettling frescoes of the Fall of Troy were no longer darkened by blood but lit with glory. *Look at us,* they seemed to cry. *Look at what we were, what we did. Human valor is never in vain.*

Then the old unwelcome prophecy flew into Zoe's mind, darkening her assurance. She willed it gone. She couldn't let anything spoil the joy of this special day, the sixth of January, the Feast of Theophany. Constantine's coronation day.

Clarions blared, drawing her attention to the entry. Constantine strode in, followed by his Varangian Guard in short red tunics and long red cloaks, their axes on their backs, their flaxen hair betraying their foreign birth. Known to the people as the emperor's axe-bearing barbarians, Norsemen had served as the emperor's elite bodyguards since the tenth century, for only foreigners were certain to give him undivided loyalty.

Looking happier than Zoe had ever seen him, Constantine ascended the steps to his throne. He was every inch the Roman emperor in his golden armor and rich coronation cloak of purple velvet clasped at one shoulder, his face framed by strings of pearls hanging from his crown. Though he blazed with jewels, however, it was an open secret that the gems were colored stones. The crusaders of the Fourth Crusade had absconded with the imperial regalia, and the impoverished Palaeologan dynasty could never afford to replace them.

Constantine took his throne and the hall broke into the blessing song *God grant you many years.* Zoe regretted that he had no immediate family present except his cousin, Theo, who had brought the crown from Constantinople. But at least George Phrantzes was at his side. Their bond was a close one. Phrantzes had saved his life at the Hexamilion Wall, and Constantine had been best man at his wedding and godfather to his two children. She pondered again, as she had often done, the source of the enmity between Phrantzes and her father. Both came from the island fortress of Monemvasia in the south Peloponnese, and both had married into the royal family. They should have been the best of friends, not bitter enemies. No one knew for certain what had happened between them, but rumors told of scandal and a dishonored girl expecting her lover's child who was forced to take the veil. The girl was said to be Phrantzes's sister; the lover, Zoe's father, Lucas Notaras.

Her gaze returned to Constantine, receiving the tributes of his bishops and state dignitaries. One by one they offered prayers, greetings, and gifts. With a jolt, she heard her name called.

"The children of His Serene Excellency the Grand Duke Lucas Notaras, Admiral of the Fleet," the herald announced. "Helena, Zoe, Maria, and Isaac Notaras!"

Zoe held her nine-year-old brother's hand and approached with her sisters, Helena, older by two years, and Maria, younger by two years. Helena had recently wed her new husband, the Prince of Lesbos, in a proxy marriage and was leaving Mistra to join him, and Maria had just arrived in Mistra for schooling.

"May God in His mighty wisdom bless you with a long reign and many victories," her sister Helena said as Constantine accepted the Notaras family gift from their servant. The giant solitaire diamond her father had chosen was as large as a Smyrna kingfisher's egg and blazed blindingly as he examined it. Zoe watched nervously, hoping he wouldn't resent this reminder of her father's immense wealth.

"Our thanks to the illustrious Notaras family for their generous tribute," he said, looking up. "I shall put its value to good use repairing the walls of Constantinople."

Zoe smiled wide in relief.

"Silver becomes you, my lady," Constantine said, addressing her. "Indeed, all the family looks splendid this night," he added diplomatically with a nod of dismissal.

Zoe felt her face flame, but inwardly she blessed her silver silk stola and diamond-studded *maniakis* collar for drawing his eye. Her pulse hammering in her ears, she fought for composure as she withdrew with her family. Not until she looked up did she see Maria's green eyes watching her like a cat. Her smile faded. She suspected that Constantine's compliment had drawn her sister's ire. She had no idea that it was something else entirely, and Maria was thinking, *I get opals from our father and she gets diamonds.*

When the last guest had paid homage, Constantine retired to the banquet table. Zoe followed with her siblings and took her place on the dais, dismayed by the sadness she felt. As her sisters feasted and giggled and her brother Isaac watched a troupe of male dancers, Zoe stole troubled glances at Constantine, who was conversing with his ministers. With a jolt, she realized he was no longer "Prince," but "Emperor."

Emperor.

Zoe found herself both happy and sad in the same moment: happy, because it was what Constantine wanted and she would have no one else as emperor, especially not his hateful brother, Demetrios. Sad, because he was leaving for Constantinople and their paths were diverging. What if she never saw him again—maybe never again in her entire life? What if—God forfend! —he took a wife before she had a chance to make him fall in love with her? Her gaze flew down the banquet table to Constantine. Sending a fervent prayer heavenward, she begged for divine intercession on all her concerns, but on this point especially.

She took a mouthful of pheasant and put down her fork. She had no appetite. Much as she tried to dismiss it, she couldn't rid herself of the dark prophecy that rattled in her head. Servants sprinted around the table, refilling goblets and offering delicacies: roasted piglet, aubergine-stuffed suckling goat and gazelles from inland Anatolia. Zoe waved them away and sipped her wine, her gaze on Constantine. She was too far away to hear what he said, but she noted with concern that he was in rapt conversation with her tutor, Greece's famed philosopher, Plethon, who had schooled Constantine as a boy. Plethon had confided to her that Constantine's first order of business would be to take a bride and birth children for the dynasty. Was Plethon even now offering him names of princesses to choose as wife? Was Constantine deciding even at this moment whom he would wed?

She nearly choked on her wine.

How can I stay in Mistra when he's in Constantinople? If I stay, he'll wed someone else. How can I live with that? I must find a way to go with him! Maybe she could speak to Plethon and have him suggest to Constantine that he take her to be with her father? Surely, Constantine wouldn't refuse a request from his beloved tutor. She set down her wine. Yes, that is what she would do.

"Zoe, are you unwell? You do not eat." Helena's voice.

Zoe was fond of her older sister despite the airs she'd assumed since her betrothal to the Lord of Lesbos. "Here, try this," Helena said, dropping a scoop of Black Sea caviar on her plate. At that instant her sister Maria knocked over a goblet of red wine, splattering Zoe's skirt. Zoe knew it was deliberate. As children, she and Maria had squabbled constantly, and Maria never lost an opportunity to mock her. When they were small, it was her red hair. Now that they were grown, it was her bosom. "Flat as plates" Maria liked to laugh, for Maria was amply endowed.

A lone flute summoned the next group of dancers. Absorbed in wiping the wine from her skirt, Zoe didn't notice until Helena called, "Hurry, Zoe!" and picked a scarf from a basket. She hastened to the floor as Zoe pushed back her chair and grabbed the only scarf left in the basket, a lavender color, scarcely flattering with her auburn hair. She snatched it up and rushed after Helena. The minstrels struck a chord and Zoe assumed her pose at the center of the circle, for she was lead dancer. Twirling her sheer lavender scarf, moving languidly to the music, she lifted her voice in song.

Lost in wine and the rippling chords of harp and flute, Constantine watched the graceful dancers, memories passing in review. Though his two marriages had been made to secure peace treaties, he'd cared for both his wives, Theodora and Catarina, and had mourned them deeply. Now, for the first time since they died, he remembered them without guilt or anguish as the red-haired siren waved a lavender veil and filled his heart with a song of exquisite beauty.

He came out of his thoughts with a start. *Red haired siren? Zoe?*

Not long ago she had been a child running to embrace him with hugs and kisses. Now, she was a woman—as she herself had reminded him that day at St. Demetrios. And not just any woman, but one with a voice that would have charmed Odysseus. Overnight the years had flown, but where had they gone? He felt now that he had slept through them. He remembered how Zoe had looked sitting beneath the orange tree. She had blossomed even as he'd gazed. He leaned forward in his chair, confounded, enchanted, trying to understand her appeal. She was tall but wispy as a water sprite, not statuesque like Aphrodite, and her features were far from perfect. Yet she had something. An innocence. A vulnerability. A luminescence ...

Those eyes.

The dance ended. Applause shook the hall. He lifted his goblet and toasted the maidens. Turning his attention to a servant with a silver urn, he rummaged for a gift. A glimmer drew his eye to a garnet brooch. He held it to the light. The deep color made him think of wine, and youth, and sunrises.

"For you, Lady Zoe. Here, allow me—" He rose from his chair and pinned the brooch to her gown, his hand brushing her skin as he gathered the silk and pushed the hasp through.

Zoe felt his touch like a burn and her breath caught in her throat. Their eyes met and held. Constantine felt a rush of inexplicable emotion, and for a moment he could not move. Fighting for control, he forced himself to focus on the gifts the servant offered for his inspection.

"Now for the other lovely dancers," he managed, not daring to look at Zoe again.

Snow dusted the Vale of Sparta, but it wasn't weather that detained Constantine in Mistra weeks after his coronation. Though Zoe's father was Lord High Admiral of the Imperial Fleet, the title was hollow, a vestige of the days when Rome had been master of the seas. But she was master no more. The fleet had been dismantled long ago, and the once-mighty empire had no ships. For that, they could thank the Venetian invaders of the Fourth Crusade.

In dire need of transport, Constantine charged his kinsman, Theo Palaeologus, with finding him passage to Constantinople. It came as no surprise when the Venetians and Genoese offered only excuses. Finally, Theo brought good news. "The Catalans have agreed to furnish three warships to afford safe passage, Augustus. They wish you to know it is their gift to you, to mark your ascension to the throne. We leave on the fifteenth of February."

A sorry state of affairs when the Roman emperor must beg passage to his own city, Constantine thought. The day of his birth, February eighth, had passed virtually unnoticed, and his name day celebration would not take place until May. He felt very much alone. Four of his brothers were dead, and he was not close to the two who lived. He had only his mother, and she was aged. Soon time would demand payment from her, as it did from all mortals.

On the eve of his departure for Constantinople, beset with sudden melancholy, he entered the silent throne room and made his way out to the great colonnaded balcony. Leaning his weight on the stone balustrade, he gazed at the lights scattered across the darkness of the Vale of Sparta and the thousands of stars in the sky above, shining down on him. When he was a boy, he had thought each was an emperor of Rome.

Now I am one of them, he thought.

"A beautiful night," a soft voice said behind him. "So many stars."

He turned to find Zoe stepping out of the shadows of a Corinthian pillar. He was surprised at the pleasure that flooded him at the sight of her. "What brings you out on such a chilly night, chi—" He caught himself in time, "—my lady?"

Zoe sensed the smile on his lips. "I was reading a book of poems by Aeschylus when I saw you. I have wanted to thank you for allowing me to accompany you to Constantinople."

"You are welcome," he replied, moving close.

It seemed to Zoe that the air took on a heady sweetness. She had finally dared ask her tutor Plethon to speak to Constantine about taking her with him to court. The reason she gave was to find a husband. Naturally, she'd omitted who exactly she had in mind. Before Constantine could question her, she changed the subject, "I shall miss Mistra."

"I know," he sighed. With its churches, monasteries, and rich cultural life, Mistra was the artistic and intellectual center of the Christian East that Constantinople had once been. Its vitality and excitement contrasted sharply with the gloom and despair of the capital. In Mistra the divisions between unionists and anti-unionists were not hotly debated; there were no empty spaces and abandoned buildings. No shortage of people and trade; no dearth of thinkers and men of taste like Plethon.

He turned to Zoe. She wore the silver silk stola he remembered from his coronation feast, and she looked lovely. The wind stirred the gown around her willowy form, and the light of the torches illuminated loose strands of her red hair that had escaped the pearl-studded curls piled high on her head. The tendrils floated in the air, making him think of embers glinting around a fire.

Zoe was right, he thought. She was no longer the little girl who had shrieked with delight and flown into his arms each time he visited Mistra. She was a grown woman, composed, intelligent, and beautiful.

Zoe caught his admiring look and gave him a smile. With a glance at the fire pots burning nearby, she hugged herself, for the wind had picked up and she had come without a cloak.

"Where is your *palla*?" Constantine said after a silence. His eyes, olive black in the dimness, held concern. "You will catch a chill."

"It was mild earlier. I didn't think I needed it," she replied. Torchlight flickered over his features, emphasizing the sharp planes of his face, and Zoe found that she could not look away. Ever since their encounter at St. Demetrios, she had dreamed of nothing else but being alone with him, and now that she was, she knew it would be another eternity before it happened again.

"Here, take mine. It is not lavender, but it is warm," he smiled, unbuckling the ornamented fibula that secured his purple cloak at one shoulder. He draped the velvet around her, his fingers brushing her skin and hair.

Thrilled that he remembered the color of her scarf, Zoe turned her face up to him. "Thank you," she whispered, clutching it close.

He did not reply. For a moment their eyes held. Then each looked away to gaze into the darkness that was lit by the stars above and the flickering torches of the city below. Zoe was distressed at the sudden tension that fell between them. "I've never been to Constantinople," she said, desperate for conversation. If they didn't speak, he might leave, and she couldn't bear for him to leave. "What is it like?"

"Magnificent. Once it was the center—and the wonder—of the world."

"Father says it's a sad place now."

"True—" Everywhere he looked, he saw *their* work. The broken columns. The empty alcoves looted of their treasures. The once splendid Hippodrome shorn of its great bronze statues. By the time the first Palaeologan emperor had driven the hated crusaders out of Constantinople nearly sixty years after they came, the treasures were gone, like the sculptures, the jewels, the gold and silver and marble, the fleet and the territories that had formed the Roman Empire of the Christian East. All that remained was the shell of the city the first Constantine had founded, and that they burned to the ground as they left.

"But," he said, injecting a brighter note into his tone, "the city is alive with history and memories of greatness. Where we step, the first Constantine walked before us, and where we pray at the Hagia Sophia, the great Justinian knelt." After a pause he added, "But I will admit what saddens me is that two hundred years ago, before *they* came, a million people lived in Constantinople. Now there is barely fifty thousand. I feel the absence of every person no longer there."

Moved by the moment, Zoe touched his sleeve in the old familiar way she used to do when she was little. "In your hands, the *Queen of Cities* has hope, Constans," she said softly, using her pet name for him from childhood. "You will make a great emperor and leave your mark." It was the truth. She felt the force of destiny around him.

Constantine took her hand into his own and brought it to his lips. "Thank you, Zoe, my child, my lovely young lady." After a long moment, he added, "I am pleased you are coming to Constantinople."

Four

Fair winds filled the sails of the two-masted Catalan galley as rowers plowed the currents of the Sea of Marmara, speeding Constantine to famed Constantinople. With his heavy purple cloak whipping about him and salt spray wetting his lips, he stood at the bow of the low-slung, armed vessel. Soon he would be hailed Emperor of Rome by his people.

Emperor of Rome.

His pulse quickened as the eerie prophecy reared up in the dark recesses of his mind. *What began with Constantine born of Helena will end with Constantine born of Helena.* In the eleven hundred years since the founding of Constantinople, Constantine was the eleventh emperor named 'Constantine' to rule Rome. But only he and the first Constantine had a mother named Helena.

He tightened his grip on the rail and stared at the wintry seas that stretched ahead, the mewing of gulls throbbing in his ears. *Rome will not end with me by God! I will not allow it. I will prove the prophecy wrong! I am the right man for the times, and I will save the empire.* It wouldn't be easy, but he had history on his side. Constantinople had been besieged twenty-three times in her existence, and only once did she fall. That was to crusaders who gained entry by treachery—an unlocked gate in the night.

But that one time changed everything forever.

Now, dismembered, weakened by plague, earthquakes, civil war and invasion, the fabulously old Roman Empire stood dangerously divided on the question of union between the two Christian churches of East and West. And this at a time when they faced the greatest threat to their civilization in a thousand years.

The division had grown more bitter with each passing year. The anti-unionists accused the unionists of forgiving the sack of Constantinople in 1204 when, intoxicated by the wealth and beauty of the opulent city and frenzied by greed and jealousy, the Venetians leading the Fourth Crusade forgot they came to liberate Jerusalem from the infidels, and instead, attacked Constantinople. A Christian city. Their own front lines against the heathen faith!

Worse, they decided to stay. For nearly sixty years they feasted in the palaces and paid no heed to the plight of the empire, until the empire was gone, lost to the Ottoman Turks. By the time the first Palaeologan emperor threw them out, little remained of the glorious Roman empire in the east except a few outposts and the city of Constantinople.

Constantine exhaled heavily. When they were rich and powerful, the Latins had resented them. Now that they were poor and in need, the Latins ridiculed them. After all Eastern Rome had done for Europe, there was no gratitude, only insult. As far as the Latins were concerned, the Roman Empire perished in 400 when the city of Rome fell to the Vandals. They treated Eastern Rome's Greek-speaking dynasty, the Palaeologans, with contempt, and Constantinople as if it were still the humble fishing village of Byzantium. This, despite the fact that in Constantinople, the city of Seven Hills founded by Rome's first Christian emperor, were preserved Roman law, Roman imperial government, Roman state traditions, Roman architecture, and Roman culture.

He remembered John's hostile reception on his return from Italy. The crowds had been sullen, their silence only broken by sporadic cries of *Apostatis,* that damning epithet denoting someone who was both a heretic and a traitor. Would they call him that because he supported his brother's decision on union?

He heaved a sigh. However it went, God had entrusted the Eastern Roman Empire to his care, and he would not fail his people. Lifting his face to the sky, he asked for Heaven's blessing.

Zoe stood aft, clutching her new lavender cloak tightly against the cold, and watched him across the deck, her heart troubled. His profile was etched in sharp relief against the dismal sky, and his sandy hair whipped in the wind.

Despite the people around him, he had never seemed so solitary, so alone. She had been right, she realized with sharpened clarity. Loneliness had formed a bond between them from the beginning.

She blinked to clear her vision, for a sudden shadow seemed to engulf Constantine. She checked the sky. Nothing had changed; it was still the color of stone. She shook herself to banish her unease. *It's naught but the confounded prophecy toying with me.*

Even for a nonbeliever, the power of the prophecy was not easily dismissed, for it foretold their doom at the hands of an emperor named Constantine with a mother named Helena. She shook herself. What mattered was how the people received him. That would be the harbinger of what awaited. If they united behind him, all would be well. Acceptance was also important on a deeply personal level. Rejection was painful, whether for a child from a mother, or a ruler from his people. Even when it came from strangers, it had the power to wound deeply. She recalled a trip to Crete where she'd experienced a hostility that had left her bewildered. Among other things, scornful whispers had claimed she was descended from a fishmonger. The lie held a grain of truth. Though her grandfather, Nicholas Notaras, was never a fisherman, he began his career as a purveyor of fish and made a fortune exporting sturgeon, caviar, and dried fish to the Venetian colonies on the shores of the Black Sea. He came to the emperor's attention when his exports assumed a grand scale.

A voice scattered her thoughts.

"Sing for us, Lady Zoe!" Theo called from the bow of the vessel. "The day is dull and we could use some merriment!" Leaping down from the cannon where he perched, he threw a Saracen rug over a bench as encouragement. Hearty cheers echoed his call. The seamen's enthusiasm overcame Zoe's shyness, and she navigated her way forward, stepping carefully, grabbing ropes, and accepting the helping hands offered. When she was seated, someone handed her a lyre.

She ran her fingers over the instrument, trying to capture the melody she'd heard at the celebration feast in Monemvasia, the night they boarded ship. Despite the cold, merrymakers had gathered outdoors to drink wine and dance around bonfires. The song they sang had drifted to her through an open window as she'd watched the tender interaction between Eirene and her mother on their last evening together. For Constantinople was a long way from Monemvasia, the fortress island that was home to the Notaras clan, and who knew when they'd meet again? At one point, Eirene's mother had secured a stray tendril of her daughter's glossy black hair lovingly behind her ear. A small gesture, but gazing on them from the high table, Zoe's heart had twisted. Her mother would never have done the same for her.

A sudden gust of wind slapped the sails, jolting her back into the present. She returned her focus to her lyre, summoned a ripple of chords, and raised her voice in a lament.

As the first sweet notes drifted to him, Constantine turned to look at Zoe. Clad in a flowing stola of pale apricot wool with a lavender cloak draped over her shoulders and a filmy jeweled veil over her auburn braid, she lit up the gloomy day like sunshine. He was reminded again that Zoe had grown up. The thought saddened him. He had enjoyed her childhood infatuation. Often, as she'd clung to him and wept in farewell, he'd found himself with a lump in his throat. There had been a curiously deep bond between them when she'd been little.

Sea traffic was picking up. He turned back to the north expectantly. They were leaving the Dardanelles and passing several great galleys entering the narrow channel, bearing bales of silks, gold-works, turquoise, wax, copper, and precious dyes from Constantinople.

Suddenly, Constantinople burst into view. Garlanded by the shimmering waters of the Golden Horn, the Straits of the Bosphorus, and the Marmara Sea, it sparkled in the dismal morning light like a jewel in a molten silver sea. This point where the three bodies of water met always made him think of a love triangle. For here, the Bosphorus rushing south from the Black Sea embraced the Golden Horn, and the Horn racing east from her inlet embraced the waters the Romans had called the "Sea of Marble." In both directions, north and south, the Bosphorus and the Marmara united to part Europe and Asia from one another, but they did so reluctantly, for the straits between them were so narrow that the two continents almost seemed to kiss.

The cry of *Land ahoy!* brought everyone to their feet. Seamen ran up from below deck and sprang to work preparing the vessel for disembarkation. Zoe laid her lyre aside and rose from her perch. Next to her, Theo pointed ahead and cried, "There! There she is, the Queen of Cities—"

The holy city of Constantinople took dramatic form as the imperial party approached along the Marmara Sea. From atop its seven hills, hundreds of crosses pointed the way to heaven from the golden domes of churches and red tiled roofs of monasteries. Zoe stared spellbound. Never had she seen so many sacred houses in one place! But as impressive as the crenellated fortifications were, Zoe found them more astounding the closer they drew to the city. Rising out of the sea, Constantinople's white walls towered so high that they blotted out the sky. Behind them she could see the tips of stone monuments, gilded columns, bronze statues, and marble palaces.

"Blessed Mother," she murmured in awe. Turning to Theo, she pointed to a massive tower glimmering like a mountain of pearls in the cold winter light. "What is that?" she asked, shouting to be heard over the flapping of the banners in the wind.

"The Marble Tower!" he yelled back. "It marks the junction of the sea and land walls. You can't tell from here, but it's faced with white marble from top to bottom."

Zoe stared at him. How could a tower be adorned in expensive marble? "But a tower is meant for fighting!"

He grinned. "Constantinople has surprised people for over a thousand years."

They moved rapidly past the city, but the length of wall seemed endless. High above on a hill, amid the imperial pennants fluttering from towers and palaces, shone a massive golden dome.

"The Hagia Sophia?" she asked.

"Yes! The Church of Holy Wisdom. Magnificent, isn't it?"

She nodded. This was where emperors had been crowned since the first Constantine founded the new capital of Rome in the year 330. With a pang, she thought, *Until now.* "What is that town that flies the pennant of the red cross?" she asked, pointing across the sea to a settlement opposite Constantinople.

"The Genoese fortress city of Pera. Some call it Galata."

"Oh." The town of Pera had been ceded to Genoa as payment for their help in ousting the Venetian crusaders from Constantinople.

They sailed past several gates to a large harbor dotted with colorful fishing boats and crowded with great merchant galleys. A cluster of masts bearing the flags of many nations rose and dipped on the waves. "We're passing the harbor!" Zoe cried taken aback when they failed to stop.

"We go to the royal landing at Bucoleon Palace," Theo replied. "It's farther up."

"Another harbor?"

"Constantinople has seven." He proceeded to name them. "Those are the ones on the Sea of Marmara. On the Golden Horn there are—"

"How many harbors does a city need?" Zoe interrupted in disbelief.

"Constantinople is not merely a city," a resonant voice said at her shoulder. "It is the *Queen of Cities.*"

Zoe looked up. Constantine grinned at her. He'd been following the exchange and found himself enchanted by her wonderment. Her innocence brought to mind a wide-eyed child delighting in her discovery of the world.

"You have much to learn, Zoe," he said, startled by the thought that flashed through his mind. He would like to be the one to teach her.

Zoe watched Constantine disembark at the Bucoleon's royal landing stage, an impressive structure that took its name from two enormous marble lions flanking the stone pier. The vast area stretched into darkness before her and was unlike anything she had ever seen: an enormous open-air hall with a marble floor, an endless roof, and as many Corinthian columns as a forest had trees. When her eyes adjusted to the dimness, she saw that a delegation awaited them. Standing behind Empress Helena was her father. She could barely restrain her joy!

In his late forties, broad-shouldered and fair-haired, with green eyes and a close-cropped light beard, Grand Duke Lucas Notaras cut a resplendent figure in a richly embroidered topaz tunic belted at the waist with a jeweled crimson sash and his velvet cloak clasped at one shoulder. Strangely, her mother was nowhere in sight. Zoe wanted to run into her father's arms, but she dutifully performed the ceremonial kissing of hands as she passed from the elegant black-clad dowager empress to Constantine's imperial brothers, hard-faced Demetrios and the more genial Thomas. Finally, she stood before her father.

He gave her a peck and she felt his short, bristly beard scratch her cheek. She smiled wide. His beard had always tickled her, and as a child she would give it a tug.

"You're not going to tug it now, are you?" her father said, reading her thoughts, his green eyes twinkling.

She laughed.

"You are a joy to behold, my daughter."

"Thank you, Father." It had been over a year since he last visited Mistra, and she had missed him terribly. "I'm so looking forward to spending time with you at last! Where is Mother?"

"I regret she was unable to come, Zoe. She has the ague. You can see her when you visit us at Blachernae Palace."

"Visit? I won't be staying with you?"

"Our palace on the Golden Mile has been prepared to receive you," She stared at him in bewilderment. Had she been excluded from participating in the imperial ceremony? "What about the Great Procession—"

"Fear not, you will have a good view," her father said, misunderstanding her concern.

Constantine was greeting his mother when he overheard the conversation between father and daughter. Turning, he addressed Lucas, "We would be delighted to have Lady Zoe join our procession."

Zoe jerked her head up and broke into a dazzling smile. Constantine grinned at her.

Standing beside her son, the dowager empress looked from Constantine to Zoe, and her eyes widened in comprehension. She laid a gentle hand on Zoe's sleeve. "My dear," she said kindly, "why do you not ride with me in my litter?"

Zoe curtsied to the empress, her heart joyful, yet uncertain. Empress Helena had always struck her as someone who did nothing on impulse. She couldn't help wondering what lay behind her offer.

Spurning a litter for a beautiful white palfrey, Zoe rode through the city with her father and his retinue, marveling at the sights that met her eyes. In every direction, there were richly clad lords on horseback and ladies borne along on gilded palanquins. Zoe picked up a gabble of foreign tongues from the strangely garbed pedestrians. One of the streets was even paved with marble, lined with tall columns, and covered with a roof to protect pedestrians from rain. She had never seen such splendor. Her father turned into a wide, yellow-colored avenue with fountains at the center to divide the traffic. As she gazed, the sun came out from behind the clouds and the street took on a dazzling brightness.

"Is the road crushed gold?" she asked in wonderment.

"Crushed yellow marble from the local mines," her father smiled. "We call it the Golden Mile."

The Hagia Sophia pulled into view. Zoe marveled at the thousand-year-old cathedral with its huge golden dome and cluster of half-domes. As everyone knew, the Hagia Sophia was built on the first hill of Constantinople, a city chosen to be the capital of the east because it had seven hills, like Rome, the capital of the west. At the entrance, on a column so tall that it seemed to pierce the heavens, stood a statue of Constantine the Great, his horse rearing beneath him, his hand raised indicating something in the distance.

"What is he pointing to?" Zoe asked her father.

"Some say his dominions in the east. Others say he points east, because from there will come our doom. But that is just foolishness."

While Zoe digested this, her father added, "From atop this very column, nearly two hundred feet high, a Roman emperor was hurled to his death by the Latin crusaders in 1204."

Zoe winced and averted her eyes. As they rode, she became aware of what she had failed to notice in her earlier excitement, beggars huddled deep in the shadows of the colonnade. Some slumbered while others watched passers-by, bony hands held out for alms. There were men, women, and children of all ages. Many were sickly with visible sores. A young mother and child caught her eye. The girl was about her age, and her aura of despair pierced Zoe. She was emaciated, too weak even to swat the flies that buzzed around her and her babe. The girl moved, and the child slipped in her fragile grip. At any moment it would slide into the open gutter and be swept away into the cisterns.

"Halt!" Zoe cried, reining in her palfrey. With neighs and protests, the little procession clattered to a stop. "Father, pray give me money—"

"What?"

"I need a coin, Father."

"You can shop later, Zoe. We have not time to stop now."

"Humor me," she pleaded sweetly, offering him a smile.

He drew out his purse and looked inside. "I have only gold pieces," he said, as if to end discussion.

"One will do." Zoe grabbed a coin quickly before he could slip the purse back into his belt and trotted her palfrey over to the sleeping girl. She dismounted and knelt beside her. The girl opened an eye that was caked with yellow discharge and Zoe showed her the shining coin in her palm. "For you." The girl looked down at the gold, then up at her. In her unfocused gaze, Zoe saw awe, and disbelief. "It is yours," Zoe explained. But the girl made no move to take the coin, and Zoe had to press it into her hand.

She rode along in silence with no heart to admire the immense plazas, grandiose monuments, forums, temples, cisterns, and baths of colossal proportions. Her thoughts were with the girl. Never had she seen such poverty. In Mistra no one huddled in the streets, and no one starved.

The famed Hippodrome drew into sight. Overgrown with weeds, it emanated a desolate, forlorn air. Zoe was conscious of the smell of urine and decay. For a fleeting instant she had an image of the glory of those long-gone days when Constantinople was a city of towering walls, marble streets, shining churches, and glittering palaces. Now, against the backdrop of the Marmara Sea, a few ragged urchins played Christians and Infidels on the crumbling walls, and a pack of stray dogs nosed for food.

The Notaras palace was set back from the road behind a high stone wall overhung with bay trees. A porter creaked the gate open. She trotted her palfrey into the inner courtyard and gave her reins over to a groom. After the squalor of the streets, she felt as though she had stepped into the Garden of Eden. Expansive walks and streams radiated from a circular stone pond, and peacocks strutted between the statuary and fountains. The cries of the street were muted here by birdsong and splashing water. Shielding her eyes from the sun, she turned to her father's palace. Built in the Eastern Roman style of cream-colored stone trimmed with red brick, it was adorned with colonnaded balconies, slender pillars, pointed arches and trefoil stonework. The cross of the Hagia Sophia on the First Hill glittered above the palace roofline like a crown.

Her father led the way up a staircase lined with empty flowerpots to a balcony that spanned the length of the house. As they stood before her bedchamber, one of the many rooms with latticed doors of intricately carved wood, her father gave her instructions on Constantine's inauguration ceremony. "The Great Procession ends at the Hagia Sophia," he concluded. "Wear something elaborate. There will be a banquet at the Daphne."

"Another palace? How many does the emperor have?"

"Too many to count, but Blachernae in the northwest is the only habitable one. The Great Palace complex in the southeast where we landed has only a partial roof and the Magnaura is so shabby, it is used by the University of Constantinople."

"Sad."

"Yes," her father sighed. "The lack of money is evident everywhere."

Zoe gave her father a farewell peck on the cheek and entered her chamber. Under Eirene's supervision, servants unpacked coffers and hung gowns on pegs in an alcove. After a trip to the bath house and a good scrubbing in a sparkling blue mosaic pool, the bath attendant rinsed Zoe off with rosewater and she made her way back to Eirene to don a gown of coral damask. But when Eirene reached for a hammered silver *maniakis* studded with diamonds, Zoe restrained her. "That one—" she said, pointing to a gold collar with topaz pendants.

"He must have told you your eyes are like topaz."

Zoe grinned.

Looping and braiding Zoe's auburn tresses at the nape of her neck, Eirene secured the coils with pearl and ivory pins and attached a sheer pink veil across Zoe's cheeks. Zoe promptly loosened one side and let it drop. Eirene gave her an exasperated look. As soon as Eirene was done, Zoe removed Constantine's garnet brooch from her jewel casket and secured it to her gown, remembering how he had looked when he had pinned it to her dress, how she had felt as his hand had brushed her skin—

"Zoe—" Eirene prodded. Zoe came out of her reverie to find Eirene holding up a mantle of golden mesh. She shrugged into it, and Eirene stood back to admire her.

"You'll be the talk of court, Zoe," she said proudly.

"And that's never good," Zoe replied, applying her perfume.

"It is, when men fall at your feet, and you have your pick."

"Eirene, do you think *he'll* notice?" she asked plaintively.

"Only if he has eyes," she said. "Now stop fretting and go."

Five

Zoe gasped in astonishment. High against the western sky rose the legendary walls of Constantinople, tiers and tiers of them, towering, massive, awe-inspiring, and invincible. She was unable to tear her eyes away until her litter bearers turned into the grounds of the Palace of Blachernae and the walls passed from view. As she wound through the palace gardens, she could see the distant waters of the Golden Horn shimmering in the sunlight. Ships large and small from many lands rocked at anchor in the harbors that dated from antiquity, their colorful pennants fluttering in the wind. From this glimpse, Zoe had a flash of discovery and felt as if she looked at a long-ago moment in time when Constantinople had stood at the center of the world.

They followed the graceful driveway for a time, passing servants, noblemen, and soldiers. Then the Palace of Blachernae came into view, tall as a white marble mountain against the azure sky. Zoe's bearers set her down near the palace steps, beside a sundial of enamel and bronze. Like everything else in Constantinople, the sundial was mammoth.

The courtyard bustled. Horses neighed, grooms checked harnesses, and servants sprinted hither and thither. Zoe took a seat on a stone bench to await Constantine. They were on the Sixth Hill, in the far northwest corner of Constantinople, and the air was different here: clear, and fragrant. She breathed deep as she lifted her gaze to the imposing two and a half story fifth-century palace. Trimmed in red brick, Blachernae was decorated with endless pointed arches, long traceried windows, and slender Corinthian columns crowned with acanthus leaves and scrolls. She marveled at a balcony ornamented with quatrefoils that wrapped the entire upper story. There, an ancient artisan's genius had tricked the eye into believing the balcony was not wrought of stone, but of a most delicate, fragile piece of lace.

She scanned the throng for other noble ladies, but none were present. As she secured her veil across her face, her gaze fell on three litters off to the side, awaiting their occupants. All were outfitted entirely in black and gold with filmy curtains tied by golden ropes. The largest of these bore the double-headed eagle emblem of the Eastern Roman Empire over its pointed canopy. No doubt it belonged to Empress Helena, and the others to her daughters-in-law. Helmeted, bare-chested bearers stood guard beside them, red cloaks fastened at the neck, muscular arms crossed. An uneasiness came and went as she wondered again at the purpose of the empress's invitation.

Church bells chimed three of the clock and the song of the monks arose, meditating on the death of Christ at this hour. Almost at the same moment, a fanfare of clarions and cheers announced Constantine. Zoe's breath caught at the sight of him. He looked more handsome than ever in his imperial armor and crown, his purple cloak flowing from his shoulder, and his strong thighs visible above his high red boots. Men clasped their fists to their breast in salutation as he made his way down the palace steps and mounted his horse, a richly caparisoned chestnut mare with white hooves, named Athena. Zoe dropped into a curtsy, unable to keep from staring.

Abruptly, she tore her eyes away. Empress Helena was heading straight for her.

"You look lovely, my child," she said, extending her hand to be kissed. For this ceremonial occasion, she wore her nun's habit of a white tunica, plain leather belt, and a wooden cross held by blue ribbons around her arms, symbolic of the yoke of Christ. A cloth veil embroidered with seraphim coiled around her head, one end dangling loose at her shoulder. The empress entered the litter.

Zoe gave her obeisance and took her seat on a black velvet bench. She folded her hands demurely in her lap, noting absently that the fabric was frayed. Heralds dressed in white velvet blared their clarions and the procession began to move, an acolyte carrying a large cross in front, followed by the Patriarch clad in gold-embroidered white silk and a delegation of clergy swinging incense. State officials fell in behind them, bearing lit candles. Zoe thought they looked like an eddy of sparkling snowflakes floating out the gates. As minstrels played, noblemen trotted their horses forward, plumes nodding, jewels flashing. They rode according to rank, those of lesser importance in front. The last to leave were Constantine's close imperial kin, including her father and George Phrantzes, for both were of equal rank.

Her litter swayed and she clutched the sides to steady herself as the bearers lifted them up. Zoe rejoiced that she faced the rear of the procession; it meant she had a clear view of Constantine behind them, bobbing in his saddle surrounded by his colorful Varangian Guard.

"A fine day for the procession," the empress said. "I was afraid it would rain. We get much rain this time of year."

Zoe smiled and contributed her share of prattle, but as they headed southeast along the endless towers and defensive walls of Constantinople to the Golden Gate, the empress fell silent. So did Zoe. Through that military gate every emperor of Rome had made his traditional ceremonial entrance into the city since the first Constantine built the arch in the fourth century. Zoe glanced over her shoulder anxiously. Soon they would know the reaction of the people. What if Constantine received a hostile reception? What if people spat, or hurled insults, or cow dung or—God forfend! —attacked him? Roman emperors had died at the hands of the people before. She murmured a silent prayer.

A few scattered cheers arose from farmers tilling the fields, and children ran to greet them, followed by their dogs. Women smiled and waved, and Zoe waved back. Then, all at once, they broke into the special hymn of rejoicing. To Zoe, it was as if a flock of nightingales had suddenly burst into song. Elated by the people's goodwill, she smiled wide as she lifted her eyes to Constantine, who had stopped to listen. They moved on, and the two-story Golden Gate with its six columns drew into sight. She stiffened.

As if to ease the tension, the empress spoke. "Once two elephants stood here. Of pure copper, and so large that people marveled."

Destroyed by the crusaders, Zoe added inwardly. She turned behind her and her hand tightened on the armrest of her seat. The entire city had turned out for the occasion. They crowded the streets, stood on walls, balconies, even rooftops. Her litter passed through the arch and a rousing cheer went up. But then, the empress had always been popular. Her eyes flew to Constantine. Astride his mare, he waited in the arched entryway of the Golden Gate. What would be the people's verdict?

Heralds blared his entrance. He trotted his horse forward.

A roaring cheer went up as the citizens beheld their new emperor. Constantine broke into a brilliant smile. Zoe's heart soared and she fell back into her seat, flooded with overwhelming relief.

The procession wound along the Golden Mile. She waved to the cheering crowds and maidens who ran alongside throwing laurel leaves in Constantine's path. She turned a loving gaze on mothers who lifted their babes for his blessing and smiled at men who bowed to him. She admired with soft eyes the windows and balconies of the city that the people had adorned with carpets and wall hangings of silk and gold. Many in the crowds bore lit torches to welcome their new emperor. Not one yelled *Apostatis.*

Zoe's heart filled with profound gratitude. *The prophecy was wrong!* There was nothing to worry about, nothing to fear. Her gaze went to Constantine cantering behind them, surrounded by his Guards. How handsome he was! How she loved him! How happy she was for him, this hero of her youth, embraced by the people he was born to rule—

The empress turned in her seat and followed her gaze. "He is the best looking of all my sons," she said meaningfully. "And the noblest."

Zoe blushed and averted her eyes.

"But love is not his portion."

Zoe struggled to hide her shock that the empress had read her heart.

"He considers himself unfortunate and not destined for marital happiness."

The knot in Zoe's stomach tightened.

"—and now the Ottoman threat grows perilous. Duty demands he align himself with strength for the sake of the realm. You must understand it is impossible…"

The empress droned on. So, this had been Empress Helena's intent. To dissuade and deter her from even hoping for Constantine's love. Zoe sat quietly, trying not to listen, her head proudly erect, her spirit in chaos. But despite herself, she heard her words.

"—the young always think everything is forever," the empress was murmuring, almost to herself. "They do not know life has a way of healing wounds, even the deepest cut of the heart." Empress Helena turned her full gaze on her. "One thing I know. With God's help, we survive."

Realization struck. Empress Helena spoke from experience. Once she had loved as Zoe did, but an arranged marriage had been her destiny. Would that be Constantine's fate? Panic froze her breath. She couldn't accept it! Somehow, she had to find a way to prevent it.

As a minstrel played, Constantine took a cup of wine with his mother in his reception chamber at the Palace of Blachernae. Not for naught was it called the Ocean Hall, he thought, for it commanded a panoramic view of the sea. Shades of night were falling, and his body servant, Aesop, moved barefooted about the room lighting candles. The highest-ranking eunuch in the imperial household, Aesop was a *parakoimomenos* of first sword-bearer status, a gift to Constantine's father from Sultan Murad II when Constantine was ten years old and Aesop thirty.

A sudden gust of wind drew his attention to the lattice doors standing open to the marble balcony where a full moon shimmered over the black waters of the Golden Horn. He found it oddly fitting that the moon should be waxing on this night of nights when he was newly emperor. For the full moon was the symbol of Constantinople.

The crackling fire in the hearth and sweet notes of the minstrel's lament soothed Constantine. The ceremonies had been long and tiring, but the people had welcomed him.

The people had welcomed him...

His mother spoke again, her voice tender with memory. "John loved it here. He called it his sanctuary. It was mine, too, when your father was alive."

Constantine nodded. The wines and pale blues of the chamber were pleasing, and the reclining couches afforded comfort with their downy cushions. Here and there the Saracen carpets that had been gifts from eastern potentates splashed color, as did a circular sunken alcove ringed by columns and statues that served as a study, filled with maps, documents, parchments, and venerable books bound in gilt and leather. Many of these were hundreds of years old, and several had been written by his father and other imperial ancestors. He relaxed into his seat, a one-armed, overstuffed chair of crimson silk embroidered with beads, and laid his head back.

Helena watched him, her thoughts on the Notaras girl. Her son was primarily a man of action; one adept at the art of war, courageous, enterprising, and deeply patriotic. The empire was fortunate to have him. But he stood alone, and never were the times more perilous. The Grand Duke's daughter was eminently suitable, and she loved him, and maybe he even loved her. But if that was so, it was unfortunate for them both. Zoe Notaras could not help him save the empire.

"We need to address the question of your marriage, Constans," Helena announced abruptly.

Constantine came out of his thoughts with a start. "You never waste time getting to the heart of the matter, do you, Mother?"

"No," she sighed, "for good reason. We have none to lose."

Constantine's smile faded. "I recognize the need and have made offers, Mother. The Lord of Taranto's sister. The Infanta of Portugal. The Doge's daughter. All have been refused. There is no one left. The western powers do not welcome an alliance with us, and no princess will come to share my precarious throne."

"Then the western powers be damned!" she exclaimed, slamming her walking stick on the marble floor. "Find a bride in the Orthodox world. You need to placate the anti-Latin feeling in any case. Emperor John of Trebizond has only one daughter, but one is all we need. Send Phrantzes to secure the hand of Princess Theodora. Give him the word and send him off!"

"The Great Comnenus is weak, Mother."

"But rich. He can supply ships and men. That is all that matters."

"How old is Theodora, do you know?"

"Old enough. Seventeen, I believe."

Zoe's age. Theodora's mother was a Palaeologina too. Did they resemble one another? Unlikely. Auburn hair was not much known in the Palaeologus family. Zoe's coloring had to come from the Notaras side. If he recalled correctly, Zoe had an uncle with red hair. He had died long ago. In his mind, he heard Plethon's voice. *She will go to Constantinople to choose her husband.*

How like Zoe to choose her husband, and not the other way around—

"I am glad the thought pleases you," said his mother.

Constantine snapped out of his reverie to find his mother looking at him with her sharp blue eyes and realized he wore a broad smile on his face. It seemed Zoe always had that effect on him. He cleared his throat and forced his mind back to the matter at hand. "I am fully prepared to do what I must. We cannot stand alone against the Ottomans."

"Ottomans! Ottomans!" a parrot shrieked.

Constantine turned behind him. A magnificent bird with sapphire and purple plumage fluttered in a gigantic gilt cage set amid green foliage near the door. He smiled. "Did John teach him that?"

"He did. He said Apollo made it seem like a jest, and that lightened his heart."

Constantine picked up a piece of quince from a silver platter and took it to the bird. Apollo munched greedily, slapping the fruit around to cut it down to size.

"We cannot stand alone, Constans, and we also need heirs," his mother continued as he took his seat. "Between all my sons, I have only two grandchildren, both of them girls, one from Thomas and one from Demetrios."

Constantine lowered his gaze. His second wife had died in childbirth, and in great agony. The guilt weighed heavily on him. His thoughts strayed to Zoe. How would it be for her?

"What do you want?" the parrot screeched, piercing Constantine's thoughts.

To protect my country, he answered silently. To go down in history as a great emperor. Everything depended on the marriage he made. So why did he keep thinking of Zoe? From across the room, he threw Apollo a pomegranate seed. It missed its target but gave him a moment to compose himself. "Very well. I will dispatch George to the Black Sea."

"You will not regret it, Constans. The princesses of Trebizond are famed for their beauty. John's wife was the loveliest woman in Constantinople."

Constantine sighed, thinking of his brother. It had been love at first sight for John and his bride, Maria of Trebizond. He was never the same after her death. Constantine asked gently, "How went the funeral?"

"Thankfully, your brothers behaved themselves during the ceremony and didn't fight." She blew her nose hard. "But it was not easy to see John laid out in the Hall of the Double Axes like that."

"John, John!" the parrot squawked. *"Who loves Emperor John?"*

An acute sense of loss swept Constantine. John must have asked that question many times in his loneliness and despair after Maria died. He shifted his gaze to his mother. She had aged since Mistra. Burying her oldest child was proving a harsh burden. He went to her side and took her hand into his own. "I am sorry, Mother."

"I cannot help grieving as I do, though death came as a relief for John." Her mouth worked with emotion.

"Did he have such great pain?"

"No. He realized your father had been right about union with the West and he had been wrong. It weighed on him heavily at the end." Helena lifted her eyes to the window where the dark sea moaned in the wind. So had it churned that dreary winter's day long ago when her husband Emmanuel had read Sultan Murad's missive to the Senate. "I ask that the friendship that existed between you and my father should continue, and that you cease supporting the imposter Mustafa against me." Lowering the missive, her husband had looked at his senators. "I agree with Murad. I want peace, and Murad wants peace. All Murad asks in return for peace is that we give him back his brother, Mustafa."

"No, Father!" John had exclaimed, leaping to his feet. "We are safer with Mustafa than without him! He is a prize! As long as we have him, we hold the threat of civil war over Murad's head and we can stir up other troubles, too. The more the Ottomans squabble among themselves, the less of a threat they are to us!"

"Aye, aye!" echoed the Senate.

Following that response, Sultan Murad had laid siege to Constantinople in 1422, and only when news came of a revolt in Anatolia did he abandon it. But he contented himself with sending an army to ravage the Peloponnese.

"Why did you give in to them, Emmanuel?" Helena had asked him afterwards. He had regarded her with his gentle brown eyes. "I was weary, and I thought maybe I was too old, and maybe they were right."

Helena blinked and came out of her reverie. "A mouse does not taunt a lion, Constans. Your father opposed union because the Ottomans would see it as threat."

"You think I should reverse course then?"

"You know my feelings on the matter. We have no money, only debts. We exist only because the Ottomans allow us to."

"For eight hundred years we have served as Europe's shield against the armies of the east. I cannot believe they would not come to our aid if we needed them."

"Your father went to England seeking aid, and your brother went to Italy. Has anything changed? The Ottomans must not feel threatened, or they will destroy us. Only friendly relations with them can ensure the survival of the empire."

"Empire? Scarcely the word. I am but the ruler of a strip of land barely a hundred miles long. We have these fourteen miles of wall, a few provinces in Greece, and some outposts on the Black Sea. The Ottomans surround us from Anatolia to the Balkans. Now they eye the morsel we stand on. We cannot beat them back without help."

"Never say that. With God's help, David beat back Goliath."

Constantine rose and went to the window. His brother's face floated in the inky night, looking as he had when he'd returned from Florence: haggard, weary, despondent. Only a few in the crowd had shouted *Apostatis,* but their sullen silence had been almost as devastating. "Do they think it was easy for me, Constans?" John had asked. "I signed because there was no other way to save the Christian East."

On that day, at that moment, Constantine had felt they stood on a tiny outcrop between Scylla and Charybdis, the two sea monsters of Greek mythology. Disaster awaited on both sides of the middle road, and the middle road was narrow and treacherous, obscured in mist and darkness.

But I am emperor now. I will tread that middle road wisely and deliver my people from peril.

His mother put down her cup and came to him at the window, her cane tapping softly as she walked. "You remind me of your father in so many ways, Constans. You seek to do the right thing, and you were ever loyal to him, and to your brother."

"I owed them allegiance. They were my emperor."

"Too bad Theodore and Demetrios never felt the same way. Demetrios was a terrible disappointment, but then, Emmanuel had many disappointments-" Her eyes misted with memory. "It is why he wrote. Writing brought him consolation. He always looked for the good in people, Constans. He rarely found it and was often punished for it."

"I know, Mother."

"I am thankful you are emperor. The empire is in good hands."

"You can rest assured that I will do my best for my people."

"John trusted in you for good reason, my son."

Constantine placed his arm around his mother's shoulder and drew her close. He laid a gentle kiss on her brow, and together they stood at the window, gazing down on the walls of Constantinople.

Six

Zoe couldn't sleep. The news that Phrantzes was leaving for the Black Sea to find a bride for Constantine had plunged her into a deep despondency, and the image of the girl with the babe haunted her. She felt like a rudderless ship, adrift on an endless gray sea, with nowhere to go, serving no purpose.

One frigid night soon after her arrival in March, the Star Wind shrieked into Constantinople, shaking the earth with a torrent of rain and fierce growlings of thunder. Curled up in a window seat, she watched the wind lash the trees and rattle the windows, hoping the girl with the babe had found refuge on this terrible night. Dawn finally arrived. Sitting with Eirene before a glowing fire, she broke her fast with a glass of pomegranate juice.

"You do not eat?" Eirene inquired, helping herself to another heaping spoonful of halva made with sugar, powdered almonds, and ground sesame seeds. She tore off a piece of freshly baked unleavened bread and fed half to an old, limping hound she had rescued and named Theseus in place of Pegasus, who had gone to live with her mother. She smeared her piece with butter and sweet quince jam and popped it into her mouth. "It's delicious."

Zoe regarded her cousin. With her pretty looks Eirene turned her share of heads, but she didn't seem to need anyone, or anything—except, maybe, a dog. She wondered at the source of her self-sufficiency. Was it a mother's love? Eirene had received a letter from her mother yesterday, buoying her spirits.

While she—

She blinked to banish the ache that was always with her. She hadn't been invited to the palace to see her parents yet, nor had she heard from her brothers who were learning the art of war in other noble households. Everyone had forgotten about her, even Constantine. Her sense of loss was acute. She found it easier to excuse everyone's neglect except her mother's. A mother's love was supposed to be a child's birthright.

Eirene laid down her napkin. "What is the matter? Is it the emperor?" she asked gently.

"Always," Zoe replied. "And the street dwellers."

"You have to stop thinking about them. You give them money when we go into town. You cannot do more."

"Does their misery not trouble you, Eirene?"

"Of course, it does, but what can I do? I'm not rich or powerful. I can change nothing."

Zoe froze. For a moment she couldn't breathe, then she slapped down her napkin and gave Eirene a joyous hug. "You are a genius, Eirene! Thank you—thank you!"

Eirene stared at her, speechless with astonishment.

That afternoon, with Eirene in tow and a guard as escort, Zoe went to the palace to see her father. Crossing the Court of the Sundial, she mounted the palace steps to the great bronze doors and identified herself to one of the imperial guards.

"The Grand Duke is in the council chamber, my lady. If you hasten, you may catch him before the emperor arrives for the meeting," he replied, assigning her a guide.

She rushed after the guardsman with Eirene as he hurried them along the open walkways and endless corridors of the sprawling palace. They passed through a garden court of tall columns and a peristyle at such a quickened pace that Zoe barely noticed the beautiful patterns of exotic leopards, lions and gazelles splashed across the tiled floors. In the north wing they ran up a splendid white marble staircase to a corridor as wide and long as a city street. Supported by gilded columns and lined with busts of Romans emperors, the passageway glittered in the rainbow-colored light fracturing through a rose window. At the end of the hall Zoe came to a breathless halt before the Varangian guards. The immense gilded doors of the council chamber were shut. She was too late.

The Great Hall where she was taken to wait was divided into two long sections. The lower end was noisy and crowded with all manner of common folk: petitioners, long-bearded priests in black robes and hats, and merchants in cloaks and tunics from knee to ankle length, some in boots, some barelegged in high laced sandals. A few women were present, mostly widows or nuns. But at the far end, on a raised gallery cordoned off for the nobles by a fleet of shining marble steps and crimson velvet curtains, a group of jeweled lords and ladies were gathered around a troubadour. Zoe checked her steps and dismissed the guide.

"Will you not join the nobles?" Eirene asked her in surprise.

Zoe shook her head. "I have no wish to raise Empress Helena's ire by making my presence known. I'll read my book until the council meeting is over. You may do as you please until then, Eirene."

Eirene left to pat a dog lying by the hearth, and Zoe settled into a window seat that commanded a spectacular view of the sparkling waters of the Golden Horn. She opened the book she had brought to read. *The Alexiad* was written nearly four hundred years earlier by Anna Comnena, daughter of the eleventh century emperor Alexius Comnenus. On her father's death, Anna made a failed bid for the throne, lost the battle against her brother, and was imprisoned in a nunnery for her efforts. There she whiled away her confinement by writing an account of her father's reign. Images of the personalities, battles and court intrigues rose before Zoe's eyes as Anna mourned the loss of the father she had loved. Zoe's fingers slackened around the book, and she wiped away a furtive tear. Four hundred years, and nothing has changed. People still love, fight wars, and suffer—

"Lady Zoe, what do you read?"

Startled, she looked up from her window seat to find Constantine standing before her and herself the center of attention. She leapt to her feet, blushing, and hid the book behind her skirts as she curtsied.

"By St. Nicholas, what can you be reading?" he teased, bemused by her confusion. "Pray, my lady, let us have a peek—" He held out his hand for the book.

Aware of the eyes on them and the sudden silence that had fallen over the great chamber, Zoe gave it to him, her cheeks burning.

He bent his head and read aloud: "To put before the public the life history of such an emperor reminds me of his supreme virtue, his marvelous qualities, and the hot tears fall again as I weep with all the world—" He looked at her.

Zoe dropped her lids. Placing a finger under her chin, he tilted her face to him.

"My lady, mourning the loss of a loved one is no cause for shame. Loss is a wound to the soul as great as a sword thrust to the body. No one is immune. Potter, shepherd, silk weaver, emperor—it makes no difference who you are."

Zoe lifted her gaze to his hazel eyes, her heart pounding, her breath catching, emotion blurring her sight. As their eyes met, Constantine took on an expression of bewilderment. He dropped his hand and returned her book. "Death is the order of things, Zoe," he said under his breath. "None can escape. For those who are left behind, there is comfort and honor in remembrance."

She fingered the book. "I prefer Vegetius—" she said hastily, to change the mood—change it, and keep Constantine with her, for he was turning to leave. "Vegetius gives practical advice."

"You have read *de Rei Militari?"* Constantine demanded in astonishment. Zoe never ceased to surprise him.

"Of course."

"But why?"

"Why not?"

He roared with laughter, displaying the dimples she loved. "Why not indeed? No doubt Anna Comnena read Vegetius. Perhaps that was why she made a bid for her brother's throne? There was once an empress named Zoe who ruled the empire alone. Do you nurse aspirations I should know about, my lady?" he teased.

"My aspirations are not for a throne." Zoe lifted her chin. "A wife can advise a husband best if she is well read."

"Advise on fighting?"

"On everything."

He grinned. Zoe might be young in years, but she had spirit, and was turning out to be very interesting. She always made him think.

Zoe bristled at the amusement she saw in his eyes. "I will wager a bet with you, Augustus—That the Empress Helena has read Vegetius."

His smile vanished. She was right, of course. His mother had read Vegetius, but somehow his mother had always seemed to him more than just a woman. Now he realized that Zoe was right.

"And the dowager empress not only counseled her husband on affairs of state, but also her sons," Zoe continued, driving home her advantage. "Is that not so?"

He stared at her mutely. Zoe gave him a sly smile that recalled their old familiar friendship and curtsied though he hadn't dismissed her. She felt his eyes on her as she left.

Zoe circled back to the royal council chamber to find her father dictating a letter to a scribe. Furnished with an enormous oak table and chairs and a marble bust of Constantine the Great, the vaulted council chamber was light and airy and commanded a stunning view of the Golden Horn. As she waited quietly at the entrance for him to finish, she admired the artwork hanging on the wall behind him; a gem-studded, gold-washed icon of the *Protection of the Theotokas,* depicting the Virgin Mary holding the veil of protection over the emperor and his city.

Her father looked up. "Daughter, good to see you! What do you here?'

Zoe's smile faltered at his reaction. "I came to see you—" Hesitantly, she added, "And mother."

"But your mother is not here. She left for Lesbos to visit Helena—I thought you knew."

How would I know? she wanted to scream. Who has told me? She banished the old wounding hurt and reminded herself why she had come. "Forgive my intrusion, Father. I have a favor I would ask of you, and it cannot wait."

He nodded to the scribe and the man gathered his papers and left. The door thudded shut. "So, my dear," her father said, relaxing into his seat, "what is this about?"

She cleared her throat. "Father, I know you have lent a great deal of money to the emperor—"

"Yes. That is no secret."

"I would like you to lend some to me."

Lucas lifted his eyebrows. "When I loan money, I ask for collateral. What do you offer?" His green eyes held laughter as he looked at her.

"You gave me a diamond necklace two name-days ago. I can offer you that. It is very valuable."

"I know," he said, rubbing his chin to hide his smile. "Are you planning to purchase necessities abroad for the empire?"

"No, Father. My needs are simple. I wish to buy necessities for the poor here who have nowhere to turn."

Lucas didn't reply immediately. Zoe knew he was thinking of the time when she gave the gold bezant to the beggar girl. "You cannot save the world, Zoe. All my money cannot help you do that," he said gently.

"I know, Father. I have no wish to save the world, only the poor and needy in Constantinople."

"The poor and needy have charities they can go to for aid."

"There are too many poor and needy and not enough charities."

"That is the sad truth. And that, I fear, will never change."

"But we cannot stand by and do nothing, Father! The poor suffer through no fault of their own—I have gone into the streets and spoken with them myself and I—"

"You what?" Lucas slammed a hand on the table. "I'll have no daughter of mine mingling with the street dwellers! How can you be so foolish? They carry disease and many of them are criminals—"

"Father, they steal to eat."

"At best they're indigents then—"

"Some are young girls who have been forced into prostitution—some are servants let go because they're old and have outlived their usefulness. Most are good people, Father. There's Agatha, who shares her meals with a stray dog—and Eugenia a former circus performer who recites poetry and walks with a limp after being thrown by a runaway horse. Now she teaches others her circus tricks so they can entertain passers-by on the street and earn a reward. They steal food because God made them to eat, and they cannot find work!"

"Anyone can find a job who wishes to work—"

"You know better than anyone that trade is down, Father. Fewer and fewer ships come to purchase our silks, dyes, gold-works, copper, and lacquers. Able-bodied men can't find work, let alone women and children! Work is scarce. That's why so many have no shelter!"

"There is naught to be done about it then. It is the way things are."

"No, Father. It is the way things are because those who can change the way they are choose to do nothing!"

Her father fell thoughtfully silent. Zoe watched as he stroked his beard, growing more anxious as time passed. Fearing his thoughts were weighing against her, she slipped into the seat beside him and laid a gentle hand on his arm. "I do not need much, Father. You know I'm not a spendthrift like Maria. For the price of a few gems, I can set up a kitchen in one of the abandoned churches and give shelter to the street dwellers."

Zoe knew it was time to employ the last weapon in her arsenal: an appeal to her father's vanity, for he loved to be admired. "And once the charity is set up, all Constantinople will bless our name. Your generosity will be on everyone's lips, and all the churches will pray for our family. It wouldn't cost much. There is nothing to be lost, Father, and much to be gained."

She waited for what seemed an eternity.

"Very well. I will make a donation to your efforts," he said abruptly.

In her joy, Zoe fell to her knees before him. "Thank you, Father! Thank you—" She grabbed his hand and kissed it.

"A *small* donation, Zoe."

"Small." She flashed him a wide smile as she rose. "But if l do well, you'll give me more, won't you?"

He shook his head helplessly. "You are impossible, child."

A few days after the feast of St. Gregory Palamas on the second Sunday of Lent, Zoe went shopping for a church.

The remnant of the storm that had howled in during the night whipped her cloak and flung icy spray into her face. Named for King Boreas, the fierce mythical ruler of the winds, the storm had nearly buried the city beneath a thick white mantle of snow, but she couldn't wait for more clement weather. Easter would soon be here, and time was short. As children made special dolls and people cleansed body and spirit in preparation for the holy event, she trotted her palfrey west on the Golden Mile, past the Forum of Constantine, to the *Mese.*

At the corner of the famed commercial avenue of *Makros Embolos* that was marked by the Guild of the Makers of Silver Thread on one side and the Dealers of Olive Oil on the other, she turned north toward the Golden Horn. Already laden with ice from the frigid Black Sea, it glittered in the sun as if blanketed with smashed glass. *Makros Embolos* was home to all kinds of merchants and artisans, and the street bustled with activity. The air was rife with the clamor of whirling wheels, banging of shipbuilders, and clanging of metal from the blacksmith shops.

Along the street city workers shoveled snow from the roadway, merchants swept their storefronts and customers from strange lands passed by, their eyes scanning the gilt and leather emblems that swung wildly in the wind. She followed their gaze to the quill of the scribe, the scissors of the tailor, and the hammer of the mason.

"It is the wine-barrel of the tavern-owner that attracts most of the business this day," she noted to Eirene, riding at her side.

"A cup of hot wine would do me no harm," Eirene replied crossly, shoulders hunched beneath her cloak. She had long ago run out of the food she always carted with her for the street dogs and thrown her last bone to a hungry hound. Now all she wanted was to go home to Theseus, her newly adopted gray hound.

"We'll be there soon, Eirene. Let's pray this church has a few walls left." Most of the churches for sale were ruins.

"Amen to that. And may the Lord show mercy and throw in a roof."

Zoe gave her an indulgent smile. The search had been wearing thin as church after church proved too dilapidated for use and too expensive for repair. St. Acacius was one of the last on the list. Zoe prayed that enough remained of the old church to make it serviceable. Located in a deserted area near the Venetian quarter, it had been founded by Constantine the Great in the fourth century and rebuilt by Justinian in the sixth. Abandoned years ago, it had fallen into disrepair and could be had cheaply.

The sleek white palfrey she had named Ariadne reared beneath her with a whinny of protest. Her eye fell on a group of horses tethered in front of a greenstuff dealer, eating hay from bags suspended from their bridles. "Patience Ariadne," she clucked. "You'll get your turn soon, I promise." As they moved on, loud voices came to her from the victualer's store.

"Three stavrata a kilo for chickpeas? You are a robber!" a woman exclaimed.

"When the supply goes down, the price goes up. If you don't wish to buy now, come back next month when the docks are full of ships."

"We need chickpeas now. We can't eat meat during Lent!"

"That is your problem. This is my price. Take it, or leave it, woman."

Zoe saw the housewife shell out the coins and heard her angry grumbling before the shop passed from view. She leaned over to Eirene. "I'll probably be squabbling like that with the Patriarch for a good rent on my church. Let's hope I have better luck."

"All I know is, if we don't get that church soon, I'll die of exhaustion, frostbite, and starvation. And a few other things," Eirene replied.

"Oh, Eirene, you should have joined the circus," Zoe chuckled. "You have such talent for drama."

When they finally reached the Church of St. Acacius, Zoe couldn't restrain her excitement. Not waiting for a hand from one of her two guards, she leapt down from Ariadne and hastened into the roofless nave. She glanced around for only a moment before she twirled in delight, laughing. "Eirene—we've found it— It's perfect!"

"Missing a few walls and roofs, but other than that, I can see it's perfect," muttered Eirene, shivering in the shelter of an overhang. "If you don't come out of the rain, you'll catch your death of cold. Then your father will kill me."

"There is a roof, if you care to look—" Zoe pointed to the west. "And one is all we need."

Eirene turned behind her. She had trouble seeing it at first, for it was hidden by a thick cluster of Aleppo pines. But Zoe was right. Of the many domes that had once covered the four points of the compass along the cruciform building, this one though stained and shorn of brass, remained intact.

Inside they found a single occupant: a hound sleeping peacefully in an arched niche set in a stone wall. Eirene saw it first and placed a finger to her lips to alert Zoe, and they continued past on tiptoe so as not to disturb his slumber. After a few turns along the passageway, Zoe came to a halt. "Eirene, do you hear that? There is a brook just beyond those trees!" She pointed to an opening where a window once stood and quickened her pace to round another corner. "And look at this—"

Eirene followed her gaze to the floor where mother-of-pearl and colored stones had been inlaid in a design that resembled a beautiful Saracen carpet.

"This place will be wonderful!" Zoe exclaimed, barely able to contain her joy. She wandered around for a long while, retracing her steps back and forth, taking careful note of what repairs were needed, where cupboards could be built, tables placed, and serving pieces hung. It was almost vespers before she was done. "I think I have everything now."

Eirene looked up from the stone sill where she sat rubbing her sore feet. "You mean we can finally go home? To a fire and a good meal?"

Zoe gave her an absent nod. Now that she had found her church, her mind was no longer filled with concerns for the poor, or even for her own physical needs. She wondered if an invitation had come from the palace.

Seven

Soon after dispatching George Phrantzes on the marriage quest, Constantine invested Demetrios and Thomas as joint rulers of the Peloponnese. Demetrios received the southeastern half of the peninsula with Mistra as its capital, and Thomas the northwestern half. At a solemn ceremony in the throne room attended by Empress Helena and the high officials of the land, his two brothers swore allegiance to him and eternal friendship to one other.

"I wonder how long that will last," his mother remarked to Constantine as they sat together by a roaring fire in the Ocean Hall.

"If it lasts any time at all, I will be grateful," Constantine replied, sinking into a chair of pale blue silk embroidered with tarnished silver thread. Thomas, his youngest brother, had never given him much trouble, but Demetrios was restless, ambitious, unscrupulous, and the self-appointed champion of the Greek faith against the Latinizing tendencies of his brothers. He thrived on discord and had been a burr in Constantine's saddle from birth. When he was eight years old, Constantine had told Demetri he would be Constantine the Great one day, and Demetri had promptly beaten him up for it.

He heaved an audible breath. "We sons of the family of Palaeologus have proven ourselves a quarrelsome lot, haven't we, *Mana mou?*"

"We Greeks are a quarrelsome lot. From time immemorial we have fought one another."

"And now we must unite against the wider threat that confronts our civilization," Constantine sighed. The clink of armor turned his attention to the captain of his Varangian Guards.

"Augustus, the Grand Duke is here to see you." Tall and clean-shaven, John Dalmata was in his thirties with a thick crop of yellow hair and clear blue eyes that blazed his Old Norse heritage. At Constantine's nod, he stepped aside and made way for Zoe's father.

"What is the matter?" Constantine demanded, taking in Lucas's expression.

"Prince Demetrios and his supporters are going to demand Patriarch Gregory's resignation at the meeting tomorrow. I thought you should know."

Constantine tightened his grip on his armrests. Patriarch Gregory III Mammas came from the island of Crete that had once belonged to the Eastern Roman Empire but was now ruled by Venice. He had supported union in Florence, but he was no Venetian in his sympathies. He was one of their own, and they could not do better in a patriarch.

"By St. Barnabas, instead of trying to resolve matters, Demetrios wishes to impede me any way he can," Constantine said, venting his frustration.

The next morning, as the winds of King Boreas wreathed the city in velvety snow, Constantine strode into the throne room and took his seat. The atmosphere was already thick with animosity, and Patriarch Gregory's glum expression spoke of barely concealed rage. As it turned out, the problem was not so much Constantine's brother, Demetrios, who was present, but the monk named Gennadius, who was not. Before he'd changed his name and taken his vows, Gennadius had been the famed scholar George Scholarius: philosopher, theologian, and former patriarch of the Orthodox church. As Scholarius, he had been pro-union, a signer of the accord at Florence, credited with resolving the most dangerous theological point of dissension between the two churches—the nature of the Trinity. As Gennadius, he was vehemently anti-union and raged tirelessly against it.

"I consulted Gennadius on my way here," announced Demetrios. "This is what he wrote—" He approached the throne and handed a rolled parchment to Constantine. "He warns that you and your government would do better to trust in God than to pin your hopes on rescue coming from the Latins. Those who betray the True Church and the faith of their forefathers for the sake of earthly rewards will forfeit His blessing and His help."

Constantine scanned the missive before passing it to the patriarch. He was always amazed how readily some claimed to know the mind of God. He himself was no fanatical advocate of the pact of union signed at Florence, but he continued his brother's policy because he believed it was their only hope. Unfortunately, Gennadius enjoyed an esteemed reputation and had many followers. Even locked away in his cell at the Pantokrator monastery, he was a formidable adversary.

"We have resolved the questions that divide us," Constantine replied wearily. "We resolved them at Florence, with Gennadius's help."

"And he has changed his mind. He wishes his right hand had been severed so he could not have signed the pact of Union."

"The West is not our enemy," Patriarch Gregory III Mamas said, rolling up the parchment. "The West is our salvation."

"The West is our doom!" Demetrios exclaimed. "The act of union will destroy us. The Ottomans will see union with the West as a threat. They will rise up and crush us."

"Nobilissimos," Lucas said, addressing Demetrios respectfully, "I am as much against union as you are. We do not differ on any point. None of us here wants to unite with the Latin church, but what choice do we have? We cannot stand alone. That much we know. Our brothers the Serbs and Russians are too poor to help us. Only the Latins can help, and that they will not do unless we put away our differences. We must unite to save ourselves. It is the only way."

A chorus of ayes arose from one side of the room.

Constantine added his voice. "Only if the West sees us as upholding union can we hope to secure from Christendom the armies we so desperately need to protect ourselves. That is why I plead for your support, Demetrios. Help me to save the land we both love, brother."

"You live in dreams! We will never unite, and they will never send help!" Demetrios raged. "And I will never accept Latin theology, and never will I abandon our Eastern traditions!"

"Brother, we have been fighting among ourselves for a long time, and while we fought, the enemy marched steadily westward. Now they surround us. Can you not see that? Do you not understand what is at stake? We must put away our differences for the survival of Christian civilization in the East—or we will cease to exist!"

"The West does not regard us as true Christians, though we were the first Christians," Demetrios retorted. "We practice the ancient traditions of Christianity as handed us by St. Paul and the Apostles, yet they wish us to bend to them as if we were heretics! We will never compromise with the Latin church. We are here to demand the resignation of Patriarch Gregory for his support of union!"

The room erupted with shouts. The aged Patriarch Gregory pushed angrily to his feet, his face as red as the rubies in the jeweled cross he wore. He opened his mouth to protest, but Constantine held up a hand for silence. "The Patriarch's authority comes from God, and only God can revoke it! Such a demand is an offence against Him and a betrayal of our faith."

"And you betray the true faith by uniting with the West," Demetrios cried. "You are a traitor! You have no right to the imperial throne! I will never accept you. No one will who is against union!"

"It is not religion that drives you to say these monstrous things, Demetri. It is blind ambition! There is indeed a traitor among us—and it is you. You sold out John for your own ends and marched at the sultan's side when he attacked Constantinople! You wanted the throne from John, and you want it from me—and you care naught how much blood you shed getting it!"

"And you, brother—you're so filled with hubris you can't see what you've stirred up. All our difficulties are your doing. If you hadn't evicted the Venetians and Genoese and built the Hexamilion Wall, you wouldn't have made enemies of the Italians and angered the sultan, and he wouldn't have invaded the Peloponnese. You and your dreams of conquest! You and your dream of union!" He spat on the marble floor.

The Varangians reached for their weapons, but Constantine shot them a restraining glance. "You condemn me for building the wall," Constantine said, "but not your friend the sultan for enslaving sixty thousand Christian captives. Do you ever give a thought to those unfortunate souls—your fellow Greeks? Do you not care that their children are being raised as Muslims to fight against us in the sultan's army? Do you ever think of anyone but yourself? Of anything but what you want?"

"If you hadn't restored the Hexamilion, he wouldn't have come! If you hadn't fought him, he wouldn't have enslaved our people. Now you're doing the same with Constantinople that you did with the Hexamilion—goading the enemy into attacking us! All you can think of is yourself. In your desire to save Constantinople, you've sold your soul to the devil! *Rum Papa* will never send the help you seek!" he cried, using the derogatory name for the Roman pope that antiunionists gave their dogs. "Better to befriend the sultan and welcome the Ottomans."

Constantine stared, speechless, unable to believe his ears. Lucas broke the shocked silence. "Better the sultan's turban than the cardinal's miter?" he breathed in horror.

"Yes! The Latins burned our city, raped our women, and murdered our children! They're worse than the infidel. So, yes—better the turban than the bishop's miter!"

"You are even more deluded than I knew," Constantine said. "Wait until your friend the sultan sends for your daughter for his harem. See how you feel then!"

Demetrios drew his sword but before he could make a move, John Dalmata had seized his arm and his Varangians had readied their axes. Demetrios dropped his weapon. At Constantine's nod, Dalmata released him. "How dare you!" Demetrios said, addressing Dalmata as he rubbed his wrist. "I am the emperor's brother, and you will pay for this!"

"I cannot see you as my brother," Constantine said. "You are too much of a fool."

Leaning his weight on the balustrade, Constantine inhaled a deep, scented breath. Twilight was falling over the earth, and by the round towers of the western land walls the darkening landscape was thick with black cypresses and the silvery foliage of laurel trees. He could smell the spicy odor of thyme and resinous woods on the wind, along with the ever-present sea-salt. Sea birds shrieked loudly, and fishermen returning from the day's catch rolled up their nets on the beach. Merchant ships sailed past on the Golden Horn, torches flaring as they headed for safe harbor in one of Constantinople's ports or the thriving trading colony of Pera inhabited by Greeks, Jews, and Genoese.

The strains of a dulcimer drifted to him from somewhere below, and he was flooded with peace. How he loved this land! Everywhere he looked, velvet waters surrounded him, and in their midst, God had laid the jewel of Constantinople like an emerald amid sapphires. The tapping of a walking stick intruded into his thoughts. He turned.

"Ah, there you are, my son," his mother called out.

He came to her side and gave her a kiss. Together they made their way inside where Aesop had laid dinner by the fire. Constantine took the steps down to the sunken alcove that served as his study and retrieved a document from his desk. Settling into the beaded chair of crimson silk that had become his favorite, he passed his mother the missive he'd received from Adrianopolis.

"I knew Sultan Murad would oblige us by accepting the truce we offered," he said. "He is a reasonable man."

She looked up when she had read. "More importantly, he is old, and tired, and wants peace. You seem to be disappointed on all fronts, except with the enemy."

Constantine gave her a wan smile. "In many ways it is easier for me to deal with the Ottomans than with my own family."

"And your own people," Helena added. She examined the plate of bite-sized savory pasties of *apotki*, selected a grape leaf stuffed with rice and raisins, and nibbled delicately.

Constantine toyed with his wine. Time was passing and he had made no progress whatsoever in his efforts to reconcile his divided country on the question of union. The Orthodox church of the East saw the Latin church of the West as adulterating the True Word with their changes. In meeting after meeting, privately, and in concert, he had tried to persuade the clergy and high officials of the land that their differences did not matter. They were still of one faith, and in union lay their only hope of saving the Christian church of the East. But he'd encountered nothing but resistance.

He took a spoonful of the Black Sea caviar he loved. "I did not expect union to be easy, but it has proven more difficult than I ever imagined. I have no idea how John and the pope brought their two sides together at Florence. That they agreed in the end would give me hope—were it not for Gennadius."

"Gennadius!" his mother sniffed contemptuously, cutting into her venison. "The man is mad."

They discussed the monk and other matters, big and small, then Constantine fell silent. It had been a long day, filled with decisions. He had attended ceremonies for the Venetian and Genoese envoys, and mediated disputes between his ministers. He had dictated letters, and met with the central tax collector and the paymaster of the troops. He had even made time for the manager of the imperial estate. What they had to say was not reassuring. The treasury was in dire financial straits. Revenues were on a downward slide and had been plunging for years.

He leaned his head back and closed his eyes.

"You are tired, my son. You must rest." His mother set her napkin down and Aesop pulled back her chair.

Constantine escorted her to the entry and Aesop threw the doors open. The Varangians saluted with a fist to the breast and a lady-in-waiting rose from the bench where she had been seated. He bid his mother goodnight with a peck on the cheek and watched as she made her way to the great white marble staircase, leaning heavily on the woman's arm, her cane tapping softly. In Mistra, he had welcomed the time alone at the end of a difficult day. Now suddenly, he found it a burden. For a moment he considered sending for a woman, but casual liaisons rarely brought him pleasure. He preferred a meeting of the mind with someone whose company he enjoyed. Someone who understood him, with whom he shared memories. Someone he could talk to freely, who could lighten his heaviness. He thought of Zoe. The image of her dancing with a lavender veil, singing like a siren, and quoting Vegetius filled him with a strange yearning. Part child, part woman, part goddess, she always managed to make him smile. Recently she had even sent him a smile through her father. "I must compliment you on your daughter," Constantine had told Lucas. "She is well read and has an excellent grasp of military concepts. We had quite a discussion about strategy. She is a brilliant girl."

"And as obstinate as a mule, Augustus," Lucas had replied. "Once she gets something into her head, one cannot persuade her otherwise. To help the poor, she had me extend her a loan using as collateral a diamond necklace I made the mistake of giving her for her name-day."

Constantine had thrown his head back and roared with laughter.

Aye, Zoe would dispel his doubts and fears with her lyre, he thought, standing uncertainly in the middle of the room. But the hour was late—

"*Who loves Emperor John?*" Apollo shrieked, blasting him out of his thoughts. He looked at the bird. Apollo stared back at him.

"Remind me never to tell you my secrets, Apollo," Constantine said. Taking him a slice of orange from a platter on a nearby chest, he watched him eat, his thoughts on Zoe.

Eight

No invitation arrived from the palace. To bury her disappointment, Zoe plunged herself into work. After obtaining a lease for her church, she interviewed stonemasons, tile workers and carpenters and secured a good price for the addition of the kitchen and storerooms. She bartered with the makers of wooden cups and bowls, copper cauldrons and ladles, cookpots and gridirons, and braziers, tables, and benches and hired men to dig a well for drinking water and install a pool for washing utensils. She engaged a crew to erect outdoor privies, roofless and made of mud to save money. Daily she checked on the progress of the remodeling, correcting mistakes and suggesting improvements. As the work neared completion, she hired cooks for the charity she named "Last Hope of the Careworn."

"I don't know what I'd do without you," Zoe told Eirene as they rode back to the Notaras palace one April afternoon after Nones.

"I admit I thought it foolish at first," Eirene confided, her cheeks rosy from the cold wind that blew from the sea. "I was afraid you'd lose interest and it would all be for naught. But it is good work we do. I am glad to be a part of it." She gave Zoe a smile as they waited for the watchman to swing open the gate to the residence. "But tonight, I want nothing more than a warm meal and a comfortable bed—I'm so famished I could eat a river horse."

"We'll feel better once Lent is over, Eirene."

In the outer court, Zoe gave her reins over to a stable hand and made her way into the inner garden and up the staircase. She was exceptionally weary this evening, and the steady splashing of the fountain, so soothing and hypnotic, fanned her drowsiness as she climbed to her bedchamber.

"Daughter!"

Her father's voice startled her when she reached the top of the stairs. She looked up to find him heading toward her from the privy chamber. "Father— What do you here?" she exclaimed.

"Have you forgotten? This is my house. Are you not happy to see me?"

"Of course. But I'm surprised," she said, embracing him. "You rarely come, and—" She searched his face, suddenly alert. "You have news— Something has happened!" Had Constantine found a bride? For a sickening moment she couldn't breathe. She reached for the balustrade.

"I do bring news, but you look exhausted, child. It can wait until after we sup."

As she read his expression, relief swept her. This was personal, something on the order of another title perhaps; news about Constantine would have taken precedence. She nodded gratefully.

They took their meal at a table set before a roaring fire, dining on Lenten soup, white bread, shining gray mullet and anglerfish, and quenching their thirst with sweet malmsey from Monemvasia. She accepted two helpings of fritters with honey for dessert, and when she was satiated, she lifted her eyes to her father's face. "I'm dying to hear—what have you to tell me?"

"Well, my dear, the news I bear is the best a father can give a daughter." He moved to stand with his back to the fire. "How would you like to be a duchess?"

"A duchess? Of what?"

"Serbia."

Zoe stared at him for a moment, not comprehending. "But Father, you know I can't leave Constantinople."

"What do you mean you can't leave Constantinople?"

"I can't leave now. I have important work here."

"Work? You mean making broth for the poor? Bah! There are plenty of poor people in Serbia. You can make broth for them."

"Father— I am not your only daughter. There is Maria. Marry her off. She would love to be a duchess in Serbia."

"They're not asking for Maria. They want you."

She dropped her lids to hide the wounding ache in her heart. She had barely arrived and already her father wanted to send her away, maybe never to meet again. She searched desperately for a way out, and the answer came to her. Her beloved father had one great flaw. Ambition.

"Father, do you love me?" she asked, unable to suppress the plaintive note in her tone. No one except her nurse had ever told her they loved her.

"Of course."

"If you love me, don't make me wed, Father. I haven't even been presented at court. If I can get an offer of marriage that makes me a duchess now, imagine what grand alliance may come our way once I am at court. I pray you, wait for a marriage that will bring you greater honor." She went to him and laid her head against his chest

Zoe could not have known what paternal emotion she had evoked with her simple gesture of affection as Lucas remembered the adoring, enthralling little girl who used to run to him with open arms, her face lit with joy. He knew he should be insulted that Zoe didn't leap to do his bidding; he was her father, after all, and daughters were supposed to obey their fathers. But when had Zoe ever done what she was told? Willful, stubborn, disobedient—all this she was without doubt, yet he had only himself to blame. From the moment she'd smiled at him in her cot, he'd been enslaved. A good beating might have taught her a lesson years ago, but he had not the heart to take the stick to a little wisp of a child when she reminded him so much of Hector, the laughing red-haired brother he had lost. Now it was too late. He had to face it. He could deny Zoe nothing.

Zoe did have a point, however. She had not yet been presented at court. It was most unusual for the daughter of the premier duke of the land to be unwelcome in the imperial presence, yet that seemed to be the case. Each time he'd requested to bring Zoe to court, Constantine had replied that he would consult his mother. But then, the answer never came. Zoe must have offended the dowager empress that day in the litter, though she seemed baffled herself. Maybe her good works would bring the imperial family a change of heart. Once she was presented at court, who could tell what suitors would come? She was still young.

She had plenty of time.

Zoe felt his stiff shoulders relax but dared not look at him as he disengaged her arms from around his neck. "Perhaps you're right, Zoe, and you can do better." He gazed down at her. "But if I bring you a prince, I will not take no for answer. Is that understood?"

"Oh, Father, thank you!" She showered his hands with kisses and looked up at him with moist eyes. "Father, I promise you this. One day I will make you proud of me."

He cupped her cheeks in his hands and laid a kiss on her brow. "I am already proud of you, child."

One good thing about Easter, Zoe thought as Eirene dressed her for the glorious resurrection midnight liturgy on Holy Saturday. She would finally see Constantine.

"Fire of Zeus becomes you," Eirene said, helping Zoe into her gown of fine Venetian velvet. It was a shade of flame that complimented Zoe's coloring and brought to mind the persimmon fruit, *Diospyros lotus,* the "Fire of Zeus." Selecting a braided cord of silver thread from a casket of ribbons, Eirene wound it around the bodice of Zoe's Grecian gown, adjusted her long sleeves, and pinned a sheer diamond-studded veil over Zoe's glossy tresses.

"Perfection," Eirene announced, stepping back to assess her handiwork.

"But will he notice me?" Zoe sighed, seeking reassurance, as always.

"He'll notice you even if the empress hides you behind a colossal pillar."

Zoe couldn't suppress a giggle. "Eirene, I adore you!" Eirene never failed her.

On the second floor with a bevy of other noble ladies, Zoe had cause to remember her words. The empress had indeed assigned her the worst seat in the imperial loge. Zoe glared at the wide marble column that obscured her view of the *Omphalion,* a sacred circle of multi colored marble near the altar where Constantine sat on his throne. In order to see him, she had to lean far to the side and obscure someone else's view. Each time she managed a glimpse, he had his face uplifted to the balcony. Though she knew it was his mother he sought, she wanted to believe that he looked for her.

She had barely restrained her joy when she'd received the gilded invitation to attend the midnight service at the Hagia Sophia on Easter Saturday and the feast of rejoicing at Blachernae Palace on Easter Sunday. But now her disappointment was acute. She fingered her beautiful flame-colored gown despondently. Three seamstresses had labored a week on the dress, and Eirene had done her finest work yet on her Grecian hairstyle, looping and twisting her perfumed auburn locks with pearls and piling the curls high on her head, because, she said, "The upswept hairstyle shows off your swan neck." But it was all to no avail. She felt as alone as she had years ago on the wharf watching her parents sail away. The empress ignored her, and her ladies followed her example.

She was an outsider, even among her own. Her mother was still in Lesbos, awaiting the birth of her first grandchild, her father was absent though he was in the city, and her brothers were too occupied with their lives to pay her much heed. She might not exchange greetings with them even on this special night, for they stood below with the men, and would, no doubt, leave immediately after Easter service to prepare for the morrow's feast.

In the misty haze conjured by burning incense and the blur of candles, as monks chanted the Resurrection liturgy, Zoe dared a peek around the column again. Constantine had left his throne and was crossing the nave. Tall and stately in a silk dalmatic, with his crown on his shapely head and his purple cloak flowing from one shoulder, he dominated the richly clad patriarch and bishops as he took his place in the procession. On impulse, throwing caution to the wind, she leaned over the balcony as he passed beneath and gave a little wave.

He looked up directly at her.

As she stared in amazement, paralyzed with shock and joy, his smile widened. Then he passed beneath the balcony and disappeared from view. She fell back into her seat, exhilarated and only dimly aware of the shocked whispers her behavior had elicited. Then she thought of the empress. She stole a sidelong glance at her along the row. Helena was staring at her with an expression of intense displeasure. Zoe wiped the smile from her lips, sat back in her chair, and clasped her hands demurely in her lap. She was saved from further embarrassment by the traditional extinguishing of the light as the last minutes of Holy Saturday passed in symbolic darkness and the church clock tolled the hour.

On the stroke of midnight, the patriarch lit a flame from the perpetual lamp and carried it to his bishops who passed it along to the congregation. A sudden blaze of light illuminated the enormous nave. Bells pealed and the church resounded with cries of "Christ is Risen". The holy procession took shape below, and Zoe's gaze sought Constantine again. She was thrilled to see his head turned in her direction. This time she had no doubt his smile was intended for her. Joining her voice to the thousands of Christian faithful and beaming with happiness, she sang her responses loudly, her heart overflowing with joy.

With the greatest excitement she had ever felt in her life, Zoe dressed for the Easter Sunday celebration at the palace. She had been excluded from participating in the afternoon entertainment, for that had been planned by the empress, but she was certain to encounter Constantine at the feast. Even Empress Helena couldn't prevent that.

Clad in the splendid persimmon gown and sheer diamond-studded veil that had won her the good fortune of Constantine's smile the night before, she gripped Eirene's hand nervously as their litter carriers bore them through the palace gates. Tumblers welcomed them with somersaults, and men on stilts doffed their hats to them in greeting. Even circus people were in attendance with their performing animals. By the time they arrived at the Court of the Sundial, Zoe had seen elephants, zebras, gazelles, leopards, and all manner of other large cats. To her delight, a chattering monkey in an embroidered cap had even handed her an apple. But as she stepped from her litter, before she had a chance to fully take in the merry scene, a page bowed to her.

"The festivities are in the imperial vineyards, my lady, and Empress Helena has sent me to escort you to your seat," he said.

With a parting hug to Eirene, who would sit below the dais, she followed the page up the steps to the lion statues, through the palace and out again into the expansive inner gardens. It was a beautiful day, mild in temperature, and the walk to the imperial vineyards could not have been more splendid, nor Zoe's heart lighter. The merry melody of minstrels playing beneath a pomegranate tree enfolded her in its lively beat. With a spring in her step, she rounded a corner to a glittering vista. Emerald vineyards fanned out in rows, and beyond the ancient city walls, the sea sparkled like crushed diamonds against the verdant hills and blossoming orchards of the Genoese town of Pera. So enthralled was she by the splendor of the scenery that she didn't notice where the page was taking her until they stood at her table. Her smile vanished. She was not seated on the dais, but far in the opposite direction, her back to the high table. In stunned disbelief, she turned and gazed past the sea of pink tables to where Constantine would sit.

"Something wrong, my lady?" asked the page.

She was about to protest that there was indeed when comprehension washed over her in a muddy flood. This was no mistake. The empress had planned it this way.

"No." She dropped down into the chair he held out for her, too stunned to say more. Guests claimed their seats around her. She acknowledged them with a strained smile and a heavy heart. When clarions trilled announcing the arrival of the imperial party, she barely lifted her eyes from her trencher as she rose in greeting. Nor did she look at her father, for then she would surely catch sight of Constantine, and that would be like pressing on an aching tooth.

Servants heaped her plate with steaming mussels and clams. Kneading a piece of white bread and pushing the shells around her plate, she barely noticed the chatter around her.

"You do not eat, my lady?" said the elderly man beside her. He looked at her curiously.

"No, sir, I—I— have no appetite." She picked up her goblet and drained her malmsey. The wine burned a path down her throat. The dinner dragged on. Soon she was forced to notice two girls at the far end of the table whose snide laughter and disparaging glances reached her where she sat.

"—grand duke's daughter… not on the dais…must be disgraced—"

"Wonder what she's done—"

"—cooking for the poor—"

"That *is* a disgrace!"

Giggles.

Zoe pretended not to notice. The dishes were cleared away and the entertainment commenced. Mummers and troubadours performed scenes from the Trojan War, and the sultan's cousin, the Ottoman prince, Orhan, recited a poem he had composed entitled, *My Name is Hope.*

I am endless. I am forever.

I am brightest in the depth of darkness.

When you are at your bleakest, I hold you closest. I am always with you, to your last breath.

The floor was thrown open for dancing, and people left their tables to mingle with one another. Zoe went to Prince Orhan's table to compliment him on his recital and then headed for the palace. She had nowhere to go and no plan; she only knew she had to leave this place.

Wandering aimlessly through the peristyles, she stumbled on a quiet courtyard of blue mosaics where a fountain trickled and took a seat on a stone bench scattered with the flaming petals of an acacia tree.

"May I bring you something, my lady?" a page inquired.

She requested a lute and accepted it gratefully. Strumming the instrument, she broke into a lament:

What good is spring when you are not here and ice entombs me?

Ah, ah, ah...

What good is spring?

She dropped her head as the last notes died away, feeling drained, hollow, lifeless. The old loneliness she had never completely banished returned with an ache, and she was swept with a yearning for Constantine and Mistra. So deep was she in gloom that she heard the applause only faintly, like an echo across a vast distance. She roused herself and looked up. The lute slipped from her grasp, and she rose to her feet slowly, unaware she moved. "Constans—" she breathed, watching in dazed disbelief as he came to her and took her hands in both his own. He smiled down, his hazel eyes twinkling, his dimples creasing his cheeks. "That was beautiful," he said.

They stood locked in one another's gaze, and Zoe had the strange sensation that she'd fallen into the stupor of a timeless dream where all sound was muffled and all vision distorted save his face. Recovering, she bobbed a quick curtsy in obeisance, for his Varangians watched from a distance. "Forgive me, Augustus— "

"For what, Zoe? For having the voice of an angel? For singing the most beautiful song I have ever heard?"

He stood so close Zoe could feel the heat from his body, and it made her senses spin. Not trusting herself to look at his face, she kept her eyes averted.

"By what oversight were you not part of the entertainment this afternoon?" he demanded. When he'd seen her quit the banquet, he'd felt compelled to follow, and it took him a while to locate her in this forsaken corner of the palace. For in truth, he had thought of her often during these weeks since their discussion of the Anna Comnena book. Zoe fascinated him and he marveled at her, this young thing who had become the talk of the town and the hope of the poor. When most girls were thinking of marriage and focusing their efforts on finding the best match they could, she had come out of nowhere to ease his troubles by alleviating poverty and injustice. He recalled his recent conversation with Lucas.

"I could not sleep last night and almost sent for Zoe to sing to me," he'd confided to her father.

"Why didn't you?" Lucas had asked. "I know she'd like nothing better."

"At that hour? She would think me mad."

"Mad? She regards you as the worthy successor of both Hector and Achilles, and probably Zeus."

Constantine had been flooded with a rush of pleasure. "How is her work coming refurbishing the Church of St. Acacius for the street dwellers?" he had asked. And having opened the subject, he found he wanted to go on talking about her.

"Expensive, Augustus. I need to find her a husband." Lucas had grinned.

Constantine had been unprepared for the tumble of confused feelings that assailed him at the thought. During the midnight service on the previous evening, he had searched for her, and when he finally saw her leaning over the balcony, he'd been startled by the rush of joy he'd felt. This afternoon he'd fully expected to share her company and was sorely disappointed to find her seated so far away. He guessed the reason. His mother. But he could scarcely fathom why. "It is not good for you to see her, Constans," his mother would say each time he asked to invite Zoe to the palace. "You must not indulge yourself." He would argue, but she wouldn't explain, and nothing changed her mind. He didn't understand his mother sometimes. What harm could it do if he enjoyed a little time with the girl? It wasn't as if he was going to marry her.

Zoe's lashes quivered. She lifted her eyes to him, and he felt as if he were drowning in their velvety brown depths. "Why were you not seated with me on the dais?" he asked gently.

"I—I—know not, Augustus— "she said, breathing hard, still dazed at the shock of his presence.

"Will you come back to the banquet and sing for me again—sing for everyone?" he corrected.

A rush of pink stained her cheeks, but when she didn't move, he said, "It would not be seemly if I dragged you there, my lady, would it? Pray allow me to escort you."

Zoe looked down at the strong sun-bronzed hand he offered. He had singled her out. He had come for her. Would she sing for him? Oh, yes, she would sing— With all her heart, she would sing!

She reached for his hand and smiled at him with the blinding radiance that suddenly filled her soul.

Nine

"The Grand Duke inquires again if you would welcome his daughter at court," Constantine said, lounging in his favorite red silk chair. He stole a glance at his mother over the rim of his goblet.

Empress Helena set down her wine. She picked up a tapestry square and began to stitch. "The subject is closed."

Constantine clapped his hands twice and Aesop appeared from the direction of the sunken study. The gold edging of his white tunica shimmered in the low candlelight as he refilled the empty goblet of Cyprian wine that Constantine held out to him. Behind him, the sea was taking on the glow of sapphires in the gathering dusk, and a soft breeze wafted from the lattice doors open to the terrace. Until this moment, Constantine had been drowsy with contentment.

He downed a gulp of wine. It was always the same when he broached the subject of Zoe. *"Mana mou,* it is not seemly that the daughter of the premier duke in the land is excluded from court. She has done nothing wrong. It is cruel—and if l didn't know you as I do—I would say vindictive."

Helena looked up sharply from her embroidery. "You must not indulge yourself, Constantine. The Notaras girl will not do."

"Indulge myself, Mother?" Constantine demanded, his voice rising in volume. "I have dispatched Phrantzes to the Black Sea and will wed whoever agrees to wed me! This is an entirely different matter. People gossip and cast aspersions. She is caused unwarranted suffering, and to what end? It is unjust. I have never known you to be unjust!"

Aesop tactfully withdrew to prepare the bedchamber for the night, bearing a candelabra to light his way along the raised marble step that ran from the bronze doors on the west to the bedchamber on the east. The minstrel followed his example and quietly slipped away.

With an audible sigh, Helena reached for his hand. "You have told me I am the only one who gives you counsel untainted by self-interest. Do you still feel that way?"

"Of course, *Mana mou,* but—"

"Then trust me on this, my son," she said gently. "You may be emperor, but you have much to learn about the human heart."

Autumn followed summer, the festivities of Christmas ushered in Twelfth Night, and Zoe's mother remained in Lesbos. With brief exceptions, Zoe was still excluded from court, and when she did attend, the empress continued to curtail her access to Constantine. There were celebrations at the palace for the founding of Constantinople on the eleventh of May, and for the emperor's name day on the Feast of the Holy Great Sovereigns Constantine and Helena on the twenty-first of May. But this time no emperor came to lead her to his court.

At odd moments Zoe relived that Easter day when Constantine had singled her out, and always her hand would still, and her heart would leap with remembrance. Sometimes it was as she ladled broth into the tin cup of a beggar at her charity of Last Hope of the Careworn; sometimes, as she sliced their bread, and sometimes as she sang for them. Always the moment was accompanied by the dazed joy she had sampled on that holy weekend.

Eirene noticed these moments, and noticed, too, the hope that lit Zoe's eyes each time a palace messenger arrived at the Notaras mansion. Zoe would reach for the missive with excitement, and as she read, the light in her eyes would dim, for it was never the invitation she hoped to receive. Each week that passed made it clear that the Easter night when she had dazzled the imperial court had not marked the end of her banishment.

As for Zoe's own name day on the Feast of St. Basil, the first of January, it had passed unnoticed by all except the Notaras servants who sang and danced for her at the residence. But her father did manage a brief visit to mark the day, and Constantine sent a gift of marchpane fashioned into tiny colorful fruits.

On this autumn evening in early September, Eirene caught the wistfulness in Zoe's voice as she sang. She suspected that she was more unhappy than she knew, despite the admiring folk who crowded the tables in the old, refurbished church of St. Acacius. An ache came to her, for it was not thus that she had expected her loveable cousin to spend her days, shunned by the imperial court and denied the love she yearned for. She had expected great things for Zoe, and sadly, she had been mistaken.

Zoe sat down on a stool and positioned her lyre as Eirene led a blind man to a seat at the dinner table, trailed by Theseus. The hound was devoted to Eirene and followed her everywhere, even if it was only from one corner of the room to another.

Though she had strained her budget to hire a dozen assistants for her charity, Eirene was its lifeblood. Zoe had expected the work to be unceasing and hard; she had known to expect difficulties dealing with dishonest merchants. But she had not anticipated that thieves would break in at night to steal supplies set aside for the poorest and most desperate of society, or that vandals would shatter windows for pleasure. All these disappointments she had shared with Eirene and resolved with her help.

She watched her cousin hand out bread around the tables. She cut an appealing figure in her blue linen gown, Zoe thought. Her glossy hair gleamed like onyx beneath a short veil, her brown eyes shone in her heart-shaped face, and her cheeks were rosy from the kitchen heat. Eirene had changed in these months; the hard edges had softened. Perhaps her work with the poor was healing the wounds she had borne in Monemvasia, but it still amazed her that Eirene, pretty as she was, felt no yearning to love and be loved.

"Greetings, O Short One—" a beggar grinned at a wide-eyed little girl, clambering over the bench and squeezing into place beside her, trencher in hand.

The remark was met with a bellyful of laughter, for the man was as tall as a cypress, and the child stared up at him as if he were Zeus come down from Mt. Olympus.

Zoe's finger rippled across her lute, and she broke into a merry ditty, her mood lightened. Poor folk sang along and clapped to the beat as if they hadn't a care in the world. Some left their bowls to dance and returned laughing to their seats. Now that she knew their names and their stories, Zoe couldn't believe there was a time when they had been merely the "street dwellers" to her.

It wasn't just Eirene who had changed, Zoe realized. St. Acacius had changed her too.

Early one morning, as word spread that the grand duke's daughter turned no one away who needed help, a young girl came to the Notaras mansion.

"Forgive my audacity for troubling you, my lady, but I am desperate and know not where to turn—" She broke off in tears.

"It is all right. Tell me your troubles," Zoe soothed.

"I am an actress," the girl said, regaining her composure. "I was taken into the theater as a child when I was orphaned… I have met a man who wishes to wed me—he is a good man, and I care for him, my lady. But the circus owner won't let me go. God forgive me, I have thought of ending my life."

Zoe regarded the pretty fair-haired girl who she guessed was around her age. A life in the theater meant a life of prostitution and odium beyond imagining. Those who worked there were once so despised that the church denied them the sacraments unless they were on their deathbed.

"Take heart, the law is on your side," Zoe said. "It has been so since the sixth century, thanks to Empress Theodora, a circus dancer herself. The theater owner cannot prevent you from leaving. Give my scribe his name, and he'll write an order. If the owner gives you trouble, let me know."

The girl collapsed in grateful tears.

Soon Zoe was deluged by other petitioners. Most were women, and to her relief, she found that she could resolve many of their ills at small expense.

"My parents would have me wed, but I wish to take holy orders," a girl wept. "I know not what to do!"

"I'll speak to your father," Zoe replied. Another girl had the opposite problem.

"My family would have me enter a convent," she sobbed. "I wish to wed the tavern keeper's son, but his father demands a dowry of two milk cows, and my family cannot pay it!"

"I will pay it for you. You will marry the one you love."

The girl threw herself at Zoe's feet and tearfully kissed the hem of her skirt.

Zoe met with success in every case she mediated, but she had no illusions. The outcome owed nothing to her oratory skills and everything to her position. Few dared gainsay the daughter of the premier duke in the land, even one banished from court.

As the months passed, not only did the poor come seeking her aid, but middling folk too. The number of petitioners grew, as did the complexity of their problems. Zoe learned about unjust verdicts issued by corrupt judges and men who stole the inheritance of female relatives. She came to understand more than she wished about marital disputes in which women had been unjustly divorced and kept from their children. Even men solicited her help whose wives refused to divorce them. She referred the more difficult matters to her father, but some only the emperor could resolve, and he could not hear them all.

"If I had more power," Zoe lamented to Eirene late one night after a particularly grueling day, "I wouldn't have to turn so many away. Why is it so hard to right a wrong, Eirene?"

With a sigh, Eirene handed her a cup of wine.

Before long the line of petitioners wound around the walls of her father's residence, and Zoe was hard-pressed to get to St. Acacius by noon. More and more, she relied on Eirene to run the charity. Whenever she arrived, she would find her cousin bustling about, the keys of the storerooms jangling at her waist as if she were a prison guard. Sometimes she'd be arbitrating a dispute or arguing with a cook about spices, whether too much or too little. Sometimes she'd be scolding a servant or haggling with a merchant to get the lowest price in Christendom. Zoe was happy to leave it all in Eirene's capable hands, especially the financial matters. She herself was a poor negotiator and frequently overcharged, for while some merchants hesitated to cheat a grand duke's daughter, others had no such scruples. They saw a woman to be milked, all the better because she was rich. She had been shorted by devious merchants with inaccurate scales and paid with shaved coin, and as she corrected for one problem, they invariably found another.

"You have worked wonders keeping costs down, Eirene," Zoe told her one day as she went over the accounts on the kitchen table that was piled high with onions, leeks, celery, and spearmint and crowded with tiny bowls of cumin spice, pepper, fennel, rosemary, dill and an earthenware pot of flour. "I think I could even found another charity."

"You wouldn't dare! I have enough to do—" Eirene launched into a fit of endless scolding. Suddenly she stopped and gave Zoe a searching look. "You're not serious, are you?"

Zoe grinned. "Just waiting for the right moment to approach my father. I'm going to need his money."

Eirene lifted a hot cauldron from the fire and brought it to the table. "Your poor father. He'll be in the almshouse by the time you finish with him."

Zoe chuckled as she rose to lend Eirene a hand pouring the broth into a copper urn. "We'll be fine, Eirene. Father has plenty of money. More than I can spend in a lifetime."

"Good to see you, Father!" Zoe said, linking arms and leading him to the fireplace. "You do not come nearly often enough."

"There is always much to do, daughter."

"Would that we had more hours in the day," she said in sympathy. Her gaze went to the chess set of lapis lazuli and carnelian set out before the fireplace. The tiny, jeweled eyes of the carved ivory figurines danced invitingly in the candlelight. "Chess?"

"Why not?"

Zoe sent for sweet wine and appetizers. She had a purpose for her invitation, but it was important she choose the right moment to broach the subject on her mind. She offered her father a wide smile and took a seat on a white velvet couch opposite his tapestried chair. He was more pliable when he was in a relaxed mood, and he relaxed best when moving his army across the board. Resting her chin in her hand, she picked up a pawn in front of her queen and moved it two spaces forward. "So, what is the news on the emperor's marriage front?" she asked casually.

"Nothing yet. We're waiting to hear. It seems that all we do is wait to hear." He made his move. "There is much talk at the palace of you."

Her heart missed a beat. "Me?"

"They praise what you have accomplished with your charity, Zoe. Thanks to you, our name is daily blessed in the churches. The emperor himself has taken note."

"Oh, Father!" she exclaimed, unable to hide her emotion.

"Indeed, he often asks after you. You've worked miracles with the poor, and there is not such unrest as before. He is grateful and intends to honor you at the palace."

She took a knight with her queen. "And that will be soon, I imagine," she said bitterly.

Before her father had a chance to answer, servants arrived with the *apotki.* They poured the wine, laid out the appetizers, and withdrew. Her father reached for her hand. "Now, now, my dear, be patient. Your time will come. When your mother returns from Lesbos, she will see to it that you are welcomed to the palace. She has much influence with the empress."

Zoe bit her lip. She tried not to think of her mother who left without bidding her farewell as soon as she'd arrived from Mistra. If Zoe didn't know better, she'd think it was intentional, but more likely, she hadn't cared enough to give her a thought. Even so, somewhere at the back of Zoe's mind hovered the thought that if she could win the approval of others, perhaps her mother would love her too. She picked up her goblet and took a long draught of wine. "How is the babe?"

Her father heaved an audible sigh. "Our first grandchild… he still lives, but he is sickly. Your sister worries. It is good that your mother is with her."

Zoe was swept with pity for Helena. Many children didn't survive infancy but that hardly lessened the pain of loss. She felt a rush of guilt for her resentment of her mother's absence.

She mulled the board for a long time. Then she said, "Father, I need you to do something for me… I need you to persuade the emperor to grant me an imperial appointment." In the motion of dipping a piece of bread into spiced eggplant, her father stilled his hand.

"You are not even permitted at court. How do you think he would agree to such a thing?"

"Officials do not always have to be at court to carry out their duties, and there is much need, Father. If the emperor is as grateful as you say, he should give me an official appointment so I can do more—" She rushed on before he could stop her. "Women come to me who are beaten by their husbands. They have no recourse—they need intermediaries to intercede with their husbands. I could be one of those if I had a title. I could even suggest new laws to protect them against abuse. With an imperial position, I could put forth my ideas—I've been reading the law—I could advise on—"

"Enough! The law is no subject for a woman."

"What about Empress Theodora? She was a woman. A mere actress until she married Justinian. All the laws that protect women are hers. Little more has been done in these eight hundred years since Theodora. It's high time we—"

"Surely you do not compare yourself with Theodora?"

"I may not be an empress, but if you can secure me an imperial appointment, I promise you won't regret it." Returning her attention to the game, she sacrificed a knight to take two pawns and sat back, waiting for her father's reply. But he made none, nor did she press for a response. She had planted the seed. That would serve for now.

They studied the board and took their turns with the game as they sipped their wine and munched *apotki.* When her father moved a knight and exposed his king, she pounced. "Checkmate," she said, moving her queen forward.

"Why am I always beaten by my own daughter?"

"'Tis nothing to be ashamed of, Father—as long as I don't tell anyone." She gave him a coy smile.

"I detect a threat there somewhere."

"No threat. But I do have a more immediate concern I want to discuss with you."

"By St. Nicholas, isn't an imperial appointment enough for one night?" He settled back in his chair. "Well?"

"Winter is coming."

"So? Last I checked there were four seasons. Has something changed?"

"Father, many street dwellers die from exposure in winter. I have been thinking—"

"Zoe, you have to stop thinking," he sighed. "It is not good for me."

She leaned forward, eyes sparkling with excitement. "The Palace of Botaneiates by the Severan Wall near Prosphorion Harbor on the Golden Horn—you know the one, it's in the Genoese quarter. It serves no purpose, Father. I can turn it into a hostel with very little expense—*very* little. For the price of some hay and cotton cloth, we can stuff pallets, repair the ceiling, buy a few charcoal braziers, and provide protection for hundreds. I've checked it out. It's perfect. It wouldn't cost much—"

He shot her a stern look, but inwardly he marveled at this child of his, amazed by her resourcefulness and startled by the sudden thought that leapt into his mind. *A shame the emperor must wed for an alliance. I could have offered him the perfect empress. Another Theodora.*

Aloud he said, "Remind me to put my efforts into finding you a prince. Otherwise, I fear you will take the entire population of Constantinople into your care. At my expense."

Zoe leapt up from her seat and flew into his arms. "Oh, Father, thank you, thank you—oh I love you so much!"

Ten

The news that Constantine had dreaded for years was brought to him on the twenty-third day of March in the year 1450. His mother had died in her sleep.

The city filled with tears and the tolling of church bells. Despite the dowager empress's treatment of her, Zoe grieved her loss, for well she knew how Constantine would miss her. Naught can compare to a mother's love, she thought sorrowfully as the solemn funeral cortege wound through the streets in the rain. She trotted her palfrey forward, her gaze on Constantine. He walked bareheaded with his brothers behind Empress Helena's horse drawn casket that was draped in the yellow and black double-headed eagle of Eastern Rome. People wept softly as he passed, their sobs mingling with the clatter of horses' hooves.

At last, they arrived at the Hagia Sophia. Constantine and Patriarch Gregory entered side by side and crossed the resplendent circular nave to their respective thrones as custom demanded: the patriarch to sit by the altar, and Constantine on the *omphalion.* Clouds of incense wafted in the air, misting the golden interior, and sunlight filtered through the high windows, illuminating the jewel-colored mosaics on the walls. From the domed ceilings that soared two hundred feet above Constantine's head, a thousand silver oil lamps dangled on brass chains, sending flickering lights into the nave. He thought of an ancient description of the Hagia Sophia: "Like the whole heaven, scattered with glittering stars."

His eyes went to the mourners gathered before his mother's coffin on a dais near the altar. A hush fell, and the patriarch began his litany. He felt a vast weariness as he struggled to rise and sing the hymns. Though he had anticipated this moment for a long time, he found himself unprepared for the weight of grief that descended on him as Patriarch Gregory's voice droned on, extolling his mother's virtues.

"Before becoming a nun and taking the name Patience, the holy Empress Helena was the wife of Emmanuel II. She honored God all the days of her life and donned the nun's habit after her husband's death. For twenty-five years, she lived a monastic life..."

Constantine's disconsolate gaze roamed the wealth of columns gilded with rosettes of acanthus leaves that rose tier upon tier until they were lost in the semi-shadows of the soaring dome. Into each pillar Justinian the Great had entwined his initials with those of his empress, Theodora, the woman he loved, but Time, the enemy of all things mortal, had silenced them both, leaving only these stone testaments to their love...

He lifted his gaze to Justinian's columns of purple porphyry, black stone and yellow marble gathered from across Greece, Egypt, and Syria in the days when Rome had owned the world. He rested his weary eyes on the second level balcony, directly across from his throne. There, between the marble pillars, his mother had sat in a high-backed ivory chair, surrounded by her ladies, watching the service as empresses had done for centuries.

Patriarch Gregory's voice came again, "Who does not know of her charity? She established the home for old people called The Hope of the Despaired at the Monastery of KiraMartha..."

Constantine gazed at her empty seat, and it seemed to him that he could almost see the vague shape of his mother's white veil and her nun's habit. He averted his eyes. Who was left that he could turn to for comfort? Demetrios, his unpraiseworthy brother, the one who stood expressionless at their mother's funeral? His brother Thomas might grieve, but Thomas would soon be back in Greece, and far away. His eye moved to his commander-in-chief, silver-bearded Andronicus Cantacuzene. He was a good man, but he disagreed with him on most matters, including union. What of Andronicus's nephew, Demetri Cantacuzene, standing beside him? He, too, was a loyal friend, someone he could rely on, but Demetri didn't agree with him on much either.

His gaze moved to Zoe's father. His elder statesman, Grand Duke Lucas Notaras, was suitably resplendent for the occasion in a multi-layered sapphire and topaz outfit. Lucas had been his brother's chief minister and had great experience of state. Constantine counted him as one of only two close friends, but the other was George Phrantzes, and George disliked Lucas, maybe from jealousy of his position, or his wealth and influence. Or perhaps he did not approve of Lucas because, with an eye on their uncertain future, Lucas kept much of his wealth in Italian banks and had accepted Genoese and Venetian citizenship.

Constantine heaved an inward sigh and closed his eyes. They all vied with one another, all his officials, his friends. There was much jostling for position among them. Only his mother had put his interests above all else and offered him advice untainted by jealousy, ambition, or desire for reward. Now she was gone. He had no wife, no child, no one who loved him for himself and not what he could do for them.

"Her fortitude in adversity is well known," Patriarch Gregory's voice droned on. "She was a woman of great intellect and learning..."

He looked back at the throng, his vision blurred by sorrow, and it seemed to him that he was surrounded by naught but gloom, but as he gazed, in the distance there came a flash, drawing his glance across the heads of mourners to someone whose face he could not see. For some strange reason, the past came to mind, and again he smelled the scent of orange blossoms and heard a little girl's laughter as he swept her into his arms. Was it a meaningless movement that had stirred these memories, a mosaic on the wall, perhaps, that had caught a ray of the sun and reflected on him memories of happier days? He peered into the dimness. A jeweled hand was lowering a kerchief from the tears it had dried, and the face in the crowd looked up at him with infinite compassion. Their eyes met across the heads of the crowds. He had never seen a gaze so luminous and tender, or a mouth that smiled yet bespoke the sadness that filled his spirit. His thoughts scattered, the people dispersed, and the walls receded. He gripped the side arms of his chair and leaned forward. It was a face he knew and did not know, one he'd seen and not seen.

Zoe's face.

Child, woman, goddess, she lit up the darkness like sunrise breaking through the darkest night.

Zoe—

Zoe, who had always loved him.

Easter services were subdued during the month-long mourning period following Empress Helena's death. But on the first day of May, Zoe's father brought her the summons to the palace that she had yearned to receive.

"Daughter, did I not say your time would come?" he beamed. "And here is a gift for the occasion."

Zoe accepted the velvet pouch he offered and tore open the thread that sewed it shut. A gasp of delight escaped her lips. It was the beautiful diamond *maniakis* that she had given her father as collateral. She embraced him with passionate gratitude.

On his way out, Lucas turned back. "In case you're interested, child, every week brings another suitor for your hand. Do you care to know who they are?"

Zoe smiled sweetly.

"I didn't think so. Very well then, we wait for a prince."

When Lucas had left, Eirene said, "You should order a new dress and not count the cost."

Zoe shook her head. "Think how much grain we could buy with the money, Eirene."

After being bathed and massaged, her hair washed, brushed, and perfumed, Zoe tried on several dresses and decided on a gown from her father styled in the Venetian fashion that had become the rage at court: a rich green velvet that swept the ground, with a stiff bodice and sleeves studded with gems. Eirene swept up her elaborate curls, entwined them with pearls, and clasped her father's diamond collar around her neck. She set a silver circlet on her brow, draped the lavender cloak around her shoulders, and arranged the circlet's trailing veil of tulle behind her over its folds.

"You are a vision. Now go slay the emperor," she laughed.

With Eirene and a procession of guards as escort, Lucas ushered Zoe into the great hall at Blachernae. Heads turned, taking startled notice of Zoe as she passed on her father's arm. Petitioners crowding the lower end of the hall fell back, clearing a path to the tapestry-hung gallery beyond the velvet curtains that separated the nobles from the common folk. Laughter, loud talk, and music floated from the glittering *dynatoi* who were gorgeously attired in brightly colored many-layered robes embroidered in silver and gold thread and embellished with gems and pearls. Scattered around the columned hall, they sipped wine and conversed, rolled dice, and played chess. Some ladies reclined on silk cushioned couches and watched a mime while others chatted or perused illuminated manuscripts.

Lucas noticed the blush that stained his daughter's cheeks and felt her tremble. "A little like going into the lion's den," he whispered, giving her hand a squeeze. Though he knew the bold curiosity of the hyper-critical court was the cause of Zoe's distress, her reaction was scarcely what he expected. With surprising dignity for one so young, she offered the staring crowd an infectious smile that sent the men bowing in admiration and the women smiling back. She is like a light passing through the room, he thought, swept with a sudden realization. His gangly, scrawny, impish little girl had grown into a beauty without shedding the innocence and fragile quality that had distinguished her as a child. This, he realized, was the secret of her charm.

Intuitively, people sensed her vulnerability and her affection and concern for them and responded with their hearts. But as is often the case, not everyone was charmed. As she mounted the steps into the nobles' area, he caught a snatch of conversation, *Ah, yes, one has heard something, has one not?* followed by a snicker, quickly suppressed. Zoe heard it, too. There would always be disapproval, whatever she did, good or bad. It was something she'd learned early in life, and it had inflamed her natural shyness. She widened her smile, for only a smile could hide her apprehension, and only a smile could make her forget.

Her father was making introductions. She greeted the Burgundian ambassador from the court of Philip the Good, and some distant relatives of Constantine whom she had met at Mistra as a child, and a group of girls around her age, two of whom buoyed Zoe's spirits with their praise of her work for the poor: Sybil Narcos, daughter of the Master of the Doves and Nightingales, and Muriel Aristides, whose husband, the Eparch of Constantinople, oversaw the administration of law and order. But before they had time to become better acquainted, an imperial messenger arrived.

"Emperor Constantine is ready to see you, my lady," he said, bowing to Zoe.

Lucas moved to escort Zoe, but the messenger next words halted his step. "*Nobelissimos,*" he said. "The emperor requests that you take his place at the Praetorium and resolve the urgent matter he has pending with the Eparch."

Lucas gave a nod of acknowledgment and stepped back.

Through courtyards and peristyles, past fountains, and statuary, up the white marble staircase and along the columned hallway of Roman busts Zoe and Eirene followed the man to Constantine's council chamber. The Captain of the Varangians stepped aside sharply and his men retracted the lances that barred their way. Zoe entered the stone-vaulted chamber. Eirene followed, shrinking inconspicuously into the shadows of the room.

Constantine stood at the window, looking out across red-tiled roofs and city walls to the shimmering Golden Horn. As soon as he turned, his expression gave way to the familiar dimpled smile that Zoe loved. "My dear lady, what pleasure to see you again. It has been a long time..."

Zoe fell into her curtsy. *One month, one week, and two days since the funeral,* she thought, *and a year since that precious Easter day.*

He stood gazing at her long after she rose. While he had imagined this meeting many times since his mother's funeral, he was unprepared for the intensity of his feelings at the sight of her. She seemed more luminous than ever with her hair glimmering like Bohemian crystals and her wide brown eyes sparkling between their thick black lashes.

Zoe waited uncertainly for him to speak.

"Pray, have a seat, Lady Zoe," Constantine said at last, finding his voice.

A cupbearer appeared with a flagon of wine on a silver tray. He set two goblets on the oak table and poured. Sipping gingerly, Zoe watched Constantine take a long draught. Abruptly, he set down his wine and leaned forward in his seat. She followed his example, thinking he would speak, but he continued to stare. In astonishment, she realized he was nervous too. The thought that even an emperor could be nervous brought a smile to her lips.

Her smile was the spur Constantine needed. "Lady Zoe, I have asked you here today to thank you for your charity work and dispensation of justice to the poor. But I am curious. What prompted you to get involved in such weighty matters?"

"Prompted me? The fact that nothing was being done." The words tumbled out like an accusation, and she blushed furiously. She dropped her lashes, aware of his eyes on her.

Constantine fought to suppress the laughter that welled in him. *That should teach me,* he thought. Little Zoe had never let him get away with anything, and neither did the goddess she had become. But he expected no less. It was true he had ignored the poor—not because he wanted to, but because there wasn't enough money, or resources, or time in the day to deal with their problems. More urgent issues kept taking precedence. But this slip of a girl—this child who not long ago had sat on his lap bubbling with laughter—had taken matters into her own hands, and with no encouragement or assistance, had worked miracles in the city.

Assuming a grave demeanor, he said, "You have no legal training in matters of justice, have you?"

The heavy lashes that shadowed her cheeks flew up. "No more than Theodora."

"I assume you mean the empress Theodora?"

"Yes. It doesn't take a genius to figure out what is just or unjust. It merely takes a heart."

"Are you suggesting I don't have one?"

"Oh, no, never, Augustus!" Zoe protested, wishing she could take back her careless words. "You are the noblest, most splendid emperor Rome could ever have—" She broke off in embarrassment.

"Am I indeed?" he asked softly. He savored the pleasure of her words as he watched her confusion, enjoying the moment of his advantage. With her cheeks blushing like roses and her eyes sparkling like topaz, she made him think of youth, and springtime, and love—

He cleared his throat. "Well, indeed, I am relieved to hear you say so. The way you tried to mend matters that I had failed to concern myself with made me think you disapproved of me."

Zoe was beside herself. Nothing was going well, and she had so wanted matters to go well! "Oh no, Augustus! Forgive me—I never meant to impugn your handling of affairs. I only meant to help—"

With soft eyes, Constantine rose from his chair and drew her to her feet. "You have helped, Zoe. So much that I can see no way to manage without you. I wish to offer you the responsibilities of the *Zoste Patricia.* Will you wear the Golden Girdle and accept the position of First Lady of the land? The honor was dear to my mother's heart, and there is no one more worthy to step into her place than you."

It was Zoe's turn to stare at him, lips parted, speechless. "The *Zoste Patricia?* But my mother— The honor belongs to her… Shouldn't she— How can I—" Words failed her.

He clutched her hand in both his own. Everyone knew her mother was a drunk, everyone except Zoe. "The Lady Daphne is not here, and we know not when she will return. Her duties belong to you in her absence. I need you,

Zoe. There is much to do, and it cannot wait. Accept my offer, I pray you."

Outside the palace walls, church bells clanged for another Mass and the chant of monks rose in the garden. Here was her dream come true, an imperial appointment! But *First Lady*—that, she had not even dared to dream! Her heart soared with joy.

Eleven

Never had Constantine felt more keenly the beauty of his land as he did that sun-drenched summer of 1450. Love painted the world with splendor. It was a time of glorious sunrises, tender blue twilights, stars, and moonlight. All God's creation seemed to celebrate with him. More dolphins frolicked in the glittering turquoise waters than ever before, and the earth promised a rich harvest of wheat, melons, and vegetables. As far as the eye could see, flowering trees bedecked with blossom sparkled with a bounty of fruit: red and black plums, golden quince, sweet white mulberries, ruby pomegranates, and a variety of purple and green grapes. Despite the troubles of the empire and the lack of agreement from the clerics on the question of union, Constantine had never felt happier, or more encouraged.

Nor had Zoe. Each day brought fathomless joy. On the twentieth day of July, as the city celebrated the Feast of St. Elias, Constantine conferred on her the dignity of the Golden Girdle of the *Zoste Patricia.* At the banquet that followed, minstrels played, wine flowed, and dancing and laughter filled the palace halls. Prince Orhan, who had written a special poem in honor of the occasion, read to the court, his dark eyes soft as they rested on Zoe. Seated on Constantine's right hand, she was in a state of such rapture that days later she could barely recall the event.

Autumn followed summer, swirling in with its own glorious loveliness. Zoe woke up to morning mist and lay down to stars and the nightingale's serenade. The knowledge that winter would soon follow only heightened the caress of the soft autumn breezes and the farewell song of the birds. She marveled at every blessing, and knew it was because Constantine returned her love. And there was more. For the first time ever, she discovered the joys of friendship and community. No longer did she feel the sting of jealous glances sent her way or snide whispers, for there was Muriel Aristides and her friend Sybil with whom to spend dusky evenings warmed by shared confidences, affection, and laughter.

Zoe also discovered new fulfillment in her work. Though her title added more duties to her already demanding schedule, her new position eased the burden. Abusive husbands often fell in line at her threat of imperial retribution, for no man wished to lose his job, have a contract withdrawn, or find himself in a judge's disfavor if he was a litigant. All this lay in her purview to arrange. Her sole disappointment was that she had to wait to improve the legal position of women because she couldn't raise the weighty issue of new legislation until she had support in the imperial council.

Not all her duties were as rewarding as the administration of justice, however, and her position entailed responsibilities she didn't relish, such as household management. The grand chamberlain now reported to her, and she had to supervise the daily menus, greet foreign dignitaries, arrange banquets, and shoulder the domestic responsibilities that, in the absence of a wife, once went to the emperor's mother. But of all her duties as *Zoste Patricia,* the one she dreaded most was a gift-giving ceremony for a hundred high and mid-level government officials. The gifts formed an important part of their stipend and needed to be chosen with care.

"The *teleti doro* is less than a month away and I have no idea what to do, Eirene!" Zoe fretted, wringing her hands as she paced back and forth in her official bedchamber at Blachernae. "How do I make sure I select the right gifts? My mother could advise me if she was here—she knows their needs—O why is she not here? Who do I ask for help? Where do I begin?"

Seated on the edge of the bed sewing a tear in the hem of a gown, with Theseus curled up at her feet, Eirene looked up in surprise. Her level-headed mistress had never indulged in self-pity before, but she was under tremendous pressure. Assuming so many new duties at once without guidance was a daunting task, and clearly it had frayed her nerves. "Your mother may not be here, but a lot of other people are. Ask them," she said gently.

"Of course!" Zoe exclaimed, swept with relief, wondering why she hadn't thought of it herself. What need had she of her mother's help when her dear friend was the wife of the Eparch? "I know just the one!"

She hastened to the great hall in search of Muriel and arrived as a fulsome, robustly built girl was leaving. The girl dropped a hasty curtsy as they passed in the entrance, and Zoe gave her a warm smile, recognizing her as one of Muriel's friends, a girl from Clarenza named Iris. Zoe made her way to the raised gallery where mummers performed for the *dynatoi.* Muriel was at the back of the hall, secluded with Sybil on a pale blue armless couch beneath an enormous tapestry of a forest scene. The cozy corner was divided from the open hall by a crimson velvet curtain tied at the waist. As always, a clutch of maidens had gathered around Muriel. Heads together, they whispered, giggled, and tittered, oblivious of Zoe's approach. She stepped into the little enclave with a smile. "What is so amusing?"

The laughter was abruptly checked. Looking guilty, they scrambled to their feet in silence and bobbed their curtsies, eyes averted. Zoe's gaze swept the group. "Something wrong?" she asked in concern.

"Zoste Patricia, it is nothing," Muriel said. "Certainly not worth repeating. We were remarking that Iris has gained a little weight recently, that is all." She exchanged a warning look with Sybil to say no more, for her explanation held only a kernel of truth. The conversation Zoe had interrupted involved a noble lady who had fallen ill and could no longer attend court. Since she was confined to bed and unable to walk, she had gained a great deal of weight, and Iris had just returned from visiting her. "It was like looking at a river horse wrapped in silk sheets," she had reported to waves of laughter.

"You have such a clever way with words, Lady Iris," Muriel had replied sweetly. "Very clever. So witty and amusing," Sybil had agreed. The stocky girl had waddled out of the hall soon afterwards. "That is the problem with *hippopotamus amphibious.* One river horse doesn't recognize another, "Muriel had tittered, watching her disappear. "The day will come when poor Iris finds herself wedged in that entry." Everyone had burst into laughter, and it was this great amusement that Zoe had witnessed.

She took a seat beside Muriel. "Dear friend, I have a problem, and I need your help."

"Anything," Muriel said sweetly. "You know I would do anything for you, Lady Zoe."

The dreaded day of the gift-giving arrived. The ceremony was lengthy and laden with protocol as one by one tribunes and logothetes from the fiscal, judicial, and civil branches came up to the dais to accept their gifts. Zoe's back ached, her feet were sore from standing for so many hours and she was mortified by the reaction of the crowd, for it was obvious that something was terribly wrong. But what could it be? She had chosen each gift in consultation with Muriel and had expected warm appreciation, but applause was scant and seemed contrived. Beneath flowed a growing undercurrent of whispering and muttering that Zoe found disturbing. For Zoe, the church bells couldn't ring soon enough to mark Nones and the end of the ceremony. And the end of this grueling day.

She called another name from the list. An official in charge of the aqueducts.

The herald sounded the clarion, and the priest blessed the gifts. Zoe read the man's titles and achievements as he came to the dais. She handed him three large sacks of cane sugar, two sacks of almonds and pistachio nuts, and an amphora of costly rosewater. In puzzlement she noticed the dark looks exchanged in the audience. Again, she was confounded. It should have been welcome. These were the ingredients of halva, a sweet confection his wife loved—a year's supply, no less! The herald blared his clarion and the priest intoned the prayers, but in an increasingly halting, uncertain voice.

More responses. More prayers. Only one gift remained to be bestowed. *Thanks be to the Holy Mother that this will soon be over!*

Masking her inner turmoil, she injected a deceptively cheerful note into her tone as she announced the last name. The man was one of Constantine's key appointees, and along with his staff of magistrates and ministers, had responsibility for maintaining roads, public baths, the water supply, and harbors. "—and for the Prefect who recovered the icon of the Presentation of Our Lord to the Temple that was stolen from the Pantocrator, and just last week put out a great fire at the soap makers guild, we have ten yards of fine black velvet cloth three yards broad—" She took the bolt of fabric the chamberlain passed her and waited for the man to present himself.

Silence. No one stirred. Nor did the herald raise his horn to his lips. She looked from the herald to the priest in bewilderment. Both wore stunned, fearful expressions, and their eyes were riveted on the bolt of fabric in her hands. Shaken, she stood helplessly before them, her eyes welling with tears.

At the back of the hall, someone moved. A feeble man, thin, with gray hair. Zoe watched as he made his way forward to the dais, every step denoting effort. At last, he stood before her, and she saw to her shock that he wasn't old. His face, though gaunt, was youthful, and his hair was thick, as if grayed by hardship, not age. He was as white as milk, and like everyone else his eyes were fixed in horror on the gift she held. *What in God's name is wrong? If he cares not for the velvet, he can sell it and pocket a handsome sum, surely—*

The man lifted piteous eyes to her face, and her heart broke. "Sir Prefect, what is it? Are you unwell? Is there anything I can do for you?"

To her shock his shoulders began to heave. Covering his face with his hands, he muffled the sobs that suddenly wracked his body. Zoe turned her eyes on the velvet she held.

"What possessed you, Zoe? How could you?" Constantine demanded, pacing angrily in the council chamber. He halted his steps and glared at her as she stood by the tenth century painting of Mary that adorned the wall. "If you knew, it was cruel! If you didn't know, you should have bothered to find out!"

Zoe bowed her head miserably. She'd been horrified to learn that the prefect who'd broken down at the ceremony had just buried his only child, and his ailing wife was likely to soon follow him into the grave. Under the circumstances, the gift of black cloth had seemed a wicked jest. Nay, worse; an omen, prophesying her death.

She closed her eyes tight on a breath. *His favorite color is black,* Muriel had said.

"As for that poor, ill woman confined to a litter because of her colossal weight—how could you mock her love of sweets?" Constantine demanded. "No doubt it is one of the few pleasures left to her in her sickness—" He continued with a litany of Zoe's missteps.

Contrite and sick at heart, Zoe listened quietly. "I take full responsibility, Augustus," she said when he was done. "My error was grievous, but you mustn't think it was intentional."

He whirled on her. "Not intentional? When you didn't trouble to seek counsel, Zoe?"

"But I did," she murmured.

"What?" In stunned amazement, Constantine closed the gap between them. "Who advised you to give the tribune black cloth?"

Suffused with shame, she looked at him mutely, unable to find the words.

"*Who* did you consult?" he demanded, his tone hardening.

"Lady Muriel Aristides," she whispered, her voice barely audible.

"The Eparch's young wife?"

"Yes."

"She suggested these gifts?"

"Yes."

"So, pray tell, my lady, why you chose to trust to consult Muriel Aristides instead of Theo's wife, or Phrantzes's, who you knew had *my* trust?"

Zoe cringed at his tone.

"I am waiting," Constantine snapped.

"Because Muriel's mother died giving birth to her, and my mother threw me away at birth," Zoe said meekly. "So I trusted her."

It was Constantine's turn to fall silent. He hadn't appreciated the extent of Zoe's self-doubt. She masked it too well. Yet there had been hints, had he cared to notice. The wispy child rose before him: fragile, wounded, bravely fighting tears as she ran in a panic after her mother. But the mother, who held her younger daughter's hand, never glanced back at her other little girl. He had thought it odd at the time; odd, too, that Daphne didn't bid her child farewell. Instead, she had boarded ship without a backward glance. It was Lucas, he remembered now, who had knelt with the child; Lucas who had kissed her; Lucas, who had entrusted his little one to Constantine's care. Later, it was Lucas, not Daphne, who had marked Zoe's birthdays with a gift—but only sporadically, when he remembered.

Constantine blinked. *Why did Daphne reject Zoe when she was a devoted mother to her five other children?* As if in reply, a young man with red hair, handsome, dashing, emerged from the dim recesses of his mind. *Ah yes, the gossip…* Daphne had begged to wed him, but Hector was a younger son, and she was a Palaeologina, a prize meant for the older brother. The heir. Lucas. Hector left for Italy soon after Zoe's birth, never to return. His name was not mentioned again, and in time people forgot. But in Daphne's heart, the birth of her daughter would forever be linked to the loss of the man she had loved. It was probably why she drank.

His gaze rested on Zoe, flooded by compassion. The child was grown now, but still fragile, still vulnerable, and still very much alone. Denied a mother's love, she had been rejected by his mother Empress Helena, betrayed by a trusted friend, taunted by a court riddled with jealousies, and chastised by her emperor. Yet here she stood with all the dignity of a queen, bearing his reproofs and admonitions with touching gallantry.

"Zoe," he said softly, gently, "you have a lot to learn about court. This is not Mistra. Those carefree days are gone. We have to be circumspect and cautious where we place our trust. Next time come to me."

Her lashes glistening, Zoe lifted her gaze to him. "I will not let you down again, Augustus."

In the ensuing weeks, Zoe set herself to making amends to those she had affronted with her blunders on that terrible day of the ceremony. But she declined Constantine's offer to punish Muriel by replacing her husband as Eparch. "Being paired with her for life is punishment enough for him," she told Constantine. He had thrown his head back and roared with laughter.

Nevertheless, he replaced the man. His wife's jealousy had to have driven her mad, for she had to know her action would have consequences. The fact that she had disregarded accountability meant she had no fear of the emperor. That was dangerous on many counts, not least because it suggested a heart that respected no boundaries. No one of that ilk had a right to be near power.

Zoe and Constantine came into frequent contact as Zoe tended her affairs, sometimes at the Notaras palace, sometimes at Blachernae. To her delight, she was invited to attend Constantine's private evenings at the Ocean Hall with increasing frequency. There was always much laughter at these gatherings. Someone inevitably taunted Apollo about something, and his responses never failed to send everyone into fits of laughter. More importantly, as time went by, Zoe found herself growing in stature with Constantine.

The first time her father had come to discuss affairs of state and found her present, she rose to leave, but Constantine had objected. "I should like your thoughts on the matter, *Zoste Patricia*— You have no objection, do you, Lucas?" A startled look had come into her father's eyes. "None at all," he'd replied, a slow smile spreading across his face. "None at all…" Zoe knew her father and realized a new dream had been lit in his heart. To see her empress. She heaved a sigh of relief to know his hunt for a prince was finally dead.

Christmas came and went, and the new year of 1451 wafted in gently on sunshine.

Constantine marked the twelve days of Christmas with a bounty of little treasures that brought Zoe much delight: a copy of *Trojan Women* by Euripides; ribbons for her hair; a tiny triptych washed in pure gold, and many other precious tokens. There had been much laughter and joy. The months passed, drawing them closer still. Many times, their eyes met, and their hands touched passing a manuscript, a missive, a gift. Zoe read his heart in his eyes and knew he felt as she did, but one thing was certain. Not until all hope of an alliance was gone would Constantine give voice to his feelings. Meanwhile, they waited for news.

On a bitterly cold evening in February, as the Winds of Boreas howled and the sea roared, Zoe sang for Constantine. *Something is wrong,* she thought. He stood staring out the window of the Ocean Hall, a fine figure in a knee length tunica of heavy umber silk with a gold sash at the hips and dark silk hose that molded his lean, muscular body and complimented his bronzed complexion. But he was as silent as his pet bird beneath the velvet cover of its cage and looked as morose and forlorn as he had at his mother's funeral. Tonight, there had been no game of chess by the fire and no laughter. He had barely spoken. This was unusual, for Constantine shared everything with her now. The problems he faced were as tangled as a Gordian knot, but Zoe couldn't help wondering precisely what troubled him this evening. Had Phrantzes sent news?

Her song ended. He turned, and their eyes met. But the joy she felt in his love was erased by the sorrow she beheld. She threw him a smile, and to lighten his heaviness, broke into a merry refrain.

Constantine gazed at her, sitting by the blazing fire, her long, elegant fingers flying over the lyre as she plucked the notes. She wore the flowing *stolla* of pale apricot silk that had served for her arrival in Constantinople, a gilt circlet at her brow, and a long, diaphanous diamond-studded veil that floated down to her silver slippers. The rich red hair he loved glimmered in the light of the fire, and the thick braid that fell over one shoulder was now the color of wine.

Following his mother's death, he had expected his days to be hard, lonely, and comfortless. But life had surprised him with the gift of love. For the first time in many long years, he knew happiness, and laughter came as easily to him as it had in his youth. For this reason, the missive he'd received earlier that afternoon had distressed him more deeply than he could have imagined.

George Phrantzes was in Thrace and would arrive in a matter of days. Soon he would know if he must marry the princess from Trebizond.

He shifted his weight and leaned against a marble pillar, his eyes on Zoe. If George's journey was successful, her visits would cease. The knowledge pained him. For a bare instant he wished the negotiations had failed, but as quickly as the thought came, he banished it. His duty was clear. To save the empire. However much he railed against it, however much he hated to face it, this was what he had to do.

"Augustus— " Aesop said. "The Grand Duke is here with urgent news."

Zoe broke off her song, a cold knot forming in her stomach at the sight of her father's ashen face.

Oblivious of everyone in the room, Lucas went directly to Constantine. "Augustus, we have just heard—" he said, breathing hard. "Sultan Murad II is dead. Mehmet is sultan."

Feeling his blood drain from his head, Constantine sank into a chair. The death of a ruler of such immense power had consequences far beyond what could be imagined in the moment, and Mehmet was linked to one of the worst disasters ever to befall Christendom. *Varna.*

Threatened by the Serbs but wishing to avert war, Sultan Murad had marched to the Danube and made a truce with the newly crowned nineteen-year-old king of Hungary and his allies. All sides swore to abide by the agreement—Murad on the Qur'an, and the Christians on the Bible. Then Murad retired to Anatolia to lead the life of contemplation he had always desired. No sooner was he gone than the young king of Hungary was persuaded to break the agreement. When Sultan Murad refused to return to Hungary, twelve-year-old Mehmet wrote his father: "If you are sultan, come and lead your armies. If I am sultan, I hereby order you to come and lead my armies." Murad returned. At Varna, on the shores of the Black Sea, he rode into battle with the text of the broken truce nailed to his standard and slaughtered the young king and every man in his Christian army.

Murad had been a man of peace. He had to be goaded into war. But his son, Mehmet—

Constantine swallowed on the knot in his throat. "I had not expected it so soon. We were the same age. What happened?"

"He died of apoplexy," Lucas replied.

Constantine pushed himself from his chair and went to the window. Darkness had fallen, and his own face gazed back at him from the black void beyond the glass. Tomorrow was his birthday. And this, he thought, was a gift he could have done without. He rubbed his eyes.

Standing by the fire, watching him, Zoe felt a chill blow through the room. She turned to the hearth and hugged herself for warmth.

Twelve

I turn a page in the holy book and rub my bleary eyes. When I look up, the blackness of the water and starless sky penetrates to the depth of my soul. The hour is late. I should be sleeping, but I cannot sleep, not on such a night. Murad is dead. Mehmet is sultan. And I am filled with foreboding. How can I not be when the wind howls, the sea shrieks and the melting candles flicker in the draft that hisses through the stone walls of my Christian refuge?

I distribute my bulk more comfortably over the scattered cushions of my wall couch and draw my blanket close. I reposition a flaming taper for better light. Once more I bend my head to the Bible in my hands to escape the darkness that presses down on me. See how the holy book is worn? The gilded brown leather cover is faded and cracked with use, the pages earmarked. I should not be reading this book; certainly, it should not be bringing me comfort. Nor should I know so many passages by heart. I am a Muslim. If *Allah* graces me one day I, Orhan, a prince of the Ottoman Empire and grandson of Sultan Suleiman Selebi—may *Allah* bless his soul—will unseat the usurper Mehmet and rule a caliphate for Islam.

I was three years old when Mehmet's grandfather stole my grandfather's throne. His death forced my father to flee to Constantinople with me. My memories of that episode in my life are dim—a few dark, confusing flashes and jumbled images. But the fear endures, and sometimes in the night I awaken like a child in a nightmare. Why the panic has not faded with time, I cannot fathom. After all, it happened so long ago, in 1411.

I have lived with the Christians for over forty years.

A lifetime. An eternity. And in these years, I have learned that their God is no different from mine. There is still a great deal I do not understand about their faith, but as regards the main tenet—that God is love and blesses peace—this, we share. Noble aspirations are difficult to put into practice, given our human failings, so it should come as no surprise that Christians fall short of their lofty goal, just as we Muslims do— The Crusades stand out for us, but there is also the present time. Witness, I pray you, the wars in Europe, where Christian fights Christian, and the bitterness and distrust between the Catholics of Rome and the Orthodox church of the East. Indeed, the divisions between unionists and anti-unionists within this very city. Yet the peace that floods me when I hear the monks' song is the same peace I feel when the muezzin's resonant tones from the mosque in this ancient Christian city summons me to prayer, especially at day's end as the sun sets, and the world stills, and the Hand of God in Creation is most tender. In that peace I find hope for myself and for the world.

I bend my head to the holy book and thumb through the pages until I find what I seek. *St. Matthew.* There is a stain in the margin and the ink is smudged, making the passage hard to read, but no matter. I know these words by heart. *Whosoever welcomes you, welcomes me. And whosoever welcomes me, welcomes the one who sent me.*

The command is not unique to Christians. It is in the Old Testament and shared by all People of the Book—Christians, Jews, and Muslims. However, I choose to read the passage as Matthew wrote it, for it reminds me of my debt to the Christians, and gives me comfort to know we differ so little, one from the other.

Lest you think otherwise, I am not so naive as to believe Roman generosity lacked a more compelling and pragmatic reason for sheltering us. The emperor desired a counterweight against my people, and that is what we were, my father and me. A threat to the sultan. Nonetheless, had it not been for Constantinople, my journey would have ended when I was three. Never do I forget that I came as a stranger to the Romans, and they clothed me and comforted me and gave me protection. At every feast they celebrate, they welcome me and applaud my humble poems. My happiest memories have been made here, in this old Christian city. Though I am, and will always be, an outsider, it matters not. One day the Romans will know my thanks: I will either repay them by ruling my people in aspiration of the ideals of love and peace that we share, or by sacrificing myself for them on their walls.

Hear my prayer and my vow. If *Allah* blesses me with the restoration of the throne of my ancestors, I will sheath the sword with my Christian friends. A new era will dawn between us, bright with hope and love and the promise of God's peace on earth.

So may it be written, *Inshallah.*

As the Winds of Mount Olympus unleashed dismal winter rains and churned the Bosphorus to the color of mud, George Phrantzes returned from the court of Trebizond.

Constantine received his lord chancellor in the Ocean Hall.

"Murad is dead," Constantine said abruptly, unprepared to speak of marriage. "Mehmet is sultan."

"I know. I heard of it in Trebizond. They thought it good news."

"But you do not?" Constantine regarded his friend.

"Sultan Murad was a man of peace. He was weary of war and had given up any thought of conquering Constantinople. I grieve his death."

"I always respected Murad. He was an honorable man. While he was sultan, we were safe. But Mehmet…" His voice drifted away.

"He is anxious to prove himself," Phrantzes said. "His mother was a slave-girl, and his brothers despised him. Their mothers were princesses. Maybe that is why he is consumed with Alexander the Great. We may not have much time, Augustus."

A silence fell.

Constantine regarded his imperial chancellor. In a green silk tunic from the famed looms of Lucca in Tuscany and a red velvet cap with gold tassels on his head, he cut a striking figure. "You have met Mehmet," Constantine said. "Tell me about him. How does he look? What is he like? Describe him."

"As far as appearance is concerned, he is of middling height and strongly built, with a red beard. His hook nose and thick red lips made me think of a parrot's beak resting on cherries… What I remember most clearly are his eyes—" Phrantzes broke off, recalling his unease. He banished the memory and went on. "He is young—nineteen, as you know—and has an extraordinary intellect. But he is arrogant and cold… He is notoriously secretive. I am informed by those who know such things that it is impossible to tell what he is thinking."

He learned this from Halil Pasha, Constantine thought. Halil had been

Murad's Grand Vizier. He was a cultured, reasonable man. Halil did not like Mehmet either.

"—his energy and determination command respect," Phrantzes was saying. "And once he makes up his mind to do something, nothing can deter him."

Constantine felt momentary distress. Had he made up his mind to conquer Constantinople? He let himself down into a chair.

"Murad had paid him little heed until both his other sons suddenly died mysterious deaths," Phrantzes said.

"Sudden mysterious deaths are a hereditary condition at the Ottoman court," Constantine sighed. "Demetrios admires the Turks, but he has not thought it through. We brothers would have banded together and made sure he was the first to go, had we been Turks."

Phrantzes roared with laughter. "May God forgive me for finding the thought engaging."

From the direction of the bird cage, Apollo cackled in imitation of his mirth and yelled, *Demetrios, Demetrios!* Changing tone, he immediately followed with *Bless you, my son.*

"What?" Phrantzes asked in astonishment. "Did I hear correctly?"

"Patriarch Gregory took John's confession here," Constantine explained. "No doubt my brother's name came up often, probably with a profanity that Apollo has the good sense to leave out." Taking Apollo a wedge of dried quince, he fed it to him through the gilt bars of his cage.

"Better cover him up if the Patriarch visits," Phrantzes chuckled. "A shame if this charming bird got himself executed for heresy."

"May fleas infest your armpits!" Apollo shrieked with a flutter, gripping the bars of his cage.

"Never know when he is going to let that one out," Constantine grinned.

When Phrantzes spoke again, his tone was grave. "Emperor John of Trebizond feared Murad, but he believes Mehmet is incompetent and poses no threat to Christendom."

"I gather from what you said that you disagree with him."

"Mehmet is a zealot, Augustus. Despite his own Christian blood—or maybe because of it— he has been an enemy of Christianity since childhood." He fell silent a moment before adding, "He is a violent man. You heard about the babe, his half-brother?"

"Terrible business." When Mehmet arrived in Adrianopolis, his father's widow came to offer her condolences on Murad's death and her congratulations on his succession. Mehmet had received her graciously, but while they spoke, he had a servant strangle her babe.

Feeling a need for movement, Constantine rose and went to the window. He gazed down at the walls where men were hard at work, laboring on repairs. Beyond the defenses, on the beach, a few fishermen passed by, dragging their nets. He sighed inwardly. He had delayed the marriage question long enough. It was time to summon courage and get to the heart of the matter. Now that Mehmet was sultan, they needed the alliance more than ever. Without turning, he said, "And Princess Theodora? Is Emperor John willing to ally with us?" The words felt like stones dropping from his lips.

"I tried every argument I know. But, no, he is not. He fears offending the Ottomans. There are still the Georgian princesses… Unfortunately, that will take more time."

Constantine bowed his head, swept with relief.

"However, Augustus, I have not come back completely empty-handed," Phrantzes said, joining him at the window. "In Trebizond, Emperor John told me that Murad's Christian widow, Mara of Serbia, was sent home to her father laden with gifts and honors. She had been like a mother to Mehmet when his mother died. He loves and respects her greatly." After a pause, he added, "She would make a fine bride for you, Augustus."

"What?"

"The *amerissa* is young and wealthy. She is much loved in the Ottoman court. And she has influence with Mehmet."

"But she is the widow of an infidel ruler!"

"Your own step-grandmother was the wife of a Turkoman lord. She even bore him children before she married your grandfather. Mara has borne Murad no children. It is said he never consummated the marriage. If you married Mehmet's stepmother, he might regard you in a different light. As family, not an adversary."

Constantine leaned his full weight on the stone sill of the elegant window. A storm had blown in. The waves were choppy, and the wind howled over the Horn. At length, he turned to Phrantzes.

"I will put it before the council," he said.

In the cheery Ocean Hall, servants lit candles and served sweetmeats. Surrounded by his friends and advisors, Constantine relaxed into his chair by the blazing hearth. The wind screeched and the ocean roared, but no one noticed. Apollo claimed their attention, for he was in the midst of a fulsome temper tantrum and refused to return to his cage.

"No! I won't go!" Apollo exclaimed, strutting angrily on top of the gilded ceiling of his cage. "But it's past your bedtime, Apollo," Aesop coaxed. "You must go, or time outside will be curtailed tomorrow."

"Whoreson! Whoreson!" Apollo shrieked, expressing his rage. "Fleas infest your armpits!"

Waves of laughter filled the hall. "Now, now," Aesop clucked, "that's no way to talk when ladies are present, Apollo. You know better than that."

Incensed, Apollo let loose a tirade of curses and grievances, only one of which was understood. "I regret you've been shorted of crackers, Apollo," Aesop soothed, "but I promise to make it up to you if you go to bed now..."

Apollo still strutted and complained, but he no longer seemed as angry. "Confounded whoreson!" he ended, hopping into his cage and settling down for the night.

With a chuckle, the ladies dispersed to converse among themselves, and Constantine convened with the men. "Mehmet says he wishes peace," he said, sipping his wine thoughtfully. "The question is, can we believe him?"

A silence.

"I recommend caution, Augustus," his silver-haired uncle Andronicus said." He is a man whose path to the throne was paved by the murder of babes."

"But he doesn't seem intent on war," Theo offered hopefully. "He is renewing his father's treaties with all who will sign... Even your emissaries are well received, Augustus."

"Indeed," Lucas agreed, "the sultan not only swore on the Qur'an that he would observe the sanctity of Roman territory, but also promised to pay the fine sum of three thousand aspers for the honorable detention of our captive, the Ottoman prince, Orhan."

"It appears Mehmet is under the influence of his father's peace-loving minister, Halil," Theo said. "That is welcome news."

A cheery chorus met this last remark, but Constantine remained troubled. "I have heard otherwise. I am told Mehmet's peaceful gestures are not genuine, and he is using the time to plan his great campaign for the conquest of Christendom."

"I agree with you, Augustus," Andronicus murmured thoughtfully. "But the memory of Varna has crushed Europe's zeal to fight the Ottomans. They prefer to believe we can live in peace with them. I fear they delude themselves."

"Only the pope understands the threat we face," Constantine said, toying with his wine, "but he is not eager to help a city that refuses to implement the agreement we signed at Florence. He believes I exaggerate the difficulty of enforcing union."

"Maybe we have no cause for concern," Lucas offered. "Maybe Mehmet is as incompetent as the West thinks he is."

"Let us pray on it, my friend," Constantine said.

Voices drew everyone's attention to the entry. Zoe was returning from her duties at St. Acacius. She handed her cloak to Aesop, peeked at Apollo, embraced each of the ladies in turn, and kissed her father. There was a cross-current of greeting as she took a seat by the fire and accepted a goblet of wine. For a while everyone indulged in amiable conversation. Then Constantine spoke.

"*Zoste Patricia,* this bleak winter's day could use some warmth. Will you sing for us?"

"With pleasure." Zoe accepted her lyre from Aesop and assessed the mood. "Here is something merry…"

Constantine picked up his wine and settled back into his seat.

They are like husband and wife, Lucas thought. And he marveled yet again at his daughter, who had a way of attaining the impossible.

Thirteen

Dawn painted the sky silver and gold. In his bedchamber, Constantine pushed aside the gauzy curtains that partitioned his prayer alcove from his sleeping quarters and knelt at his prie-dieu. Candles burned before an icon of the Virgin, and its gold and jeweled tones gleamed with a mysterious light in the flickering flames.

He concluded his devotions and kissed a precious ninth century cloisonne enamel crucifix of agate and lapis, gratitude in his heart. After the two-week celebration of the Feast of the Procession of the Venerable Wood on the first day of August, when the True Cross was taken out of the imperial treasury and borne through the city streets, rumors had reached him of trouble brewing for Mehmet. He made his way to the council chamber with a spring in his step.

"Augustus," Theo said, "God be praised, welcome news awaits you this day!" He indicated the messenger.

"The Karamanian emir has raised a rebellion against the sultan, and the Lord of the White Sheep has invaded Ottoman territory. Princes are arriving from all directions to claim their ancestral thrones in the lands Sultan Murad conquered. The Ottoman's finest troops, the Janissaries, have also revolted, demanding higher pay."

"And this time Murad is not here to save him," Constantine grinned, remembering the strife that had forced Sultan Murad out of retirement when he'd left twelve-year-old Mehmet in charge of the empire.

"Perhaps it is time to make some difficulties of our own for the sultan,"

Lucas offered. "A simple threat might suffice to bring us a concession."

"What do you suggest?" Constantine demanded.

"What do we need?" Lucas replied.

"Gold!" everyone laughed.

To remedy the dire state of his imperial treasury, Constantine had increased taxes on ships coming into Constantinople's ports. But he was forced to repeal them when the Venetians threatened to close their quarters in Constantinople. If they had transferred their trade elsewhere, the suffering economy would have been devastated.

"We know what we want, but what can we use against Mehmet?" Demetri Cantacuzene said.

"We have the pretender, Prince Orhan," Lucas offered. "Mehmet hasn't paid the monies he promised for his maintenance. Perhaps we can send him a reminder that our Ottoman pretender could replace him as sultan?"

"Indeed, matters seem suddenly hopeful, Augustus," Theo chuckled.

But the elderly Andronicus didn't share his mirth. "I urge caution, Augustus. Emperor Emmanuel tried something similar with Sultan Murad. It did not go well."

Constantine winced, remembering. He had been seventeen when Sultan Murad besieged Constantinople. Never would he forget the fearsome spectacle of tens of thousands of Ottomans amassed before the city gates. It was a horror he could not banish from memory.

"But the Queen of Heaven protects the Queen of Cities," Patriarch Gregory offered. "By her grace, a rebellion broke out in Anatolia, forcing Murad to return home. We have nothing to fear by making the request."

"I don't like it," Andronicus said, blowing his nose loudly, for he had caught a chill. "This is a ruler who deals ruthlessly with threats. What he did to the babe his brother should give us pause. If he sees us as a danger, he'll use the ploy as an excuse to break the truce. Even with his troubles, we would not last a week against his might."

"Unlikely," Lucas demanded. "To go to war over so trivial a matter would be reckless folly."

"I agree with my uncle," Demetri said. "Perhaps we should wait and see what develops for Mehmet? That would be the wisest course. He has made treaties with Serbia and Hungary. If—God forfend! —he broke his truce with us, we would stand alone."

"There is little chance of that," Lucas said dismissively. "Mehmet is no Murad. He is young. He is new to the throne. He has his hands full. He will want to appease us. As for the chance we take, nothing comes without risk."

Constantine listened thoughtfully. Andronicus was wise and experienced; his nephew Demetri was level-headed, sensible. They had a point. But so did Lucas. Murad had been a seasoned warrior, long established on the throne. Mehmet had no experience. What could he do but pay up? And how they needed the gold! He tried to imagine what advice Phrantzes would give if he were here. But he would agree with Andronicus, if only to avoid siding with Lucas.

His mother would have known what to do.

He lifted his eyes to the golden icon of the Virgin that dominated the council chamber. As the story went, in the tenth century a man had a vision of Mary spreading her veil over the city of Constantinople to save it from a Slavic invasion. In the jeweled icon, she stood with the angels, her hands outstretched over Constantinople and its emperor, her veil of protection shielding them. As Patriarch Gregory pointed out, the Virgin had not failed them in eleven hundred years.

"Make the ploy," he said.

Constantine took a cup of wine with Zoe on the balcony of the Ocean Hall where he'd been amusing himself discussing military strategy. "How do you know so much? From Vegetius?"

"No. I have been reading Maurice's *Strategikon.*"

Constantine roared with laughter. Maurice was a sixth century emperor who had compiled a handbook of war. But his laughter died on his lips. Lucas stood at the entrance of the balcony, ashen pale.

"What is it?" Constantine said, unease stirring at the pit of his stomach.

"We have had a reply from Brusa. It is not good." Lucas turned to the messenger with him. The pallor of his complexion did nothing to stem Constantine's anxiety. The man clamped a fist to his chest.

"The Vizir, Halil Pasha, was enraged, Augustus. He called us stupid Greeks."

"What?" Constantine said, coming to his feet. He didn't comprehend for a moment. Expecting a payment of gold from Mehmet, he had been looking forward to the arrival of the emissary he had sent to Brusa. "What exactly did Halil say?"

The man cleared his throat nervously. "He said we were reckless and impertinent. He asked how we dared threaten them when the ink on the treaty is barely dry. He shouted that we had ruined everything he had tried to do for us. He said that he's had enough of our devious ways. That the late sultan had been a lenient and conscientious friend to us, and the present sultan is not of the same mind. He said you, Imperial Majesty, had signed your death warrant—that if you, Augustus, escape with your life, it will be a miracle—" He broke off and swallowed visibly.

Zoe came to her feet with a gasp.

"He said they are not ignorant, nor are they powerless," the messenger resumed. "If you think you can start something, you should do so. If you wish to proclaim Orhan sultan, you should do so. If you wish to bring the Hungarians across the Danube and recover the lands you lost, do so— But you should know this. Whatever happens now, you have brought it on yourself."

Constantine's mouth went dry as he listened. These were strong words, more so because they came from a reasonable man. Like his master Sultan Murad, Halil Pasha had always been fair. But why would he react this way? To win concessions, the two empires had played the same cat and mouse game with one another for over a century. What had changed?

The answer came unbidden. *Mehmet.*

Halil Pasha sounded like a man distraught, losing his grip. Constantine had little idea what went on behind the scenes at the Ottoman court, but one thing he knew. If Halil Pasha was under threat, it boded ill for them. He looked to the East, his heart in his throat.

No further word came from Brusa.

"I have been thinking of pocketing my pride and groveling before the Venetians," Constantine told Lucas as they bathed together in the imperial bath house. He was seated on a stool half-immersed in water and a servant was lathering a loofah to scrub his back. Light flowed through small high apertures in the ceiling, sending rays of sunlight dancing through the mist-filled bath house and the Roman pool lined with blue mosaics.

"I am considering offering them valuable concessions if they help us. They have the most to lose if we—" He broke off, unable to finish the thought.

"They will help, if you pay them," Lucas replied quietly. "For a good price, they will sell you their souls."

In the silence that fell, time streamed backwards, and again Constantine saw himself with his mother at Mistra. "The Latins are not to be trusted!" he'd exclaimed. "They are the Trojan Horses in our midst. They may be Italian by birth, but they do the bidding of the Turks—I will drive them out and rebuild the Hexamilion Wall!" And his mother's voice came back to him across the years, "They are Christians, like us. Do not anger them, my son. You may need them someday."

Time had proved his mother right. He blinked to banish the memory.

"—but for us, Venice would never have grown rich and powerful," Lucas was saying. "And look how she repaid us. By turning the crusaders on us."

"The Venetians do not trust us anymore than we trust them," Constantine said, barely able to raise his voice above a whisper. "The distrust between us has been centuries in the making."

"Be that as it may, one thing is clear. They will always put their own interests foremost. They will hedge their bets against the day when Constantinople might be in Ottoman hands."

"All this I know," Constantine agreed, "but a starving man cannot afford to pick and choose whose coin he will accept for food. We stand alone. We have to look for allies wherever we can."

Nor did Constantine's anxiety wane over the next days. As he signed documents, met with advisors, attended daily services, and made his ceremonial rounds, he couldn't shake the sick feeling that he was guilty of a grievous error.

On a fine spring day in April, as the wind blew in from the sea, Constantine received a visit from his old tutor, Plethon.

"Shall we walk in the garden? The day is fine—" Constantine broke off, his eye going to Plethon's staff. "That is, if you feel up to it, my illustrious friend." Plethon was nearly eighty years old, but he carried himself erect and possessed a mind so sharp that one could be forgiven for forgetting the might of his years. A scholar of Plato and Aristotle, he had studied in Florence as a youth and taught at Mistra for three decades.

"Not to admire nature when she has adorned herself so richly for us would be an offence, Augustus," Plethon said with a smile, pausing to inhale the scent of a Persian lily breaking through the earth.

Constantine gazed fondly at his teacher. He was a large-framed man, almost as tall as he was himself, with a striking and memorable face. From beneath his round, colorfully embroidered cap, wavy locks of hair white as freshly fallen snow straggled to his shoulders. His features were strongly hewn, his eyes a piercing blue, and his magnificent white beard reached to his chest.

"Tell me, Plethon, are churches, monasteries and mansions still being built in Mistra as they were before I left?"

"Aye, new buildings go up daily, and old ones are given new life with decorations and wall paintings. It is a busy beehive, our little Mistra. Libraries are collecting books and copying manuscripts for posterity, and silk weavers can barely keep up with the production of their silkworms. Makes me think of how it must have been here in the Queen of Cities once upon a time." They walked, his staff tapping the garden path that had been solid marble and was now cracked with weeds.

"It is good to see you, Plethon. I have had little opportunity for such pleasures lately and no longer recall the last time we strolled together."

"It was in '42 after your royal brother Demetrios joined forces with the sultan to attack Constantinople."

"Ah, yes... Indeed. How did that slip my mind?"

"Perhaps because you don't wish to remember, Augustus."

"I have never understood my brother, Plethon. How he could justify such a shameful pact is beyond me."

"That is because you lack the driving ambition for power that eats him from within. Forgive me, Augustus. I am not one of his admirers, and I will confess that Mistra is not the same without you. Nowadays, there is always discord, thanks to Prince Demetrios."

"I know... I spend much time mediating his disputes with our brother, Thomas." After a long pause, Constantine added, "Demetrios resented most bitterly that John made me his heir."

"To be sure, it was nothing personal," Plethon said, throwing Constantine a wry smile. "Prince Demetrios was violently opposed to anyone but himself being named."

"To the point of almost tearing the land in two?" Constantine heaved an audible breath. "And now, somehow, we must unite against the wider threat that confronts our civilization."

"That will be no easy task. You tried once before, as I recall, Augustus."

"The Hexamilion Wall..." Again, Constantine heard the shouts of battle and saw himself lying prostrate on the rampart, staring up at the sky through a smear of blood, the dark shadow of a Turk looming over him, scimitar raised for the kill. He saw death in that moment before Phrantzes cut the man down and saved his life. He shook the memory gone.

"My head was filled with dreams of uniting the Peloponnese. I was certain we would vanquish the enemy, certain that God was on our side." The defeat had taught him a hard lesson. He did not know the mind of God. No one did. God worked in mysterious ways and in His own time.

"Wisdom is the daughter of experience," Plethon replied softly.

Constantine turned his gaze on his old friend. "If you were to advise me now, what would you say?"

"The enemy surrounds us, and all we have are our walls. We need to ally with the West. At all costs, Augustus. And soon."

Constantine nodded.

A rattling sound drew their attention to the sky. A stately procession of storks was coming in from the Bosphorus. Constantine watched them with soft eyes. This was their home too, and soon they would be seen throughout the city, on all the highest monuments of the Hippodrome, the towers, the soaring church steeples. It was the sight he loved most about Constantinople—storks returning to their ancestral nesting places year after year. The eternal permanence of God's creation had always been a source of great comfort to him.

He turned to Plethon. "Will you be visiting Lady Zoe while you are here?"

His friend brightened. "Naturally. No visit would be complete without beholding her beautiful face. How is her hunt coming for a husband?"

Constantine averted his eyes. "I do not believe she has found one yet."

"Lucky the man who wins her, Augustus. She is a most remarkable young lady."

"Augustus!" a voice said.

A messenger hastened up the path between the narcissus and the anemones. The man saluted with a fist thump and held out a rolled parchment that was sealed with red wax and tied with a ribbon. "I bear a missive for you from the Imperial Chancellor Phrantzes."

Constantine broke the seal, hoping Plethon didn't notice the tremor in his hand as he unfurled the missive. "Your Imperial Majesty Constantine Palaeologus in Christ, Emperor of the Romans, I greet thee full reverently," Phrantzes had written. "Knowing well how anxiously you await my news, I have dispatched this missive to report the tidings thus far. You may hope, Augustus! Prince George Brankovic of Serbia and his wife, Princess Irene, welcome an alliance with full hearts and are most anxious for the match to take place as soon as possible. They see a great future for their daughter, Mara, as Empress of Rome. God in His mercy has sent us a way out of our desperate plight."

Constantine rolled the parchment up.

"Good news, I pray," said Plethon, his blue eyes sharp.

"Good news," Constantine said quietly.

After a wild boar hunt to break the building tension, Constantine returned to his privy quarters as sunset poured orange and gold into sea and sky. Theo was already there, clapping for Zoe and a group of maidens who danced to the song of minstrels on the terrace, dark silhouettes against the sparkle of the sea. Fastened to a perch nearby by a fine silver chain, Apollo hopped from foot to foot, bobbing his purple head to the beat of the music and eliciting much laughter.

Constantine settled down to watch. A servant brought a platter of sweets, and he took one. Phyllo dough stuffed with crushed almonds and drenched with rose water was one of his favorite sweets, but today it had no taste. He threw it to a gull.

"A fine evening," Theo offered.

"Indeed," Constantine replied. The Storm of the Turning Windmills had swept through the darkening cypresses and cedars, sweetening the air with spring and whirling the sheeted windmills on both sides of the Golden Horn. Yet he found it hard to smile.

"Augustus," Aesop said, bowing. "You have another messenger from the Lord of the Imperial Chanceries."

Constantine felt a sudden tightness in his chest. His glance went to Zoe, absorbed in the dance, laughing and waving a scarf. For a moment he flashed back to his joyous coronation banquet in Mistra when the future had stretched ahead bright with promise. "Have him come to the study," he said, lowering his voice.

Crossing the Ocean Hall, he made his way to the sunken area that was encircled by red marble steps, black Corinthian columns, and statues of Greek gods and goddesses. At his desk he accepted the missive from the messenger, grateful that the statues hid him from view on the terrace. He broke the seal, skipped the greeting that listed his titles, and went directly to the tidings.

"Knowing full well how anxiously you await word," Phrantzes had written, "I have dispatched this report before I leave Serbia. The marriage that had won the blessing of the king and queen and looked so promising has foundered on the objections of the Lady Mara Brankovic herself. For she took a vow that if God ever released her from the chains of the infidel, she would lead a life of chastity for the rest of her days. Nothing will change her mind."

Torn by both intense relief and shattering disappointment in the same moment, Constantine lowered himself into his chair and read on. "Only King George of Georgia remains with whom we might forge an alliance. Pray, Augustus, inform my messenger as to your wishes. Should I return to the Queen of Cities, or should I leave directly for Georgia?"

Constantine lifted his head. "Georgia," he barked at the man. "Tell him to make haste to Georgia."

The messenger withdrew. He laid his head back against his chair and closed his eyes.

"Ill tidings?"

Constantine looked up. Theo stood on the steps. He waved him to a seat. "Serbia is gone. Georgia is all we have left. I am told not to worry, that Mehmet is incompetent. But I begin to have my doubts."

"Why? He is only nineteen, after all."

"So was Alexander the Great."

A silence.

Constantine spoke again. "In the same breath that they tell us Mehmet is no threat, they refuse to ally with us because they fear him. We have only one chance left, Theo. We must pray that Georgia does not spurn us."

"Why so solemn?" Zoe's voice. "Has something happened?"

Constantine jerked his head up. Zoe stood between two black marble columns, her hair a wine halo in the filtered rays of the sunset, her golden belt of rank glinting around her slender hips and her silver silk stola fluttering in the breeze from the balcony. How he loved to look at her!

"Well?" She moved down the steps toward them, a floating vision.

"We were discussing Mehmet," Constantine said, avoiding mention of Georgia. "Whether he is as immature and inept as they say."

"No."

The ease of her answer sent a wave of apprehension coursing through him. "Go on."

Zoe draped herself on a scarlet silk reclining couch with a gilded half-arm and examined the fruit in a silver urn before her. She chose an apple and took a bite. "Mehmet is dangerous," she said, nibbling thoughtfully. "Far more dangerous than he appears. He conceals his aggression behind a facade of good will."

"How can you know?" he asked, a sickening sensation tightening his stomach.

"He is my age, nineteen. I understand the mind of someone nineteen. Everyone thinks you immature and easily manipulated. If you are intelligent and ambitious, you resent that. More so when you are the son of a slave and have been dismissed as inconsequential all your life. You are compelled to prove them wrong. Therefore, you are dangerous. Especially if you think they are trying to cajole or outwit you."

Constantine stared at her in bewilderment. She was the one he should have consulted before making the ploy. She had explained what only Andronicus had suspected. Now he understood Halil Pasha's agitation. Halil knew his master and his ambition. He knew Mehmet would take the threat as an insult. And an opportunity.

Constantine's breath caught. Hs mistake was not just a grievous error. It was a strategic miscalculation. Pray God it didn't prove deadly! Extracting gold from Mehmet was not like taking candied rose petals from a child. It was like taking meat from a tiger. "The Sultan received our ambassadors with great respect," Constantine said, desperate for Zoe to allay his mounting fear. "He put their minds at ease with declarations of his good intent. Do you think he lied?"

She considered a moment. "When the Serbs broke their truce with Murad, he was cosultan with his father and still a child. He sent his father a message, did he not? Varna was the result. You do not play games with someone like that. Mehmet is not to be believed."

Constantine stared at her, and it was not of Grecian goddesses and muses that he was thinking, but of Cassandra on the walls of Troy, speaking the warning that no one heeded.

In her bedchamber in the Notaras privy quarters of the *Soros Triklinos* at Blachemae, Zoe reclined on a couch by the fire, deep in thought, a hand to her brow. Outside the palace walls, the waters of the Golden Horn glimmered darkly in the dusky gloom.

Eirene watched her, thinking how lovely she looked on the sapphire couch with her long auburn tresses falling in waves around her. Since Zoe had become *Zoste Patricia* and moved into the *Soros,* she had been happy. Until now. She took a seat at the edge of Zoe's chaise. "What is it, dear one? Are you sick?"

Zoe shook her head.

"Is it him?" She took her hand.

Zoe sighed. "Is it so obvious?"

"Let me put it this way. It doesn't take an astronomer to figure it out. It is probably safe to say anyone paying the slightest attention knows how you two feel about each another."

"I have always wanted love, Eirene, but not like this. Never like this—" Tears sprang into her eyes.

Eirene gathered her into her arms and smoothed her hair. "There, there... Nothing has been decided yet." All that marriage talk; it was everywhere. In the streets. In the shops. In the palace. Phrantzes was on his way back from Georgia, and it was said his news was good. Eirene thought again, as she often did these days, how grateful she was to have evaded cupid's arrow.

"What am I to do?" Zoe whispered, looking at Eirene, tears rolling down her cheeks.

"You can do nothing, and neither can he. He must find the strength to marry for Rome, and you must find the strength to bear your burden when he does." She pulled out a handkerchief and gently dried Zoe's tears.

Fourteen

On an autumn day in mid-September as the leaves turned crimson and mist shrouded the sea, George Phrantzes sailed into port. With him came an emissary from the Kingdom of Georgia. Constantine received them in the throne room where his axe-wielding Varangians created a path from the entryway to the throne. Clarions blared. The Varangians extended their lances and snapped to attention, and Phrantzes and the thick-bearded Georgian envoy passed through their ranks.

Phrantzes swept his gold-tasseled red velvet cap from his head and gave a ceremonial bow. "Imperial Majesty, be it known that your quest for an empress is at an end! I have here a marriage contract with the king of Georgia for the hand of his daughter, Princess Medea. With this alliance, His Majesty King George promises armaments, horses, a hundred ships, and an army of forty thousand men to aid us against the infidel!"

The relief that flooded Constantine was so intense that for a moment he didn't breathe.

"We are indebted to Georgia for the successful negotiation of our alliance," Phrantzes resumed, bowing to the Georgian ambassador, who was richly arrayed in massive jewels and four patterned silk tunicas of various lengths. "For it is the custom in Georgia that the bridegroom provide a dowry to the bride and not the other way round. I explained this was an impossibility, given the state of the imperial treasury, and His Majesty King George graciously agreed to provide a dowry to us."

"Pray accept our profound appreciation," Constantine replied. "We join with you in happiness and hope. May God bless our alliance and save Christendom in the East!"

"May God save Christendom! May God save Rome!" the black-bearded Georgian echoed, flourishing a deep bow with a rustle of silk and flash of jewels.

"Let us drink to our accord," Constantine said. Servants entered with silver trays laden with goblets of wine. As they made their rounds, Constantine looked at the faces that thronged the hall, his gaze passing from one to the other casually, negligently, until it fell on Zoe, half-hidden behind her father. Their eyes met in a long unsmiling look and their hearts flowed into one another. She was ashen pale, and inwardly he felt her shocked anguish at the news of his intended marriage. Though he knew his duty and was determined to make every sacrifice that fate demanded of him, he felt utterly wretched. Tearing his eyes from her face, he rose from his throne and raised his goblet high. "To the alliance!" he called, upending his cup.

"To the alliance!" came the resounding cry.

Without delay and in the Georgian ambassador's presence, Constantine signed the marriage contract with three crosses in red ink on the upper corner and sealed it with gold, providing the confirmation demanded by Georgian custom. He handed the agreement to the envoy. "With God's help, my Imperial Chancellor Phrantzes will arrive next spring and bring Princess Medea to me."

"Thank you for your tireless efforts, my friend," he told Phrantzes in the privacy of the Ocean Hall when the emissary had left. "You have saved the empire this day. When this is behind us, whatever you desire is yours."

Phrantzes eyed him with concern. "Are you unwell, Augustus?"

"What makes you think that?"

"You look pale and seem distracted, not pleased."

Constantine tried to keep his gaze from the empty couch by the fire where Zoe used to sit.

"It is nothing. Something I ate didn't agree with me. It will soon pass. If I seem distracted, it is because tomorrow we meet with Patriarch Gregory and Gennadius."

Phrantzes frowned. "Very unpleasant. I am glad I am here to lend you a hand, should you need it."

Constantine squeezed his friend's shoulder. "I can always rely on you in my hour of need, George. I received the letter you wrote on the twenty-eighth of May about the failure of the Serbian match—odd that I should remember the date… For all these months since, I have placed my hopes in you, and you have not failed me."

"Augustus—" Phrantzes said in a troubled voice. Constantine waited.

"You mentioned the twenty-eighth of May. I had a dream that night. A most curious dream. So extraordinary that I wrote it down and had my account witnessed." After a long hesitation, he went on. "In my dream, I was in Constantinople. I came to take my leave of you—and this is what is strange, Augustus— I made a motion to prostrate myself before you and kiss your feet, but you restrained me. Raising me up, you kissed my eyes instead."

"Strange indeed," Constantine said. "That ancient custom of final farewell between emperor and loyal subject fell into disuse hundreds of years ago."

"Exactly. I told everyone sleeping by me to note the date. The feeling I had, Augustus—it was like nothing I'd ever known before. Unsettling… As if I were seeing you for the last time."

Constantine forced a smile. "Thanks be to the Virgin it was just a dream."

Not until the moment of the Georgian marriage announcement did Zoe realize how deeply she loved Constantine. Her eyes red-rimmed from weeping, she sat at the window of her chamber in the *Soros.*

Standing at her chair, her father said gently, "It is unfortunate that times are what they are, and the emperor must wed for reasons of state, Zoe…" He spoke quietly, his disappointment evident, for he knew that Zoe would surely be empress had matters been less urgent. He waited for a response, but she continued to sit silently, as if he weren't there. "Child, have you not heard a word I've said?"

No response.

He heaved an audible sigh. When he looked up, his eye fell on Eirene, watching from a respectful distance.

"How long has she been like this?" he asked.

"Ever since the announcement," Eirene replied softly.

"Has she spoken to you, Eirene?"

"No."

"It has been two days. How much longer can she keep this up?"

"She is not ready for the world yet. It has been a devastating blow."

"One she must accept."

"That doesn't make it easier, my lord," Eirene said, grateful again that Cupid had passed her by, for love always seemed to walk hand in hand with grief of one kind or another.

"What about her duties?" Lucas demanded.

"Aesop has assumed the responsibilities with the palace household, and she has good people managing the charities. I go to Botaneiates and St. Acacius daily to take care of matters."

"I was at my residence yesterday. A crowd of people awaited her with their petitions. She cannot ignore them forever."

"She won't. She merely needs a little more time."

"It is important work she does," Lucas said. "Now that Zoe has given the people a voice, they will not take kindly to having it silenced. There could be trouble in the streets."

"She will not let the emperor down, my lord. But when the body is dealt a cut, it requires stitches and time to heal. It is the same with the heart."

Lucas cupped Eirene's face in his hands and kissed her brow. "Thank you, Eirene, for being a good friend to my daughter."

The next morning when Constantine strode into his council chamber the atmosphere was thick with tension. He took his place at the head of the table, opposite Patriarch Gregory Mammas at the other end, surrounded by his bishops. Lucas, Phrantzes, Theo, and the Cantacuzenes were gathered in a group by the window. Zoe wasn't present. She hadn't answered his summons. Perhaps it was for the best, he thought. He had appointed her a councilor but the presence of a woman wouldn't sit well with the fiercely conservative monk Gennadius, who stood with his adherents near the door, as if to bolt at any moment.

"We are here this day to resolve our divisions," Constantine said, taking in the glowering faces of the clerics. "The enemy may be preparing for war as we speak. To survive, we must unite."

Patriarch Gregory lost no time voicing his concern. "I have been boycotted by my clergy since my arrival from Rome! You, Imperial Majesty, have done nothing to implement the agreement of the Council of Florence. You have not pressed union!"

"We have not done so, Your All Holiness, because we do not want riots in our streets," Constantine replied. "We must stand united against the Ottoman threat. Civil war must be avoided at all costs."

"Difficult as it may be, I see no other way. You must enforce the accord. Not until the terms of the Council of Florence are met will the West send the aid you need."

"Your All Holiness," Lucas said, addressing the patriarch, "you know my sentiments. I am anti-union, but I am prepared to support it to save my church. If we force the issue, however, our bishops will revolt. Nor will any Orthodox church east of Rome condone such a move. We would stand alone. What assurance can you give that the pope and the Christian West will rally to our cause if we impose union on our people by force?"

"The only assurance I can give is that there will be no help unless you do."

Gennadius, who had been silent during this exchange, slammed his fist on the table. "We will not unite with you! We will not accept your Latinizing ways, your unmarried priests, your corrupt popes! We will not buy earthly security at the cost of eternal salvation! If disaster befalls us as you say, it is God's punishment for our sins. It is written that the end of the world is coming in 1492. Union with the West cannot save us or alter our fate. What is written, is written!"

"By not enforcing union, we Romans are proving ourselves fools and obstinately committing suicide!" Patriarch Gregory shouted, red-faced.

Lucas turned on the patriarch. "The Latins are the fools. They practiced a Holy War that was dangerous and unrealistic. When we didn't support their crusades, they turned on *us*! Until they came, we lived side by side with Muslims in respect and tolerance. The Latin crusaders brought their hatreds with them and made us enemies. The disasters that have befallen us are their fault—"

"Enough, Lucas," Constantine commanded.

"The dynastic civil war between Palaeologus and Cantacuzene that precipitated 1204 was their fault?" Patriarch Gregory hurled back, too angry to heed Constantine. "How convenient to blame others for the troubles we cause ourselves! We feuding Greeks have always fought, and we never needed help finding a reason to kill each other."

"I said enough!" Constantine roared, slamming a fist on the table. A shocked silence fell at this rare display of temper. "We come to this table today with our long history standing between us," he said more calmly. "Some of our problems were our creation, but not all. It is true the West was offended by our lukewarm attitude toward their crusades and appalled that the city dedicated to the Virgin held a mosque and a synagogue where Jew and Muslim prayed side by side. They called us heretics. They excommunicated our emperor, and we excommunicated their pope. Nor did the Muslims thank us for restraining the crusading ardor of the West. None of this can be denied. But let us not forget one thing—"

His glance moved from face to face. "It is history. What matters now—*all* that matters now—is the future! What we do here this day will decide the fate of Christendom in the East." He turned to Patriarch Gregory. "Your All Holiness, you are correct. Our dynastic civil war invited the Venetian invasion of 1204. But Palaeologus and Cantacuzene stand united now—" He gestured to Demetri and Andronicus, who nodded assent. "Let us not repeat the same mistake again! All of us here must put aside our differences knowing that what unites us is far more fundamental than what divides us. We are not adversaries. To fight among ourselves is to invite destruction! Let us heal the rift before it is too late. Let us unite and find a way out of our dire plight."

"Augustus… Your All Holiness," Phrantzes said, moved. "Our doctrine allows us to overlook minor differences in the interest of the House of God—"

"The marriage of priests is not a minor difference!" Gennadius exploded. "The supremacy of the pope is not a minor difference! *Rum Papa* is a bishop like all other bishops, but he wants supremacy over us. I will not give it!"

Phrantzes turned to Patriarch Gregory. "We are willing to bend," he said, hoping for a concession to defuse Gennadius's objection. "Will Rome meet us halfway?"

Before Patriarch Gregory could reply, Gennadius yelled, "We are not meeting them halfway! We follow the True Word as handed us by the apostles. These heretic Latins have adulterated God's Word and want us to follow them into damnation!"

It was Patriarch Gregory's turn to leap to his feet in anger. "How dare you insult us in this manner! Your arrogance will not go unpunished!"

"And your arrogance makes me agree with those who say, "Better a caliph's turban than a bishop's miter!" Gennadius shouted.

"My brethren in Christ, do you not understand what is at stake?" Constantine cried.

"I have had enough," Patriarch Gregory roared, whirling on him. "You hear this and do nothing? You will not receive an ounce of Western aid! I am returning to Rome at once, and I will tell what transpired here this day. If you will not save yourselves, I wash my hands of you!" He turned on his heel and stormed out, his retinue in tow.

"Good riddance to him," Gennadius spat as he followed him out.

The room emptied. Constantine passed a hand over his face and crumpled into his chair.

"The man in the middle gets no thanks from either side," Phrantzes murmured. "And we are the man in the middle."

"Send a message to Venice," Constantine said, his voice thick, unsteady. "Unless reinforcements are dispatched at once, Constantinople will fall to the Turks."

The estrangement with Zoe and the row with the patriarch and the monk took their toll on Constantine. For the second day in a row, he spent a fitful night, sleeping poorly, tormented by bad dreams. In his dream, Gennadius's fist had pounded a table, and with each blow, pain had shot through him. Then he saw it wasn't a table at all, but his own dead face that Gennadius punched. The monk vanished, and Zoe stood in his place. "What do you here?" he asked with joy. She had replied without moving her lips. "You dream. I am not here. You are alone." Even Halil Pasha made an appearance. "You stupid Greeks. You have slain me and killed yourself."

Constantine watched the sheer bed curtains flutter in the breeze that blew in through the lacy doors standing open to the terrace. He inhaled a long breath and sat up. For some strange reason, he remembered Phrantzes's dream on the twenty-eighth of May, the one his friend had related to him after the Georgian emissary had left. He shook himself to clear his head. When he looked again, darkness was lifting, and birds had begun their sweet chorus to greet the dawn. He threw back the bedspread of silver silk embroidered with peacocks and roses. Flinging the lattice doors open wide, he went out on the terrace. The wind blew hard, whipping his hair and woolen nightshirt, and gulls mewed as they circled overhead seeking their breakfast. He rested his hands on the stone balustrade and watched the sunrise. Magenta, crimson, and orange streaked the sky and melted away into the palest of blues, drenching the shimmering waters with their reflection. Zoe's face rose before him, arms lifted, laughing as she twirled, auburn hair mingling with the crimson dawn. Constantine tightened his hold on the stone balustrade. *Zoe.* He closed his eyes. When he opened them again, a dimming moon looked down on him; then it faded, chased away by the rising sun.

Fifteen

In the Palace of Botaneiates, Zoe looked around the crowded dormitory and brought her gaze back to the monk she'd put in charge.

"As you can see, there is no more room here for pallets," he said. "Nor is there space in the antechamber."

"How many more do we need?"

"At least a hundred. People have been streaming in all morning. There seems not to be any end."

"I thought we had made room for all the refugees from Struma?"

"We did. These refugees are farmers from the western Marmara coast."

She stared at him, not comprehending. Western Marmara was in Europe— It was Roman land!

"Mehmet has evicted them from their property," the monk said. "He has set his horses to graze in their fields and ravaged their crops."

"But it's harvest time. They've worked all year for their crops!" Zoe exclaimed. She looked at the cluster of new arrivals: old men, young men, women, and children. In the short time she'd been talking with the monk, more had streamed in to swell their ranks, carrying their few possessions in bundles on their backs, little ones clinging to their mother's skirts. A few children held their pets in their arms: a cat, a dog, a baby goat. Their eyes were pools of entreaty as they gazed at her across the hall, and she caught the sparkle of their tears. "We will find shelter for them. The roof in the treasury hall has a few leaks, but we can patch some and set buckets under others. I will speak to the linen merchant about cloth for the pallets. Can the nuns help sew?"

He nodded.

Zoe hesitated. "Does the emperor know about this?"

"He knows about the farmers from Struma, *Zoste Patricia.* I'm not sure about these new refugees."

"Then you'd better tell him." The monk inclined his head.

Constantine summoned his advisors to his study to receive a messenger with a report of a sensitive nature. It was late in the evening, and everyone was present except Andronicus, who had been taken ill. And Zoe.

"What do our spies in Adrianopolis say?" Constantine demanded.

"Augustus, as soon as the sultan returned, he expelled the Greeks from the towns of the lower Struma and confiscated their lands and revenues."

"We know that. We learned it from the refugees who came to us." From Zoe, who gave them shelter. He winced.

"Mehmet is nothing if not crafty," the man continued. "He holds his thoughts close beneath his turban, and no one knows what he plans. But all are agreed on one thing. He models himself on Alexander the Great and is bent on conquering Rome—*Rum,* as he calls us. He has been so inclined since childhood. I am told we underestimate him at our peril."

Nausea churned Constantine's stomach. His mother's words. Words he had forgotten until it was too late! He gave a nod of dismissal and turned to his advisors, noting with an ache Zoe's empty seat. "What do we do? Any ideas?"

"Perhaps you should consider enforcing union," Phrantzes said.

"My ancestor, Michael VIII, tried that—" He had imprisoned and persecuted his opponents in order to unite with the Roman church and save his people, and he died excommunicated by both churches, condemned as a perfidious bungler by Rome and a traitor to his faith by Constantinople. "The anti-unionists will martyr themselves before they give up their orthodoxy. I will not kill my own people because they believe in taking a different path to God."

Lucas spoke. "If we cannot unite with Rome, then we must make the papacy understand what we are up against. They might relent and send us aid."

"The papacy will do nothing without union, Notaras," Phrantzes said. "And you are dreaming if you think they will."

"I see the situation as clearly as the next man, Phrantzes," Lucas bristled. "The papacy has been lulled into a false sense of security by the news from Adrianopolis. They wish to believe Mehmet is as incompetent as they hope he is. I'm saying we have nothing to lose by stripping them of their illusions, either about union or about Mehmet."

"You are responsible for all of this!" Phrantzes exclaimed. "It is because of you and your hair-brained scheme to threaten Mehmet that we are here!"

"For God's sake, put the past away for once and think of the realm!" Constantine said. "We are all in this together. We cannot fight the enemy and one another at the same time! How do we convince the papacy, Lucas?" he demanded.

"Send the pope a document from the clergy stating their objections to union," Lucas replied.

"Are we decided?" He looked at Phrantzes.

Phrantzes gave a reluctant nod.

"Augustus— " Aesop said.

"What is it?"

"Another messenger to see you."

"At this hour? Very well, send him in," Constantine sighed.

Zoe's monk entered.

For three days Constantine had hoped to run into Zoe, but he never did. Now he was certain she was avoiding him. Nothing had prepared him for her reaction, and it tormented him. They had never spoken about his impending betrothal—why would they? All the realm knew an alliance was vital to their survival, for they could not hold out alone against the menace from the East.

Struggling with his emotions, Constantine took the marble stairs up to the Ocean Hall. Zoe might no longer come with her father to dine with him or share a cup of wine before compline, but she still discharged her responsibilities honorably, managing everything from her quarters in the *Soros.* The problem was that the Blachernae grounds were rambling, enabling her to come and go without ever encountering him. That was why he'd summoned her to give him a report. At least, that was the reason he gave in his summons. But the simple truth was that he needed to see her.

More than anything in the world, he needed to see her.

Aesop greeted him at the entry, his pearl earring dangling as he bowed low. "Is she here?" Constantine asked under his breath, ignoring Apollo's screeches of welcome and his excited cry of "Constans! Constans!"

With a discreet movement of the head, Aesop indicated the terraced balcony. Constantine gave his shoulder a squeeze and headed in that direction. He pulled up sharply at the threshold. Zoe stood gazing out over the Golden Horn, her hands resting gracefully on the stone balustrade. She did not turn though she surely heard his steps. Her gray silk gown fluttered around her willowy form and the golden girdle of office hugged her slender hips. Her upswept hair, bright as burnished copper in the sun, was twisted and knotted with strings of pearls, exposing her long white neck. He went to stand at her side. His heart pounded. For a long moment, neither spoke, letting the ebb and flow of the tide, the shriek of sea birds and the sweep of the wind through the trees fill the silence for them.

Then Zoe said, stiffly, with averted eyes "You wished to see me?"

"I wondered how the preparations were coming for the emissary from the Lord of the White Sheep," Constantine replied.

"His welcome will be lavish. I have arranged an elaborate feast and chosen gifts of perfume and silks for his retinue and a dagger with a hilt of ivory and carnelians as a gift for His Excellency."

"That is good. Very good. He is a powerful man. A foe to the sultan. Maybe a prospective ally. His territories border the Ottoman empire on the east—" He broke off. Never had he felt so awkward.

"I know."

He searched his mind for something to say. He had no wish to bring up the subject he knew they must discuss. Not yet. Not so soon. "How did the matter go with the *vestiarios?*"

Zoe had just that morning arbitrated a dispute over payment between the wardrobe-keeper and a silk merchant. She was surprised Constantine had heard about it since it was a small matter involving the palace staff. "I found in favor of the silk merchant. He was underpaid. He had almost come to blows with the man by the time I got there." She smiled to herself, remembering the joy of the merchant as he collected what he was owed.

"I appreciate everything you have done, Zoe. The people love you. Can you—will you stay?"

She stiffened. "Your empress will assume my responsibilities. I will stay until she arrives. After that, I do not know… "Her voice faltered. In a low tone, she said, "I cannot remain in Constantinople."

A silence.

"I have missed you," he said.

"You will have company soon enough."

He heaved a deep breath and brought his gaze to their hands, so close together, their fingers almost touching, yet as far apart as the two continents separated by the Bosphorus a short distance away. What could he say? What words would close the chasm between them?

"It is my destiny, Zoe. What I would give to change what must be—" His words came like a cry on the wind. At the same moment, he placed his hand over hers. He heard her gasp, but she didn't pull away. His heart pounded violently. He closed his eyes. If only he could hold this moment forever.

Zoe felt his touch like a burn. Her breath caught in her throat. She turned to look at the tall brown-clad figure beside her who stood as pale and still as a marble statue, his mouth tight with emotion, his shoulders drooping with misery. Sudden realization swept her. Neither was it easy for him. She had thought it was, and she'd been wrong—so wrong! An intense aching need engulfed her. She wanted to throw herself into his arms, to kiss and be kissed; to feel, to touch, to hold and be held forever; to never stop, never let go—

"I can't stay," she whispered hoarsely, pulling her hand from his, backing away. "I can't stay–"

"No, Zoe—do not leave me!"

"I must—"

Before he could stop her, she had fled. He caught a glimpse of silver silk as the door thudded shut. Steeling himself against the anguish that flooded him, he bowed his head and gripped the stone balustrade with all his might.

The messenger thumped a fist to his breast in salute. "Augustus, I bring dire tidings. The sultan is demolishing churches and monasteries and tearing down the dwellings of farmers who live in Thrace. Forty men from the village of Epibatai protested the destruction of their property. A fight broke out between them and Ottoman soldiers. They were brought before the sultan, who said they would be suitably punished."

Constantine felt the blood drain to his feet. "They have every right to protest! That is our land—" First, Mehmet had invaded them to the south; now he invaded them to the north, as if to surround and isolate them. Crushing his mounting fear, he turned a questioning gaze on his councilors. Three places sat empty at his table: one belonging to the patriarch, who had returned to Italy; another to Andronicus, who had died after his sudden, brief illness; and the third to Zoe, who remained absent.

"It is an act of war," Phrantzes said, his face pale.

"It can only mean one thing. He is preparing to besiege the city," Lucas said.

"We could be leaping to conclusions. It could merely be the impetuosity of youth—" Constantine said, clinging to hope.

"Unfortunately, I can find no other explanation," Phrantzes replied. "His own grandfather, Sultan Bayezid, asked your father's permission before he built his fortress on the Asian side of the Bosphorus, Augustus. Yet the land belonged to him. But this—" He broke off, leaving his thought unfinished.

"We can send an embassy to ask about his intentions and remind him of our past amity," Lucas said, ever ready to take the opposite side of Phrantzes's position. "Point out that we have a solemn treaty. Couch our message in the language of friendship. Anything to avert hostilities—"

The sound of footsteps drew their gaze to the door. Another messenger stood framed in the entry, his face ashen pale. He clasped a fist to his chest. "Augustus, the sultan has decided the fate of his Greek prisoners. They will be beheaded before our walls."

Constantine stared at the man in sick disbelief. Around him his councilors were a frozen tableau of pale faces and shocked expressions. All at once, fury exploded in his veins, and he slammed a fist on the table. "Lock the gates! Round up the enemy! Behead them all!"

"Augustus, we are not ready for war," Lucas said quietly. "We can't fight Mehmet yet."

"Perhaps we should imprison them instead?" Theo offered hastily, his troubled gray eyes dark as slate in his ashen face.

Constantine scraped his chair back and went to the window. He ran a hand through his hair helplessly. He needed to do something, but what in heaven's name could he do? The Ottomans had all the money, all the lands, all the men. If he humbled himself to Mehmet, would that mollify him? He turned back to his councilors. "Very well. Let me think on it."

That night Constantine slept fitfully. As he tossed and turned, he heard something on the wind, a strange sound, faraway. He strained to listen. What was it? *Whispers?* No. Drums, and men singing…

He couldn't make out the words. Abruptly the song ceased, and he saw that he lay in the dirt. He tried to rise but lacked the strength. He turned his head and peered into the darkness where shadows lurked, and the shadows drew closer, and they were men stamping their feet to a martial beat. White cloth fluttered from their headgear, and a terrible realization washed over him. *These are Janissaries! Mehmet's elite troops.* Drawn from the strongest and bravest of the enslaved, they were taken in childhood, indoctrinated, forcibly converted, and raised to fight for Islam.

The Janissaries knelt and thrust their laughing faces into his. He stared at them, his bewilderment turning to horror. Beneath their helmets, they were all children. Christian children, raising their swords to behead him—

He screamed and opened his eyes to find Aesop shaking him awake.

Like everyone in Constantinople, Zoe received the news of the events at Epibatai with chilling foreboding and a nauseating sense of despair. The old prophecies of doom were revived and embellished. Not only did people whisper that what began with Constantine born of Helena would end with Constantine born of Helena. They also remembered that it was not to his dominions that the statue of Constantine the Great pointed, but to the East from whence their doom would come.

Though she did not weep and wail, and beat her breast, and call out the prophecies as the townsfolk did, she felt the moment keenly. The world had changed. Nothing would be the same again, and nothing could be taken for granted. Not the next instant or the next sunrise. All they had was the present. Not one grain more.

In her chamber she stood at the open window that overlooked the Golden Horn. Mist was rising, and she could hear the sea moan. The white fog was damp and smelled of burnt salt. When she looked in the direction of Constantine's imperial balcony, she couldn't see the walls, only the flower urns on the terrace and the vague outlines of the palace, fading in and out. It was seven o'clock. The day's end was at hand, and monks were singing Vespers and meditating on

Creation, but instead of the golden beauty of sunset, the mood was one of fear and oppression.

For Zoe this past week had been filled with not only emotional turmoil but with a depth of despair and wretchedness of mind she had never known before. Her distress had been so acute at times that it was almost a physical pain. Her father, suspecting what she endured, had tried to help in his fashion by talking of duty and the exigencies of life. But unable to voice her pain, she had sat silently, barely listening. She knew all that. She understood the chasm between dreams and reality. It didn't help the despair. Nothing helped, except being with Constantine. For all her anguish, yesterday on the terrace was as close to happiness as she had come since the marriage treaty. Despite the pain, despite the impossibility of her hopes, the touch of his hand on hers still flamed in her memory—

Gently, so very gently, she laid her cheek on her hand, pretending it was his. *Oh Beloved, where has the time gone that should be ours?* Through the autumn mist a man's voice drifted to her, singing to the sweet notes of a flute, a song filled with yearning and lament:

Midnight is here. The moon is no more,

Time passes, and I sleep alone.

The words sliced through her like a sword. She closed her eyes on the aching sorrow, and as she did, a new knowledge came to her. Shadowy at first, it gathered force until it submerged her like a giant wave. The old world was gone, and with it, the old ways. From now on, the rules they'd lived by no longer applied. Her eyes flew open. If she couldn't have a full draught of joy, she'd take what she could get. She would seize the cup and drain it. Before it ran dry.

Before the chance was lost to her forever.

While Zoe was contemplating her future, Constantine was in his council chamber, reading the pope's reply to his entreaty for help.

You must make greater effort to convince your people that the price of further help from western Christendom is their acceptance of the pact of Florence, he wrote. *The Patriarch Gregory Mammas must be reinstated, and our name must be properly honored in your churches.*

"What does he say?" Lucas inquired, taking a seat at the table.

Constantine slid the missive across the table. “Same thing popes have always said. Do my bidding, or there is no help.”

Leaning back in his chair, he gazed out the window. The light was fading. Soon it would be sunset. Oranges and lemons gleamed in the orchards, and from the undulating fields came the bleating of sheep and sweet tinkling of bells. He thought of his ancestor, Michael VIII. He did not want his fate, yet what choice did he have but to enforce union? He rubbed his bleary eyes, remembering the prophecy. *What began with Constantine …*

There had been eleven emperors named Constantine, and not one had a mother named Helena, except for him and Constantine the Great. He made a fist. It could not be true. He would not be the last emperor of Rome! He would not accept it. There had to be a way to save his people!

He heaved an audible breath and looked at Lucas helplessly. “I have done my best to enforce the terms of union without causing riots in the streets. I have tried to make the pope understand—” He broke off, at a loss.

“Our best wager is still Venice,” Lucas said quietly. ‘They have the most to lose if we fall.”

“I will send to Pera as well and ask if they are with us.” Constantine frowned, knowing what their answer would be. If war broke out, the Genoese colony of Pera would be in the thick of it, but they would behave with the same cautious ambiguity and self-interest as the Venetians. “John’s words keep coming back to me. ‘We do not believe in the Roman Church; how can they think we do? It is only to save Orthodoxy that we even contemplate it. To save our city. Our people. Our Christian faith, and the Church of the East. Why can they not see it?’ I have the same question, Lucas. How can they be so blind?”

Before Lucas could reply, the sound of shuffling came at the door. A messenger stood at the threshold. Constantine stiffened. A glance at the man’s face told him his tidings were evil. *Can someone not bring me good news, just once?*

“What reply did the sultan make us?”

The man saluted. “None, Augustus. He refused to see us.”

Constantine clenched a fist. He had laden the envoys with gifts. He had returned the Ottoman soldiers he had taken prisoner. He had made every gesture of amity there was to make. He had done all this though Mehmet had murdered his people. Nothing had worked.

He gave the messenger a nod of dismissal and sat silently, oblivious of the falling darkness, or Lucas's request to depart, or the gentle hand he rested on his shoulder as he left. He had no wish for company, no appetite, no desire for anything, except to think. To find a way to…

Servants entered. Quietly, they lit the candles. The room flooded with light. He rose and went to the window. Thousands of stars glittered above, water washed the shore, and the wind blew. Lit by torches, the great curved walls Emperor Emmanuel Comnenus had built in the twelfth century stood guard over the blackness outside. Walls that had repelled Avars, Persians, Arabs, Slavs, Bulgars and Attila the Hun. For over a thousand years they had stood guard and kept a Christian civilization safe. Maybe they could be made to serve them one more time—

He rubbed his eyes and lifted his gaze to the sky. God was still there in His heaven. He might yet work a miracle. He bowed his head in prayer.

At last, he roused himself. Followed by his ever-present Varangians, he went downstairs and navigated the empty passageways and colonnades with bowed head, absorbed in his thoughts, oblivious to the beautiful mosaic designs at his feet and the splashing fountains he passed.

He took the wide marble stairs up to the Ocean Hall, vaguely surprised that Aesop was not there to greet him. He didn't care enough to wonder why. He made his way to his bedchamber. A fire burned in the hearth, casting flickering light over the room. The silver peacocks on the silk coverlet glinted in the low light, and the sheer curtains around the canopied bed fluttered in the breeze that drifted through the lattice doors of the terrace. He unfastened his cloak, undid his sash, and took off his outer tunica. He cast them aside and was about to remove his short inner tunica when he sensed that he was not alone. He stilled his hand and looked up. A figure stood in the darkness, a tall, slender figure with long, unbound hair that fell to her waist and glistened like embers in the light of the fire. His heart exploded with a wild joy.

"Zoe?"

She came out of the darkness into the half-light, her filmy nightdress and long auburn hair stirring in the breeze. For a moment, she stood perfectly still, a shadow among shadows, so that he thought he only imagined her.

"Yes," she said.

In an instant he closed the distance between them and pulled her roughly to him. He kissed her savagely. "Zoe— O Zoe— Zoe…" Between each word he kissed her shoulders, her lips, her neck. Her blood sang and her body flamed. Burning with fire, aching with desire, laboring for breath, Zoe grabbed a fistful of his hair and held him to her, returning his kisses with fiery ardor. Weak with passion, her knees crumpled, and she fell into his embrace. He swung her into the circle of his arms and carried her to the bed. Tearing off her shift, thrusting his tunica from him, he lowered himself over her. She gave a cry at the first surging, shocking contact of their flesh and arched her back to receive him. Her senses spinning, she dug her nails into his flesh and clung to him as the storm of passion bore them up one moment and down the next, swept them high into the clouds and plunged them down to earth, flowing and ebbing like the waves that crashed against the rocks beneath the starry sky. And there, in the vast, celestial glory of the heavens, their souls met at last, and touched, and entwined, and flowed into one another, never to perish, but to mingle for all time as one.

Sixteen

Zoe and Constantine exercised great caution in the coming months. Only two confidantes knew of their liaison. One was Aesop, who escorted her along a secret passageway from Constantine's bedchamber to the royal library on the lower floor. The other was Eirene, who fended off the ladies of her chamber with excuses why Zoe had no need of them for the night. Though Eirene clucked with disapproval, Zoe believed she took a vicarious delight in her secret love affair.

All seemed well enough until the arrival of a new peril. Maria.

She arrived from Mistra soon after the troubles at Struma. Her father, citing the dangerous times, wished to have all his children close. Now Maria resided at the Notaras Palace on the Golden Mile, along with their two brothers, who had finished their training in the art of war, and Isaac, who had just begun his. But they often came to spend the night at the *Soros*, and Zoe found this distressing, for it provided Maria an opportunity to snoop.

Maria's jealousy had not abated during their time apart. If anything, it had worsened, and now her sister's interest bordered on obsession. Zoe had caught her rifling through her belongings on several occasions, and items had gone missing. They were of no consequence—a ribbon, a book, a perfume dispenser. But it was unnerving, nonetheless. She could only hope that Maria never learned her secret.

On his part, Constantine found in love an armor that girded him for the ordeals each day unleashed. Though little good news followed the great happiness he had found, there was always hope, and both he and Zoe clung to it, even as messengers came and went with troubled tidings. Seated together on the balcony, they delighted in the beauty of their ever-changing land, where black cypresses grew by round towers and giant plane-trees spread dappled shade, where fishermen sang mending their nets, and shepherds played their flute grazing their sheep. They listened to the nightingale's serenade beneath the summer moon and to the monks who chanted the hymns of the midnight office that sent them comfort on the wind. Many nights Zoe played the lyre and sang for Constantine, all the while laughing at Apollo, who tried to imitate them, and made light of heavy matters.

Too quickly the seasons changed. Summer yielded to autumn, and autumn to Christmas. The Winds of King Boreas delivered the new year of 1452 with a special fury and were speedily followed by the ice-cold Winds of Mount Olympus. Darkening sea and sky, they released the dismal winter rains of February. On Constantine's birthday, the eighth of February, Zoe tossed and turned, unable to sleep, for the situation had grown desperate. No ships, no help, and no word had come from Georgia. The people in the outlying areas, incensed that they were being driven from their lands and that Constantine did nothing, had taken matters into their own hands and there were daily incidents. It had reached the point where the mere appearance of a messenger sent waves of apprehension coursing through them

The Storm of the Swallows wafted in from the Marmara in early March, announcing the arrival of spring. Soon after Easter, as storks built their nests and schools of dolphins leapt joyfully in the sea, Constantine left to inspect the walls. Blossoms adorned the trees, and wildflowers bloomed in the meadows; birds sang, dogs played, and children laughed. But for Constantine, the beauty only underscored the magnitude of what was at stake. Six months had passed since the Georgian emissary had left with the marriage contract, and Venice had yet to reply to his plea for help.

I will write them again, he thought, as he rode from gate to gate and tower to tower along the Golden Horn. I will ask the Venetian *Bailo* to deliver a personal plea. The West will not abandon us once they appreciate the urgency of our situation.

Turning southward, he arrived at the Charisian Gate and dismounted. The city of Constantinople was triangular in shape. On two sides, it was protected by the sea. On the only side that faced land, the defensive walls ran triple for most of their length from the northwest comer on the Golden Horn all the way down to the Marmara. Only around the ruins of the Church of St. Mary of Blachernae was it single for a short space. It was originally thought that the Holy Mother had no need for triple walls because she could protect her own church. But St. Mary's had burned down in 1434, and the wall was still single.

After examining the fortifications for damage, he dictated his findings to a scribe before moving on to the next southerly gate of St. Romanus. Between the gates of Charisius and St. Romanus wound the River Lycus. This stretch, commonly called the *Mesoteichion,* was about a mile long and represented the most vulnerable portion of their defenses. To this area Constantine gave special attention.

After a long day of inspection along the Western battlement, he reached the Golden Gate, near the Marmara Sea. Blue shades of twilight were falling, and birds shrieked loudly as they flew overhead. In the city quarter known as the Studion that housed the university and the patriarchal academy, he supped with members of the faculty. It was late by the time dinner was over, and he decided to spend the night at the nearby Castle of the Seven Towers, instead of returning to Blachernae.

The next morning, he awoke abruptly to cries, shouts, and curses. Instantly awake, he flung back the covers and bolted to the nearest window. Pandemonium had broken out in the streets. Women wailed and crossed themselves, their faces upturned to heaven; children ran this way and that as fast as their little feet could carry them, and men shouted and gestured, pointing in the direction of the Marmara Sea.

The captain of his Varangians, John Dalmata, appeared at the door, fair hair tousled, his cloak askew. "What has happened?" Constantine demanded, pulling on his boots, heading for the door.

"The sea is filled with Ottoman ships! The people fear the sultan comes to lay siege—"

Leaping on his horse, Constantine galloped to the Marble Tower, followed by his Varangians. The tower that stood at the junction of the land walls with the sea commanded a panoramic view of the traffic that went to and fro on the water, bearing the commerce that was the lifeblood of Constantinople. He ran up the stairs. A flotilla was sailing up the Bosphorus. To his shock and disbelief, all flew the pennant of the Ottoman empire, the Crescent Moon on a bloodred background.

A clatter diverted his attention to Phrantzes, Lucas, Demetri and Theo bounding up the stairs. From their sickly pallor, he knew instantly that something was terribly wrong.

"These ships—what do they mean?" he demanded.

"Mehmet plans to build a fortress on our side of the Bosphorus," Lucas said, breathing hard. "His ships bear masons, laborers and building supplies to the site he has selected." He turned to the north, where the Bosphorus curved toward the Black Sea.

Ashen pale. Constantine followed his gaze. "The narrowest part of the straits," he said, through stiff lips, barely able to breathe. A gaggle of ships choked the harbor, and mules and pack animals stretched up the hill in a thick line across the horizon. Did Mehmet truly plan to blockade Constantinople by land and sea? He would not—could not—allow himself to believe such a horror. But already on the slopes of the hills along the Bosphorus, men were felling trees to clear the land of orchards, and where there had once been lush green beauty, a dark stain now formed.

Beside him Phrantzes stared ahead, looking as if he were caught in a spell. *"Laimokopia—"* he whispered. *Throatcutter.* "Mehmet means war."

Constantine gave an inward shudder. Pray God Phrantzes was wrong. Pray God, this was not what was taking shape before them.

From his balcony in the Ocean Hall, Constantine had an eagle's view of the enemy laboring like ants on Mehmet's fortress. *Rumeli Hisar.* The "European Castle." Spies had confirmed its purpose. Situated directly opposite Mehmet's castle in Asia, *Anadolu Hissar,* it would enable him to close the channel to the Black Sea and starve Constantinople of food supplies and the commerce that was its lifeblood. More importantly—the spies said—more importantly, *Rumeli Hisar* would be the base from which the Ottoman siege of Constantinople would be waged.

Already the foundations were visible, rising before his eyes. *Laimokopia.* Throatcutter.

Was there nothing to be done? Could it be sabotaged somehow—Maybe burned, perhaps? It was six miles away. Mehmet had teams of men working night and day. It was never unattended. The men he sent would need to take Greek Fire with them. They would have to pass through multiple guarded checkpoints. They would be searched—

He passed a trembling hand over his face. *Impossible.*

Resting his weight on the stone balcony, his gaze swept the villages nestled in harbors dating to antiquity. There, beyond those beautiful green hills and glittering golden crosses, the formidable might of the Ottoman army was being arrayed against him. And all he could do was protest, send gifts, and plead.

Zoe's eye kept stealing to him as she stood by the open doors of the balcony, going over the next day's menu with the chamberlain. "—and for *deipnon,* we shall have roasted pheasant, seasoned with honey and saffron. For vegetables, grape-hyacinth bulbs in vinegar, and sweet and sour aubergine—" She handed the list of dishes back to the *koubikoularios,* the eunuch in charge of the imperial household.

"And for dessert?"

"The usual," she said curtly, anxious to be done. He withdrew with a bow.

"Anything else?" she asked Aesop, her gaze stealing to Constantine.

"One of the palace cooks wishes to marry the daughter of a miller. He requests a recommendation."

"Tell my scribe to write him a glowing one." She hurried out to the balcony. The wind blew, scented with the fragrance of spring, and sea birds squawked overhead. But she knew Constantine had not come to admire the splendid day. She rested her hand on his.

He regarded her with pained eyes. With everyone else, even Lucas and Phrantzes, he had to feign optimism, for he was emperor, and they looked to him for strength. But he was swept with a desperate need for comfort, and Zoe was the only one he could turn to. "I fear for us, Zoe. No one heeds our plea—"

"We may be tilting with phantoms, Constans. Have you thought the fort may not be what we think? Mehmet may simply want the land and takes it because he can. Maybe the fortress is merely meant to show us he is master."

That had occurred to him. It was his greatest hope. He heaved a long breath, and they stood quietly, side by side, gazing at the sea. Out on the Horn, two great galleys headed for Neorian Harbor, one bearing Venice's emblem of the Lion of St. Mark, the other the pennant of the red Genoese cross on a white field. In the wharf, around a French ship flying the red banner of Saint Denis that had been the personal flag of Charlemagne, men heaved aboard bales of silk, wax, copper, gold-work, wormseed, lacquer, and other treasures that were the lifeblood of Constantinople.

"The Eastern Roman Empire is little more than one decaying city," Constantine said, permitting himself to confide another fear. "If Mehmet is intent on war, we cannot stand alone against an empire with territories that span the greater part of the Balkan peninsula and Asia Minor."

"A grand Christian alliance can unseat them. You will make that happen."

With a sinking heart, Constantine nodded absently, unnerved by her confidence.. Night and day, Halil's words rang in his ears. *Whatever happens next, you have brought it on yourself.* Not even to Zoe could he confide the guilt that smoldered in his breast—a guilt he could barely admit to himself. That he was responsible for the predicament they found themselves in. That he had brought this evil to pass. If he hadn't needed money— If he hadn't threatened Mehmet— There would be no Ottoman fort on Roman soil.

If only he had listened to his mother! She had tried to warn him. Swept by a need for action, he went to his study and sent for a scribe. As he began dictation of yet another letter to Venice, Aesop appeared.

"Augustus," he said, "a messenger is here to see you."

"Send him in—" Constantine barked, coming out from behind his desk. He had anxiously awaited Mehmet's reply to his plea for peace and amity between them, but a week later, to his bafflement, the envoys still hadn't returned. The wait had weighed heavily on his nerves.

"Augustus—" The ashen-faced messenger swallowed visibly. "I am the bearer of foul tidings. The emissaries you sent to Sultan Mehmet have been beheaded. The sultan says— He says the next one you send will be flayed alive!"

Constantine stared at him in horror. His knees crumpled beneath him. He stumbled backwards and fell into a chair.

This was Mehmet's answer to him.

A declaration of war.

Seventeen

Stone by stone over the summer of 1452, Constantine and his people watched Mehmet demolish churches and monasteries to build his fortress. And all Constantine could do was write missives to the West begging for help.

"We have received a reply from Rome," he told his advisors gathered around the council table. "The pope is sympathetic and will send us three ships in aid. But he cannot muster the forces we need to oppose the formidable might of the Ottomans. Therefore, we should approach the other Catholic rulers of the West. The Genoese give the same reply."

"They will come to our aid if the other Christian powers do the same," Demetri said. "They will *all* come to our aid only if the others come! At least they are clear on that point. May the devil take their confounded souls!"

So it went, day after day. Constantine and his advisors met with clerics to persuade them to change their minds on union and wrote dispatches to the crowned heads of Europe. He sent emissaries to Venice, Rome, Genoa, Spain, Hungary, Ragusa, and Serbia, pleading for help.

One day an emissary arrived from England's mad-monk king, Henry VI, with a missive for the "Emperor of the Greeks," providing the court a rare light moment. Constantine eyed the man, a monk in homespun cloth and sandals. "We fear the messenger from England is lost. We know not where he can find the Emperor of the Greeks. Here, there is only the Emperor of the Romans. We suggest he return to his king in England and request better directions."

The hall erupted in laughter. Constantine allowed himself a small smile.

In his council chamber later that day, he sorted through the missives that had arrived, selected the most important, and broke the seal.

"We have received a reply from Venice," Constantine announced, bending his head to read, "We sympathize with the Emperor's plight, but we are engaged in a war against the Lombards. The best we can do is ship to the Queen of Cities the gunpowder and armor the Emperor requests."

Constantine turned his head to the window and closed his eyes. "More and more, it looks like we stand alone," he said on a breath.

Constantine stood with Phrantzes on the ramparts, watching men dig up headstones in the graveyard outside the city walls. It was a beautiful summer evening in mid-August, and the True Cross was safely back in the imperial treasury following the first of the Three Feasts of the Savior.

"Heartbreaking work," Phrantzes murmured. "For many, these are the headstones of recently buried loved ones."

"We have no choice. The enemy would use them as missiles, and we must stockpile stone while we can. The quarries are far away. We cannot rely on them to repair the walls if he—" Constantine broke off and looked at his friend with pained eyes. "I still cannot believe it has come to this, George."

Silence.

A bird sang in the branches.

"We should scrounge materials from old buildings and abandoned churches while we can," Phrantzes said quietly. "That will assure a ready supply of stone. Trees should be felled. We will need wood."

Constantine nodded. "I have dispatched an imperial transport to purchase foodstuffs and munitions. If we are besieged, we will need everything—wheat, wine, olive oil, spears, arrows, shields— But there is not enough money to buy it all. I am thinking of asking for donations."

"Let us hope Notaras makes a hefty one. He can well afford it from the immense wealth he keeps in Venetian and Genoese banks," Phrantzes said bitterly.

"I am sure he will be generous. I am hoping the churches will help with donations of plate."

Phrantzes nodded. "The more we collect, the more supplies we can buy, and the longer we can hold out."

Church bells chimed the hour of seven, and from the monasteries rose the chant of the monks at vespers, saluting the glories of creation and the day's end.

Constantine rested a hand on Phrantzes's shoulder. "Time for supper, my friend."

A sudden commotion and shouts of men drew Constantine's attention to the tower steps. In the gathering darkness a long-bearded man in a dingy gown was being hustled away by the Varangians. "What is happening?" he demanded.

"A Hungarian named Urban has been trying to see you for weeks, Majesty," Dalmata said. "He claims his invention will save the empire. He refuses to tell us what it is, but we think him mad."

"Bring him to me," Constantine commanded. Moments later, the Hungarian panted up the steep steps and fell to his knees before him. "Thank you, Basileus. Thank you for seeing me!"

"Well?"

The man scrambled to his feet. "Basileus, I am a maker of bombards. I would like to make you one— the biggest one in all the world!"

"How big?"

"One that throws a stone ball twelve hundred pounds in weight and eighty-eight inches in circumference!"

Constantine's eyes widened. "Such a ball would reach as high as my waist!"

"It would indeed, and it would destroy the enemy—I can do that for you, Basileus. I have the design here—right here—" He pointed to his head. "All I need is the money."

"How much?"

"Ten thousand bezants."

"You have taken leave of your senses! If I had that kind of money, I would purchase the finest galleys ever built!"

"Basileus, with my bombard you can vanquish hundreds of the enemy with one shot!"

"And where would we put your great gun? These walls would collapse beneath such a weight." The man wilted, and Constantine felt a stab of compassion. "Take my advice and go home," he said gently. "You don't want to be here when war comes."

Guards hustled him away, and moments later, Constantine and Phrantzes followed a torchbearer to their waiting horses. "Eighty-eight inches in circumference…" Constantine shook his head. "He is dreaming."

"Poor old man, age has addled his brain," Phrantzes laughed as they came down the tower stairs.

From where he sat unseen in the shadow of an arch mulling his bitter disappointment, the Hungarian lifted his head. He was a proud man, and the scorn cut deep. Constantinople had been his last hope. He had wandered west to Spain trying to sell his idea, then east across Europe, seeking a warrior-king who would grasp the brilliance of his design. But his genius had gone unappreciated, and door after door was slammed in his face. A realization struck him forcefully. It was a man's birth, family name, and connections that opened doors, not merit. Not genius. The minds of kings and emperors were as blind to new ideas as the night to the brilliance of the sun—unless it was presented to them by one of their own. He had designed a bombard so technically advanced and powerful that it verged on the miraculous. But he was an outsider of low birth, and they understood little of science or mathematics. They couldn't fathom such a grand invention, so they mocked him and called him mad.

Swept with despair and hopelessness, he wiped a tear from his eye. His invention had fueled his dreams and given his life direction. As the North Star guides a weary wayfarer home through hunger, travail, and deprivation, it had kept him afloat in the face of persistent and devastating rejection. Now he had come to the end of the road. There was nothing left for him but to die.

He was about to rise when all at once his gaze fell on the torches of Pera where the sultan's men labored night and day, and an idea lit up his mind like a beam of light. His heart stilled. All was not lost! The Ottomans would receive him! It was merit that mattered in the East, not birth. Many of the young sultan's highest officials were Christians and Jews of low birth. Even slaves could rise to the zenith of power in the Ottoman Empire and hold the ear of the sultan. New hope flooded him, and he shed the ashes of his despair.

Sultan Mehmet was young and as rich as Midas. He was brilliant, maybe even a genius, like himself. He would understand his invention. They would have a meeting of minds. The sultan would appreciate what his gun could do for him!

Urban rose from the wall, beaming. With joy in his heart and excitement in his step, he turned his face east and hastened into the night.

At the Ocean Hall, Zoe and Constantine took a cup of wine together on the terrace. A warm breeze stirred, and moonlight danced on the dark waters of the Horn. Constantine reached for her hand.

"You are very quiet this evening. What are your thoughts?"

"People are whispering, Constans… They say I am your concubine." She dropped her gaze. "I am thinking I am what they say. A shameless woman. They claim there is nothing worse in the world than a shameless woman."

"They are right," Constantine said.

Zoe jerked her head up. She went to pull her hand from his, but he tightened his hold. "There is nothing worse than a shameless woman," he grinned, flashing his dimples. "Save another shameless woman."

Despite herself, Zoe laughed. After a while, Constantine spoke again, but this time his tone was grave.

"Mehmet's fortress is nearly complete." Complete, and more terrible than he could have imagined. A monumental structure running the full length of the steep hillside. Seventeen towers roofed with lead and built in four months at a cost he couldn't have managed in ten years. He suppressed the memories of the Hexamilion Wall that always dredged up the old familiar pain in his gut.

Zoe made no reply.

"In spite of everything, these past months have been the happiest of my life, Zoe." He drew an arm around her shoulder.

"And mine," she murmured, snuggling close. A silence fell.

"I love you, I love you," Apollo clucked on his outdoor perch. Zoe and Constantine shared a smile.

Zoe spoke. "You heard from Thomas and Demetrios. What did they say? Will your brothers help?"

"I can rely on Thomas. He will send troops as soon as he returns to Clarenza."

"And Demetrios?"

A hesitation. "I am unsure."

Zoe fell silent. How hard it was for him to know that his own brother would not help. She felt sickened by the thought. After a silence, she said, "What about Pera? Will they be with us?"

"Yes… and no… They have orders from Genoa to play both sides."

Zoe hesitated to bring up the subject but saw no other way to lift his spirits. "Georgia has promised a hundred ships. That will turn the tide in our favor when they come."

Constantine made no reply for a long while. At first, she thought he had not heard. Then he said, "Mehmet knows it takes time to build ships. That is why he rushed into clearing the land and building his fort. It is to prevent King George from coming to our aid."

So, there will be no wedding, Zoe thought. She didn't know whether to be happy or sad. After a while, she said, "The Holy Mother protects Constantinople. She will not let her city fall." She rested her head on his shoulder, and they sat together, listening to the water lapping the walls of Constantinople.

Constantine thought of the single wall around the ruins of St. Mary's at Blachernae. He hadn't the heart to remind her that the Holy Mother had let her church burn down.

At first light Zoe awoke after a fitful night. Beside her, Constantine slept. She rose from bed and laid a gentle kiss on his brow that he acknowledged with a soft grunt. She went out to the balcony.

The nip of autumn was in the air, and mist floated over the silvery water that was taking on a copper glint in the breaking dawn. Sea birds circled overhead, their cries shrill in the serenity of the morning. She hugged herself as she stood in her filmy shift, admiring the colors of the rising sun.

Constantine stirred. Finding Zoe's place empty beside him, he raised himself on an elbow. He saw her on the balcony, silhouetted against the flaming sky, her glorious hair stirring in the wind, casting sparkles of fire around her form. He thought of Paris, who had doomed Troy for love of Helen, and understood the passion that had driven him. Never again would he see the sunrise with the same eyes; always it would be entwined in his heart with Zoe standing there, drenched in the colors of the dawn.

He came up behind her and locked his arms around her waist. He laid his cheek against her silken hair and kissed her brow. "Zoe," he murmured, "how I love you."

She turned in his arms and pressed herself hard against him. A rush of heat soared through him; his heart jolted, and his pulse pounded. He swept her up in his arms and carried her back to bed.

Much later, after they had said morning prayers and broken their fast with a flask of pomegranate juice, freshly baked unleavened bread, and sweet persimmon jam, Constantine left for his council chamber and Zoe set out for her quarters in the *Soros.* Bearing a torch aloft, Aesop led the way as Zoe followed him up and down flights of narrow stairs and through the musty secret passages that connected the imperial privy chambers to the library.

At last, she reached the exit. She took silent leave of Aesop, and with utmost caution pushed through a turning panel lined with books. Quietly, she secured it back into place. The whispers that she was the emperor's mistress had grown louder, and already her brothers had been obliged to defend her honor. Tiptoeing through forgotten rooms and empty corridors, with many a surreptitious glance behind her, she made her way out of the imperial residence into the palace grounds. Only once had she feared she might have been seen, and that was yesterday, when she thought she glimpsed Maria in the gallery. But it must have been her imagination, for when she looked again, no one was there.

She hastened back to the *Soros*, but when she reached her chamber, she halted in stunned surprise. Her father was pacing back and forth like a caged tiger, and Maria was with him. He whirled on Zoe, green eyes blazing as Maria watched with a smirk, her expression telling Zoe everything she needed to know. "Where have you been?" he roared, shaking with anger.

"I had hoped to keep it from you," she said quietly.

"You foolish girl!" he exploded, striding toward her, hand raised, ready to strike.

Zoe closed her eyes and braced herself, but the blow never came. When she looked again, her father had checked his steps and dropped his hand.

"Thank you, Father, for not hitting me. I know I deserve it, but it would do no good."

"Have you no shame?" he yelled.

"Shame?"

"How can you ask such a question? You're my daughter! You're the most desirable woman in the empire. You could have had anyone—the emperor—anyone! Helena married the Lord of Lesbos, and she has not your charm. Now you'll never be able to hold your head up again— You are a ruined woman!"

"Father, I love him."

"What difference does love make? Love has nothing to do with marriage!

Even if it did, you cannot wed him—he is betrothed! As for you, no one of any consequence will take you now. You are no better than a whore!"

"Emperor Justinian made a whore his empress. As for Constantine, you can be assured I never forget that he is betrothed and not free to wed me."

"So, you willfully threw your future away? You stupid, selfish girl! Even if he could marry you, he wouldn't take you now, when you have nothing more to give him. You have ruined everything I tried to do for you and tarnished your sister's chance of securing a good marriage! Maria won't be thanking you for it."

Maria glared at her from the corner of the room with her cat eyes.

"Father, Constantine is betrothed to a phantom. No ship dares bring her. The fortress on the Bosphorus has us by the throat, and the Sultan will not let go until he gets what he wants. Nothing can be taken for granted. The world we knew is gone, and so are the rules we lived by."

"Zoe, Zoe—how can you say such things? How can you think such fearsome thoughts? We must believe that God will save our city—otherwise we cannot go on!"

"We cannot know God's mind, Father, but we will go on, whatever we think. I tell you this. Constantine will never give in to the sultan. He will die fighting for his people. Then I will be left with nothing. At least I have snatched what happiness I can. I am twenty, Father—" She broke off, and looked at him. "My life should be beginning, but this may be all there is. I cannot continue to deny the present for a future that may never come. Wish me well, dear Father—"

Her father's expression melted, and he put out his arms to her.

The captain of the Varangians, John Dalmata, snapped to attention in the Ocean Hall, a fist to his breast. "A youth is here to see you, Augustus," he announced to Constantine, who was ensconced in his study with Phrantzes. "He says he has information of utmost importance."

At Constantine's nod, the boy ran to him and knelt, eyes round with fear. "*Autokrator— Basileus*—Grand Emperor—" He broke off, uncertain how to address him.

Constantine laid a gentle hand on his shoulder. "What is it, my son?"

"I come from Pera," he panted. "Sultan Mehmet is on the march and is headed this way with his Janissaries!" He threw a terrified glance at the city walls beyond the windows.

"Headed here?" Constantine exchanged a startled look with Phrantzes. "To what purpose?"

"I know not, *Basileus*," the boy said, settling on the old Greek name for a king that came from the Persians. "But he finished his fortress this day!"

"How do you know this?"

"A shepherd passed the word to my cousin in Pera. He is a friend of the Greeks—"

Buckling his sword belt, Constantine grabbed his helmet from Aesop.

"We leave for the walls immediately!" Phrantzes, Dalmata and his Varangians fell in behind him as he strode to the door. "Bring the people into the city from the villages! Bring their crops to safety behind the gates!" he said, barking orders as he went. "Lock the city gates!"

One by one, guards raced off to carry out his orders. In the Court of the Sundial, Constantine and his men leapt on their mounts and galloped out of the palace gate with thundering hoofs. Through the city they flew, bent low in the saddle, Constantine in the lead, looking neither to right nor left.

Young and old ran out of shops and dwellings to stare after them. Potters looked up from their clay, and blacksmiths came out of their fiery smithies, glowing irons in hand. In the streets men dropped the burdens they carried, nuns kissed their crucifixes, and monks fell to their knees and crossed themselves. Everywhere people froze at the terrible sight of an emperor galloping through the streets in panic without regard to safety and ceremony.

At the Gate of Eugenius on the acropolis by the Golden Horn, the imperial party dismounted. Constantine took the steps two by two to the parapet. He entered the tower and ran up the stairs to the ramparts. With the banner of the double-headed eagle beating in his ears, he looked past the slopes of Pera and scanned the northeast. Mehmet's fort was just visible, an ominous dark smudge against the distant sky. He tore his gaze away and followed the curve of the wall to the north where the inlet of the Golden Horn dead-ended into land near Blachernae Palace. He stiffened. The shepherd was right. Shrouded in dust kicked up by their horses, a large enemy party was swooping down towards the city's western defenses like a dark storm cloud.

"Surely Mehmet doesn't plan to attack with such a small force?" Phrantzes said. "But why else would he come?'

"To inspect the walls." Constantine said, a sick feeling in his gut.

Barely did the villagers make it safely behind the locked gates of the city when Mehmet's men arrived to pillage and burn the hamlets. As the pungent smell of smoke wafted into the air, the newly homeless villagers inside the city beat their breasts and wept.

For three days in rain and wind, Mehmet rode the length of the walls, carefully taking notes as Constantine and his men watched from the walls. Working his way south from Blachernae, he followed the western land walls down to the sea, past the Gates of Charisius, St. Romanus, and others, to the Golden Gate.

On the third day, Zoe went searching for Constantine. As twilight fell, she spotted his guards. They lined the steep staircase that led up to the ramparts near the Gate of St. Romanus. Stepping carefully between them, she climbed to the top and paused to catch her breath.

Resting his foot on a turret, Constantine stood alone on the rampart, gazing out over the Lycus Valley and the meandering river, a forlorn figure against the vast gray sky, his purple cloak whipping in the wind. She followed the direction of his gaze and gave a shudder. A party of riders had dismounted at the Charisian Gate, just north of St. Romanus. Watched by a sinister, black-hooded rider on a black horse, they bent to examine the base of the walls. She went to Constantine. He slipped an arm around her shoulders and drew her close. "This is where he will concentrate his forces," he said quietly.

Zoe swallowed hard on the constriction in her throat. Until now, it had just been talk. Suddenly it took on a frightening reality. "How do you know?"

"It is the weakest point. The ground is soft. The wall is low. It is where we are most vulnerable. Because of the river."

They stood together, gazing at the horsemen in the distance. In the gathering gloom, the wind felt more chill than before. Zoe shivered.

"You'd better go."

"Are you not coming?" she said, holding back the hair whipping her face.

"Not yet. I shall be in soon. Go, before you catch cold."

He watched her disappear like a torch into darkness. The sound of hoofs drew his gaze back to the Ottomans. The black-hooded rider had broken away from the pack and was galloping in his direction. At the river's edge, he drew rein. For a long moment, the black figure stared down at the water. Then he turned his stallion and slowly advanced to the base of the stone tower where Constantine stood. Constantine thought he heard the wind hiss and felt a piercing chill as he watched, for the man's black wrappings flapped eerily around his formless shape, stirring a sense of menace. When the figure reached the gate, a gust blew his hood back from his face, revealing a jeweled turban framing a round face with a long beaked nose, thick lips, and a thrusting chin covered with a red beard. *A parrot's beak, resting on cherries,* Phrantzes had said.

Mehmet.

Constantine stiffened. He came out from behind the tower and peered over the edge of the wall for a better view of Mehmet inspecting the ground below. There was a coldness to his movements, a sharpness, a ruthlessness. Mehmet must have sensed his presence, for he looked up suddenly, and Constantine found himself staring into two piercing eyes of such intensity that for a moment he didn't breathe. Then Mehmet turned his horse and galloped off like a shade in the night, his robes flapping wildly behind him, whipped by the wind.

Eighteen

Zoe rose in the darkness before dawn, long before the palace stirred, and glanced at Eirene, asleep on a pallet in her bedchamber. Moving quietly, she donned her stola of pale apricot wool and gathered her hair into a pearl net. She pinned Constantine's garnet brooch to her gown, took her wine cloak and sheer tulle veil from the peg, and slipped out of the bedchamber.

For three distressing nights she had slept in her own room at the *Soros* and had not seen Constantine, at his request. He had been brooding all week, and she had been unable to engage him in conversation or coax a laugh. Then mysteriously one evening, he announced that he wished her not to come to his chamber for three nights, but to meet him on the ramparts of St. Romanus an hour before matins on the fourth day. The appointed hour had finally arrived.

She threw Eirene an apologetic glance as she tip-toed past her slumbering figure, for Constantine had bid her come alone. Making her way along the darkened corridors and peristyles, she continued past the few men-at-arms who stood silent guard at the top of the palace steps and went down to the garden, half-expecting Maria to jump out at her. Except for the groom who brought Ariadne, the Court of the Sundial was deserted, and the night lay silent beneath a few frosty stars.

Constantine. Her pulse quickened and she trembled. What would he say to her? Was he planning to send her away? She mounted Ariadne and trotted her toward the palace gate, so absorbed in her thoughts that she didn't notice

John Dalmata until he called her name. She halted her palfrey and looked around in confusion, for Dalmata was ever at Constantine's side. "Is the emperor here?"

"His Majesty awaits you at St. Romanus," Dalmata said, falling in at her side, accompanied by two Varangians. "I am to escort you there."

The few sentries on duty at the palace gate recognized the Captain of the Varangian Guard and stepped aside with sharp salutes. They cantered through the empty streets of the sleeping village of Blachernae, past the shuttered shops of the silk weaver, jeweler, bookbinder, herb seller, and the glassblower whose ancestors had made lamps for the Hagia Sophia. As they neared the soothsayer's shop, Zoe heard a nightingale and hoped it was a good omen. At the gate of St. Romanus, Dalmata helped her dismount and fell back.

"This is as far as I go, my lady," he said.

Her heart pounding, she took the steep staircase to the ramparts. A light rain fell. Pennants flapped wildly in the wind. She crossed the parapet to the tower, stepping carefully in her thin leather slippers, and took the stairs to the top. Drawing her cloak tight against the cold autumn morn, she stood for a moment at the entry, scouring the darkness for Constantine. She didn't see him at first; then he came out of the shadows, the sapphire fibula that secured his purple cloak glinting in the torchlight. Clad in high laced boots and a short, belted tunica of cerise silk, he strode toward her, almost concealed by the night. When she finally saw his face, relief flooded her, and she ran into his arms with a cry of joy. His mouth came down hard on hers.

"Constans— 1 have missed you so!"

"My love," he whispered, covering her eyes, her cheeks, her lips with kisses.

She felt his heat and her body flamed. She lifted her hand and traced the lines of his face. Her fingertips rested lovingly on a dimple before moving to his scar. "Why did we have to part, Constans?"

"I was preparing a surprise." He moved his hand out from behind his cloak.

She looked down, and gasped. The ring he held sparkled like a cluster of stars in the flaming torchlight.

"This belonged to my mother," Constantine said, taking her hand.

"I recognize it. But I do not understand."

"It is very simple, Zoe. This ring says I love you. This ring says—" He tightened his hold of her hand. "Will you be my empress?"

Joy exploded in Zoe's breast. Before she realized what was happening, before she could help herself, she burst into a fit of sobbing and covered her face with both her hands. "But-y-you cannot-y-you are betrothed— It is not-p-possible—"

He took her by the arms. "Zoe, we must stop deluding ourselves. The alliance with Georgia is dead." He had not heard a word from King George since the emissary's departure and had received no help, not one ship, nor one bezant, even secretly. "The future is not ours to see, but the present is ours to do with as we will. I love you and want to marry you. I want to make you as happy as I can for as long as I can."

Zoe sobbed louder.

"Zoe—Zoe— I thought you'd be gladdened!" He loosened his hold of her.

Zoe fought to rein in her emotions. "Gladdened?" she cried, finding her voice, "Gladdened?" she managed on a sob. "I am overjoyed!"

"Then why do you weep?" he asked in bewilderment.

"It's simply that—I cannot—believe! Oh, Constans, tell me this is really happening!"

"It is happening, Zoe. I am asking you to marry me."

She sniffled and wiped her tears away roughly with the back of her hands. "I have loved you all of my life. I have dreamed of this all of my life—and now—now—" She looked down at the ring he held. "And now my dream has come true."

"Then you will wed me?" he said uncertainly.

She laughed wildly. "Yes, my love, I will wed thee—" She held out her hand and he slipped the diamond on her finger. Radiant with happiness, Zoe gazed at him, at the sandy hair stirring in the wind, the hazel eyes, the rugged, sun-bronzed face and the dimples she so loved.

"I wish we could be married at Mistra," he said softly.

Her breathing quickened. "Mistra?"

"Where I fell in love you, though I did not know it at the time."

"And I with you—" Zoe laughed, interrupting him as exquisite happiness coursed through her, making her light-headed. Again, she saw him in Mistra, bending down to receive her and saw herself running into his open arms. Now he would be hers forever, this man she had loved as far back as she could remember. She felt she could not bear the joy of it. "Mistra—"

"No, it is a dream," he sighed. "I made inquiries and found ships to take us. I thought we could stay a day or two and honeymoon in Monemvasia. But there is no way I can leave Constantinople. Not now—" He took both her hands into his own. "I am afraid we must wait, Zoe. I promise you that when this is behind us, we will have our honeymoon—and the state wedding that should be yours as empress. But now we must wed secretly—"

"Secretly?" Her lashes flew up and she was flooded with doubt and crushing disappointment. Would a secret marriage even be legal? To marry the one she loved had always been her dream, but there was her father. Honor and image were so greatly important to him. How would he feel when it was whispered ever more loudly that she was the emperor's whore? She didn't know what to say.

Constantine's voice came gently. "When the danger is passed, we will announce our marriage to all the world, but it must be kept secret until then. Meanwhile, it would probably be wise not to wear my ring. For with this marriage, I share with you my own great peril." His hands tightened their hold of hers, but his gaze remained steady. "Should Constantinople fall, as my empress Mehmet will hunt you down and take you into his harem—"

Zoe gasped. He drew her to him and held her tight, stroking her hair. "I say this to make you understand what you risk by wedding me, my beloved Zoe. If you wish to reconsider, I will understand."

She drew away and looked at him. Her gaze ran lovingly over the silver touches at his temples, the crinkles around his eyes and mouth, the scar on his cheek. "I am not afraid. You are all I want—all I ever wanted. Mehmet be damned."

Constantine drew her close again and laid his cheek against her hair. "Very few can know… your family, a few close friends… "But not Phrantzes, he thought. For his own good, so he will not think he has been cast aside. When the troubles were behind them, he would make it up to his friend. "I was thinking we could be wed at the church in Chora." He gazed down at her. "It is a beautiful church, built by my Comnene ancestors… It would be a good memory, Zoe."

She melted in his arms and raised her lips to his.

As far back as the fifth century, the little Church of the Holy Savior in the Chora had stood on the same plot of land near the palace of Blachernae, untouched by the centuries. In its early days it was a simple country church located outside the first Constantine's city walls, but by the time of Emperor Theodosius, the city had grown and the western land walls near the Gate of Charisius came to enclose the small church. What it lacked in physical size, however, the Chora made up for in the sheer beauty and splendor of its fabled interior, which had been refurbished in the thirteenth century.

With bells chiming the midnight hour, dressed in her bridal finery, Zoe took her father's hand and stepped out of her litter. Torches flared, throwing light and shadow over the entry. Leaning on his arm, she lifted the hem of her silver gown that was sewn with pearls and diamonds and made her way down the sloping path. At the great doors of the church, her father dropped her sheer veil over her face and smiled at her, his eyes lit with pride.

She entered the outer narthex. A tall priest approached along the hall and there was a crosscurrent of greeting. "Daughter, may God bless you this night and always," he said, making the sign of the cross over her, his crucifix flashing in the torchlight. "Pray, follow me. The emperor awaits ..."

Zoe had never seen the Chora in the dark of night with so many candles blazing. Though she knew the intent of every Orthodox church was to create a spiritual space where earthly cares were banished and heaven glimpsed in the touch of man's wondrous artistry, still she was awed by the beauty and splendor of the holy place. She made her way from the outer narthex to the inner, past marble columns and walls, beneath ceilings and domes covered with glittering mosaics depicting the life of Jesus and the Mother of God, the *Theotokis* Mary, all heavily studded with tiny gold chips and semi-precious stones. The smell of incense assailed her, poignant and sweet. When she reached the central doors of the nave, the chant of monks singing the prayers of the midnight office fell on the night, enfolding her in an ineffable lightness.

On one side of the altar stood Eirene, Aesop, Maria and her three fair-haired rosy-cheeked brothers, Alexander, Jacob, and Isaac. On the other, before the central door of the *iconostasis,* the altar screen studded with icons and pierced with three openings, Constantine awaited with his cousins Demetri and Theo, magnificent in a golden circlet, purple cloak, and a red and azure tunic tied at the waist with a golden sash. She saw him through a dreamy haze: so tall, majestic, and handsome, hazel eyes shining in his sun-bronzed face. Their gaze locked, and he broke into a wide, open smile, flashing the dimples that bracketed his generous mouth. Flooded in the glow of his smile, she floated up the aisle on her father's arm.

As she passed beneath the blue and gold central dome of the *Koimesis* that depicted Jesus at Mary's Assumption, the glint of armor drew her glance to Constantine's Varangians, vibrant in their tunics and red cloaks. They stood to the right of the altar, barring the entrance to the *parecclesion,* the funeral chapel. A shiver touched her spine. Constantine had wished their witnesses to be drawn from his side of the family, so they could confirm their marriage, should something happen to him. She blinked to banish the dark thought and drew to his side, only dimly aware of her father stepping back, and her family smiling, and Eirene sobbing, a handkerchief at her mouth, her muffled sobs at times drowning out the words of the wedding liturgy the priest intoned. All that mattered was that she would be Constantine's empress, and he would be her husband, and they would belong to one another forever in the sight of God. Together, side by side, they would face their destiny, whether long or short, bitter or sweet.

Constantine took her hand, filling her world with his touch. In the glowing arc of light that reflected down from the ceiling, he was bathed in shades of shimmering blues and golds, and she thought of the many twilights they had shared on the terrace of the Ocean Hall, and the many more she hoped the years would bring them as man and wife, God willing.

Zoe and Constantine stood on the balcony, admiring the tender autumn night. "Are you happy, my love?" he asked, pushing a tendril of hair back behind her ear. She turned her lips to kiss his palm. "Happier than I ever dreamed I could be."

He drew her close and she laid her head on his shoulder. In the darkness, the white flowers of jasmine vines that covered the slopes of Pera across the Horn took on an iridescent glow, and the violets, narcissus, and lilies cascading from the pots on the balcony shone with starry brightness, their sweet perfume mingling with the drift of citrus from the dark groves.

"The scent of orange blossom has reminded me of you ever since that morning at St. Demetrios," Constantine said, his love shining in his eyes.

Zoe wrapped her arms around his neck and Constantine swept her up and carried her to bed. She felt his heart beating against her own as she clung to him, and her senses leapt to life. Never had the song of the nightingale felt so piercingly sweet beneath the autumn moon or the fragrance of flowers so intoxicating. As he laid her on the silken sheets and lowered himself over her, the walls melted away and time barreled backwards and she was a child again, casting off her embroidered tunica and finery, running into the woods far from nurses and bondage into an enchanted forest where birds of jeweled plumage flitted among the foliage and luscious fruit hung on golden trees. Reaching up, she picked a ripe persimmon and bit into it. A delicious sweetness sang through her veins, and she burned with exquisite fire. She savored the ecstasy, wishing it could last forever and knowing it would not. As it faded, she heard the wind moan and the rain fall, but she knew that she had found what she had come to find and was where she was meant to be. Cradled in love, she drifted into dreamy sleep in her husband's arms.

Nineteen

The twenty-sixth day of November in the year 1452 dawned dismal and gray. Dreary clouds threatened rain, and the sea picked up the gloom and reflected it back over the earth like a giant mirror. So it was as the large Venetian galley sailing from the Black Sea to Constantinople approached the bend in the Bosphorus.

"Holy Mother of God, what in Heaven's name is that?" a seaman cried.

Captain Antonio Rizzo came to the bow and peered into the distance. A look of stunned bafflement settled over his features. Turrets, massive walls, and at least a dozen towers covered the hillside, flying the pennant of the crescent moon on a blood-red background. "A fort?" He looked at his men in bewilderment. "I was here not four months ago, and there was only the Church of Asomatoi."

His officers came to his side, straining for a better look in the gloom. "It's huge!" one said. "It's not possible to build such a large fortress in so short a time—"

In the water, a small black speck took shape: a boat, speeding toward them. They watched it pull alongside. "The sultan demands you lower your sails and heave to!" a Turk bellowed.

"We bear goods for sale to Constantinople! We are within our rights to sail these waters!" a Venetian yelled back.

"Sultan Mehmet owns these waters now, not Rome. He knows you bring supplies to his enemy and demands you heave to! Ignore his orders at your peril!"

"We are a Venetian vessel! We are protected by our treaty with your sultan!"

"If you do not obey, you will be destroyed by the sultan's guns!"

"Your warning is taken!" Captain Rizzo said. The boat sped off.

All eyes went to the captain. Would they turn back, or proceed as planned? The helmsman at the wheel waited to learn his orders.

Still stunned by the sight of the enormous fort that had risen on the slopes of Pera seemingly overnight, Captain Rizzo assessed the situation intently. Large cannons on the European side of the Bosphorus aimed straight at them. He turned behind him. More guns lined the eastern shore in front of the Ottoman fortress of Anadolu Hissar. He examined the current; it was swift, rushing headlong downstream to Constantinople. That was good; it afforded them a fair chance of making it through the checkpoint safely. His glance went to his rowers; they were in fine form, having rested well in Selymbria. They were sailing the narrowest part of the Bosphorus, to be sure. But it would be well-nigh impossible for a cannon to strike its target at this distance.

"We continue," he called to the helmsman. "Full speed ahead!"

The oarsmen redoubled their efforts and the galley lunged forward. Angry shouts came from Mehmet's fortress and the cannons let loose a volley of shot. A plume of thick black smoke appeared in the distance and a monstrous, thunderous roar shattered the calm. Cannon balls sped across the water. The men aboard fixed their gaze on one in particular. Eyes stretched wide with disbelief and growing horror, they watched helplessly the sight unfolding before them: A colossal, monumental iron ball such as they had never seen, churned the waves violently as it hissed its way inexorably toward them.

In Constantinople men-at-arms ran up the tower steps at the sound two at a time and strained their eyes into the distance. In the streets, the marketplaces, palaces, churches and monasteries, life came to a halt. Gazing up at the dismal skies, people asked one another, "What was that?"

No one knew, but somewhere, someone said, "The roar of a beast—"

"No beast sounds like that," replied a merchant visiting from Crete.

"The Beast himself—Satan—surely sounds like that!" exclaimed a butcher stepping out of his shop, wiping his bloody hands on a towel. Children screamed. They ran to their mothers and clung to their skirts. "Stop that talk!"

a woman said, crossing herself. "You're frightening the little ones."

An old beggar with one arm and one leg who had fought at Varna and had experience of war muttered under his breath that they all had good reason to fear. On the Tower of Eugenius at the junction of the Marmara with the Golden Horn, soldiers ran down the tower steps and vaulted on their waiting horses. People who saw their ashen faces crossed themselves in dread. The men galloped off, ignoring the cries of the gathering crowd pleading for reassurance. When they reached Constantine, they found he already knew of the attack on the Venetian galley. The awful, shattering noise of the cannons had reached him as far away as Blachernae Palace.

"Did you see if the ship made it safely through?" Constantine demanded.

"No, Augustus! We saw only the ungodly smoke that rose up in the distance, and we heard the cries that rent the air."

"You saw no ship after the cannons fired? No sign of a ship?"

"No, Augustus. Nothing."

An hour later, a breathless shepherd boy brought news.

"Basileus, my father sent me to tell you— A Venetian galley was captured by the infidels. They sent many shots flying across the water, and one giant stone ball struck the ship."

"The men— What about the men?" demanded Constantine, a sickening feeling taking hold in his gut.

"Some drowned but many others made it safely to shore. The Ottomans put them in chains and marched them off to the sultan in Didimotkon."

Constantine sank down on a stool. Maybe they could ransom those that survived. He drew a thick breath. "Get me the Venetian *Bailo*," he said in an unsteady voice he scarcely recognized as his own.

The Venetian *bailo,* Girolamo Minotto, the Republic of Venice's ambassador to the court of Rome, lost no time rushing to the sultan, but it was to no avail. Before the walls of Constantinople, the thirty sailors were lined up and beheaded. First, however, they had to watch their captain, Antonio Rizzo, suffer death by impalement. One of the most heinous methods of execution ever devised by man, its purpose was not merely to kill, but to prolong suffering for as long as possible. Sometimes a victim lingered for days, fading in and out of consciousness.

Captain Rizzo's body was left to rot as a warning to the townspeople. There was one survivor, the young son of Rizzo's clerk, whom Mehmet sent to his seraglio to await his pleasure. If his intent was to sow panic, he succeeded. Utterly aware what it would mean to be enslaved by the enemy, men, women, and children gathered outside the walls of Blachernae, wailing and beating their breasts. "Save us, *Basileus!* For the pity of God, save us!" they cried out to Constantine.

Inside the palace Constantine sat in his room, alone, disheveled, a hand covering his face, an empty wine flask on the table. This was how Zoe found him when she returned from the Hagia Sophia where she had gone to pray. At the sound of her footsteps, he dropped his hand and lifted his head. A look of such anguish contorted his features that Zoe froze in her steps, seeing Constantine again when she was a child of eleven, and he had arrived home after his defeat at the Hexamilion Wall…

She had cracked the door open to his chamber to find him sitting alone, his side bandaged, cradling his head in his hand, the gash on his cheek a violent red. A flask of wine stood empty before him. He had looked up and met her eyes. "Did I ever tell you your hair reminds me of the sunrise?" he had said haltingly, his voice weak, barely audible. "A beautiful crimson sunrise…"

His anguish had broken Zoe's heart. "I am glad you like my hair," she had said, her tone belying her heavy heart. "No one else does."

"Oh?"

"They say I look like a barbarian."

He gave her a tremulous smile. "They are jealous, Zoe. Pay them no heed." She came to him and took his hand.

His eyes grew moist. "You make me smile, little Zoe. It is good to have something to smile about."

"They say it was treachery. Was it?"

Constantine heaved a sigh. "Perhaps… Or perhaps the wall was bound to fall sooner or later beneath the pounding of artillery."

"Why don't you get one of those bombards, and bombard the enemy with it?"

His mouth lifted a little. Then his smile vanished, and the tight expression of strain returned. "Guns are good for beating down a wall, but not for much else. The problem is—"

Zoe waited.

"The problem is that times have changed, and I know not what to do."

Zoe returned to the present with a jolt. She went to Constantine and knelt. She took his hand.

"I could do nothing for him—nothing. Nothing—" He closed his eyes on a breath.

"Only God could help him, Constans You must not fault yourself."

He regarded her piteously. "Who understands the ways of God, Zoe?"

"Hush, hush, my love—it is not for us to judge… I know not for what sins Captain Rizzo died such a fearsome death, but God will take his suffering into account."

Constantine staggered to his feet. "What lies ahead for us, Zoe? For all those people out there—the mothers, the babes in arms, the old men—the young men. All they want is to live their lives in peace. Peace I cannot buy them— Not with gifts to Mehmet, not with offerings to God!"

"It is not your fault, Constans. There is only one thing you can do. *Believe.* In God. In yourself. If you do not believe in yourself, how can others believe in you?"

Constantine went to the window. He ran a hand through his hair. The sea was choppy, the night dark. Zoe was right. The trouble was, he had never doubted himself. Even after the Hexamilion Wall, he'd thought he'd learned a grand lesson and would rule his people wisely, like Solomon. Had he not garnered wisdom from experience?

And here he was, responsible for the most monstrous miscalculation in history. *You have brought it on yourself."* Halil's words. He shut his eyes on a breath.

He would believe in God because he could no longer believe in himself.

In a dark tavern in Pera, two men huddled close, speaking in hushed tones.

"How much did you say?" one demanded. He was a man neither young nor old, with eyes hard as beads, a fleshy countenance, and a black beard. He wore the clothes of a Greek merchant, and he would have been nondescript save for the brown bird perched on his shoulder.

"Fifty golden bezants."

The man with the bird gave a murmur of appreciation. "How do I send you the information?"

"Look for a blind beggar with two missing fingers on his left hand who sits on *Makros Embolos* street. You'll find him in front of the Guild of the Makers of Silver Thread, next to the felt makers. He is always there at noon each day. Do we have a deal?"

The man with the bird gave a nod. Without another word he gathered his cloak and was gone.

The night was dark and bitter cold, and the waves high on the Golden Horn. The crossing to Constantinople was so rough that he was never so relieved to see the city gates. He dug in his pockets for a small silver coin with a bust of Christ on one side and Constantine XI on the other and handed it to the ferryman. Heaving his bundle on his back, he made his way to the gate.

"What is your business?" the guard at the Gate of Eugenius demanded as soldiers watched from the walls.

"I have wares to sell in the market tomorrow."

"What kind of wares stink like that?" The guard leaned close to examine the bundle he carried.

"Sheep's intestines," the man replied. "They are used for casing."

"Caw!" The guard covered his nose and waved him in.

The man with the bird took a room for the night at an inn near the Marmara, trudged up the creaking stairs, threw his bundle on the soiled pallet, and headed back downstairs. The tavern at the inn was almost deserted and wouldn't serve his needs. He hurried along the *Mese.* Shops were closing for the night. He turned into a narrow street near the Genoese quarter and perused the wooden signs he passed. The open book of the scholar. The onion of the greenstuff dealer. The lamb of the butcher.

At last, he found what he searched for. The wine-barrel of the tavern owner.

He went inside. The place was crowded with people, laughing, talking, and drinking, but mostly drinking. Tradesmen were known drunks. With some luck he'd find one who was besotted with wine and filled with information of value to the sultan.

After Captain Rizzo's death, Constantine dispatched messengers to the West with ever increasing urgency. He appealed to Aragon and Naples, to the

Genoese on the island of Chios, to Ragusa, Venice, and yet again to the pope. "Our situation is dire," he wrote. "Save us, so we can save you." He made extravagant offers of land to any who would send help. To Hunyadi, the ruler of Hungary, he offered Selymbria or Mesembria on the Black Sea, but Hunyadi's hands were tied by his three-year truce with the sultan, and after Varna, no Christian ruler would break a treaty. But he promised to see what he could do. Of the others, none promised help, though they now understood the threat that faced Constantinople. Genoa understood so clearly that they ordered their representative at Pera to make the best arrangement he could with the sultan, should Constantinople fall. When the information was relayed to Constantine, it cut him like a dagger to the heart.

Sea traffic into Constantinople had thinned with the closing of the Bosphorus. Only one lone galley had successfully made it into port from the Black Sea since Rizzo's death, but ships still came from the south, though that, too, was growing more perilous. On an icy day in early December, six Venetian vessels and three large ships from Crete arrived in the harbor, and early the next morning, Constantine received word from Minotto that the Venetian captains wished an audience. He hurried to receive them, his councilors and nobles at his heels.

Clarions blared. "The Captains Gabriel Trevisano and Alviso Diedo of Venice," a herald announced.

Constantine watched them approach the throne along the pathway between his axebearing Varangian Guards. Both captains were tall and broad-shouldered, and both were bronzed by the sun and exuded vigorous energy. Constantine felt immediately that here were men he could trust. Of the two, the one called Trevisano was clearly younger. Constantine guessed him to be in his late twenties and the other man ten years older, and while Trevisano was clean-shaven in the fashion of the Latins, the older captain wore a short beard that gave his patrician face an even more noble appearance.

Richly clad in the fashion of an Italian knight, Trevisano strode purposefully, his sword clanging at his side, his helmet under his arm. He came to a halt and gave a reverent bow.

"Welcome to our city," Constantine said. "Trevisano... Your name is familiar. Have we had the honor of meeting your family?"

"You know of them, Majesty. I regret to say my ancestors came to Constantinople with the Fourth Crusade."

The hall erupted in shocked murmurs and Constantine's smile vanished. Now he knew where he'd come across the Trevisano name. It was inscribed on a marble plinth at the Hippodrome with an inscription that read, "Here once stood four gilt horses, now in Venice."

"What brings you here this day?" Constantine said.

"I have heard you are short of men. I come to offer my service."

"That is very generous of you. But why should a Trevisano wish to help us?"

"Per amor de Dio et per honor de tuta la Christianitade," Trevisano replied in his native Italian. For the love of God and the honor of all Christendom.

Trevisano's words, spoken with touching fervor, warmed Constantine's heart. *Dwell not on the past. Only then can you move forward.* How many times had his mother said that?

With a grand gesture, Trevisano indicated a man at the back of the hall. "With me I bring my first officer, Nicolo Barbaro, a skilled surgeon to whom many of us owe our lives—"

Barbaro bowed deep. He was an older man with white hair and kindly blue eyes, humbly clad in a sleeveless leather doublet.

Constantine turned his attention to the stately dark-haired man at Trevisano's side, the captain, Alviso Diedo. He hoped—but dared not take for granted—that he, too, was offering, life, limb, and liberty to save Constantinople. "Captain Diedo?"

"Majesty, with the agreement of my men, I offer our services to your great Christian city."

Constantine broke into a grin. "How many men have you?"

"A total of a thousand on our nine ships," Captain Diedo replied. "Everyone aboard puts himself at your disposal, Imperial Majesty."

A thousand men! Constantine thought, swept with euphoria. A thousand men…

Constantine's joy over the unexpected addition of so many men to his forces was short lived. The next day, as he conducted the business of state with his councilors, the sharp thud of boots intruded on his deliberations. He knew whoever it was brought urgent news.

Lucas appeared at the door. Constantine looked up, the question in his eyes unspoken.

"Mehmet sent his general to attack the Peloponnese and ravage the countryside," Lucas said. "Your imperial brothers, the princes Thomas and

Demetrios, have their hands full defending themselves. Thomas cannot deliver the troops he promised."

Constantine scraped his chair back from the table and went to the window. Mehmet's fort was just barely visible in the distance, a black blight on the water's edge, sowing the seeds of destruction. He turned back to his councilors.

"I know not how—but somehow, we must let bygones be bygones and forget the excommunication of our prelates in 1054. Somehow, we must set aside the sack of Constantinople by the crusaders in 1204. Somehow, we must forget the differences in our dogmas—forget our hatred of the Latins that has become part of our spirit. We must do this because we have no choice. We must unite with the Latin church in order to save our Christian city. Are we agreed?"

No one raised an objection. Constantine turned to his scribe, and dictated, "To His Holiness, Pope Nicholas V—"

The anti-unionists rose in force when they heard what Constantine had done.

"Apostatis!" they shouted in the streets. "Constantine Palaeologus is no emperor of ours! We will not pray for him. We curse him!"

The spiritual father of the anti-unionists, the monk Gennadius, left his cell at the Pantocrator to add his voice to theirs. From his window at Blachernae two miles away, Constantine watched Gennadius rant and rave to his followers gathered before him. He couldn't hear his words, but he knew what he said. The fist Gennadius shook made that clear.

In response to Constantine's letter to the pope that he was ready to enforce the pact of union, the pope announced he would send as papal legate, Isidore of Kiev. Born Greek, Isidore was an admired theologian and a great orator who had represented John VIII at Florence. For his efforts in favor of union, he had been imprisoned in Russia, but he escaped to Rome and found gracious welcome with the pope who promoted him to cardinal. It was one of the few instances where a person not of the Latin Rite was raised to such rank.

"Isidore is the best man the pope could send," Zoe said, smoothing Constantine's hair as he lay on the couch with his head on her lap late one cold night.

"Let us hope he fares better than Gregory," Lucas offered, standing by the fire, mulling his wine.

Constantine sat up. "I will drink to that. May God help him in Constantinople, though He chose not to in Kiev."

"God, God!" Apollo cried from his perch. *"Fleas on Mehmet!"*

"You are quite right, Apollo, as always," Constantine said. He picked up his goblet from the inlaid table nearby and toasted his friend, the bird.

Cardinal Isidore arrived on a sunny December day. The waters of the Bosphorus and the Golden Horn shone like blue satin and sea birds hovered overhead, crying shrilly. He brought with him a glittering retinue of two hundred archers, to the delight of the populace who thought it was the advance guard of a substantial force. "See the army of archers—he brings us help!" someone cried. "And more is on the way,' exclaimed another. "We will be saved!" they cried in their euphoria, cheering and showering his procession with flowers.

In the Ocean Hall, Lucas smiled. "Now the people are all for union. The talk everywhere favors you, Augustus, and the anti-unionists are spat on. They're the ones called traitors for a change."

Constantine was buoyed by his report.

A few days later, with the emperor and all his nobles present and the people of Constantinople crowding the streets, Cardinal Isidore, dressed in gorgeous vestments of silver and gold, conducted a liturgy at the Hagia Sophia to celebrate the union of the two churches.

For all her acceptance that this was the way it had to be, Zoe watched in distress as the decrees of union were read, for the language of the service was Latin, and she, like many others, had little knowledge of the Latin tongue. Furthermore, the consecrated Host consisted of unleavened bread and wine diluted with water.

"A great success... a great success, Serene Majesty," Isidore announced when the service ended. He was a slender, brown-eyed man of medium height with dark hair, a silvery beard, and a thin, ascetic face. "Only Gennadius and a few monks refused to participate, that is all. Everyone else attended. I shall write to the pope and let him know that the union of the churches is complete. A great success indeed."

"And when will he send reinforcements? Do you know? Did he say?" Constantine demanded anxiously.

"He didn't say. Not to me anyway. But he will send reinforcements. You have no need to worry now. You are saved."

But Constantine did worry. No further word had been forthcoming from Rome. The people were growing anxious, and so was he.

After foretelling the end of the world and nailing a manifesto of doom and apocalyptic prophecy to the monastery door of the Pantocrator Monastery, Gennadius retreated into self-imposed isolation to reaffirm his condemnation of the service of union. No one paid the old monk much heed as long as there was hope, but as the weeks passed and no mighty fleet sailed up the Marmara in defense of Christendom, it became clear that Gennadius had been right after all. They had paid the price demanded by the West, and the West had betrayed them yet again. They had given up their beliefs for a barrel of empty promises.

People shunned the Hagia Sophia, muttering it was no better than a heathen temple now, and railed against Constantine. *"Apostatis! Apostatis!"* some jeered when they saw him in the streets. Zoe knew it broke his heart. While a few unionists huddled before the sanctuary, and a few trapped birds fluttered mournfully around the nave, most people attended the Orthodox divine liturgy in churches where it was still offered. The sound of prayers in the Hagia Sophia died away, and the great church darkened and fell silent.

Seated by the fire following the celebration of the Feast of St. Stephen after Christmas, Zoe laid down her book. "Gennadius refuses to come out of his cell, yet people still crowd the Pantocrator," she said, stealing a glance at Constantine as he sat staring morosely at the fire, toying with his goblet of wine. He didn't acknowledge her comment, and she thought he hadn't heard. Then he said, "Would that he remains there forever."

Zoe dropped her lids. He had been buoyed by the change in his people before the service of union, but his mood had soured with theirs.

As Constantine watched the shadows that danced on the wall, the old monk's words churned in his mind. "Wretched Romans, how you have been led astray! You have trusted in the pope, and now you will lose not only your city, but your souls— You will lose everything! O miserable citizens, to avert slavery at the hands of the infidel, you have denied the true faith handed down to you by your forefathers. The end of the world is nigh. Woe to you when you are judged!"

A vision of his grandfather Michael VIII Palaeologus rose before him. He upended his wine. Resting his head back on his chair, he shut his eyes.

The new year of 1453 arrived on a fierce hailstorm the likes of which had not been seen in living memory. It was, people murmured, as if the Daughters of the Night, known to the ancients as the Three Furies, had come to torment the earth and avenge some great wrong. The sea raged violently, the wind shrieked, and hail fell from the sky. Fierce squalls hurtled down from the Black Sea, and there were snowstorms, fog, and strange shakings of the earth. Weeks of dismal rain churned the mud in the streets, and flash floods swept many of the city's narrow streets, damaging the property of the impoverished citizenry.

A few days after Theophany on January 6th, as the cold Black Wind blew from the north, the Notaras clan gathered at their palace on the Golden Mile. The Throatcutter had halted shipping from the north, but the Marmara was still accessible from the south, albeit growing ever more perilous. From time to time, despite the fearsome weather, a stray ship had straggled into port, and finally, one brought Zoe's mother, the Duchess Daphne.

Zoe felt her mother's eyes on her. "So, you are *Zoste Patricia.*"

Standing with their father who warmed his hands at the fire, Alexander and Jacob turned to Zoe accusingly, as did Isaac, who sat at his mother's feet. From her seat by Duchess Daphne's couch, Maria fixed her with an unsmiling look.

"Only because you were not here, Mother," Zoe said nervously, accepting an *apotki* from a servant. "The emperor plans to restore the dignity to you whenever you wish." Clearly the death of Helena's babe had taken a huge toll. Clad in black mourning attire, her mother was pale and drawn as she lay on a silk reclining couch, drooping in grief.

"You are empress," her mother replied. She emptied her wine and held her cup out to the servant for another refill.

"We could share the duties, Mother." Zoe gazed at her hopefully, thinking they might bury the past and start anew as mother and daughter.

Duchess Daphne made no reply. After a long silence, Lucas answered for her. "That would require your mother to move to Blachernae, and she has decided to reside here, at our home. She needs to rest."

Zoe's eyes fixed on the servant refilling her mother's outstretched goblet, yet again.

Twenty

The twenty-sixth day of January dawned gray and dismal. The dank cold penetrated to his marrow as Constantine made his way to the throne room, followed by his omnipresent Varangians, his nobles bowing as he passed. He strode through labyrinthine passageways and mounted the marble staircase to the second floor. Sweeping his purple cloak aside, he took his throne.

Cheers outside the palace walls announced the arrival of the man from Genoa. Constantine felt a thrill of anticipation. The pope had sent no reinforcements, nor had Venice or Genoa, but men were flocking to his side. Yesterday it was a contingent from Pera who, appalled at the pusillanimity of their government, came to offer him their swords. The week before, the Venetian colony in Constantinople, led by the Doge's chief diplomat in Constantinople, the *bailo* Girolamo Minotto, had responded nobly by offering to fight for the city and go before the Venetian Council to plead for help. Before that, a single Spanish grandee named Don Francisco de Toledo, who claimed kinship with Constantine through his descent from a Comnene ancestor, came to volunteer. On the same day came a party of Catalans and three Genoese brothers, the Bocciardis, with a small company of their countrymen. All this in addition to Trevisano and Diedo, the two Venetian captains who chanced to have anchored in Constantinople on their way home to Venice and volunteered to remain.

Only a captain of seven ships from Crete with seven hundred men aboard had evinced any reluctance. Desperate, Constantine forcibly detained him, but the captain argued to have his cargo of cloth loaded on to his ships, claiming it was safer than the warehouse. "If I agree," Constantine had said, "what assurance do I have that you will not flee?" Only when the man swore on the Holy Bible that he would not depart, did Constantine consent.

No more ships had arrived since then, and no one else was detained under duress. These Genoese who came now were here of their own accord and would probably be the last. Whether they sought fortune or came to fight for God made no difference to him. Though few in number, they were all the more precious, for they swelled his meager ranks, and he was grateful for each and every one. But this man who came today was extraordinary. If the reports were even half true, he was a prize in himself.

A professional soldier with expertise in siege warfare, he was born into the House of Doria, a famed patrician family of Genoa. Everyone who knew the Genoese soldier of fortune—or knew of him—regarded him with awe. No Venetian ever praised a Genoese, yet all praised him. Constantine was anxious to meet a man who had won accolades from both friend and foe.

"Giovanni Justiniani Longo of Genoa," the herald announced to a fanfare of clarions.

As soon as he appeared, Giovanni Justiniani Longo dominated the hall. Tall and broad-shouldered, with hair as tawny and thick as a lion's pelt, he wore a brown leather doublet, a gold belt with two swords at the waist, and a red velvet cloak at his shoulders. Tight dark hose and ankle-high black leather boots displayed the manly shape of his legs.

Standing near the dais, Zoe watched him approach the throne. He was clean-shaven in the Western manner and ruggedly handsome, and there was about him an air of command. Yet, at the same time, his smile suggested a sense of humor and a mischievous charm. She felt a shiver of recognition. With his compelling dark eyes, strong square jaw, and generous mouth, he bore a strong resemblance to Constantine as he had looked in youth. Except for his mantle, the colors Justiniani had chosen for his imperial reception were as subdued as a dull winter's day, yet his sun-bronzed skin and tawny gold hair imparted a splendid richness to his attire.

It is the man one notices, whatever his garb, Zoe thought.

With princely grace, Justiniani crossed the room. Sweeping his jeweled black velvet cap from his unruly hair, he bowed to Constantine.

"Welcome to you, Giovanni Justiniani Longo," Constantine said in Italian. "We have heard nothing but the highest praise of your person and accomplishments, and we are honored that you have heeded our plea to help save our Christian city."

Justiniani responded in fluent Greek. "The privilege is mine, Imperial Majesty. I come of my deep desire to offer my sword in your hour of need. I am appalled that my land and other Christian nations have chosen to ignore your great peril. I bring with me three great galleys and my private army of seven hundred of the finest fighting men the world has ever known—" With a wave, he indicated the back of the hall where a crowd of soldiers stood. They inclined their heads in greeting. "May I present to you my first officer, Johannes Grant—" he said, singling out a fair-skinned, stocky, middle-aged man, large boned and built like a warrior. "Johannes Grant hails from the land of the Scots and has expertise in matters of siege warfare, especially artillery and tunneling under walls." Grant bowed low.

Zoe regarded him with special interest, for he was red-haired.

Justiniani turned back to Constantine and spoke again. "Everyone here has taken a vow to fight to the death for the honor of Christendom and the glory of God. Either we leave this fabled city as victors, or we die in its defense. For we honor and cherish with all our strength and soul this Queen of Cities that was founded on our Christian faith and is God's finest jewel in His earthly cross."

Zoe applauded fervently as thunderous cheers erupted. Justiniani bowed in acknowledgment, and his gaze sweeping over the nobles touched and held on her. She found herself unable to look away. Only by the utmost exercise of her will did she manage to tear her gaze from him at last.

That evening, at the great feast of welcome Zoe had arranged for Justiniani, the conversation touched on many subjects, including war and strategy, poetry, history, and philosophy. Zoe was impressed that a soldier of fortune should quote poetry with such ease and discourse so well on Plato and Socrates. As they drank malmsey and fine wines and dined on pheasant stuffed with figs and mulberries, she found herself riveted by his tales of his far-flung travels and the many perils he had survived. From her seat on Constantine's left, she peered at Justiniani, who sat on Constantine's right, and addressed him directly. "Have you ever been taken captive, noble sir?" she asked, taking a spoonful of *baklava,* a honied pastry sprinkled with finely crushed rose petals.

"I have indeed. In Dutch land. They are a fierce people, but fortunately, I spoke their language," he said gravely. Suddenly, a grin lit up his face. "Gold is a language all the world understands."

Zoe laughed. Picking up a stuffed date, she dipped it into a dish of yogurt as Constantine leaned back to speak to his cousin, Theo Palaeologus, who held the rank of *domestikos* of the imperial table. The date was exceedingly sweet, and the sugar clung to her hand. She licked her fingers before wetting them with rosewater and wiping them dry on her silver-edged napkin. When she looked up, she found Justiniani watching her.

"Have you never seen dates eaten with yogurt?" she asked, raising her eyebrows.

"Not by a beautiful Roman lady with hair the color of wine," he replied. "It is my first time in the city."

As Zoe and Justiniani shared another laugh, Theo took his leave and Constantine turned to Justiniani. "My cousin Theo Palaeologus suggests that I take you on a tour to inspect the walls as soon as it can be arranged."

"I am at your service, Majesty."

"Very good. Now to other pressing matters—" Constantine pushed his chair back. *"Zoste Patricia,* would you care to dance?"

"Always," Zoe smiled, taking his hand. The minstrels picked up a bright tune. Following their lead, others rose and clapped their way to the center of the hall.

Justiniani watched Zoe from the banquet table. Clearly the emperor favored her, and why not? She was nobly born, intelligent, hauntingly beautiful, and impossibly alluring. In a word, unforgettable. But the emperor was betrothed to the princess of Trebizond and could not marry her, however enamored he was. Duty demanded he wed for an alliance, and by all accounts, the emperor was a man who knew his duty.

The thought elicited a smile.

He leaned back in his chair and sipped his wine. He was at a loss to understand himself. He had loved once in his life—when he was young and too foolish to know better, barely twenty. It had proved a mistake he was determined never to repeat. And he never had. Not until he'd strode into that hall to make his holy promise to save this city and lifted his eyes to that unforgettable face. Then everything changed. The sparkle of her eyes and the radiance of her smile had knocked his breath from his body. Unable to move, he'd stood rooted to the ground as if by a sorcerer's spell. Had she not looked away, he would probably still be there, staring into her eyes, so helpless had he been, he thought, laughing at himself inwardly.

He inhaled a long, deep breath and upended his cup. If anyone could make him forget his vow never to love again, it was this auburn-haired Roman beauty, in this deadly game of life and death, in this dangerous place that perched so precariously on the edge of extinction.

A few days after Justiniani's arrival, as the Winds of Boreas delivered snow, the seven Cretan ships that Constantine had forcibly detained fled in the night, men who had sworn to defend Constantinople. But not everyone left. One man remained behind to fight with them. A Jew named Daniel Navarro, from the Basque kingdom that occupied lands on both sides of the western Pyrenees, between Spain and France.

"Bring him to me," Constantine told Dalmata. "I wish to thank him."

He looked up and his eye fell on Justiniani. Pushing his chair back from the council table, he rested a gentle hand on his shoulder. "Time to show you Constantinople, my friend."

In the gathering dusk, they stood together on the ramparts of the sea walls in the city's northeast corner, near the Tower of Eugenius, where the Golden Horn emptied into the Bosphorus and the Marmara. Constantine pointed out the Golden Mile and the forums of Constantine and others. He noted the many cisterns and the Basilica that was nicknamed *The Sunken Palace* for its three hundred and thirty-six Roman underwater columns. "There, to the west, is the Aquaduct of Valens and the Golden Gate of Constantine the Great. And these are the palaces—" He indicated Blachernae and Prophyrogenitus in the north and the Great Palace and many others in the south. He listed the multitude of places of worship: the monasteries and churches that covered the city, their glittering crosses piercing the gloom of the dismal winter's day. Since Justiniani's ancestor was one of the marauding crusaders of 1204, Constantine omitted the abandoned Hippodrome that bore silent witness to their deeds. Nor did he point out the Hagia Sophia with its dominant golden dome, for her fame had spread across the world.

"I have never seen so many churches in one place," Justiniani marveled.

"The Queen of Cities has had eleven hundred years to build them," Constantine smiled.

"I have heard much about the Chora. I should like to visit someday."

For a moment, Constantine was silent, remembering his blessed wedding day. "I would take you myself, but that is not possible. Perhaps Lady Zoe can oblige. Shall I inquire?"

Justiniani bowed, his heart thumping in his chest. "Nothing would please me more."

Unfurling a map, Constantine rested it on the flat surface of the wall, smoothed it out, and set a stone on top to secure it from blowing away in the wind. Across the water, the land mass of Asia Minor meandered darkly, its minarets piercing the landscape.

"As you can see, the city forms a triangular peninsula. On the west we are protected by land walls that run north and south. I will show you those another day." Constantine traced a straight line with a fingertip. "Here, along the Marmara we have two harbors and eleven gates that open to the water. The harbors are small and well-fortified. This wall, where we stand, rises almost straight up from the sea all the way to the Marble Tower, and the currents are dangerous. I have no concern about this side."

Justiniani held down a corner of the map that flapped in the wind. "What about the Golden Horn?"

Constantine turned his gaze in its direction. "That is a problem. It is pierced by sixteen gates, and the foreshore allows the enemy a landing place." His gaze rested on the warehouses along the beach. Once they had bustled with activity and poured wealth into the city. Now, thanks to Mehmet's blockade, they stood silent and presented only danger.

Justiniani scrutinized the area. "We should dig a moat along the length of the beach. Even with a ditch, the wall will be vulnerable. Have you considered closing the Horn?"

"I have." Constantine glanced at the Tower of Christ across the water in Pera. It was there he had hoped to secure the other end of the chain. "But we need the Genoese to agree, and the *Podesta* has informed us that Pera will remain neutral."

"God's blood, they are short-sighted! If the city falls, what will become of them? Majesty, may I take a delegation to the *Podesta* to persuade him to close the harbor?"

"I should like nothing better."

As Justiniani rolled up the map, Constantine's eye rested on the brave and genial man who had not asked for any reward, though he risked life, limb, and liberty to fight at his side.

"If we are successful," Constantine said, "you shall have the island of Lemnos and the dignity of a prince, Justiniani."

Justiniani gave a deep bow.

In a silver silk stola and lavender cloak, with her hair upswept beneath her veil and Eirene in tow as chaperone, Zoe rode with Justiniani to the Chora Church. He looked splendid in a sapphire doublet embroidered in gold thread, with a wine cloak over his broad shoulders, his two swords at his side, for he was ambidextrous. They had arrived at Nones, and the sweet singing of the monks drifted from the church as they meditated on the death of Christ, filling the afternoon air with poignant beauty.

"The full name is the Church of the Holy Savior in Chora," Zoe explained, gazing at the shimmering, richly decorated stone and red brick edifice where she had been wed. With its arches, balustrades, enormous bell tower, domes and scalloped, undulating roofline, the church seemed to dance in the sunlight. "Beautiful, isn't it?" She threw Justiniani a radiant smile.

Adjusting her filmy half-veil across her cheek, she led the way inside. Illuminated by rays of light filtering through the windows of the domes and semi-domes, the gloomy interior glittered with gold flecks. They moved past nuns, priests, foreign pilgrims, and citizens, old and young, who stood gazing on the wondrous artistry of the old church. Passing from one treasure to another, Zoe explained the colorful mosaics and frescoes from the Life of the Virgin to the Infancy of Christ. Justiniani followed closely behind, listening carefully and examining the pieces intently so as not to miss any detail of the sculptures, marble screens, domes, frescoes, mosaics, and vividly decorated scenes that she pointed out. Before the mosaic of Joseph taking the Virgin to his house, he came to a halt.

"The portrayal is so real, I can almost feel Mary's hesitation as she stands outside Joseph's house wringing her hands," he said.

Zoe gave him a smile as they moved on to the frescoes of the ancestors of Christ from Adam to Jacob, thinking it strange that she should feel so comfortable in his presence, as if she had always known him.

"Magnificent," he murmured reverently.

She led the way into a side chapel of the Chora Church. "We are in the *parekklesion* now, what you call the funeral chapel. This fresco is very famous."

"Christ's Descent into Hell," Justiniani murmured in awe.

"Yes, from the *Anastasis.* Under Christ's feet are the gates of Hell, and Satan stands before him—" She broke off in horror. She had seen the fresco countless times, but never had its chill significance permeated her soul the way it did now.

Justiniani looked at her and understood. The parallel with their situation was too dramatic to miss. Taking her firmly by the elbow, he steered her to the altar. He lit a candle, and they knelt together in prayer. She was still trembling when she stepped from the church back into the brightness of day. They walked together in the garden, wrapped in silence.

As Eirene and the guards followed at a discrete distance, Zoe sat down on a stone bench beneath a lemon tree, and Justiniani took a seat beside her. Deep in the foliage, a bird sang above their heads, and gradually the cold Zoe had felt before the *Anastasis* dissipated in the sunshine. She stole a sidelong glance at Justiniani. She was curious about this man who had dedicated himself to saving her city. She knew little about him, save that he was the youngest of four children from the noble House of Doria, beloved by his men, and a friend to kings.

"Why did you come?" she asked, voicing the question on everyone's mind.

"Why?" he echoed in surprise.

She blushed. It was an impertinent question, but she knew he wouldn't mind. "We are at this moment staring doom in the face. You braved great danger to come. Not only death on our walls, but the living death of slavery if we should lose. What made you do it?"

"Faith. What else?"

"Reward," she said, dropping her lashes to hide her disappointment. He hadn't been honest with her.

"Ah."

"The Isle of Lemnos will be yours. You came for the same reason your forefathers did two hundred years ago."

"So that's it. I've noticed a strange expression on your face when you look at me. Now I know why. You don't believe that my sole intent is to save God's city from the infidels. You think it is to enrich myself that I come."

Zoe took her time responding. "You are a Latin. You know what the crusaders did to us. It is hard for us to trust the Latins. While they sat around feasting in our palaces, the Ottomans took our territories, leaving us as helpless to defend ourselves as a man without limbs."

"That is in the past."

"We cannot get away from the past. The past is why we are here."

"True. We can never make up to you for what we did," he admitted with a sigh. "Can you forgive?"

Zoe shook her head. "Not when the guilty flourish, and there is no remorse."

"What if we are remorseful— At least, some of us are? What if we come to make amends for the crimes of our forefathers? Would that make a difference to you?"

"Perhaps—" She looked at him then. For some inexplicable reason, she wanted to believe. His dark eyes clung to hers, compelling, magnetic, and she couldn't look away. She realized as she gazed that they were not brown, but a rich, deep olive, flecked and ringed with gold. Summoning her will, she tore her eyes from his.

Justiniani broke the long silence that fell between them. "Lady Zoe, we don't have to live with hate. We can choose to forgive, and if we can't forgive, we can see the good in others and choose to tolerate our differences."

"Tolerance leads to heresy," Zoe gasped.

"You mean, to tolerate anything different from what you believe is heresy?"

"Yes."

"Is it heresy not to have a beard?" He rubbed his chin.

She dropped her lids. She had never considered that before. Not all Greeks wore their beards full. Many, like Constantine, kept them so short that they were barely a beard at all. But if it wasn't heresy, it surely had to be wrong. "Jesus had a beard, and so did the saints. Here, only eunuchs are clean-shaven," she said, finding an answer that didn't commit her, one way or the other.

"And whose fault is that— I mean, that they're eunuchs?"

"What do you mean?"

"We don't have eunuchs in the West. We think castration is cruel and wicked. We think people who do that to others are barbarians."

She stared at him mouth agape. Barbarians were the wild, unwashed, terrifying tribes of the north! That anyone could call Romans "barbarians" would have been amusing had it not been so insulting. "We are the most literate and civilized people in the world! Women here had rights in the fifth century that your women still don't have today! We ate with forks and bathed daily as far back as the tenth century. We were writing philosophy when your ancestors were painting their faces blue and killing one another. Everything you know, you learned from us! We protected you and safeguarded Christian knowledge until you came out of the Dark Ages! We had the first free hospital for the poor, the first university, the first orphanage! Look at our art and architecture—are they the work of *barbarians?"*

"We have some splendid literature of our own, too," he said lightly, to change the subject and defuse her anger. "Have you read Dante?"

She saw the amusement in his eyes and was infuriated that he didn't take her seriously. She lifted her chin. "No. Nor do I want to. And for your information, the only eunuchs here are those who were castrated by the infidels. We abandoned the practice long ago. It is a thing of the past."

"Ah. The past. So, we go in a circle and meet up with the past again. And what punishment should we assess your forefathers for their cruelty to their fellow man for which they cannot be forgiven?"

She felt her face flame. "What we did to eunuchs is not comparable to what you did to us. You invaded our land and oppressed us for sixty years, as if we were heathens!"

After a silence, he said, "You may be right… Some of my people see our differences as a chasm that cannot be bridged. Like married priests, for example."

"Priests *should* wed. Celibacy is unnatural and leads men astray. Besides, unmarried priests can't counsel their flock on what they do not know."

"By their sacrifice of this important part of human life," Justiniani replied, "our priests dedicate themselves to God in body and soul. Isn't it worse to make treaties with the infidel against the interests of fellow Christians, as you are known to have done during the earlier crusades?"

"Unlike you and the West, we *prefer* treaties. For us, war is a *last* option. The least desirable. You, on the other hand, revel in war. You have priests who wear armor and do nothing but fight for God."

"We fight for God now, do we not?"

"Yes. We fight to defend our faith, and our lives, and our freedom, and our right to exist! We fight because we are given no other choice."

"I grant you that. But we digress. We were talking about heresy. That tolerance is heresy. How do you know you are the only ones who are right?"

"Jesus spoke Aramaic. His sayings were recorded in Greek, not Latin. We Greeks were the first Christians. We practice our faith as the apostles gave it to us, but you changed many things." She spoke heatedly, propelled by a need to refute him "That is why you Latins are seen as heretics in the East."

He laughed. "Will you burn me then?"

"We don't burn heretics here. *Barbarians* do that," she said, stressing the word. "We send them to monasteries so they can repent of their evil ways."

"Oh, I forgot—you blind people instead."

"Only for treason. A blind man can't be emperor. By blinding him, we don't have to kill him."

"Wouldn't death be more merciful than a life in darkness?" Justiniani asked.

"No. Life is always precious because it is God-given."

"But you hang a man who steals your horse," Justiniani insisted.

"Only to deter others."

"Is his life not God-given?"

The hint of a smile hovered around his mouth.

"Maybe we should burn heretics!" she said, leaping to her feet, frustrated that she kept losing the argument. "That would take care of you!"

As she left him sitting by the lemon tree, she heard him call out after her, "What can I do to convince you I come only to fight for God?"

Twenty-One

"The Venetian *bailo* to Constantinople, Girolamo Minotto!" The herald announced.

Clad in a crimson robe with open sleeves, a scarf of scarlet silk over his shoulder, and the black velvet cap that identified him as a Venetian official returning from abroad to report to the *Collegio* of the Republic, Minotto strode into the Venetian Senate.

He bowed to the Doge and the nobles gathered on the dais. "*Serenissimo Principe … Eccellenza,* I bear an urgent dispatch from His Imperial Majesty, Constantine XI, *Imperatore di Roma.* As your representative to the Eastern Roman Empire, I come to beseech your help for Emperor Constantine and his Christian people. They face great peril. The enemy will soon be at the gates of Constantinople."

The Doge leaned forward in his seat, the pearls in his tall conical cap glistening, the jewels on his fingers flashing. "We have received many entreaties from the Emperor of Rome. Is the situation truly so dire?"

"It is, *Principe.* Emperor Constantine is David fighting Goliath. He has implored Sultan Mehmet to make peace, but the sultan is determined to bring siege. Without help, Constantinople will fall, and if it falls, the threat to all Christianity and our trade and colonies in the Mediterranean cannot be overstated. The sultan has made his intentions clear. Captain Rizzo's fate was our warning. To avert catastrophe, Venice must send men and munitions with utmost speed. Constantinople will not hold out long. What answer may I take back to the emperor?"

"Assure him of our goodwill. Tell him Venice will send a fleet to assist him in his dark hour. But inform him that it will take time to organize the flotilla and place command in worthy hands."

Minotto considered whether to convey Emperor Constantine's final warning, for fear it might give offence and do more harm than good. But he decided it was too important to omit. He braced himself and spoke. "Emperor Constantine urged me to add one last thought for your consideration. Appeasement is dangerous. Today they come for Constantinople. Tomorrow they come for you."

"Indeed, we understand," the Doge replied, nodding his pearl encrusted bonnet in dismissal.

Minotto could only hope he understood.

The first day of February dawned bright and sunny. But help did not arrive from the pope or any Christian nation. "Mehmet will soon be here. I can feel it in my bones," Constantine told Phrantzes as they walked the western ramparts together.

"And the Venetian fleet has yet to come," Phrantzes murmured.

Constantine winced. Time was running out. When would they be here—would they even come? His heart missed a beat at the terror of the thought. "We must decide how to deploy our men. Take a census of all able-bodied fighting men in the city, George."

As Phrantzes left, Captain Dalmata strode up. "Augustus, Daniel Navarro, the Jew who stayed behind to defend Constantinople, is here, as you requested."

Dalmata stepped aside, and Constantine found himself gazing into a face older than he had expected, with dark hair graying at the temples and a thick short beard flecked with silver. Navarro had a strong build and was of middling height, but it was his eyes that held Constantine's gaze. They were full of life, pain, and unquenchable warmth.

"You stayed when everyone else left," Constantine said. "Why? You are not even Christian. It is not your fight."

"Injustice is everyone's fight, Augustus."

"Ah, yes... The history of your people is fraught with injustice." He averted his eyes, finding himself touched by the man in a way he couldn't explain. "Life is a struggle," he murmured, surprised at his admission. Never had he spoken so intimately to any man, especially a stranger.

"I believe our struggles have a purpose. They are meant to make of us better men. That is why our choices are so important," the Jew answered.

Constantine looked into his soft eyes. A faint light twinkled in their brown depths. Only the wise could make such comforting sense of a senseless world, he thought. "Where are you from?"

"Kiev, originally." Navarro hoped the emperor would not ask why he'd left Russia. He had no wish to explain that a mob had broken into his walled ghetto one night and slaughtered his wife and child for no discernable reason. He'd left his village then and wandered the world, trying to forget, never staying long in one place until Navarre in the Basque country where he became a fisherman. It was a peaceful time, spent among people with a troubled history much like his own. There, at last, he found both the healing and the enlightenment he sought.

"You have come to the right place," Constantine said. "There is important work to be done here, and we can use your help, Daniel Navarro. I thank you and bid you warm welcome."

Constantine thought about Navarro over the next few days and followed his progress intently. He knew he had a good man in him, one he could entrust with important responsibilities. But first he needed Phrantzes' assessment of their situation.

A week after his encounter with Navarro, when he was in his privy quarters, as church bells struck the hour and monks chanted compline, Aesop finally announced Phrantzes.

"I come to report on the task you assigned me," he said.

"Yes?" Constantine replied, swept with sudden tension.

Phrantzes did not speak. Instead, he threw a meaningful glance at Zoe, who was going over the accounts of her charities on a couch by the fire. Constantine understood. Taking his friend by the elbow, he led him out to the balcony.

"That bad?" he asked when they were alone.

"Worse," replied Phrantzes. "Worse than anything you can believe."

"How many?"

"Barely five thousand."

Constantine felt the words like a sudden violent punch to the gut. His knees sagged beneath him, and he almost fell against the stone balustrade. "How many?" he said thickly, breathing hard.

"Five thousand," Phrantzes repeated.

"We must draft the monks and clerics."

"They are already included in the count, Augustus. With the foreigners who have come to fight for us, that makes seven thousand men to defend fourteen miles of wall."

Silence.

"No one must know," Constantine said when he could breathe again.

Phrantzes gave a nod. "Only God can help us now."

"Or the Venetian fleet," Constantine said. He turned and looked out into the dark night.

The dreadful knowledge spurred Constantine to redouble his desperate efforts to get help from the West and work feverishly to speed up his preparations for the siege he knew was coming. He stocked the warehouses on the wharves with munitions and collected arms and all manner of missiles, shot and arrows. He gathered men to repair the city's defenses. He had already stockpiled huge quantities of stones and timber and filled the cisterns with water. Now he sent another imperial transport to the Aegean islands to buy wheat and foodstuffs.

"It has been a bitter winter," said Lucas as he rode with Constantine to inspect the sea walls on the Golden Horn.

"Bitter indeed," Constantine replied, scanning the shoreline on both sides of the water. No sign of the Venetians. The day was bleak, the sea sullen. There was thunder in the air, but not a drop of rain or a breath of wind. The leaves of the citrus trees hung listless in the groves of Pera, as if waiting for something. Children dragged the kites that refused to fly behind them as they ran in the sand, and an old man with a long white beard sat on a rock, fishing for the family dinner. It was noon, the sixth hour of the day, and only the song of monks drifting from the monasteries on the hills of Pera bestowed any comfort. Yet they, too, were melancholy, for they meditated on Christ's crucifixion, which took place at sext.

All along the Horn, where the Venetian and Genoese commanders had staked their emblems on their portion of beach, men labored to repair the walls, their tools clinking. Donkeys laden with sacks of sand and rocks stood by patiently as men mixed water, limestone, and sand, and carried pails of mortar to those repairing the walls. His eye fell on Prince Orhan and the newcomer, Navarro, laboring together. The two men had struck up an unlikely friendship, and where one was, the other could be found. Constantine stopped to thank them.

"Small service can we offer," they replied. "But we do so gladly."

Trevisano and his crew, aided by Alviso Diedo, captain of the three Cretan vessels, looked up from their work digging the moat by the pennant of the Winged Lion of St. Mark that they had fixed into the sand. Constantine was surprised to find Justiniani already there with them. The man didn't spare himself, he thought. In addition to shoring up the defenses and preparing the city for siege, he spent hours each day instructing the Greeks and the Genoese from Pera in the martial arts and was quickly fashioning an impressive army out of tinkers, tailors, bureaucrats, shopkeepers, and shepherds.

"You have made excellent progress," Constantine said, admiring the sixty-foot-wide ditch they had dug.

Trevisano wiped the sweat from his brow with the back of his hand. "Majesty, our Genoese friend here informs us that he persuaded Pera to close the harbor, but I know not whether to believe him, since he is Genoese." A chorus of chuckles met this remark.

Constantine smiled as he dismounted. "He speaks truth. On occasion, both Venetians and Genoese may be trusted." Laughter made the rounds among the men. He placed a hand on Justiniani's shoulder. "Our thanks to you, noble friend. The ditch adds a level of protection, but it is the closing of the harbor that will save us. We owe that to you. Now we can make do with fewer troops here—troops we desperately need elsewhere."

From the top of the wall, Zoe stood with Eirene observing the party on the beach. She had seen little of Constantine in days and had left her work at St. Acacius and Botaneiates to be with him the only way she could—from a distance. His terrible burdens were taking an enormous toll. He brooded, picked at his food, and slept fitfully. Where once he had been confident, now he battled the prophecy that said he would be the last emperor of Rome, and he labored day and night to prove it wrong. All this she understood, but try as she might, she could do nothing to help him. He rarely confided in her anymore.

She heard snickering. As usual, her appearance had caused a stir. There were elbow jabs as she passed and pointed looks exchanged that said, *There goes the emperor's whore, for shame!* No one dared express overt hostility to the first lady of the land, but their resentment was thinly veiled. After the curtseys and polite greetings came the quickly suppressed laughter and disapproving stares of the women. Well she knew what they thought of her, for the campaign of whispers was led by Sybil, who had never forgiven her for Muriel' s banishment from court. Muriel and her husband had defected to Mehmet after he lost his position with Constantine. For that, too, she was blamed.

She turned her eyes back on the beach. As she gazed, one of the two Venetian captains looked up in her direction, and gave a wave. To her great surprise, Eirene waved back, smiling broadly. Zoe stared at her in puzzlement. "You know him? I mean, well enough to wave to?"

"Yes," Eirene replied. "I've spoken with Gabriel a number of times."

So, it was *Gabriel,* Zoe thought, not *Trevisano.* She looked back at the tall, wind-blown Venetian knight digging a ditch on the beach. Trying not to frighten Eirene with her tremendous interest, she said, "He's handsome. Do you know much about him?"

"I know he is the youngest son of a prominent family," Eirene answered. "Much like the *Protostrator.* "

The Deputy-Commander. Justiniani's new title. Zoe fell silent. In these weeks he had worked miracles with the defenses and become indispensable to Constantinople. His worldly experience, enthusiasm, high spirits, and expertise in military matters instilled confidence in everyone he met, and his charm was undeniable. Men smiled and laughed with easy camaraderie in his presence, and wherever he went, all eyes followed, especially those of women. She had to admit that he had won her over too, despite his sometimes-exasperating ways.

"The *Protostrator* is a godsend to us." Maria's voice. "And most charming. Do you not agree, sister?"

She turned to find Maria at her elbow. Her sister had an uncanny way of reading her thoughts, but whether Zoe agreed or disagreed, she knew enough to keep it to herself. Maria was perverse and a mischief-maker who thrived on discord. "If you say so."

Zoe returned her eyes to Justiniani. Maria was right: he was a godsend to them. As an outsider, the *Protostrator* was immune to the petty rivalry for imperial favor that marred an emperor's relationship with his magnates. As a result, he had Constantine's trust, and the two men had become fast friends in these short weeks. Only Justiniani could cheer him. Somehow, he had managed to bring a smile to Constantine's face yet again.

Zoe's gaze moving away from the beach touched, and held, on Maria. Her sister was staring at Justiniani with an expression of such longing that Zoe was swept with pity. She looked back at Justiniani who was inclining his head in acknowledgment of something Constantine had said. How could Maria help falling in love with him? No knight ever bore himself more nobly, with such princely grace.

When she looked up, Maria was staring at her with daggers in her eyes.

As bells rang for prime on a snowy March morning, Zoe rode to the Gate of St. Romanus with the Venetian physician, Nicolo Barbaro, heavily cloaked in her hooded mantle of lavender wool. Several hospitals were needed for the war effort, and she had offered to help set them up. Since she knew only the rudiments of nursing, such as all maidens are taught before marriage, she had been receiving instruction from Barbaro on caring for the wounded. Now she wished to hear his plans for the hospital at the Gate of St. Romanus.

Despite the early hour and the snow and icy wind, the streets of the Blachernae region were crowded. People bustled hither and thither, and she passed many carts and donkeys laden with building supplies and timber. From all directions there came the relentless pounding and chiseling of those who repaired the walls and the sound of sawing as men felled trees. She dismounted by a tiny chapel beneath the tower stairs of St. Romanus, and her gaze fell with dismay on the formidable tower steps that rose sixty feet high against the wall and stood open on one side. She had never realized how steeply vertical they were. Bringing the wounded down from such a height would be no easy task.

"This way, my lady," Barbaro said.

Head bowed against the snow flurries, she followed him briskly to a small field opposite the tower steps. They had almost reached the clearing when a voice called out to her. She turned to find a handsome, red-cloaked figure striding in her direction. *Justiniani.*

"I'll take it from here, Barbaro," Justiniani said. Excusing himself, Barbaro withdrew as Justiniani gave Zoe a courtly bow. "The memory of our last meeting burdens my conscience, my lady. Am I forgiven?" he grinned, staring at her boldly.

"No," she said.

But Justiniani was not to be deterred. "I have missed you. Did you miss me?" he teased.

"Is this what you stopped me for on such a day? To prattle about nonsense?" She had no wish to be harsh, but she had to discourage his interest.

"My apologies, dear lady," Justiniani said in a changed tone. "Since you will manage the hospital facilities with Barbaro, I wished to consult you before we erect the buildings. We need to make haste, no matter the weather."

"What can I do?" Zoe said, softening.

"I am considering distributing tents along the perimeter of the walls, especially around the *Mesoteichion* where we expect the fighting to be fierce. One will be here where we stand. These trees will be felled to make room for the tent and to protect against the danger of fire from the enemy's missiles."

Zoe looked around the field, and her gaze went to a broad olive with a gnarled and twisted trunk standing at the edge of the circular clearing near a pile of crumbling stones that had, in ancient times, bordered a building. "Can you spare that tree? It must be a thousand years old." She indicated the olive, its branches shivering in the wind. "We shall need shade in the sun." It felt strange to be speaking of heat when it was so bitter cold, but changes in seasons were often sudden. As sudden as the turn of Fortune's Wheel, she thought.

Justiniani's voice banished her moment of whimsy.

"—medicines must be stockpiled, and potions, and bandages," he was saying. "We'll need pallets, of course, and wine."

"What about the churches and monasteries? They already have quantities of medicines on hand."

"Their stocks will not be enough. You should co-ordinate with them to see what we need, but remember, you are the final authority. The churches will disagree with one another, and there will be argument."

"Do you wish to approve the decisions I make?"

He relaxed his taut expression, and for a moment it seemed to Zoe that he was about to make a jest. But his tone was formal when he replied. "I have full faith in your judgment, my lady. If you need another opinion, consult with Barbaro."

She gave a nod. There was no more to be said. They walked back to the walls in silence. “By the way, I have a gift for you—” Justiniani withdrew a package from inside his cloak.

Zoe took it from him in puzzlement and turned it over in her hands uncertainly. Sewn in rose silk, it was solid, and heavy. “What is it?” she asked.

“A surprise,” he said gently, lifting her onto her palfrey. “Let me know what you think.”

Zoe lost no time assembling a small army of children and old folk to gather the weeds of the field required for the medications needed. But first they had to learn how to identify the herbs that were to be boiled, mixed, and pounded into potions and salves.

Flanked by a small retinue of palace administrators and wearing the formal white robes of the *Zoste Patricia,* her golden belt of office around her hips, Zoe addressed a group of clergy and university scholars. “The people require instruction on all aspects of preparing the healing medicines and poultices we will need,” she said, her glance roaming over the abbots and abbesses, and doctors of medicine, chemists and herbalists from the University of Constantinople. “Your assistance is vital to the effort. Pray give your names to the *koubikoularios,"* she concluded. With a rustle of movement, everyone turned to look at the chamberlain with the gold-hilted sword of office who stood with the sword bearers at the back of the room. “That is all. May God be with us in our hour of need.”

“Amen,” they murmured fervently, making the sign of the cross.

But it was help from an unexpected source that proved of greatest value to Zoe.

“I did not realize you were a scholar of the healing arts,” she said when Prince Orhan came to offer his services. “I know I shouldn’t be surprised. For many centuries, Islam led the way in medicine.”

Prince Orhan bowed from the waist, sending her a kiss from his fingertips. “I am gratified to be of assistance, however imperfect my knowledge. If I may make a suggestion?” At her nod, he continued. “Many survive amputation only to die of infection. I have found Juniper berries boiled with bitter aloes and Achillea—which as you know, Achilles discovered himself—to be especially helpful as an antiseptic against infection.”

Zoe regarded the dark-bearded, turbaned man with the soft brown eyes. He was an outsider and different in many ways, yet despite the distrust of many at court, he had proven repeatedly that he was one of them in all the ways that mattered. "Thank you, Prince Orhan. I am very grateful for your assistance in these trying times. If you need anything, let me know."

Prince Orhan hesitated, and then he said, "*Zoste Patricia,* Daniel Navarro is well versed in the healing arts. May I have your permission to appoint him my deputy?"

"Of course," Zoe said, surprised.

Following Phrantzes's devastating news, Constantine slept little. Nor did Zoe. Most nights she watched him through the open door of the bedchamber as she lay in bed, her heart breaking to see him poring over maps on his desk and brooding over a table filled with sand on which a scaled model of the defenses had been built, this man she had loved all her life, alone in the dark night, struggling with a burden no one should have to face. He needed sleep, he needed nourishment, but more than this, he needed victory. Only God could grant him that. She felt her helplessness keenly, and the realization that she could do nothing to comfort him overwhelmed her with a special sorrow.

One night when Constantine was at his desk and she couldn't sleep, she removed Justiniani's gift from her coffer. Ripping open the silk covering, she found a small book. She opened the worn brown leather cover and glanced at the title. *La Vita Nuova.* The New Life. It was written by a man named *Dante*, who related the story of a poet's love for a girl he could not have. As she read, she lost awareness of time, and all at once it was morning and she was stirring on the couch where she had fallen asleep. The sound of shovels and voices filtered up to her through the open windows. In the darkness before dawn, men were already working on the walls by torchlight She heard movement in the room and saw Constantine in the dimness. He was fully dressed and buckling on his sword.

Raising up on an elbow, she rubbed her bleary eyes. "You can't leave yet. You haven't eaten or said matins—"

"I am fasting for Lent. I will pray later." He turned his back.

She hastened to her feet, anxious to stop him, to make him see reason: that he couldn't go on like this—toiling ceaselessly, not sleeping, and fasting for days in the hope of gaining God's favor. "Come, let me—"

"Leave me be, woman!" he shouted, crossing the room with long, angry strides. Dismayed by his harsh rebuff, she watched his retreating back, wounded to the core.

After a long day making the rounds of her charities, hearing petitions, and receiving instruction from Barbaro in the healing arts, Zoe went directly to the warehouses on the Golden Horn. She needed to collect supplies for the hospital tents—blankets, fabric for sewing pallets, gauze for bandages, coal for firepots, buckets, soap, jars, bedpans, and other necessities. Everything was required in enormous quantity to serve the ten hospitals being erected along the fourteen miles of wall.

Though Eirene's duties at the charities took precedence and her services as chaperone were rarely required, she'd insisted on accompanying her to the wharf. Zoe knew the reason. Gabriel Trevisano had offered his services as guide. Despite her exhaustion, the knowledge that her cousin was falling in love brought a smile to her face, and she found cause to leave her alone with Trevisano at every available opportunity.

As gray twilight fell and monks chanted for vespers, Zoe returned to the palace so weary that her bones ached. She hugged Eirene farewell at the entrance of the *Soros* and made her way to the Ocean Hall. Fountains no longer splashed, and to conserve fuel, few torches lit the walkways. The shadows and silence sent a cold knot forming in her stomach as she hastened through the empty peristyles and tangle of chambers. Fear was everywhere in town, a contagion poisoning all chance of joy as old men ate in silence at the tavernas and children played quietly in the streets. Here, too, it permeated the very air she breathed. Spreading its ghastly tentacles, it darkened the present and filled the future with dread.

Her footsteps echoed on the marble hallway, and she saw that she was passing the cavernous Hall of Nineteen Couches. She halted. Now it was an expanse of darkness, but once it had been alive with banquet tables of gold and ivory where men had laughed loudly, calling for wine, song, and celebration with the carefree laugh of those secure in their land. She could almost hear the music of the minstrels, almost see the tumblers performing their leaps. A glimmer of marble caught her eye from the statues of Roman emperors and Greek gods that stood between the tall columns like phantoms. She wished she could sweep away the centuries and bear witness for herself how it used to be in that long-lost world of security and opulence. She blinked and moved on.

Her thoughts went to Constantine. She wondered if he was up. Most likely, she thought. He slept little these days. She gave an inward sigh. At night he studied his maps or brooded over the sand table with the replica of the defenses. Sometimes he went out to the balcony and stared at the dark sea. Sometimes he paced, up and down, up and down. When he did sleep, he was troubled by evil dreams. As a result, he had lost much weight, and there were circles under his eyes.

Indeed, Constantine had little desire to go to bed, thanks to the nightmares that plagued his slumber. On this night, awakened by one of these, he'd risen and gone to the balcony. That was where Zoe found him.

"Tell me about your dream," she said, pouring him a goblet of wine. She had put away her hurt and anger from the morning, for there was no longer time for grudges. Constantine took the goblet from her and toyed with it for a while. Then, in one gulp, he emptied it. "Always they begin and end the same way—with the marching of boots and a Janissary staring into my eyes."

"It is a battle dream then."

"No. Worse."

"How?"

"The Janissary is always a child wearing a Saracen helmet. A Christian child, like the ones playing in the streets as I ride about the walls." Like the ones taken into slavery in the villages around the Hexamilion Wall, he thought. *Because of me.*

Zoe gave a shudder.

Constantine said, "Mehmet's Janissaries alone number twelve thousand. They are our people and equal to us in every way—except that they are better equipped. His army is said to be a hundred and fifty thousand strong, perhaps more. We are a handful, outnumbered at least twenty to one. I fear for my people."

"God will help us," Zoe offered, regretting she had nothing to offer but a platitude.

"I know not where God stands in this," Constantine said softly.

"How can He not be with us, Constans? He protects the righteous."

"They say I am not righteous. That I am a heretic. A traitor. An *Apostatis*—"

"Pay no heed. Do not doubt yourself."

"What began with Constantine born of Helen—"

"No! Prophecies mean nothing! Once they said the statue of Constantine the Great pointed to his dominions in Anatolia, and now they say it points to the direction of our doom— Prophecies have no credence. Do not believe—"

His eyes held a faraway look, and she wasn't sure he'd heard, but he had confided in her for the first time in many months, and she was grateful. She leaned close and took his hand into her own. "Hark! It is the nightingale. It has been a stormy winter, but spring is on its way..."

She'd hoped he would embrace her and give her a chance to enfold him in love, but he was already gone. She felt as if she stood by a dark lake and he was drowning in front of her eyes, and no matter how far she struggled to extend her hand, she couldn't reach him. She watched him rise and turn to leave, and as he passed, he said nothing to her, and she saw that his eyes were the eyes of a stranger, looking past her to an inner hell she couldn't share. She watched as he went inside and crossed the marble hall, watched as he took the steps down into the sunken study and stood at his desk, his head bowed over the maps. Never had she felt more acutely the burdens that weighed on his shoulders.

Twenty-Two

"This is our Achilles heel. This is where he will attack," Constantine said to Justiniani as they stood atop the great wall between the gates of Charisius and St. Romanus that overlooked the Lycus Valley. The fierce wind blew their cloaks around them, entwining Constantine's purple with Justiniani's red.

Justiniani had always been fascinated by legendary Constantinople, the city of seven hills founded by the Roman emperor, Constantine the Great. Even as a child he'd dreamt of one day visiting this ancient bastion of Christian civilization. Never had he imagined it would be under these circumstances. When he heard of the sultan's plans to besiege the Roman city, he knew he had to come. What he didn't expect—and had not bargained for—was to meet an auburn-haired Roman beauty who set his heart to pounding with thoughts of tender, tremulous love. Only once before had he felt that way. The girl he loved had promised to wait for his return from battle, but when a duke had asked for her hand, she'd lost no time breaking her promise and his heart.

And broken promises had far-reaching consequences. He winced.

When he was a young boy, he had begged his mother not to visit her dying father in plague infested Chios. "Fear not, I will be back soon… I promise," she'd said, embracing him tightly in her arms. But she had died there of the pestilence, and her death had changed his life. His father's second wife was a cold and carping woman who had resented him and manipulated his father. When he was twenty, his mother's family offered him a ship and two hundred men. He'd accepted their offer and set out to win fame and fortune. He had never looked back.

Until now.

As he gazed over the crenellated ramparts that rippled from the earth with a silken sheen all the way from the Golden Horn on his right, down to the Marmara on his left, he thought of Zoe, whose rose scent and topaz eyes reminded him of the two he had loved so deeply in youth. He blinked to banish the memories and forced himself to focus on the present.

Yellowed by time, the triple Theodosian walls ran from north to south as far as the eye could see. On the land side, a moat protected the twenty-foot outermost wall; next came one about forty feet high with many towers, some square, some octagonal. Where he stood was the Great Wall, the innermost and highest of the three. Rising sixty feet with numerous bastions and towers, it was taller than any in Europe. He turned his gaze on the Lycus valley and the river meandering serenely into the city. In this central section, the ground fell to its lowest point. Directly across stood a hill. On the rise of that hill, Mehmet would command the high ground, for even at sixty feet, these walls could not compete with such elevation. No wonder this stretch was considered the Achilles Heel.

Constantine spoke again.

"This gate at Charisius is where Mehmet's father attacked us, and his father before him. That is why the walls are triple here. The moat is eighty feet wide all the way along. Even with these defenses, it is still our weakest point."

"If I were Mehmet, this is where I'd concentrate my forces." Justiniani turned to Constantine, "I request to be assigned this position, Majesty."

"But the greatest danger lies here," Constantine said, taken aback.

"I did not come to hide from peril. It will be my honor to defend this position that is so vital to the survival of Constantinople."

Constantine regarded Justiniani for a long moment. Some vowed to help and fled in the night. Then there was Justiniani. He rested a hand on his shoulder, swept with affection for this man who was so much like him in so many ways. "The Gate of Charisius is yours, Justiniani. Mine will be beside you, my friend. At the Gate of St. Romanus." He indicated a short distance to the south. It was debatable which of the two gates was more vulnerable; they shared the peril equally between them. A hesitation. Then, softly, he added, "I marvel that you came when you know the risks."

"If Rome is vanquished, the heart of Europe will be laid bare. How could I not come?"

"If only others understood as clearly what is at stake."

"I have but one question. Why has no one heeded your call?"

"I have done what I can to make Europe understand that this new threat we face is unlike any we have ever known. They all turn away. They consider it another crusade, and they are weary of crusades."

"God's blood, if Mehmet succeeds where others have failed for a thousand years, he will think himself another Caesar! Then his victory will not be the end—it will be the beginning. Europe will never be rid of the threat. How can they not see that?"

Constantine heaved a weary sigh. "They think that once Mehmet is done with us, he will be satisfied to trade with them as before. But I foresee endless war. We have always had our differences with the Ottomans, but until now no one called for the destruction of our civilization. Mehmet comes for us first because he views Rome as the torchbearer of the West, but when he has taken our lives, our homes, our land and our freedom, he will come for them. As for Constantinople—" Constantine drew a thick breath. "If we lose, it is the end of Rome."

"I did not come to lose, Majesty," Justiniani said with quiet emphasis.

Justiniani's confidence lightened Constantine's heaviness, and a rush of gratitude warmed his heart.

"Another weakness is there—" Justiniani said, glancing north to where the Golden Horn ended and the triple walls became single at Blachernae. At that point the line of ramparts made a right turn to skirt some ruins. "I fail to understand why more defenses weren't built there."

"That heap of stones is the Church of St. Mary. The belief was that the Virgin didn't need our protection and could defend herself and the city. It is said she saved us from the Avars last time."

Justiniani fell silent. How could they believe she would save the city when she failed to save her own church? Aloud, he said, "At least we have dug a moat now." Shielding his eyes from the sun, he strained to see the fortifications that ran west along the glittering Horn. "Who will you assign to the middle section? That is a position of great strategic importance."

Constantine followed his gaze. "I was thinking of Gabriel Trevisano."

"The Venetian? An excellent choice."

"I am relieved to hear you say that. Genoese usually have nothing good to say about Venetians." Constantine allowed himself a small smile.

"We are all Christians. Whether we come from Venice or Genoa, we fight for the same thing. The survival of our faith."

"If more thought like you, Justiniani, the Queen of Cities would not stand alone." He bit down on the emotion that flooded him. "With God's help, we shall hold out until the Venetian fleet arrives. They have promised twenty ships. A veritable armada."

"What about the Marmara?"

"I don't believe Mehmet will attempt a landing from the sea, what with the currents, shoals and reefs. Prince Orhan is in charge there, supported by monks and archers."

They stood quietly for a spell. Then Constantine said, "An old Hungarian once offered to build us a gigantic cannon."

"I know of him. They say he is a mad dreamer."

"When we turned him down, he went to Mehmet. Mehmet welcomed him and gave him the money and men he asked for. The reason he has not yet attacked is because he awaits the gun. It is almost ready."

After a long silence, Justiniani turned his gaze on Constantine. "Europe has no idea what awaits them if Constantinople falls. Mehmet's ambition will be on fire."

Here is a man after my own heart, Constantine thought; he grasps what is at stake. His gaze swept the walls and the gates, and the church steeples and monuments; it moved out to the water and Mehmet's fortress, and beyond, to the limitless sea. He heaved a soft sigh. "We have served as Europe's bulwark against the East for a thousand years. If we fall, there will be nothing to stop Mehmet. He and his descendants will march into Europe along the pathways we are no longer here to defend, century upon century, until nothing is left." Suddenly weary, he leaned his weight on the wall. "There will be no rest for Europe, only war."

On Lazarus Saturday, the day before Palm Sunday, Zoe gazed around the hospital tent she'd equipped with pallets, stacks of blankets and sheets, small coffers, and tables laid with scissors, candles, wash basins, towels, bandages, and potions. Her eye went to the screen that hid the axes and surgical instruments from plain sight. She rose to her feet and adjusted it. The wounded had no need to see the fearsome utensils that the surgeon would use to amputate their limbs.

Her eyes went to the tent opening. Such a beautiful spring day. Easter, the greatest festival in the Orthodox Church, was fast approaching, and the word was that Mehmet would soon attack. The prayer on everyone's lips was the same. Let us have Easter in peace. Let him not come until after the Savior's resurrection. She picked up a basin of water, took it outside and emptied it, blinking against the bright sunlight.

A blind beggar swathed in rags sat at the foot of the tower steps that rose steeply before her, but otherwise few were around. She noticed he was missing two fingers on his left hand. She dug in her bodice for a coin and gave it to him. From the parapet above the tower steps the voices of men came to her, along with a distant scraping of shovels. They were deepening the moat. There had always been menace in the valley beyond these defenses, but now it pressed close against the walls, a palpable presence, dark and forbidding. With a shudder, she pulled her gaze away and made her way back to the tent.

The makeshift tin roof that was intended to protect against the flaming arrows of the enemy flashed in the sun as she passed beneath the branches of the old olive tree she had asked Justiniani to spare. Now that spring was drawing near, it bore a sprinkling of young fruit the color of lime. She turned her gaze skyward. A pair of storks were passing overhead, returning to build their nests in the high rooftops of the city, and long lines of other migratory birds were streaking in the opposite direction, heading to their summer homes far in the north. She lingered in the dappled sunlight, listening to the song of the birds, reluctant to return to the gloomy interior. The world was so beautiful, so peaceful… A sudden unbearable yearning came to her for she knew not what, and she balled a fist against the emotion that threatened.

"Here!" she called to a passing servant, "Fetch more barrels of wine and more cups— Tin, pottery, whatever you can find. And water— They forgot the water! Bring lots of water. Get the other servants to help you."

The man bowed and hurried away. "We need water too," said a deep, pleasant voice.

She turned to find Justiniani coming down the tower steps toward her. He closed the distance between them with long strides.

"We need it for drinking and for putting out fires."

"I'll send some barrels up to you when they arrive."

"How is it going here?"

"Well enough. How about you?"

"Same. I long to revisit the Chora and keep hoping to do so, but I haven't yet had the chance," he grinned.

Zoe's smile faltered, and she averted her gaze. For her, that first encounter with Justiniani remained a charged and unsettling memory.

As if he guessed her thoughts, he changed the subject, "I suppose it will have to wait until we've beaten the Turks."

His words brought a smile to her lips. Justiniani's bright outlook on life was so endearing that she almost forgot he was descended from the same crusaders whose invasion was in large part responsible for their present plight.

"Have you read *Dante* yet?" he asked softly, dazzled by the radiance of her sudden smile.

She hesitated. "Yes."

"Well, what do you think?"

"He can't compare with Euripides, of course—" She flashed another contagious smile. "But his verses are deeply moving… Even if they are in Italian."

He chuckled. "In Dante's hands, Italian becomes the language of love, and love the portal to heaven. He believes that love teaches us much… I agree with Dante that there is nothing more important for the soul. But I'll add one thing. A heart once given must be forever." He met her eyes.

Zoe dropped her lids. Justiniani didn't know what cruel irony his words held. He thought it applied to them, but it only reminded her that she had given her heart to Constantine, and there was no going back. *A heart once given must be forever*… No longer could she doubt Justiniani's feelings for her. But this couldn't go on. She had to divest him of his illusions—for his own sake, and for Maria's. Though she had little patience for her difficult sister, she was still her blood. "Justiniani, there is something I—"

His eyes widened, and he took a step closer expectantly, hopefully. "Yes?"

She opened her mouth to speak and fell silent, unable to summon the words. What if she told him and he left? He, and all his men— If he left, it would be her fault. If he left, Constantinople would fall. But if he stayed, they had a chance. She dropped her lids.

When she remained silent, Justiniani spoke. "Even though it is a tragedy, we in the West think it a great story," he said gently, changing the subject.

It was a gallant gesture. Zoe knew he was relieving her of responsibility; letting her know he understood. But he didn't understand at all. He had no idea. She would have to tell him some day—it was too cruel to let him hope. But now was not the time. She would tell him later. When the war was won.

"It is a good tale," she said softly, gratefully. "I read it three times."

The sudden leap of joy in his eyes suffused her with unbearable guilt. He was about to speak again when laughter drew her attention to a litter approaching from the direction of the royal baths. Two young noble maidens, barely past childhood, peered out from behind their curtains. Giggling as they passed, they lowered their sheer veils demurely across their cheeks as they gazed at Justiniani. He returned their giggles with a devastating grin and a courtly bow. Zoe's mood veered to anger. It was said that women found him irresistible. Despite his clean-shaven looks, he could have his pick of them; young or old made no difference. Her gender, she thought, should show more decorum.

The girls disappeared around the curving path, leaving only the defenses to fill her gaze. In a low tone that was barely audible, she said, "Do you think we can win?" It wasn't a question she could ask her father or Constantine, for both grappled with doubts. But Justiniani would assure her of victory because he himself believed it. And she needed to hear him say it.

"If Satan doesn't interfere, we will win," he replied gravely.

It was his stock answer, usually delivered with a disarming grin. Though he wasn't smiling now, she was swept with disappointment. She hadn't expected the same glib answer he gave everyone else. "Why do you always say that?" she said testily.

"What?" he leaned back against a post and folded his arms across his chest. He wore a sleeveless jerkin that exposed his hard muscles, and his eyes were soft with admiration.

Zoe felt herself blush. She wanted comfort, not a flirtation. "'If Satan doesn't interfere.' You never say, 'With God's help,' like everyone else."

"Because they—" he jerked his head behind him to the invaders, "say that too, and God can't help both sides win, can He? Besides, war is the devil's game."

"Our triple walls have been invincible for a thousand years," she retorted.

"And they would be still, if we had enough troops. As it is, we can only man one of the three walls. The emperor must decide which. None are perfect, though all three together would be."

A silence fell. It was the truth, but she didn't want the truth. She wanted reassurance, and Justiniani couldn't give it.

His voice came again. "Those walls can be an impediment to us too. It makes it hard for us to get out and do them mischief. If only we had a postern gate."

"What is a 'postern gate'?"

"A secret gate."

Suddenly Zoe became aware of an old man pushing a cart toward them and was reminded of the cups she had requested. The man drew to a halt at these words, and she realized they had been conversing in Greek, not Italian, and he had overheard their conversation. Even the beggar had turned his head and seemed to be listening.

The old man set down his cart. Speaking rapidly and gesturing with excitement, he said, "There is one that way—" he pointed north, toward Blachernae.

"What? A gate? Where?" Justiniani no longer slouched against the post. His casual demeanor was gone, and he was every inch the alert warrior as he turned his full attention on the old man.

"There is a gate," the man said, lisping through his gapped teeth. "A small gate. My father showed it to me when I was this big—" He held his hand to his waist. "Down that way, where the triple Theodosian walls becomes single at Blachernae."

"Show me," commanded Justiniani.

"I don't know if I can find it—it was so long ago. They called it the *Kerkoporta.* It was used when Sultan Mehmet's father attacked Emperor Constantine's father. It must be well hidden by shrubbery by now. But I'll do my best."

As Justiniani strode off with the man, Zoe called out to his retreating back, "Good fortune to you!" Justiniani raised his hand in a wave without a backward glance.

Zoe turned back to the tent, and her glance fell on the blind beggar, seated by the little chapel in the wall. There was a sharpness to the turn of his head that she found disconcerting, even sinister. She halted abruptly, flooded with the strange feeling that he was watching her. But how could that be when he was blind? Unless he's not what he seems, came the thought. She shook herself. She was seeing demons everywhere. *He's naught but a poor beggar… A poor beggar is all.*

Chastising herself for her lack of charity, she went to him and placed another coin in his tin cup.

Twenty-Three

The last day of March ushered glorious spring into Constantinople. Seemingly overnight orchards burst into bloom. As zephyrs scented the air and birds of every hue sang in the gardens, the chanting of monks soothed the earth and church bells chimed sweetly, proclaiming all was well with the world on this Easter Sunday eve.

The rejoicing of the people, though subdued, was even more sincere because everyone knew what lay ahead. As the sun set and rose twilight fell over the city, people put aside their differences. Unionists and anti-unionists lit candles and carried them side by side through the city streets down to the Hagia Sophia to hear the service that began on Saturday evening. For the first time in many months, the dark, cavernous interior of the ancient church filled with glittering light, song, and incense, lending sparkle to the many filigreed lamps of brass and golden mosaics of saints and angels as young and old knelt on the cold marble floor together and prayed fervently for the protection of the Holy Mother.

When the service was over, noble ladies stepped into their litters and lords mounted their horses to return to their palaces and ready themselves for the imperial Easter feast on the morrow. But the common folk lost no time making merry. Grateful for God's mercy in allowing them to celebrate this most precious holy day, they broke their Lenten fast by roasting oxen in the fields, breaking open vats of beer, and dancing, drinking, and laughing until exhaustion claimed their bodies.

The next morning was a rush of activity as Zoe arranged the final touches to the garden feast with the chamberlain and palace staff and withdrew to her chamber to dress. Eirene secured her freshly washed burnished masses of hair in an upswept style with pearls and diamonds and helped her into her favorite gown, the persimmon silk that complemented her coloring.

"What will you wear?" Zoe asked Eirene as she donned her golden girdle and wide cuff bracelets.

"My green linen and my gray palla," she replied.

In the motion of securing a drop earring, Zoe paused. Eirene had been fussing over her dress all week, sewing, mending, and cleaning the fabric late at night, but even at its best, the gown was painfully simple. "You need something pretty," she said. "Why not wear one of mine?"

Hastening to the alcove, she selected a rich sapphire silk and held it up against Eirene as Theseus barked. "Perfect. It compliments your dark hair and creamy complexion. Even Theseus approves," Zoe laughed.

Eirene fingered the gorgeous gown. "But I can't. It is too fine. I might spill something—"

"The gown is yours now, Eirene. Do with it what you will. You can wear my turquoise pendant and silver *palla* with it. Here, sit down and be still. I will do your hair for a change." She met her eyes in the mirror and smiled. "He won' t stand a chance, Eirene."

As in the days of yore, tables covered with silk cloths and laden with silverware and urns of flowers shone once more in the sunlight, and fountains splashed in the imperial courtyard. War, austerity, and fear were forgotten.

Zoe's gaze dwelled on Constantine's tall figure as he welcomed his guests, resplendent in a golden crown and a tunic of crimson silk tied with a silver sash, his purple cloak secured at his shoulder with a giant carnelian fibula. He had slept well for once and looked rested. She was grateful for that.

Wine flowed, and there was malmsey from Monemvasia and spring water that was pure and sweet. Constantine' s favorite caviar from the Black Sea was absent, but olives and dried fruits were plentiful, and so were grape leaves stuffed with rice and pine nuts. Since it was no longer safe to fish at sea, the catch was augmented by a variety of broiled and baked freshwater fish from the lakes. But servants proffered only a small selection of venison, for meat was now in short supply. As the nobles drank and nibbled on *apotki,* the hub of conversation grew boisterous until it was silenced by the entertainment. A troop of dancers filed in, and Zoe saw her brothers, Alexander and Jacob. She glanced at her mother who watched them dance, a goblet never far from her lips.

Before sweets were served, Zoe rose to entertain the guests. Curtseying to Justiniani, she dedicated the first dance to the Latin warriors and led her troop of maidens in the steps of an old Greek dance. To the lilting tune of flutes and drums, they slapped their knees and waved their scarves, entwined arms, and circled languorously. Everyone clapped to the music, and Justiniani and his Genoese sang along lustily, waving their tankards of beer.

When Zoe and her ladies took their seats, Justiniani leapt to his feet to make a surprising announcement. "My noble friends, we perform for you a belly dance that comes to us directly from Mehmet's harem!" Calling on the minstrels to play a Saracen melody, he and his men tied scarves around their hips and launched into their version of harem concubines performing for a sultan.

In view of Genoa's duplicity regarding their impending ordeal, Zoe feared they would be jeered, but everyone rocked with laughter at their antics. She hadn't realized until this moment what a storehouse of goodwill and affection Justiniani had amassed for the Latins with his hard work on the defenses and his success in persuading Pera to close the Golden Horn. That, in addition to his great personal magnetism, had charmed Venetians, Greeks and Genoese into working together for the common weal. His attributes had elevated him to near mythic proportions.

He could charm a snake into working with a mouse, Zoe thought in admiration, watching with utter delight and incredulity as the well-built warrior, immersed in his womanly dance, swayed his hips, snapped his fingers and wiggled his shoulders as if he vied for a sultan's favor. When he slithered close and wagged an eyebrow at her with a come-hither look, she collapsed with laughter, tears rolling down her cheeks.

The melody ended and everyone leapt to their feet in riotous applause, hooting and calling for a repeat performance.

"Very well—" Justiniani announced. "But this time we do something different—" He whispered to the head minstrel and turned to his men. "We will perform a courtly Latin dance with the lovely maidens of the Roman Empire. Men, claim your partners!"

As Trevisano hastened to Eirene, Justiniani strode to the head table and requested the grand duke's permission to dance with Zoe. After exchanging a look with Constantine, Lucas gave a nod. Ignoring Zoe's protests, Justiniani drew her to the floor. His men fell into formation behind them.

Amid much glee Justiniani and his Genoese instructed the Grecian maidens in the steps as everyone marked the beat, laughing when they stumbled, and even raising their voices to sing along. Justiniani was not Constantine, and the dance was not familiar, but as Zoe held his hand and moved with him forward and back to the music, passing to his left and his right and twirling under his arm, she recalled the days of yore when she and her beloved had danced together, happy and in love. And though Justiniani wasn't Constantine, yet there was something about his sun-bronzed face and deep compelling eyes that brought to mind the old, laughing Constantine of her youth before the burdens of empire had furrowed his brow with worries of war.

In a few short months, he has become one of us, Zoe thought as she twirled beneath his hand. She glanced at Constantine. Even he was in Justiniani's thrall, applauding and encouraging him on. She dropped her hand and stepped to the side, and her gaze moving over the banquet table fell on Maria, who watched her with hurt, reproachful eyes. At that moment Justiniani passed between them, momentarily blocking Maria's view. "What is it?" he whispered, registering her expression. "Maria—dance with her," she pleaded. With an imperceptible nod, Justiniani gave a half-turn and winked at Maria. Inwardly, Zoe blessed him for his gallantry.

When the music ended, Justiniani escorted Zoe back to her seat and requested her father's permission to dance with an elated Maria.

The evening ended soon afterwards. Constantine was the first to depart, and everyone followed according to rank. Zoe left with her family, discreetly taking the peristyle that led back to the *Soros.* She didn't know why, but she was acutely aware of Justiniani laughing with his men as he turned in the opposite direction to his quarters in the Palace of Manuel Comnenus.

When she finally arrived in the imperial quarters, she found Constantine seated on the edge of the bed, removing his boots. Aesop was nowhere in sight. He rose to don the calf-length silken tunic he wore to bed and caught sight of her. Gently, he gathered her into his arms.

"I watched you dancing with Justiniani. If I didn't know better, I would be jealous. You looked so happy."

The desire in his eyes elicited a flood of emotion. All her loneliness and doubts melded into an upsurge of yearning, and she entwined her arms around his neck and kissed him savagely. He swept her up and carried her to the bed, his lips searing a path down her neck, her shoulders, her breasts. Her senses reeled as his hardness pressed into her. Dimly she heard a shutter slam open. The tang of the sea rushed to engulf her, waves crashed on the shore, and the wind whistled and moaned. The world spun, the tang grew heavy, and the wind wilder. Moving together in timeless harmony, her body became one with his. Surrendering herself to the turbulence, she shuddered with an ecstasy she knew could come only once in a lifetime, and clung to him until the winds had died, the sea had calmed, and the world was still once more.

Constantine slept soundly all night, and each time Zoe roused herself to check on him, she heard his deep, regular breathing, and lay back on her pillow in relief.

Easter had been granted them in peace, as they had prayed and hoped. But on the next day, Monday, the second of April, a detachment of Ottoman troops came into view across the Golden Horn under the command of the renegade Christian general, the Albanian, Zaganos Pasha. From the roofs, parapets, and the tops of their towers, as women wailed and monks cried out to heaven, the people of Constantinople watched them arrive on the crest of the hill above Pera. Over the course of the next two days, the ugly black scar that had appeared on the hillside with the arrival of the enemy troops grew wider as more trees were felled and grapevines ripped out by the roots. Then, the dark stain of humanity oozed down the slopes, blotting out every blade of grass, every inch of soil, every grain of sand, and still they came, no end to their numbers, spreading south to the Horn, and east to the Bosphorus, surrounding and isolating Pera. Only then, hemmed in by the sea, did they halt their march.

On the balcony of the Palace of Blachernae, as Eirene helped her dress at first light, Zoe watched the ghastly sight with Maria. Hand in hand they stood, hypnotized by the sight, unable to move. Here, before them, unfolded their nightmares of harems, human slavery, and terrors beyond imagining. No one uttered a sound; the chilling silence spoke for them all.

A man's voice reverberated in the horror. From somewhere on the western walls, as dawn faded and the sun rose on a new day, he could be heard calling,

"Everyone to their positions!" Zoe rushed to the balcony. Leaning over the edge, she peered into the distance. Constantine's tall, armored figure was visible on the parapet where the triple wall met the single of Blachernae, his purple cloak fluttering in the wind. She could feel his tension even across the distance. Clarions blared his command, and the order echoed back from all directions. Taking up arms, men leapt into action and jumped over obstacles, scrambling to obey their emperor

On the third day of April, cries from the garrison on the land walls alerted the city to the enemy's arrival on the western front. As church bells clanged wildly sounding frantic alarms, stampeding hoofs carried the message throughout the city. The warm spring air rang with clamor and the urgent prayers of monks. Youths climbed the high places to gain a better view of the enemy troops, even church domes, but fell silent when they saw the great clouds of dust kicked up on the horizon by the line of Mehmet's endless army. In the streets, sobbing women clutched their babes in their arms and hastened to the churches to plead for the Virgin's help, accompanied by old men and small children.

Zoe rushed out of the hospital tent where she had been conferring with Barbaro and his helper, Daniel Navarro. Prince Orhan had done them a service by recommending Navarro to her. He was so well schooled in the healing arts that he could handle most of Barbaro's own responsibilities except surgery. Surrounded by a throng of horsemen both Greek and Genoese, Constantine and Justiniani sat on their mounts by the Gate of Charisius, Constantine on Athena, his brown mare with the white hooves, and Justiniani on an enormous black stallion that snorted and pawed the ground restlessly, eager to be off. Unlike the fine-boned, elegant Greek war-horses, Justiniani's beast was huge, larger than any Zoe had ever seen, and he had difficulty restraining him as he conversed with Constantine. Zoe pushed to the front of the crowd beside Maria, who was already there.

"—and don't take any chances," Constantine was saying. "Station the clarions two hundred feet apart and heed my signals. I will direct you from the tower. And for God's sake, retreat when I give the order! We can't afford to lose a single man."

"I'll be in and out in no time," Justiniani grinned. He was about to close his visor when he spied Zoe. He trotted over to her. "Fair lady, it is the custom in our land, when a knight goes jousting, to take with him a token from a lady for luck in the melee. I wish to beg one from you." He lowered his sword.

Her face aflame, Zoe stared at the steel glittering before her. While touched to the quick by Justiniani's light-hearted pretense that giving battle was akin to jousting, she was aware of the eyes on her, especially Maria's. From the proud Greek youths sitting their mounts came tittering and lecherous smiles, for it was evident to them that Justiniani had not heard the gossip that Zoe was the emperor's whore, and they found the spectacle amusing.

"What is the matter, fair damsel? Are jousts unknown here?" Justiniani teased when she made no move to give him a gage.

Recovering her composure, she lifted her chin. "I am familiar with jousts. Emperor Emmanuel Comnenus held them in the Hippodrome before your ancestors looted it."

Justiniani's smile vanished. The hurt in his eyes was more than Zoe could bear as he moved to sheathe his sword. It wasn't his fault; he couldn't know of her secret marriage.

Constantine trotted his horse to them. "Noble Justiniani," he said, reprimanding Zoe with a look. "The *Zoste Patricia* meant no offense. She would be delighted to give you a token and wishes you safe return."

Justiniani hesitated before offering his sword again, but this time Zoe gave him a green ribbon from her hair. He closed his visor and turned his reins. Men pushed open the Gate of Charisius. Spurring his horse, he galloped out the gate and across the bridge, his men thundering after him.

Justiniani's sortie against the enemy was a great success. He killed several of the enemy and wounded many others without losing a single man. As more and more of the Ottoman troops appeared, however, Constantine sounded the retreat. As soon as Justiniani and his men were safe inside, he ordered the bridges over the moat destroyed along the length of the land walls and locked the gates of the city. The distant marching of Mehmet's great army grew to a loud, dull roar, and the sounds of men, horses, and oxen pulling creaking wagons filled the spring air with a hideous cacophony of noise from all directions. Constantine and Justiniani watched for a while, and then left for the Gate of Eugenius at the mouth of the Golden Horn.

"Time to stretch the boom across the harbor," Constantine said, his eyes scanning the northern slope around Pera that teemed with Mehmet's turbaned soldiers, horses, tents, mules, and carts bearing supplies for war.

"Johannes Grant—" Justiniani called, summoning his best engineer. A red-haired man pushed forward out of the crowd at the gate. "Is the boom ready?" Justiniani demanded.

"Aye, my lord. Our end is already secured. We have only to attach the other to the Tower of Christ in Pera."

"How will you support it across the water?" Constantine demanded.

"On logs, Majesty."

"How long will it take?"

"Not long. The logs are already secured to the boom."

"Make haste, then."

Soon men were in boats, draping the heavy chain across the mouth of the Horn. As Constantine and Justiniani strode across the rocky beach back to the gate, Constantine said in a low voice, "About the *Kerkoporta*—who knows of it?"

"The secret gate?" Justiniani considered for a moment. "You, Lady Zoe, me, and my man, the Scotsman, Johannes Grant. And, of course, the old fellow who showed it to me."

"Swear them to secrecy. Place a guard on the tower above. Make sure that at least one man watches the gate at all times."

"You're that concerned?"

"Spies roost in Pera and gold buys many ears," Constantine said, throwing a glance behind him as they passed through the gate back into the city. "The walls have been penetrated before through treachery. The gate is vulnerable."

"We are Christians, defending our faith," Justiniani muttered. "Yet our own intrigue against us."

With a taut nod, Constantine placed a foot in his stirrup and mounted his horse. It was Christian trade and Christian talent that had enabled the invaders to amass the might they now dedicated to destroying Christian civilization. "I go to check on Trevisano's position on the Horn. Where are you headed?"

"To Charisius. I wish to see how Mehmet deploys his army—though I suspect I already know. He is no fool."

"And that," Constantine replied, turning his horse, "is our misfortune."

The wind in his face, Justiniani stood on the ramparts, gazing over the enemy. He hadn't been completely truthful with Constantine. Yes, he came to assess the foe, but he also came to be alone. He was a man in love and in turmoil. Well he knew what they said about Zoe: that she was the emperor's whore. But he didn't believe it, and even if she was, he didn't care. All that mattered was how she felt about him. Surely, she knew he loved her. Surely, she loved him back. He saw it in her eyes when she looked at him. He couldn't be wrong about something like that. The episode before the sortie was a miscalculation on his part. He should never have put her in that position. It made a spectacle of her, and she'd had no choice but to react as she did. Constantine had been gallant in coming to their rescue, but then, Constantine was nothing if not gallant. He admired Constantine. He'd lay down his life for him, if it came to that, and he knew Constantine would do the same for him. He was the finest of men, the noblest of emperors. But that was the point. He was emperor.

Even if he loved Zoe, he couldn't give her a future. He had to marry for an alliance. When the war was over, that is what he'd do. Then Zoe would be free to wed him. He'd take her to Lemnon. There, they'd rule as man and wife and laugh in the sunshine, and make love beneath starry skies, and have a brood of little ones to run through the palace halls. Meanwhile, he had to be circumspect and do nothing that might cast aspersion on her. He must not push her for a commitment. It was not the time. Not until the war was over could they speak of their love.

Zoe left the hospital tent, crossed the circle of green in front, and made her way up the tower steps of the Gate of Charisius. Thankfully, there had been no deaths and no wounded among the soldiers from the sortie. Golden twilight was descending, church bells were ringing, and the chanting of monks was lifting the melancholy of the heavy day. *We carry the symbols of victory and cry out to you, the Victor over Death,* they sang, *Hosanna in the highest.* But the din of battle would soon drown all beauty, and Zoe felt the need to climb as high as she could and reach as close as possible to God.

When she came to the top of the tower stairs, she drew up sharply, surprised to find Justiniani on the ramparts. He stood alone by the tower, deep in thought, resting a foot on a step and gazing down on the enemy massing before the walls. In the dying rays of the sun, his hair shone like gold and his breastplate glinted so that he seemed bathed in light. She halted, uncertain whether to retreat or to continue, the memory of their confrontation fresh in her mind. As she debated with herself, he turned and saw her. "Come—" he said with a wan smile. "I only bite foes, not friends."

He looked suddenly very boyish with his tawny hair stirring in the breeze. And vulnerable. Zoe was taken aback at just how vulnerable. She returned his smile and drew to his side. Clearly, he was not a man who held grudges. Together they stood looking down on the enemy, who now covered all the territory west to the horizon, and south to the Marmara, and north to the Golden Horn. All at once, the chant of Christian prayer rose from the enemy camp.

"Christians?" Zoe exclaimed, taken aback.

"Yes. Mehmet's European divisions. Christian families must give up a son, if asked. It's a tax they pay in return for the grant of their lives and the right to practice their faith."

Zoe returned her gaze to the Christians forced to fight for Islam. It was too vile, too terrible, too abhorrent. "And we must kill them?"

"Yes. Before they kill us."

At the expression on Zoe's face, Justiniani said gently, "Such is war, Lady Zoe."

Silence.

"But not all Mehmet's Christians are unwilling," Justiniani went on. "See there, behind the European divisions—"

Zoe followed the direction he indicated.

"Those are his irregulars, the *Bashi-Bazouks,* a rough bunch of men with little training who come from all over the world to offer their arms for Mehmet's money and the chance to win booty. There are plenty of Christians among them."

Zoe's stomach churned. She rested a hand on the wall to steady herself.

Justiniani turned to the southern part of the Lycus Valley where it led down to the Marmara. "And down there, from the Golden Gate south to the Marble Tower, are more *Bashi-bazouks.* These come from Anatolia and are under the command of another Christian traitor, Mehmet's friend, Mahmud Pasha. He's a half-Greek half-Slav renegade from the old imperial family of the Angeli that failed to wrest the throne from Emperor Constantine's line... And see those strange white hats directly ahead of us? They are the famed

Janissaries. Christian children who are taken from their mothers at a young age and raised as Muslims. They are the sultan's crack troops."

The ones in Constantine's nightmares. Zoe swallowed the despair in her throat.

"His best guns will be positioned there," Justiniani went on. "Can you see Mehmet's tent?"

She squinted into the setting sun. She had trouble making it out at first, but then the sheen of red and gold silk caught the rays of the sun and glinted a quarter mile away, behind the Janissaries.

"I see it, directly across from the Gate of St. Romanus where—" She broke off.

"Yes, where the emperor will fight." His eyes pierced the distance between them. "He cares for you, doesn't he?"

She didn't reply because she didn't know what to say. But Justiniani took her silence for assent and was comforted. *It is as I thought.*

From the enemy divisions to the south the muezzin's call to prayer shrilled on the gentle twilight and was picked up by an answering chorus of male voices. *Allah Akbar,* they chanted, *Allah Akbar... Bismillah Al-Rahman Al-Rahim...*

"God is great. Let us praise Him," Justiniani translated. "In the name of God, the All-powerful and All-merciful—" He looked at her, a brooding expression in his olive eyes, his tawny hair whipping in the wind. "All prayers begin the same way. It's how they end that's the problem." He looked away.

"How do they end?"

"Kill the infidel."

Zoe stared at his strong profile, framed against the sky. The skin bronzed by sun, pulled taut over the elegant ridge of cheekbone; the generous mouth, the jaw set with determination; the carved line of forehead and nose as smooth as a marble statue. He presented a charming, light-hearted front to the world, but behind the façade was a man of deep sensibility. Where others sold their soul for a piece of gold, he had, at great personal expense, brought men and ships to Christ's city in its darkest hour. Where they fled from danger, he had, at great personal risk, come heedless of danger, prepared to brave the evils of war and share the terrors of defeat. Knowing full well he might never return to his land, yet he had answered the call. This man she had tried with every fiber of her being to disdain.

Zoe tore her eyes from his face.

Twenty-Four

Standing atop the innermost land wall of his western defenses, Constantine scanned the vast army of his enemy. The invaders covered the landscape in all directions, across the valley, over the hills as far as the eye could see, and beyond where the eye could not follow. A warm wind blew, and the morning held promise of fair weather. Below the walls where his yellow and black pennants of the Double-Headed Eagle of Rome flew in the wind, Mehmet's men labored to put up tents, dig ditches, build earthen ramparts for themselves, and fill the moat that protected the western land walls of Constantinople.

The sun passed behind a cloud and the scene before him fell into shadow. He thought of Mehmet and the shadow he cast over them that differed little from a raging pestilence. For here, at his feet, toiled the rancid sores of that pestilence, each striving in his own way to drive the infection into the marrow, the aim to threaten the corpus and still the beating of the heart. Beneath his velvet sleeves, his shoulders sagged and hope waned.

Justiniani came to his side. Softly, he said, "Where is he, and what does he wait for?"

"Our spies say Mehmet is waiting for Urban's gun," Constantine replied quietly, his gaze on the Anatolian troops led by Mehmet's bosom companion, Mahmud Pasha, a half-Greek renegade. Another Christian traitor, like Urban.

"Cannons didn't help them last time," Justiniani offered.

"Last time they were not half the size."

Justiniani gave him a measured look. Under his breath, he said, "What do you really think of our chances?"

Constantine tensed. Everyone looked to him for answers. He was God's anointed, after all, the shepherd of his people. When he was young, before the Hexamilion, he had thought the world was his to conquer. After the Hexamilion, he believed he could mold it to his desires with what he'd learned from defeat. Now all he had were doubts he hid behind a front of confidence. Neither George nor Lucas, his closest friends, knew the depth of his concern. He would hide it even from Zoe if he could, but she bore witness to his ghastly dreams of marching boots and Janissaries. Her words beat in his mind: *If you don't believe in yourself, how can others believe in you?*

Be that as it may, he owed Justiniani the truth. Justiniani had become his bosom companion, his right hand, the one who shared his every burden. With every breath he labored to save a city not his own and did not spare himself for an instant. Here on these walls, they would fight together, and maybe die together. He rested a hand on Justiniani's shoulder.

"Before you came, I felt the odds we faced were impossible and there was no way we would last a week against their might. Now, thanks to you, that has changed. If we can hold out until the Venetian fleet arrives, we will win this war."

"Did your spies tell you where Mehmet is?" Justiniani asked.

"He occupies himself by attacking our outposts, Therapia on the Bosphorus and Studion on the Marmara."

"They're small garrisons. They have no chance against his army."

"But they will never surrender. I know these men." Brave and fiercely independent, they would fight to the death to protect their homeland and freedom. But even as he spoke, something changed in the scene before him. The enemy filling the moat and others who were building an earthen rampart nearby ceased their work to watch a troop of men approach. Words were exchanged, and the ditch-fillers melted away. The troop of men drew closer to the walls and halted just beyond the reach of arrows. Constantine felt unease ripple through him. Something was very wrong.

A clatter drew his attention behind him. He turned to see Lucas taking the tower steps two at a time. The expression on his face stirred his worst fears.

"Studion and Therapia have fallen!" Lucas panted, ashen pale. "The defenders fought fiercely, but seventy-six men were captured. The enemy has brought them here."

Constantine' s gaze went to the manacled prisoners the enemy was dragging forth and moved to the stakes being readied. Realization struck, and a wave of horror sent him reeling. These men were going to suffer Captain Rizzo's fate. His breath caught in his throat, and he was aware of a sensation of ice at the pit of his stomach. He turned to Justiniani, hoping he' d say it wasn't so, but the Genoese hero was as pale as a phantom. Constantine knew his pallor mirrored his own.

As if to quell all doubt and all hope, in one body the enemy emitted a rhythmic chant and shook their fists at the defenses, crying, "*Death to Rome! Death to Rome!*"

Constantine bit down on the bile that flooded him and reached out to the stone parapet for support. "Fetch Cardinal Isidore! Summon every priest in the city! Ring the church bells—" Men ran down the stairs, scrambling to obey.

There was nothing more to be done. Nothing but prayer and monk song. He forced a deep breath against the tightness in his chest and passed a trembling hand to his dizzy head. "May God have mercy on their souls," he murmured through white lips.

Shaking with wrath, sickened to the pit of his stomach by the savagery he'd witnessed, Constantine ordered the enemy soldiers held in the Anemas prison to be brought up and executed in retribution for the impalement of his subjects before the city walls.

"Majesty! Is it true?" Justiniani demanded, pushing through the crowd of men around Constantine with Cardinal Isidore at his side. "Do you plan to execute our captives?"

"Yes."

"Majesty, I beg you to reconsider!" Justiniani said.

"Why?" Constantine shouted. "For what reason on God's earth should they be spared?"

But it was Prince Orhan, not Justiniani, who responded, "Emperor of the Christians, I beg mercy! Forgive the great wrong done in the name of *Allah*—killing is all Mehmet understands! The captives are innocent and have committed no crime—"

"They are the enemy. That is their sin," Constantine hissed through clenched teeth.

"We all want revenge," Lucas said quietly. "But this is not the time, Augustus."

Justiniani leaned close. In a low tone he said, "Once we embark on that road, there is no going back. Our position is akin to a man with a broken sword waving a red banner before a bull. I beg you to keep our options open—at least for the present, Majesty."

Constantine regarded him a long moment. Only Justiniani gave him the benefit of advice untainted by self-interest… As his mother once had. The fire seeped out of him, and his shoulders sagged. He shut his eyes and nodded.

The following day, from atop the walls at the Gate of St. Romanus, Constantine watched a party of turbaned Turks approach under a white flag of truce, their horses' hoofs kicking up a cloud of dust as they galloped.

Mehmet had arrived the previous day and Urban's gun with him. With a team of sixty oxen drawing the enormous cannon and many a shout and cry, the enemy had finally positioned it to Mehmet's liking. Now it pointed directly at one of the two most vulnerable sections of the land walls. Justiniani's position on the Gate of Charisius.

The party of Ottomans reached the foot of the walls. Constantine waited.

"In accordance with the laws of Islam, we bring you an offer at the behest of mighty Sultan Mehmet, God's Shadow on Earth!" the leader cried. "As the Qu'ran commands, he will spare you and your city, harming neither the inhabitants of New Rome, nor their belongings, if you voluntarily surrender. Otherwise, you will be shown no mercy, just as they were shown none yesterday before your walls!"

"Hear ye—" Constantine called down. "We Romans live as free men, ruled by council. We do not answer to one man. To surrender the city to you is beyond my authority. We reject your offer. We fight to the death for our freedom!"

"Brave words from those about to die!" the Turk shouted back, turning his horse.

Constantine watched the small party gallop away, their long robes billowing behind them in the dusty wind.

"Everyone to their positions!" he shouted.

Men leapt into action. Seizing javelins, bows, arrows, swords, shields and battle-axes, Justiniani and Constantine's other military commanders, Lucas and Trevisano, his admiral Diedo and his cousins Theo and Demetri, left for their command stations. As Johannes Grant turned to follow them down the tower steps, Constantine called out to him.

"Majesty?" the red-haired Scotsman said, striding up.

"The terrain here is soft. They will try to tunnel under the walls. I want you in charge of ensuring they fail. What do you need?"

"A few dishes, some water. And boys to sit and watch," Grant said.

"Boys?"

"To watch for ripples in the bowls of water we place around the walls. Tunneling operations can always be detected by the movement of water," Grant explained.

Constantine gave him a tight smile. "I am pleased you do not need men."

Grant turned to leave when a thunderous roar crackled through the air, setting the ground aquiver and sending a flock of birds clattering from the walls. A flash of fire in the Ottoman camp accompanied by black smoke and the vile smell of sulfur announced the monstrous iron ball pummeling toward them from Urban's cannon. Everyone took cover. Moments later, from the direction of the Charisian Gate, came the shouts of men. The gun had hit its first target.

It has begun, thought Constantine.

"Where did it strike?" Constantine shouted. "Down there, on the battlements," someone yelled. Constantine peered over the wall. "Where?"

Justiniani's voice came from along the parapet. "Ten meters south of you—near the Gate of St. Romanus," he called, hastening to his side. "They've taken out a whole section of wall. We have to erect a stockade!"

Now Constantine saw the damage. His heart sank. He had hoped to lessen the impact of the gun by hanging sheets of leather and bales of wool over the walls, to no avail. The ball had struck the wall, crumbling the masonry into a thousand pieces. "That is dangerous work. The men will be exposed to the enemy."

"We'll keep torches to the minimum and hope the enemy doesn't attack. But we have no choice."

After nightfall the defenders went to work mixing lime and sand. The area was congested with mules drawing carts laden with the trunks of the trees felled before the siege began. Working hastily and quietly in the darkness, women and children cleared the rubble while men dug holes. Placing tree trunks close together, they piled earth around the base and secured them into place. Stone masons standing on planks of wood held by ropes were lowered down on the walls to repair the damage to the battlements too high to reach from below, and others went outside to fix those at ground level.

"You have made great progress," Constantine called down to Navarro, who was overseeing the work. He had turned out to be almost as great a blessing on them as Justiniani himself. He had vast knowledge of ships, medicines, and building repairs. There seemed to be nothing he couldn't do. Navarro threw him a smile. "We will have the job completed by morning, Sire!" he called up, slapping mortar on the masonry.

Phrantzes said, "At least Mehmet didn't follow up with an attack."

So that is his strategy, Constantine thought with sudden realization. Bombard the wall by day. Wear us out with repairs by night. And then, when we're exhausted, strike. "No one is going to last long if they work by night and fight by day," he said. "These men need rest. From now on, priests will do the non-military tasks,"

"You're right," Phrantzes sighed. "I'll get the order out."

Constantine placed a hand on Phrantzes's shoulder. "I am going to get some sleep. You should do the same."

In the royal bath, Zoe massaged Constantine's back as he sat in the shallow Roman pool of blue mosaics. "Your muscles are tight," she said, rubbing tenderly. "This should help you sleep, Constans."

"Knowing we survived our first day with no deaths or injuries will help me sleep," he said softly.

As dawn broke on the twelfth of April, fighting men were in position again. But where walls no longer stood ran a long stockade set with huge barrels of earth that served as crenellations. At Blachernae, Constantine was donning his armor when Lucas appeared.

"Augustus, the ships Mehmet was awaiting from the Black Sea have arrived! His admiral, Baltoglu, is going to try to break through the chain."

Constantine hastened to the balcony. A quick glance revealed Baltoglu leading several large galleys to the Golden Horn. Constantine grabbed his sword and dashed off with Lucas.

In the Palace of Botaneiates where she'd gone to minister to the street dwellers and refugees, Zoe heard the clarions, drums, and trilling cries of the infidels. She went outside to see what was happening and glimpsed the black sails of the enemy approaching the mouth of the Golden Horn. She ran back and gathered everyone into the little chapel she had refurbished. Kneeling before an icon of the Virgin and Child, she led her flock in prayer for their homeland.

On the ramparts of the Tower of Eugenius overlooking the Golden Horn, Constantine was sheltering from the rain when Baltoglu appeared on the Bosphorus leading an armada around the landmass of Pera into the Horn. From north to south and east to west, the Ottoman ships devoured the blue waters of the Bosphorus and the Marmara with their black sails and red pennants. Closer in, Christian galleons and warships watched them warily as they guarded the chain.

Constantine sneezed. Someone handed him a handkerchief. He had caught a chill and was feverish, but he dared not let anyone suspect for fear the knowledge might unsettle them. Glancing to his left, he caught sight of Gabriel Trevisano's tall figure hastening to him along the parapet, his dark hair blowing in the wind. The Venetian captain guarded a position on the Golden Horn midway between Lucas on the far west corner and Constantine's newly appointed admiral, Alviso Diedo, at the mouth of the Horn. If the enemy broke through the boom, he would be in the thick of the fighting.

Constantine's gaze locked on Baltoglu's ships approaching the chain. He sneezed again.

Trevisano drew alongside. "Majesty, are you unwell?" he asked in concern

"It is nothing."

A hail of flaming arrows whined through the air, speeding toward the Christian ships. The Ottoman guns fired their cannonballs and hurled fire brands onto the galleons. Smaller vessels drew close and tried to cut their anchor ropes while others threw grappling hooks and attempted to board with ladders. The arrows ignited a few fires, but the cannonballs were too low to harm the much larger Christian ships and their hooks fell short. As a result, the enemy ladders were easily dislodged, hurling their occupants into the sea

"Grand Duke Lucas has done a splendid job of organizing the defense," Trevisano said, allowing himself a smile as he watched men on the beach below pass pails of water in relays that speedily put out the fires the enemy attempted to set.

"And God helps us with the rain," Constantine added.

The Christian ships aimed their javelins at the enemy and let loose their arrows. Fired from the greater height of their decks and crows' nests, they proved effective. Many enemy sailors fell to their deaths, their screams reverberating in the air. Now the Christian sailors followed up with stone-throwing machines and Greek Fire shot from their crossbows, rejoicing in the terror they unleashed as their flaming arrows hissed through the air. One after another, Ottoman ships burst into flames.

"Lower the chain—lower the chain!" Diedo cried, his voice faint in the distance.

Constantine grinned, buoyed to see him go after the Ottoman ships. The command was passed along until it reached the men controlling the chain in the Tower of Eugenius. A massive creaking and clanging of metal on metal filled the air as they turned the winch. The chain dropped and the Christian fleet moved out to attack the Ottoman ships.

Anticipating the disaster about to befall his fleet, Baltoglu sounded an immediate retreat. The Ottoman ships turned their sails and sped for the safety of the Port of Pillars near the Throatcutter. Constantine exhaled in relief. Only then did he realize he had been holding his breath. The battle was over. The enemy had been repelled.

They had won the sea battle against the mighty, invincible Ottomans! So stunning was the knowledge that for an instant there was utter silence, and no one moved. Then all at once men cheered, embraced their comrades, and fell to their knees, jubilant faces upturned to heaven.

Constantine gripped the parapet and bowed his head. *Se charisto, Theé mou,* he murmured. I thank Thee, my God.

The rain proved a double blessing for the people of Constantinople, for it hampered the firing of Urban's cannon, which had not rested day or night. Now the defenders on the land walls enjoyed a brief respite and could repair the defenses without fearing for their lives.

After sunset, when the rising wind drove out the rain clouds, there was celebration in the Queen of Cities. The streets, taverns, palaces, and dwellings filled with music, dancing and merry making such as had not been seen in months. Fires were lit in the fields, and the smell of meat roasting on the spit wafted in the air. Monks chanted hymns, church bells rang, and old men sat beneath trees budding with greenery, smiling and sipping wine.

At dusk, after a small private banquet, Constantine strolled with Zoe in the palace garden near the Blachernae wall, followed by his ever-present Captain of the Guard John Dalmata and his Varangians.

"How good it is to see my people rejoice," Constantine said as the sounds of joyous celebration drifted over the palace walls. He mopped his face with his handkerchief.

Zoe was about to check his brow when her father appeared, striding toward them out of the torchlight. "Augustus," he bowed. "We are informed by our spies in Pera that Urban is recalculating the aim of the sultan's cannons to make them more effective against our tall ships."

Constantine cursed the Hungarian. Without that one Christian Mehmet would never have posed the threat he had become, even with his army of a hundred and fifty thousand men. "God take his soul," he muttered bitterly.

Though Constantine had uttered the words in anger, Lucas rubbed his chin thoughtfully. "Send him to his Maker… Excellent idea, Augustus. It can be arranged… expensive, but not too difficult." He looked up. "Whatever it takes to buy us time, we must do."

Constantine rested a hand on his shoulder. "Yes, time… Time for the Venetian fleet to arrive. Once it is here, our problems will be over."

No Venetian fleet came, this week or the next. The victory bought them exactly six days. On the eighteenth of April, in the fullness of the spring sunshine, Constantine and his men watched from Eugenius as a cannon with a higher trajectory was placed just beyond Pera Point. Soon it began firing at the ships anchored along the boom. Most of the shots fell short, sending up fountains of water as they dropped into the sea, eliciting cheers from the defenders. Then, all at once, a speeding cannonball came hissing across the distance. Like a serpent sighting prey, it struck a direct hit at the heart of a Christian galley. A thunderous roar shattered the calm, and shouts of joy went up from the enemy on the shores of Pera.

Aboard the Christian ships there was bedlam. Screams rent the air as the doomed galley heeled to her starboard side. Water rushed through the gaping hole. Equipment and men were swept overboard. The mast snapped with a hideous groan and slammed into the deck, crushing the people beneath and impeding escape. Slowly the ship sank. Men flailed as the wreck took on water. The sea filled with bodies floating face down.

Diedo's clarions sounded the alarm. "Pull back—pull back to shelter!" he ordered his ships, and they withdrew out of range of the sultan's guns behind the curved land mass of Galata. A messenger came running up to Constantine. He saluted quickly, a fist to the chest. "There is considerable loss of life, Augustus! There were fifty men aboard when the cannonball struck."

Constantine felt suddenly hot. His head swam. Mopping his fevered brow, he fought the nausea that churned his stomach. Fifty men— *Fifty!*

"Find out the names of the dead… Send each family… a gold bezant," he managed haltingly. That would ensure they wouldn't starve. At least not yet. Leaning against the tower wall, he turned to Cardinal Isidore. "Your Holiness, see that prayers… are sung for them." The cardinal inclined his head and withdrew. Constantine looked at Justiniani. "He may… launch an attack on… the entire length of wall. Are we ready on… the Mesoteichion?"

"As ready as we can be," Justiniani replied, drawing to his side. "Here," he said, under his breath, "let me give you a hand."

Constantine made his way down the tower stairs with Justiniani's help and paused as another wave of nausea swept him.

On the parapet, Zoe watched them take their leave of one another, Justiniani to vault on his horse and gallop south, and Constantine to struggle on his mount with the help of his Varangians. She sighed inwardly. The strain was telling on him. He'd slept fitfully again last night and was fasting again to win God's favor, but he was a difficult patient, and no one could make him rest or eat if he chose not to. Not even Justiniani, who was the only one he listened to these days.

She made her way down to the hospital tent. Barbaro might have need of her now. This was the first time they had lost men. She knew it would not be the last.

Twenty-Five

Two hours after sunset on the following day Ottoman horns blew, announcing an attack and church bells clanged, summoning the defenders. Constantine was going over final battle plans with Lucas and Trevisano on the walls of St. Romanus when he heard them. A painful spasm bent him double, and he sank down on the parapet.

"Augustus!" Lucas said. "You are not well. You need to leave!"

"I am fine—"

"You're in no condition to fight! Go, I pray you, there is no time to lose—they will charge at any moment!" When Constantine refused to listen, Lucas sent for Justiniani.

"Should an arrow claim your life, the city will fall," Justiniani said, appealing to his sense of duty. Constantine, seeing the wisdom of this, left for his quarter.

No sooner was he gone than enemy drums and clashing cymbals sounded. They charged the western land walls. Shrieking *Allah Akbar* and ululating the chilling enemy war-cry, the archers released a hail of flaming arrows, lighting up the night.

The defenders leapt for cover. When it was safe to expose themselves, they returned fire on the enemy javelin throwers and Janissaries who were sweeping over the filled-in ditch up to the stockade along the length of the Mesoteichion, between Justiniani's position on the Charisius Gate and Constantine's on St. Romanus. Setting fire to the wood, they sent up grappling hooks to topple the earthen barrels that protected the Christian soldiers and placed ladders against the parts of the wall that still stood. Some managed to get over the first wall, but the narrow terrain between the outer and middle wall where the fighting took place meant the enemy's superiority in number did not help them.

Thrusting off the scaling ladders with long poles as soon as they were raised, Justiniani's men poured ladles of seething pitch on the attackers and hurled Greek Fire with their crossbows. Blinded, screaming, enemy soldiers fell to their deaths. Risking themselves boldly, Justiniani and his defenders fought them back inch by inch by the light of the torches. All at once distant enemy horns sounded a retreat.

Zoe, who had been on duty at the hospital all night and was holding water to the lips of a wounded man, put down the cup and ran outside. She found Navarro coming down the tower stairs. He collapsed on a step. She ran to his side. "Are you wounded?"

He shook his head. Taking out a scarf, he wiped his brow.

"I heard the horns! Did we beat them back?"

Navarro nodded assent.

"Then why are our clarions not announcing victory?" She looked up at the empty ramparts in confusion.

"No one has breath …" he said haltingly. "We have… been fighting … four hours."

"How many wounded? We must help them—"

"Need sleep…not…potions." He laid his head against the wall and closed his eyes.

"Navarro, is Justiniani all right?"

No answer. He was already asleep. Zoe hurried up the stairs, followed closely by a press of women, children and priests who had been listening to the exchange. As she stood at the top seeking Justiniani, they rushed past her to their loved ones. Cries of joy went up as they beheld their sons, husbands, fathers, and brothers, alive and well.

Now Zoe understood. Men had collapsed where they had fought. Some sat with their heads dropped on their chests in utter exhaustion; others lay propped against the walls, eyes closed, barely sitting up. When she asked for Justiniani, she was met with a shake of the head, or a finger raised with difficulty to point farther along. She finally found him near a tower midway along the Mesoteichion. He had removed his helmet and lay on his back on the stone parapet, sound asleep in his armor. Untying her lavender scarf from around her hips, she folded it into a square and knelt beside him.

Gently, very gently, she slipped it under his head with a tender touch.

Zoe gazed into the darkness. Soon it would be dawn. Waves broke on the rocks with a dull roar, and the wind stirred, laden with the tang of the sea. On the hillside opposite, the enemy campfires had burned out and were now surrendering their last glinting embers to the night. She glanced at Constantine, bundled up against the cold as he reclined in a chaise longue with his feet up. He had slept through the battle, but not through the boisterous celebrations that followed the victory at midnight.

"Not one Christian killed," he'd beamed as the noise of revelry filled the night. He had spoken slowly, as if to savor each word. She'd pressed the small clay cup with its thick black liquid against his lips. "And two hundred enemy dead. That is cause for joy, beloved. Now take your potion—no more excuses."

"Vile," he'd complained, making a face as he swallowed the concoction. He'd slept soundly afterwards and awakened in the darkness before dawn, when at his insistence, they had come out to the balcony.

Throwing aside his blankets, Constantine rose from his chair and went to the balustrade. Resting his weight on the stone, he inhaled a long, deep breath and listened to the cadence of the sea. So magnificent, he thought. At this hour, before the break of day exposed the enemy to view, he could pretend all was well with the world.

Behind the hills of Pera, a faint glimmer of light streaked the sky. Another uncertain day was dawning. No one except God knew what it held, but each new sunrise represented a victory to him. The failure of Mehmet's first assault on the walls coming so soon after the failure of his attack at sea filled him with hope. *If we can just hold until the Venetian fleet arrives, we will survive this…*

"You love the dawn," Zoe said softly, coming to his side.

He smiled and drew her close. "It is my favorite time of day because it reminds me of you… See, here it comes—rose, fiery orange, violet. These are your colors, painting all the world with beauty and peace."

She leaned her head against his shoulder. It felt good to have the old Constantine back. *Victory cures all ills*, she thought. *May God send more victories.*

The news cheered Constantine so much that he felt strong enough to pay Justiniani a visit later that morning after confession. Zoe found him donning his armor by the time she'd organized her own departure for the hospital.

"You cannot go to the walls yet," she exclaimed. "You had a raging fever yesterday. It is too soon. The doctor from the university said so."

"I cannot lie in bed like a child while others fight to defend my city," he protested, accepting his sword from Aesop and strapping it on. Zoe knew there was no dissuading him.

Surrounded by his Varangian Guard, Constantine mounted the tower steps up to Justiniani's position at the Charisian Gate, followed by Zoe with a troop of servants carrying baskets of food for the defenders. The men on the walls watched Constantine arrive with a cordiality tinged with awe.

"*Kalimera*, Augustus," said a Greek. "Good morn to you."

"Good morning. Keep up the good work," Constantine responded.

"Good morn, Imperial Majesty. Glad you're feeling better," said an Italian.

"My thanks to you. Splendid job yesterday."

Ignoring the hideous vultures circling the walls and the smell of burning flesh from Ottoman funeral pyres, Zoe and the servants trailed Constantine along the parapet, handing out bread and wine to the men.

"A fine morning!" Constantine suddenly exclaimed.

Zoe looked up to find him greeting Justiniani, whose back was turned to them, Maria at his side, pouring from a jug of wine. "Did you sleep well after your victory?" Constantine demanded, beaming.

Justiniani turned around. "Far better than I ever expected," he grinned back. His gaze went to Zoe and lingered on her face.

Zoe blushed and looked away, but her glance sweeping the parapet caught on a length of crumpled lavender silk resting on a stone ledge. Weighted down by a helmet, the edges fluttered in the wind. Her breath caught in her throat. She moved to block the sight, but Maria's eyes had followed her gaze.

"Is that your scarf, Zoe?" she demanded, her tone deliberate and as cold as ice water.

Zoe looked down at her hips, feeling herself turn as red as poppies under Maria's gaze. "I couldn't find it this morning—I must have left it somewhere—"

In two long strides Justiniani retrieved both his helmet and her scarf. "Then this must be yours, my lady. You likely dropped it on the ramparts when you were aiding the wounded last night," he said, giving her cover. He handed the scarf back to her with a courtly bow.

Zoe managed to murmur her thanks. When she looked up, Constantine was regarding her with a strange expression. She had no chance to dwell on it for a sudden thunderous *boom!* shook the parapet. Urban's gun was firing again. Everyone sought cover. Constantine took shelter behind the wall and pulled her down with him.

The shot fell short.

"His gun is aiming at St. Romanus," Constantine noted in surprise as he drew himself erect. "Not at the Charisian Gate."

"Mehmet moved it this morning. Fifty pair of oxen and hundreds of men dragged it to where it should have been in the first place," Justiniani offered with a wry smile.

"Opposite me," Constantine said.

"Indeed, Majesty, but on the bright side, Urban's gun is so unwieldy it can only fire every three hours," Justiniani grinned. "Surely you are a most fortunate emperor."

Justiniani couldn't know the irony of his words. Constantine's smile vanished. Zoe bit her lip. The first Constantine had been called "the Fortunate" for winning a battle he should have lost and founding a city that became the refuge of the Christian world. But even before the eleventh Constantine took the crown, he was nicknamed "the Unfortunate" for the tragic deaths of his two young brides and the defeat at the Hexamilion Wall. Now it fell to him to disprove the ancient prophecy that hung like a noose around his neck.

"If fortune favors me," Constantine replied, "the Venetian fleet will arrive soon, and we will win this war."

The sound of hoofbeats and shouts of men drew their attention to John Dalmata striding up to Constantine with all urgency. "A messenger, Majesty!" The Varangians stepped aside, and a man appeared on the tower steps. He hastened to Constantine and saluted with a fist thump. "Augustus, Admiral Diedo wishes to inform you that ships have been sighted on the Sea of Marmara! They approach from the direction of the Dardanelles!"

Joy exploded in Constantine's breast. From the direction of the Dardanelles into the Sea of Marmara would come the Venetian fleet! *The Holy Mother be thanked!*

"What are we waiting for?" he said joyously. "Let us give them welcome!"

Flanked by Lucas and Justiniani on one side and Phrantzes, Prince Orhan, and his royal relative Don Francisco de Toledo on the other, Constantine stood on the Marmara sea wall, peering into the distance as Zoe claimed a place next to the Spaniard. With broad smiles they surveyed the progress of the few scattered specks on the horizon that represented the approaching Christian fleet. It was a beautiful April day. A fair wind blew and the sea, though choppy, shimmered like crushed aquamarines. Sea birds swooped and dove for fish, squawking fiercely, and servants passed around wine and *apotki* in celebration of the arrival of the Venetian fleet. Except for the usual smattering of Ottoman vessels standing watch near the Golden Horn, there was no sign of the enemy.

"Where is Mehmet?" someone asked.

"He is probably still snoring," Prince Orhan snickered in response, accepting a cup of pomegranate juice and a grape leaf stuffed with rice and spices.

"I will drink to that!" Francisco de Toledo chuckled, downing his wine.

Too tense to eat, Constantine declined the offer of food and drink from a passing servant. "Can anyone make out the banner they bear?"

Munching on a mouthful of flat bread and chicken, Justiniani took a goblet of sweet spring water from a proffered tray and squinted into the distance. "All I can tell is they may be red and white."

"The winged Lion of St. Mark is red and white!" Don Francisco exclaimed, his deep brown eyes searching the horizon for more ships than the four they counted.

Zoe gazed at him affectionately. He had come to help of his own volition, though all Spanish Castille, Aragon, and Navarre chose to ignore their plight.

Trilling war-cries drew her gaze north.

With a blare of horns and an unnerving drumroll, the Ottoman fleet rounded the bend on the Bosphorus. Zoe froze at the sight that met her eyes. Composed of biremes and triremes with double and triple rows of oars, and the smaller *parandaria*, as well as large transports, the ships kept coming. Fitted with guns and protected with shields and armor, their decks crammed with rowers, archers, and the unmistakable elite troops of Janissaries in their strange white headgear, they poured into the Marmara, shrouding the blue seas in black sails. With shields, helmets, and long lances flashing in the sun and shrieks of *Allah Akbar!* echoing on the wind, the behemoth fleet of at least a hundred ships bore down on the four Christian galleys visible to them.

Zoe choked back her fear and glanced at Don Francisco. "Where is the rest of the fleet?"

"Dear lady, only God knows. *Por el amor de Dios*, wherever they are, they need to make haste!"

Constantine stood grimly, his mouth clamped shut, his gaze fixed. He had the same thought. Why did the Venetian fleet lag so far behind their vanguard? If they didn't make haste—

His chest felt tight, and his head pounded. To release the tension, he accepted a goblet of wine from a servant and glanced behind him at the city. Men, women, and children crowded the hilly slopes and rooftops all the way to the Hagia Sophia. Others had claimed the highest points of the ruined Hippodrome. All eyes were fixed on the four Christian ships. Their numbers meant that every man who could be spared from the defense of the walls had foregone sleep to watch. He turned his gaze back to the Bosphorus shores. The figure of a lone bejeweled man on a black horse flashed in the sun just beyond the walls of Pera. Constantine shielded his eyes and peered into the distance. Mehmet? Clenching his jaw, he tore his gaze away.

The Christian ships were just off the southeasterly corner of the city, their large square sails almost brushing the Marble Tower, and still no fleet was in view. He blinked in confusion. One ship flew his banner of the Eastern Roman Empire, the black double-headed eagle on the yellow background.

Lucas gave voice to Constantine's thought. "But this is the imperial transport you sent to purchase grain and supplies under the command of Captain Phlatanelas. Why is he with the Venetian fleet?"

"Perhaps he joined the advance guard for security?" Demetri offered hopefully.

Constantine stared ahead. The other three galleys bore the pennant of Genoa, the Red Cross of St. George on a white background. There were no Venetians among them. What did it mean?

"Lower your sails!" someone shouted from an enemy ship.

Constantine's eye sought Mehmet's admiral, Baltoglu. The renegade Bulgarian stood aboard a trireme, richly dressed in the robes of a Turk, the long plume in his turban blowing in the wind. Constantine cursed him under his breath. The Christians ignored Baltoglu's command. With the wind in their favor, they continued their course toward the mouth of the Golden Horn. Baltoglu issued another order that was passed along his front line.

As Constantine watched, the leading enemy vessels moved in on the Christians, but the current was against them, and they had trouble maneuvering their triremes and biremes around one another in the crowded waters. They released a volley of arrows, and the Christians returned fire from the decks, crow's nests, towers, poops and prows of their tall ships. Enemy soldiers fell to their death, their screams piercing the soft spring morning. In the ascendancy now, the defenders hurled javelins and dropped stones on their foes from great heights. A monstrous creaking and groaning ripped the air as wood splintered, oars broke, and Ottoman ships cracked apart.

Constantinople's jubilation was met by wild jeering from the shores of the Bosphorus.

Shaking his fist and shouting orders, the bejeweled figure in the distance rode his horse into the water until his robes floated up around him. Now there was no doubt. This was Mehmet. Hatred coursed through Constantine so fiercely, he tasted bile in his mouth.

But Baltoglu didn't seem to notice his furious sultan. Intent on the fight, he issued new orders. Shooting their cannons and throwing fire brands at the Christian galleys, the infidels tried to board with grappling hooks. The air filled with black smoke and a pungent, burnt smell.

Constantine watched anxiously. Undeterred, the four Christian ships sailed on, heading for the safety of the chain, impeded by the enemy, but able to shake them off. They turned to round the point below the Acropolis, and the call rose in the Tower of Eugenius, "Lower the chain! Lower the chain!"

Thanks be to God; they will soon be safe! Constantine thought. Heaving an enormous sigh of relief, he rubbed his neck and looked up at the sun. They had spotted the Christian ships at ten in the morning. Now it was almost one o'clock. Nearly three hours had passed, and still no Venetian fleet had come to back them up. He was exhausted from the anxiety and his throat was dry as tinder. Someone passed him a flask of wine. He took it gratefully. As he drank, a loud gasp went up. Removing the flask from his lips, he looked down at the sea and froze. The wind had dropped. The four Christian ships were trapped in the waters by the Marmara wall where they idled, their sails drooping, unable to move. And the behemoth enemy armada of a hundred strong was closing in.

He glanced over at the Dardanelles. No sign of the Venetians. Nothing!

The monks on the wall fell to their knees and beseeched God for help. In the Tower of Eugenius, the shout went up: Raise the chain! Raise the chain!

Tense, silent, Constantine put out a hand to the parapet to steady himself. The old familiar pain he had felt at the Hexamilion Wall was back, throbbing in his gut. The air hissed with flaming arrows and thundered with the boom of cannon. The cacophony of noise, both sharp and muted at the same time, echoed violently in his head. The memory of the seventy-six men impaled before the walls of Constantinople floated before him. He felt dizzy; he could scarcely breathe. How would he bear it if Mehmet caught these hundreds of brave sailors—

He closed his bleary eyes. He could not watch. It was too easy for Baltoglu to take his prey now.

A short distance along the parapet, Navarro joined Zoe and Prince Orhan. She offered him a smile. There was something about the friendship of these two men that brought her comfort, as if it told her in some strange unspoken way that appearances and birth were of no consequence, that in the end all that mattered was the human heart. Navarro's soft eyes met hers, and there was such a light in them and such compassion that she took his arm. His gentle eyes met hers in understanding, and he patted her hand. Then his glance went to Constantine, and Zoe knew he understood.

Prince Orhan's voice came to her. "May *Allah* save them!"

Zoe returned her gaze to the battle. Even as Orhan spoke, the Christian traitor, Baltoglu, brought his larger oared vessels forward to encircle the galleys and readied his cannon balls and flaming arrows. She understood what was happening, and so did the watching townsfolk. They gave a giant groan. Once disabled, the enemy would board the galleys and that would be the end. From the slopes of Pera and the shores of the Bosphorus, the enemy leapt up and down joyously, ululating and yelling *Allah Akhbar!*

Zoe watched in growing horror. If it wasn't bad enough that their ships were trapped in the open sea, now they were caught in the current drifting north to Pera! O Mother Mary, have mercy on our men, she screamed silently.

But the current, as if powered by Satan himself, bore the Christian ships toward the very spot where Mehmet watched the battle. From the crowds on the Acropolis arose a tumult of prayers and incantations to the Holy Mother, and from the invaders on the north shore of the Bosphorus a deafening trill, as if a thousand tongues cried out in joy with one voice. She shielded her eyes from the sun and searched the distant horizon. No sign of ships from the Dardanelles. Where is the rest of the fleet? How can they be so far behind? A thought struck her with sickening force: What if these Genoese ships were not part of the Venetian fleet? What if no help was on its way, and this was all there was?

She glanced at the sun. Three of the clock. She balled her fists as the din of battle rose to a feverish crescendo with the jarring clash of metal on metal, the beat of drums, the slamming of wooden vessels against one another, the whine of arrows, boom of guns, and the periodic blasts of clarions. The shrieks of dying men reverberated in her head, wrapped in Christian hymns and heathen cries of *Allah Akbar.* The smell of gunpowder, burning wood and human flesh sent her stomach heaving. Grasping the parapet with all her might, she leaned her weight on her hands and bowed her head. Save them, Holy Mother, she intoned, *save them, save them—*

Beside her, she heard Prince Orhan praying in Turkish, and Navarro in Hebrew, and again, she was comforted by the bond between them.

Twenty-Six

Zoe lifted her head. Not daring to look at the ships, she scanned the faces of those around her. Their eyes were lowered to the sea, and strain was evident in their expression. Forcing a breath, she braced herself and followed the direction of their gaze.

Her eyes widened in disbelief. The Christian galleons were still intact! She turned to Don Francisco, jaw agape.

"The Ottoman cannons, they are too low! The shots, they have fallen short!" He grinned. *"Dios esta con nosotros,"* God is with us.

She flashed her gaze on the Christian crews. They were magnificent. Superb. Putting out fires as quickly as the enemy's fiery arrows struck their decks and lit them. But then the renegade Bulgarian admiral called out, "Advance and board!"

What was happening?

Constantine cursed. Baltoglu had targeted the most helpless of the four Christian vessels, the imperial transport. A deafening thud of wood on wood sounded as the faithless traitor ran the bow of his trireme into the poop of the imperial vessel. She was the largest of the Christian ships but only lightly armed, being a merchant transport and not equipped for war. Other Ottoman ships drew alongside and tried to fasten themselves to her with grappling irons and hooks flung onto her anchor chains. But the imperial transport, though less prepared for the fight, carried barrels of Greek Fire, the inflammable incendiary device that had saved Constantinople in many a sea battle over the last thousand years. As flaming arrows whistled overhead, her men fought to put out the fires and worked feverishly at the prow to loosen a brass canister in the shape of a lion's mouth. At last, their efforts met with success. Liquid poured out, igniting as it hit the water.

"Greek Fire burns in water?" Don Francisco marveled, turning to Constantine.

"Water is an accelerant," Constantine replied, excitement in his voice at the turn of events. Several Ottoman ships burst into flames as he spoke, and plumes of black smoke clouded the air. He smiled. "It burns even underwater. For this reason, it requires great skill to apply, so only enemy ships are destroyed and not our own. Greek sailors are masters in its art."

The flash of armor caught his gaze. The Genoese were fighting fiercely, swinging their axes, lopping off the hands and heads of the boarding parties, putting out fires and sending volleys of arrows whizzing back at the enemy. Silently he cheered them on. So crowded were the enemy vessels that their oars were entangled with one with another, and the javelins and stones the Genoese hurled from above splintered more than a single enemy boat at a time. Tirelessly and valiantly the Christians fought on. Remembering his father's Italian blood, Constantine's heart swelled with pride.

Jubilant cries went up from those on the hills, towers, and walls of Constantinople.

Zoe cheered with them until her throat ached. One after the other, disabled, and unable to row to safety, the Ottoman vessels sank with a fearful creaking and loss of life. But as each ship fell away, another took its place, and the fight that had already lasted six hours continued. Now five triremes surrounded one of the Genoese ships, and a multitude of much smaller boats filled with armed men, the *fustae* and *parandaria,* surrounded the third. Like sharks encircling prey, she thought. Turning away from the dread sight, she fixed her gaze on the imperial transport. The fighting was intense. God damn him, the traitor Baltoglu would not let go of her! Waves of enemy soldiers tried to board and were driven back by Phlatanelas and his crew, but the transport was running short of weapons. Help them! Zoe cried inwardly, directing herself not to a Divine Power this time, but to the Genoese ships.

As if they heard, the Genoese captains noticed the transport's plight. Despite their own difficulties, somehow they brought their ships to her side. As the imperial ship deployed Greek Fire to fight the enemy, the Genoese cut them down as they tried to board their galleys and let loose a hail of arrows, all this while casting ropes to the transport and to one another. Incredibly, as the sun dropped lower in the sky, the ships managed to lash themselves together. To Zoe, they looked like a great four-towered castle rising out of the confusion of the Ottoman fleet.

All through these many hours, Zoe, Constantine and the townsfolk were riveted on the battle, sometimes groaning with anxiety, sometimes cheering. Mehmet, too, watched in excitement, now shouting words of encouragement, now shaking his fist, now yelling instructions that Baltoglu pretended not to hear.

"Mehmet wishes to manage the battle from shore," Constantine noted to Justiniani, watching him hurl deprecations at his admiral. "He knows nothing of seamanship. If only Baltoglu would do as he is told!"

"Mehmet should take part in the fighting like a real leader," Justiniani replied. "And give us the chance to kill him."

"It is not his way. He does not risk himself," Constantine said, watching Mehmet ride out into the water again. If only the current would sweep him away, all would be righted in the world; such a simple thing— For an instant he wondered why God, with all His power, knowing how much was at stake, why He didn't take this one life when he took so many others. This one life that had already exacted such suffering and would exact an appalling price if the fight were lost. He shook himself. Who was he to gainsay God?

Glancing up, he saw that the sun was dropping, and silver streaked the sky. The water had turned the dark blue of sunset. Soon it would be twilight. And still the battle raged. He was drained. How much longer could these brave ships survive? They had fought gallantly; they had done great damage to the enemy. But they'd had no rest, food or drink all day, and for every vessel they destroyed, more drew up to attack. With a sore heart, he bowed his head in prayer.

Zoe was also praying when she felt it. A change.

She caught her breath. Could it be— Was it— A touch. Soft as a caress. Light as a shower of flower petals. She turned behind her and stared. Her eyes widened in wonder.

The cypresses were stirring in the wind!

God had sent a wind!

She could scarcely breathe for joy. Before her eyes the great sails of the Christian ships puckered and lifted. She stared spellbound as the galleys began to move and men hastened to untie the ropes that bound them to one another. The ships separated; their sails swelled to bursting. Gathering speed, they broke through the Ottoman fleet and headed for the boom.

Zoe looked at Constantine. He had covered his face in his hands. *To hide his tears of joy,* she thought. Prince Orhan followed her gaze. Smiling gently, he bent his head to hers. "We have a saying in our land. 'Only he who has worn the crown of sorrows can ascend to highest bliss.'"

"Lower the chain!" came the joyful Christian cry. "Lower the chain!"

The fierce cranking of metal rent the air as the winch turned furiously in the Tower of Eugenius. The chain sank into the water and disappeared. In the gathering darkness, Baltoglu could not bring his fleet together. With Mehmet still hurling commands and curses, he ordered his horns to sound the retreat. Setting their sails, his ships returned to the Port of Pillars from whence they came. As he dispersed, a fierce blaring of clarions from the Golden Horn blasted the evening air. Like a cat toying with a mouse, Trevisano had decided to frighten Baltoglu by sallying forth with his Venetian galleys.

"See how Baltoglu flees! He thinks our fleet is about to attack!" Constantine laughed. Our massive Christian armada of ten ships! The ridiculous thought flooded him with mirth. He threw his head back and roared with laughter until pain split his sides. It felt so good to laugh, so wonderful to laugh! "Mehmet will have the traitor's hide for this!" he said, drunk on joy. He gripped the parapet and laughed some more.

"*Allah* be praised," said Prince Orhan, grinning broadly as he watched Constantine.

"Here, have a drink—" Constantine thrust his flask into the prince's hand.

"Wine is forbidden by my religion, as you well know. But this once I will make an exception, Emperor." He downed a gulp and smacked his lips. "Surely *Allah* will not mind."

After the stunning triumph on the Marmara, the city lost no time celebrating its great victory. Barrels of beer were opened in the streets, freshly baked bread was handed out, and torches and fire pots were lit, adding a starry, almost ethereal glitter to the night. The rejoicing of his people sang in Constantine's veins with unbearable sweetness as he stood on the ramparts, marveling.

When he fully embraced the knowledge that glorious victory was indeed theirs, he felt hallowed by the miracle that God had wrought and humbled by the monumental affirmation of His love. It seemed to him that he had climbed to the peak of a vast mountain: behind stretched the darkness of the chasm through which he had passed, and ahead shone the way forward, illuminated by God's love. He had advanced a step closer to a destiny yet unknown, but never had he felt so assured of His favor or so close to God. He wanted to take Zoe into his arms and tell her of the love that burned in his heart and his hopes and dreams for the future that they would have together; he wanted to beg her forgiveness for all the times he had been harsh with her and hurt her with his thoughtlessness. He wanted to shout to his people that all would be well, that God had heard their pleas and was with them. But he knew the fight was not yet over, and danger remained.

He lifted his gaze to the one person he knew would understand. Zoe returned his smile, tremulously, joyfully, with tears in her eyes. Time hung suspended between them. Then, abruptly, came a flicker of movement and the moment vanished as if he had turned the page of a prayer book. The Scotsman, Johannes Grant, was taking the tower steps two at a time and the expression on his face hurtled Constantine back into reality, dimming the dazzle of victory in his heart.

Grant drew up and whispered in his ear. Swiveling on his heel Constantine left Zoe and the revelers on the parapet and hastened down the stairs, followed by Dalmata and his Varangians. Justiniani, suspecting what had transpired, fell into step behind him, a hand on his sword hilt. Lucas did the same, as did Phrantzes. Making all haste, the imperial party galloped back to the western defenses. Zoe stared after them, her heart so light a moment before, now troubled and anxious once more.

Laughter filled the night. Now that the fighting was over, families broke bread together on the western defenses and celebrated the great sea battle. Few noticed Constantine and his commanders surveying the Blachernae wall by torchlight.

"The damage is considerable. Far more than I expected," Constantine said in a hushed tone, so as not to disturb the mood of his people.

"They didn't cease the bombardment for a moment while the sea battle raged," Johannes Grant replied. "It must be repaired by morning, or we will be in difficulty."

"I am loathe to cut short the celebrations, but you are right. Gather everyone you can and get it done." He turned to leave, and his eye fell on Justiniani. While one of the four ships was his own imperial transport that he had tasked with the purchase of foodstuffs months earlier, the other three that had fought so bravely were Genoese. "Come with me, dear friend. I'd like you at my side when I thank your victorious countrymen for the great service they have rendered us this day."

Constantine passed through the Gate of Eugenius and halted, unprepared for the sight that met him at the Harbor. In a scene reminiscent of the early days of Rome, drunken Genoese soldiers lounged on marble steps, reclined on silk cushions, and sat propped up against pillars as minstrels played and women danced for them. Each man was surrounded by countless adoring females who poured wine, held cups to their lips, wiped their brows, and stroked their hair. Murmuring sweet nothings in their ear, they kissed them and fondled their thighs. No one seemed to pay the imperial party much heed.

"I see they have no need of our thanks," Constantine grinned, "since they are being amply rewarded by the womenfolk of Constantinople."

"Indeed, they are each an emperor for the night," Justiniani grinned.

"May those days come again, for I have not known them yet," Constantine laughed. "Perhaps they will be able to greet us tomorrow, when they can stand."

As they withdrew, they passed a sailor lolling against a pillar. "Twelve thousand confounded infidels dispatched to hell—and not one Christian lost," he said, his words slurred with wine. Not one—" He belched loudly.

Constantine threw a smile in his direction. "It will not hurt the city to hear that, even if it is a bald-faced lie," he said to Justiniani.

"My countrymen are nothing if not bald-faced liars," Justiniani chuckled. "God keep them safe."

The bombardment of the land walls resumed at dawn, and by sunset a great tower had collapsed. A portion of the outer wall below it was also destroyed.

Constantine looked over the edge of the parapet, surveying the destruction. It had been a long, rough day for many reasons. The tension of the sea battle had taken its toll, and there had been little chance to rest. When he'd finally managed to get to bed for a few hours, the evil dreams of marching children had broken his sleep and kept him tossing and turning for much of the night.

"They breached the walls," Constantine said wearily. "We have been fortunate. Had Mehmet ordered a general assault, it would have been impossible to hold them back."

"We were indeed fortunate that he wasn't here today," Justiniani said with a small smile. "Probably still chopping heads for his disaster at sea. Is it true he wanted to impale Baltoglu?"

A gasp went up on the ramparts. Men hushed to listen.

Constantine nodded. "He was enraged. Upbraided him as a fool and a coward, but in the end he heeded the pleas of his officers and bastinadoed him instead. It is said he is impoverished and has nowhere to go."

"A fate the traitor has richly earned," Justiniani snapped.

But Baltoglu's fall from grace gave Constantine little satisfaction. Nothing could erase the damage the Christian had wrought, no matter what became of him. Justiniani's voice came again. "We can repair most of the walls if we work through the night."

The sound of crunching boots interrupted them. Constantine turned. Lucas was climbing the tower stairs. "The cannons behind Pera have been firing all day against the boom," he said, striding up. "But we don't think they've managed to do much damage."

"Think?" Constantine demanded, his tone sharp.

"We can't tell what's going on. Black smoke obscures our view. Mehmet is up to something though. He's put thousands of laborers to work. They've been pounding all day, but we can't see what they're doing."

"What about our spies? Have they sent no reports?"

"Nothing yet," Lucas replied

"Come to think of it, something felt different here, too," Justiniani said. "Their attack lacked heart."

"Where's Mehmet and what is he up to?" Constantine said tersely, his unease growing. "I don't like it. See what you can find out, Lucas."

"Meanwhile, we have enough to worry about right here," Justiniani sighed. "There's not a moment to lose if the wall is going to be rebuilt by first light."

"I need to consult with Trevisano on the repairs to the Genoese ships," Constantine said, rubbing his eyes. "I will be back later to check on your progress."

As he left, he passed men bringing supplies to the to repair the walls: mules laden with sacks of earth and rocks, carts piled high with wood beams and shovels, and lime and sand for mortar.

There would be no rest for them this night.

On the twenty-second day of April, two days after the great sea victory, Constantine stood on his balcony as the first glimmer of dawn broke across the sky. He tensed and peered into the gloom. He blinked and looked again. He rubbed his eyes. *By all that is holy—*

"Aesop!" he bellowed, clapping loudly. The eunuch rushed in, bleary-eyed, disheveled.

"Augustus—" He broke off, his gaze fixed on the view behind Constantine. Mouth agape, he turned stricken eyes on his emperor.

Now Constantine knew it was no hallucination. He turned back to the evil sight in bewilderment, his brain in tumult, aware of a growing sense of horror as he stared, and of horror turning to despair. Ships flying the blood-red banner of the crescent moon sat in the Golden Horn and were moving across dry land on carts pulled by teams of oxen, sails hoisted, oarsmen paddling oars as if they rowed in water. His blood ran cold to see the weird, unearthly spectacle. In the violet sunrise that broke over the hills of Pera, Ottoman drums rolled, announcing to all the world that they had found a way around the boom. As full realization came, the shouts of the watchmen on the walls tore through the dawn. *Enemy ships on the Horn! Enemy ships on the Horn—*

Constantine sank down on a stool, the old familiar pain back again at the pit of his stomach. Already he could hear the consternation in the streets, the screams of women, the wailing of children. Zoe ran out of the bedchamber, drawing her chamber robe around her. She looked at the scene on the Golden Horn and blanched. Her eyes opened wide in horror and her lips parted, but no words came. In terror and bewilderment, she turned her gaze on Constantine. She had dreamed of water pouring through her fingers and had awakened gripped with unease. Now she knew why.

Lucas rushed into the chamber. "August—" He broke off.

Constantine rose from the stool and their eyes met. For a frozen instant, they stared at one another. Then Constantine burst into action. Firing questions, not waiting for answers, he swept past Lucas into the bedchamber, Lucas following close on his heels.

"How many ships? How could this happen? How did they get in?" He grabbed his clothes from Aesop and pulled them on. He donned his breastplate and armor and waited for Aesop to tighten the straps. "This took all night—why did no one notice? Why did no one warn us?" He buckled his sword belt and pulled on his red boots. "Get the Venetians! Get Theo and Demetri!" He grabbed his helmet. "We need answers, Lucas. We need a plan—" Lucas was almost out the door when Constantine remembered to add, "But no Genoese— Except Justiniani." The Genoese of Pera had sent him no warning. He was stung by their betrayal.

Lucas disappeared through the bronze doors, and with a last, disbelieving glance at Pera, Constantine followed him out. The Varangian Guards fell into step behind him. Zoe watched them leave. For an instant red bathed the white marble staircase like a pool of blood, and then the vision vanished. She blinked and rubbed her eyes. She returned to the window and sank down on a stool. With her gaze on the Ottoman ships, she listened to the clamor on the sea, the shouts of men and the crash of waves breaking on the rocks. She had a sudden, stupid desire to cry. From behind the walls of Pera they kept coming, the ghastly procession, down to the Valley of the Spring, ships borne on carts, drawn by teams of oxen, with men to help over the steeper, more difficult parts of the road, as cannons boomed, drums beat, and clarions blared.

Twenty-Seven

By noon, as monks chanted their prayers for Sext, the last Ottoman ship slithered into the water. In the council chamber at Blachernae, with the Golden Horn glittering in the distance, a somber-faced Constantine went over his options with his sea captains. Only now did he fully realize what he was dealing with. *Mehmet the Ambitious. Mehmet the Cruel.* He was also *Mehmet the Genius.*

"How bad?" he demanded, forcing his stiff lips to move. How bad could it be? As bad as it could get. Never would they recover from the loss of the Golden Horn. He looked at Trevisano, and Trevisano looked at the Venetian *bailo,* Girolamo Minotto. Minotto turned to his countryman, the Venetian captain, Alviso Diedo. No one wants to be the bearer of evil tidings, Constantine thought.

The tough blue-eyed captain, Diedo, spoke. "Mehmet has a total of seventy ships on the Horn, Majesty. They include triremes, biremes, and the smaller *fustae* and *parandarias.*"

To Constantine, it felt as if his heart had stopped beating. "What do we do? Any suggestions?"

"We can invite the Genoese of Pera to join in a general attack on the Ottoman fleet. With their help, we could beat them in open battle," Demetri offered.

"They failed to help when three Genoese ships came under attack," Minotto said. "They failed to tell us Ottoman ships were being readied to land in the Golden Horn. What makes you think they will help us now?"

"Even if they agreed, one of them would tell the sultan. A nest of Genoese spies, that's what Pera is!" Diedo said.

Slamming a fist on the table, Justiniani leapt to his feet. "How dare you? Have you considered Pera may not have known? The sultan was firing his cannons at the boom all day. Maybe they were blinded by the smoke. Maybe they were fooled, as we were—" Justiniani's face had turned red as a beet root. "As for condemning all Genoese out of hand, I am Genoese, and I came to fight with you when my government refused. A thousand Genoese from Pera did the same. Pera is holding up their end of the boom. What about Venice? Where's the Venetian fleet your Doge promised?"

"Friends," Constantine entreated. "The sultan is known to employ Greek spies here in the Queen of Cities. Does that mean we Greeks are all spies?"

Justiniani and Diedo looked at one another. After a hesitation, they each took their seats again. Lucas broke the silence that fell. "Even if Pera is willing to join us, it would take far too long to negotiate a deal. We'd lose our chance to surprise the enemy."

"The point is moot," Constantine said. "Pera is not going to abandon their neutrality. Anyone have another plan?"

"If we could land troops on the shores of the Valley of the Springs," Lucas offered, his eyes on the Horn, "we could take out their cannons and burn their ships."

Justiniani jerked around. "That's a suicide mission!"

"I have a plan. A good one," said a one-eyed captain standing behind Diedo. Giacomo Coco commanded the lone Venetian galley from Trebizond that had successfully eluded Mehmet's guns after Rizzo's ship was destroyed in November. The cunning sea-captain had survived the guns of the Throatcutter by sweet-talking his way through the Bosphorus and pretending he would comply with Mehmet's demands. But as soon as he was out of range of his guns, he sped away.

Constantine regarded the wily captain. If the marriage to Princess Theodora had gone through, he would have dozens of such men at his side now. He banished the thought.

"I propose we leave immediately," Coco said. "If we don't waste time, we'll have the advantage of surprise."

And Mehmet's spies won't have the chance to inform him of our plans,

Constantine thought. "I am listening. What do you have in mind?"

"Here—" Coco said with excitement, positioning the map so all could see. "We'll send out two transports, their sides protected by bales of cotton and wool. Two large galleys will follow—" He pointed out the route. "Hidden by these ships, two *fustae* will oar into the midst of the Ottoman ships. They'll cut their anchor ropes and fling Greek Fire aboard. The Ottoman Serpent will awaken in the morning to find his confounded little vessels burning!"

As he listened, hope lifted Constantine's spirit. Here was a brave and clever man with a good plan and the courage to make it work. "What are our chances of success?"

"Fifty-fifty," Justiniani said, studying the map.

"I will lead the expedition myself. That will make it a hundred percent," Coco grinned.

Constantine found himself smiling. Coco's enthusiasm was contagious. Aye, there were traitors in their midst, men like Urban the Hungarian, Baltoglu the Bulgarian, and Mehmet's general, the renegade Albanian, Zaganos Pasha. But there were also heroes, too, men like Coco, Justiniani, and Trevisano, who placed their lives at terrible risk to fight for their faith and save a city not their own. "How soon can you be ready?"

"In twenty-four hours," Coco replied.

"Twenty-four hours is not enough time to prepare four warships!" Justiniani protested. "It can't be done."

Affronted, Coco turned flashing eyes on Constantine. "I have vast experience! If Giacomo Coco says he will be ready, he will be ready, Majesty!" he said, referring to himself in the third person.

"We can't afford to lose ships or men," Justiniani insisted. "Majesty, may I ask that you leave final approval of readiness up to me?"

Constantine rubbed his chin thoughtfully. He trusted Justiniani implicitly, but he couldn't offend the Venetian captain. "You all know how much depends on this effort. I have complete faith in you, Coco, but it does not hurt to be certain we are fully prepared for this mission. The *Protostrator* will advise if the ships are ready to leave. Report back to me in twenty-four hours."

The captain gave a bow and gathered up his maps.

"The man is blustering," Justiniani exclaimed when the Venetians had left. "There is no way he can be ready."

"But we must hope that he is," Constantine sighed. "We have to regain the Golden Horn. Otherwise, we will be obliged to divert men from the defense of the land walls, and we cannot afford that. We are undermanned on the *Mesoteichion* as it is... Incidentally, I know how Mehmet came up with the idea of transporting his ships overland. Urban the Hungarian told him."

"Urban?"

"The gun-maker. Mehmet was brooding on his failure to force the boom. Urban told him about the Lombard campaign where Venice had carried a whole flotilla of ships on wheeled platforms from the river to Lake Garda. The terrain there had been flat, and the Valley of the Springs around Pera is hilly for more than two hundred feet but—" He broke off, the old familiar spasm tightening his gut.

"But Mehmet has the men and the means," Justiniani finished for him.

"Yes."

"They should have been here long ago," Justiniani muttered angrily. "What in the Devil's name is keeping them?"

Constantine caught his meaning. The Venetian fleet. Always the Venetian fleet. Everyone dreamed of the Venetian fleet.

Justiniani fell silent. After a moment, he looked up and met Constantine's eyes. "If our plan is to be successful, we must have absolute secrecy. If my countrymen find out, Pera will know. If Pera knows, the sultan will know. We cannot tell any Genoese."

Constantine lifted a questioning eyebrow.

"I am first and foremost a Christian in this fight," Justiniani replied.

Constantine gripped his shoulder. "I have said it before, and I will say it again. It is too bad for the Christian race that more are not like you, my good friend."

To Constantine's deep disappointment, Justiniani proved correct. The ships were not ready.

"Every night we delay makes the chance of success that much less," Coco protested, his distress evident.

"It is only for two nights." Constantine consoled.

"The Genoese always want to steal the glory!" Coco spat.

On the following day, the twenty-fifth of April, the problem Constantine had feared presented itself. At the window, hands clasped behind his back, he gazed over the Golden Horn. On the beach, children were fighting one another with their wooden swords, and a man with a bird on his shoulder was selling grilled meat and chattering with the sailors.

"How did the Genoese find out?" Constantine demanded, addressing Justiniani, the sick feeling at the pit of his stomach gnawing at his gut.

"The Genoese ships saw the activity aboard the Venetian ships. They asked what they were doing," Justiniani replied. "A Venetian sailor boasted that it was a secret known only to the Venetians because you didn't trust the Genoese. One thing led to another, and a fight broke out. Now the Genoese captains are demanding they supply at least one of the boats, or they'll brave the blockade to leave, just as they braved it to come."

"For God's love!" Constantine sank down on a stool and put a hand on his brow to still the roaring in his head. Justiniani squeezed his shoulder.

Constantine looked up. "Then we have no choice. We must delay so they can prepare."

"The moon is waxing," Justiniani said softly. "We can't risk it until it wanes. That means we have to wait four days."

Constantine suppressed a groan. Four days! He could only pray Mehmet didn't learn of their plans in four days.

In the darkness before dawn on the twenty-eighth day of April, two great war ships, one Genoese, one Venetian, each with forty oarsmen, crept out from the protection of the walls of Pera, accompanied by two more Venetian galleys under the command of Diedo and Trevisano. With Trevisano was his deputy, Zaccaria Grioni. As they cast out from shore, Trevisano noticed a torch wave from one of the towers of Pera. "What's that?" he asked, instantly alert.

"It could be a signal to the enemy," Grioni replied. "Should we abort?"

Trevisano glanced at the three light *fustae* that followed his galleys, each with seventy-two oarsmen. Coco was in the lead boat, and with him were several small boats carrying combustible materials. If they aborted, they'd lose the chance to ever win back the Horn. What if it was nothing?

"Let's get closer," he said. "We can turn back if it doesn't feel right."

Quietly, slowly, the ships inched through the blackness. The waters were still and smooth, and the Ottoman ships rocked sleepily at anchor. Nothing seemed out of the ordinary. But aboard the *fustae*, unaware of the reason for

Trevisano's abundant caution, Coco was growing impatient.

"God's Balls, what's the matter with the cowards?" he cursed. "They're slower than a tun of honey!" Barely able to contain himself, anxious for glory, he turned to his men. "Enough of this! We'll show them how real men fight. Full speed ahead!" He shot forward and made straight for the Turks.

A sudden cannon roar shattered the silence of the night. "God's Blood—they knew we were coming!" Grioni cried.

A terrible groaning rose as Coco's boat was hit. Shouts and yells came from the other *fustae* and small boats as they hastened for the protection provided by the galleys.

Constantine stood on the *Mesoteichion*, grim and pale in the morning light, looking out on the Ottoman army that covered the hills as far as the eye could see. Beside him, Trevisano's face reflected his gloom. They had suffered a costly defeat. A galley had been lost, and a *fusta*, and only one enemy ship had been destroyed. Coco had died, and many of the sailors who were killed with him had been Trevisano's men. The knowledge that he could have saved them hung heavy on him. Worse, the enemy had caught twenty defenders. Now, before the walls of Constantinople, they were preparing their punishment.

"No family members are to be permitted on the walls to see this," Constantine commanded through frozen lips. "Ring the church bells to drown the cries and summon the priests to pray for them. Get Cardinal Isidore—" He broke off. After a pause, he said grimly, "Bring me all the enemy prisoners we have."

Trevisano inclined his head and men smiled coldly. No one protested this time.

Church bells tolled. On the ramparts soldiers stood silently, ashen faced, fighting for composure as they watched the grisly sight. When the enemy had finished their macabre work and the last man had been dealt with, Venetians, Genoese and Greeks wiped their eyes and fell to their knees in prayer.

Inside the hospital tent Zoe made a round of the injured. She could do nothing for those beyond the walls, but here at least she could help ease suffering. She bathed their wounds, and if they were awake, gave them potions and soothing words. One fair-haired youth, little older than her brother Isaac, was burned in the sea battle. His name, she had learned, was Thomas. He suffered dreadfully and, in his anguish, cried out for his mother. Zoe gave him the tears of the poppy flower for pain, and when her duties allowed, she sat at his bedside and sang to him. Now he mostly slept, though fitfully, but whenever he awoke and saw her, he smiled. That, more than anything else, broke her heart.

She smoothed his fair hair back from his fevered brow and mopped his face with a damp cloth. It was a hot day, humid and close. Flies buzzed inside the tent, and vultures hovered outside, waiting patiently for the meat they knew would soon be theirs. *This is all spring has brought this year,* she thought. No bird song, only the raucous cawing of vultures. No scent of flowers, only death and the acrid smell of smoking cannon fire and the burning flesh of Ottoman funeral pyres.

She wiped the sweat from her face with her elbow and pressed a wet compress to Thomas's brow. Bloodcurdling screams and a fearful wailing came to her from beyond the walls. She swallowed on the nausea that swept her. The disaster had cost the lives of ninety of their best sailors. But they had been blessed. They had died quickly.

Her eye fell on her lyre propped up against a coffer. She put the compress back into the basin, retrieved the instrument and returned to Thomas's side. Strumming the chords of a popular refrain, she raised her voice in a lament. Men hushed to listen, and the cries of the dying faded.

Leaving the tiny one room church that was built into the wall at St. Romanus Gate where he had gone to pray and compose himself, Justiniani paused his steps. The achingly sweet melody enfolded him in its loveliness, stirring feelings long since buried. Like a man in a trance, he turned and followed the music to the tent. Shouts and cries floated to him from beyond the walls, but they seemed very far away. Someone asked him a question which he neither absorbed nor would have answered if he had. He came to a halt near the olive tree. The tender notes plucked on the lyre and the celestial voice that sang of love rippled over him, bathing him in memory. Again, he felt his mother's silken touch on his cheek and recalled the smoldering passion of his first kiss, and again he remembered his joy the first time ever he sailed the seas. But over the remembrances soared one thought and one all-encompassing desire. His love and need for Zoe. Engulfed in emotion, he stood listening to the vast beauty of that melodious voice, and he was suffused to the core of his being with an acute, unbearable yearning for her arms, her touch, her kiss.

The song died away, and Zoe stepped out of the tent, tears in her eyes, the lyre in her hand. She froze when he saw him, and their eyes locked. Justiniani leaned a hand against the olive tree and bowed his head as he fought for composure over the surging, intense emotion that swept him. Not trusting himself to speak, he said nothing and was the first to turn away. With long, rapid strides, he headed to the battlements of St. Charisius.

Shaken by the encounter with Justiniani, Zoe returned to the tent to find Barbaro changing a soldier's bandage. She knelt beside him and dipped a sponge into a basin of water, but Justiniani gazed back at her in the ripples. She closed her eyes. Seeing his love for her clearly written on his face broke her heart. She forced herself to focus and washed the wound.

"Healing nicely," Barbaro said.

Zoe barely heard him for the shouts, clinking of chains and the scuffle of men that diverted her attention to the defenses. She rose and hurried outside. Turks were screaming, calling to *Allah* as they were shoved and dragged up the tower stairs. Barbaro drew to her side.

"What's going to happen to them?" Zoe demanded.

"They are to be executed."

Zoe returned her gaze to the Turks. One was sobbing and crying out in Turkish, his terror and anguish evident. He limped as he struggled against his captors, and she saw blood.

"But that man is wounded," Zoe exclaimed. "Why are they taking the wounded?"

"They are taking everyone," Barbaro replied.

Seeing Zoe's gaze on him, the Turk called out to her, his tone desperate, pleading. "What's he saying?" she asked Barbaro, for he knew the Turkish tongue.

"He's begging for his life. He says he never wanted to fight, but he had no choice. He says he's the sole support of his elderly mother, and she'll be turned into the streets if he doesn't return."

Zoe looked back at the man. He had collapsed on the steps, sobbing, unable to go any farther. Never had she thought of the enemy with pity. A

Christian soldier gave him a hard kick in the side. Dragging the man to his feet, he pushed him up the steps.

Zoe remembered something Justiniani had said. *War is the devil's business.* "I am going to the emperor!"

Barbaro placed a restraining hand on her arm. "Lady Zoe, you cannot prevent it. The emperor must execute these men. He has no choice."

She shook him off. "You're wrong."

She hastened across the circle of green, past the horses and a throng of men at the base of the walls. "Take me to Captain Dalmata," she commanded a man in charge of the prisoners.

The man hesitated. "He's on the ramparts. It is no place for—"

Zoe gave him a hard stare. He swallowed. "This way, my lady."

Zoe followed him up the tower steps, past startled prisoners, soldiers, and guards. The parapet was crowded with men standing silently, backs turned to her, watching the enemy encampment where distant shrieks of suffering could be heard piercing the song of the monks. As soldiers became aware of her presence, they stepped aside to open a path. She saw Dalmata hastening toward her, his face pale and pinched. Behind him coils of rope and an array of fearsome axes and swords were strewn in a pile.

"I need to see the emperor, Dalmata," she said quietly, averting her eyes from the instruments of death.

That hesitation again. "Follow me, *Zoste Patricia.*"

Resting a hand against the tower wall, Constantine stood deep in conversation with someone whose face she couldn't see. Even from the back, he looked weary. Before Dalmata had a chance to announce her, Constantine turned, and Zoe's gaze fell on the one he was with. Justiniani. She glanced away.

"What do you here, *Zoste Patricia?*" Constantine exclaimed, as if disbelieving the evidence of his own eyes.

"I seek a boon, Augustus."

"Speak."

"I understand these prisoners are to be put to death."

"You understand correctly."

"I beg you to reconsider."

"What?"

"Many of these men are wounded. Many more are innocent of any crime. I beg you to wait until they can receive a fair trial."

Constantine closed the distance between them angrily. "You have no right to be here, Zoe," he muttered under his breath. "This is not your concern."

"Augustus," she said, "I beg mercy for these men."

"Zoste Patricia, your sympathy is misplaced," he hissed. "Mercy for them who spared none for us? In case you have forgotten, we are at war! Go back to the sick and wounded where you belong!"

"Augustus, I beseech you not to do this—we are not like them."

"Go!" he commanded, shaking. He turned to Dalmata. "Take her away! You had no right to bring her here!"

Zoe fell to her knees and looked up at him beseechingly. "Noble Emperor, if you will not save them all, I implore you to grant me one life— A single life. Surely one life can be spared? God will look with favor on your clemency!"

As Constantine stared at her, Justiniani stepped forward and whispered something in his ear.

Zoe couldn't make out what it was, but Constantine's expression softened. "One life?" Constantine repeated. "Which?"

Zoe scrambled to her feet. "That one," she said quickly, pointing to the wounded Turk. Constantine regarded the prisoner. He gave a nod. "Take him to his cell."

A guard pulled the man erect. As the Turk struggled to his feet, he stared at Zoe in joyous wonder.

"Allah sizden razz olsun—" he wept. May God bless you always, always—

Holding herself stiffly erect, Zoe navigated the tower stairs, tears stinging her eyes. At the base, she came face to face with Prince Orhan. His eyes were moist as he gazed at her. "I heard." Falling to a knee, he took her hand to his lips. *"Allah size odii, guzel bayan."* May God reward thee, beautiful lady.

From her mission of mercy saving the Ottoman's life, Zoe rode to the Genoese quarter with Eirene and a guard. Though her mother had declined the position of *Zoste Patricia,* she had shouldered some of Zoe's responsibilities for the poor, and Zoe felt the need to make certain all was well.

She passed a small crowd that had gathered around a cold-eyed man with a bird on his shoulder near a butcher's shop. She had seen him before, and each time she was assailed by a strange disquiet. The man fell silent and watched her pass. Feeling the usual distress beneath his gaze, she spurred Ariadne into a gallop.

The man with the bird smiled to himself. He knew Zoe by sight and had relayed to *Rumeli Hisar* the rumor that she was the emperor's wife. Yesterday the blind beggar had relayed his orders from the sultan. He was to track her whereabouts until arrangements could be made for her abduction. The sultan was a clever man and left nothing to chance, he thought. Whether the Greeks won or lost, he would have Constantine's empress.

He watched Zoe flee past, thinking how richly she would adorn the sultan's harem. He would have good sport with her. Turning his attention back to the mischief he was fomenting, he yelled, "The confounded Genoese! May the devil take their souls! All this is their fault, the traitors!"

"Aye!" the crowd exclaimed.

"Yet they go unpunished!"

Nodding heads and shaking fists, they shouted agreement.

"So let us take our own revenge! Are you with me?"

"Aye!" they cried in a chorus, grabbing knives and hatchets from the butcher's shop, pots and pans from the tinker's cart, and clubs from a carpenter who came out of his stall to distribute them.

"Onward then—to the Genoese quarter!"

He smiled inwardly. This day's work would fetch him a fine price. With his bird fluttering on his shoulder, he marched along, leading the angry mob. At the Gate of St. Romanus, he heard sobbing and glanced up at the ramparts. But all he saw were white-faced soldiers standing silently, watching the grisly spectacle of Christian suffering.

Twenty-Eight

Amid the tolling of church bells and chanting of monks, the Ottoman prisoners were lined up on the ramparts. "Collect the heads in buckets!" a captain ordered. "They are to be sent back to the infidels, courtesy of our stone-throwing machines!"

A volley of cheers arose, and men stepped forward to offer themselves as executioners. "I wish he had two heads," the first man said, readying his axe over an invader's neck. "One for my brother, Zeno. And one for my friend, Ari." He slammed the axe down. Picking up the bloody severed head, he held it high. The enemy jeered. He threw them a mock bow. "Our archers welcome you to get the body! Rubbish should always be burned!"

Men rushed to help him heave the corpse over the ramparts. Applause broke out along the length of the walls. Vowing vengeance, the enemy shook their fists at them. One of the Bocchiardo brothers who spoke Turkish yelled, "You godless bastards! A special place in hell awaits you! With God's help, we'll send you there!"

The next volunteer executioner stepped forward. He wielded a sword. Another head rolled and another headless corpse was hurled over the wall for the Ottoman funeral pyre.

Standing by a tower wall, Constantine watched the bloodletting, his mouth grim. It changed nothing for a single soldier who had died a brutal death at Ottoman hands, but his men needed vengeance. So did he. Three times he had watched Mehmet's diabolical display. Now, finally, he was addressing it in the only way he could.

He became aware of shouting and scuffling along the parapet.

"This is all your fault," someone cried. "Our men died because of you Genoese! Because of your treachery!"

"The plan failed because of you Venetians! Coco disregarded orders and forged into the fray too soon. He was seeking glory for himself—that's why it failed!"

Constantine cursed as he followed the shouts to a melee in progress at the Charisian Gate. Two men already lay injured on the ground, and Justiniani was nowhere in sight. For an instant, Constantine wondered if he was with Zoe. Anger flooded him.

"Halt!" he shouted.

The men froze. Then one said, "But Majesty, it's their fault we lost the Horn."

"No," protested another. "Majesty, it's their fault."

"And if we agree whose fault, do we get back the Horn?" Constantine roared, trembling with fury.

They bowed their heads.

"For the pity of God, don't do the enemy's work for them! Save the killing for the fight that is coming—" A commotion drew his attention back to his position at St. Romanus. He looked at the men at Charisian uncertainly. "Can you be trusted if l leave?" A sheepish chorus muttered assent.

When he reached his post, he found guards barring entry to a group of teary-eyed boys. "Leave them be!" Constantine barked, striding up.

The guards stepped aside, and the boys ran past them, yelling for their fathers. Two men opened their arms wide, but the boys had no time for hugs. "Come quickly, Father!" one cried, dragging his father by the hand. "They broke into our house—they beat Grandpapa! You have to save him!"

Constantine closed the gap between them. "Who broke in? What is happening?"

The boys answered in unison. "They called us traitors! They said they'd kill us because we're Genoese!"

The clank of swords and armor drew Constantine's attention to Lucas, striding up from the tower stairs. "Augustus, there's rioting in the Genoese quarter! They're looting and killing people!"

"Come with me," Constantine commanded.

Constantine galloped to the harbor quarter with his Varangians, followed by Lucas and his Greek guard, Trevisano and his Venetians, and Justiniani with his Genoese. He arrived to find men battling in the streets and a mob kicking in doors and smashing windows. From the rooftops children hurled stones. One struck Athena. She reared angrily.

"Halt!" Constantine bellowed, pointing to them. "Halt—"

Zoe heard Constantine's voice through a broken window in the church at Botaneiates where she huddled with the poor. When the riot had broken out, she'd been seized with nausea and was in the alleyway, retching. In horror she'd watched people flee screaming through the streets and armed men beating those they caught. Taking refuge in the church, she'd barred the doors and shepherded the terrified women, children, and old men to shelter behind a dilapidated screen in an alcove. Now she rose to her feet. "Take comfort, the emperor is here!" she told her frightened flock. "All is well. We are safe!"

Together they pushed open the creaky church door, but her smile died on her lips at the sight that met her eyes. Resplendent in his purple cloak and red boots, his golden regalia of office shimmering in the sun, Constantine sat astride his charger, his hand raised, pointing to the east.

The East. From where their doom would come.

In that devastating pose, he breathed life into the statue of the first Constantine atop the column at Hagia Sophia and force into the ancient prophecy they had always feared.

"—the Ottomans are the enemy," Constantine was saying. "Yes, some Genoese in Pera are guilty of treachery, but not these men at my side. They fight for you! They fight for your children and your unborn. On these brave Genoese—and Venetian, and Greek—rest your futures and the future of your faith. These men volunteered to share with us the same fearsome dangers we face. Will you call them traitors? No, they are heroes! Who can forget the bravery of the Genoese ships? Who can forget the first assault that Genoese and Venetians and Greeks repelled side by side? The enemy surrounds us. They howl at our gates— Do you not hear them? This is our Armageddon! If we fail to unite, we perish from the face of the earth. My people, I beg you, help me to save our holy city! Do not fight one another! Christian must not kill Christian—" His voice cracked. Weary to exhaustion, distraught by what he had witnessed on the wall, unable to hold back his anguish, Constantine bowed his head and wept.

The image of the stricken emperor drew pity from all sides. Quietly, men sheathed their swords and dispersed. Her heart breaking for her husband, Zoe left the people she had sheltered and made her way to his side.

After nightfall, by the light of torches, the defenders repaired the day's damage. Constantine watched them from the battlements, his gaze gentle on Prince Orhan, who labored side by side with his unlikely friend Navarro. He had no doubt that the future boded bright if victory was theirs. For Orhan would mount the sultan's throne, and amity and peace would bind their kingdoms, perhaps forever. A dream, but one to cherish, he thought.

"Lucky for us Mehmet didn't follow up with an attack," Justiniani whispered.

That is twice now, Constantine thought. One day, their luck would run out. "I am going back to the palace. You should get some sleep, too, my friend." He turned behind him, south, to the Marmara. The fleet had not come today. "Maybe tomorrow," he murmured, unaware he voiced the thought aloud.

"Maybe tomorrow," Justiniani echoed, following his gaze, catching his meaning.

Turning to leave, Constantine heard a familiar female voice. He halted his steps. Zoe? He leaned over the ramparts and caught sight of her by torchlight, face smudged with dirt, auburn hair secured in a net, sleeves rolled up, helping Prince Orhan pass a heavy rock to one of the masons. Admiration swept him. After all she'd been through this day, she still found strength to do more. *"Nobelissima—"* he called down. "You've had a long day. You should rest now!"

Rubbing her aching back, Zoe straightened up and looked at him. "So should we all, Augustus. I will come when I can be spared." Behind Constantine, Justiniani's face came into view, and her heart flooded with the now-familiar ache of guilt.

Constantine turned behind him to see what had caught her gaze.

On the third day of May, Zoe awoke in the middle of the night. Dragging herself to the privy, she retched. The nausea that began last week had not left her. With a blush, she remembered the Easter night of passion. She turned the golden lever in the marble basin and washed her mouth with salt.

Returning to the bedroom, she drew on her chamber robe and hastened into the hall.

Constantine was nowhere in sight. When she'd returned from her labor on the walls, he'd been at his desk, poring over his maps. She'd bid him good night on her way to bed, but he'd been too engrossed to hear. Her glance caught on a tray of dried bread, half-eaten olives, and humus left on a coffer. Her heart sank. Once again, he'd barely touched his food. Her eyes searched the balcony. Sometimes when he couldn't sleep, he went out in the quiet of the night, and she would find him there, leaning on the stone balustrade, listening to the wash of the sea. She drew her robe close around her and hastened outside. He was seated behind a Corinthian pillar in the darkness between two torches, and it took her a moment to make him out. Soon it would be dawn. Had he been up all night? She touched his shoulder gently.

He dropped his hand from his brow and looked up. "When are they coming? We cannot last much longer, Zoe."

Her heart broke for him. That was all anyone thought about now. The Venetian fleet. They had waited so many months, and prayed so hard, and held out longer than anyone thought possible. All for the Venetian fleet. She sank down beside him. Dear God, how much change! How could she have failed to notice how thin he'd become, how much he'd aged? Gone was the magnificent, confident emperor she'd known. Merciless lines carved his cheeks from his nose to the comers of his mouth, and silver dusted the brows over his hazel eyes, once bright with hope, now tortured by doubt.

Abruptly, Constantine rose and moved to the balustrade. Zoe felt a moment's wounding hurt but dismissed it as unworthy. She watched him rest his elbows on the stone and lean out over the water. The old sorrow assailed her that she could do nothing for him. She joined him at the balustrade, knowing he had forgotten she was there, and for the first time, she did not mind.

The sea reflected the glimmer of dawn, and a fierce wind blew. Across the Horn, the dying embers of enemy campfires glowed darkly. Soon the sun would rise, and guns would blacken the sky with smoke.

Constantine ran a hand through his hair. "All the people out there—all the ones I see each day— not just them, but those yet unborn for generations to come, will they be enslaved or free? The men on the walls who fight at my side, the children I see when I ride in the streets, will they live or die? If Constantinople falls—"

"We must never stop believing we can overcome. Never!" Zoe cried, speaking quickly to interrupt his dark thoughts.

A silence.

"I need to speak to your father and Minotto," he said wearily. "And Justiniani… And all my councilors."

"Now?" It was the middle of the night.

He didn't answer. He had retreated into his thoughts and lost awareness of her again. She bit down on her helplessness.

In the Ocean Hall, Zoe conveyed Constantine's orders to a sleepy, bleary-eyed Aesop, and he left to pass the command to Dalmata. The great bronze door thudded shut. She returned to the bedchamber, threw on the plain cotton gown she wore on duty in the hospital tent and tied a clean silk scarf around her hips. Hastily, she braided her hair. When she came out, she saw Constantine cross the balcony to his desk in the sunken study. For a long moment he stood with head bowed and shoulders hunched, his weight resting on his hands, gazing at his maps. She wanted to comfort him but could think of nothing to say. Behind her, Apollo knew no such hesitation. "Where-is-the-Venetian fleet, where-is-the-Venetian fleet?" he muttered, pacing back and forth.

She went to his gilded cage and picked up a raisin left over from the night before. She fed it to him and watched him nibble. Sudden footsteps and the voices of men came from the stairwell. Aesop hastened to the door and she turned to the entry with anticipation. Clad in his breastplate, his helmet under his arm, Justiniani strode purposefully to Constantine. Trevisano followed, hair tousled from sleep, sword clanging at his side. Minotto and her father brought up the rear. The men rushed past without noticing her. She joined them in the study, and Justiniani gave her a nod of greeting. She realized he wasn't surprised to see her there and remembered that she was a councilor, too.

Constantine spoke. "I have asked you here because our situation has grown desperate. Provisions are almost exhausted. The Venetian fleet should have been here long ago. I fear something has gone terribly wrong. Minotto, give me your thoughts."

"I delivered my letter to the Doge on the nineteenth day of February,

Majesty. The Senate voted quickly to dispatch their fleet to us. Admiral Loredan was given command. I cannot think of any reason why he has not arrived, except for treachery."

"From Loredan?" Constantine said. "All reports are that he is a brave Christian commander. I have utmost faith in the captain of the Venetian fleet. What other explanation can there be—"

"Perhaps he's unaware of the order?" offered Trevisano.

"Or unaware of the urgency," Justiniani added.

"That has to be it," Lucas said. "He must be loitering in some port somewhere, unaware of our predicament."

Constantine nodded thoughtfully.

"Even if that is the case, what can we do?" Lucas said.

"We can send a party to look for him. To inform him of our dire need and beg him to hasten to the relief of the city."

Justiniani and Trevisano exchanged a look.

"Majesty," Trevisano said, his green eyes dark, "you realize how perilous that is? If they are caught—" He broke off, unwilling to finish the thought.

"I know what I ask, but I can think of no other way!" Constantine cried. Imposing an iron control on himself, he added more evenly, "That is why I will not order anyone to go. This must be a volunteer mission."

After a hesitation, Justiniani said. "We will put it to the men."

At midnight, in the garden of the ruined Great Palace, with the sighing of the sea heavy on the night, Constantine reviewed the twelve volunteers by the light of torches. In Turkish garb and turbans, they looked indistinguishable from the infidel. He noted the absence of Genoese among the Greeks and Venetians with sorrow. The treachery of Pera had taken a toll on trust, and recriminations against the Genoese hadn't ceased. Fights broke out regularly, but fortunately not with the same ire that had required his intervention in the Genoese quarter. He supposed it was understandable, given the tremendous strain they were all under.

"Are you Greek or Venetian?" Constantine asked the first man in line.

"I am Christian, Majesty," the man replied. "And Venetian, also."

A chuckle went down the line. Constantine smiled. "My brave Christian, I thank you for your courage. God bless you for undertaking this mission."

He passed to the next man. "I know you—you are Greek. From Mistra." His mouth softened in memory. *Mistra …*

"I saw you crowned, Basileus. Will never forget it. A worthy emperor you make."

Constantine felt a rush of emotion. "Do you have children?"

"Two, Basileus. A boy and a girl."

"If we win this fight, their futures are assured." The man bowed his head, and Constantine moved on. "What is the dearest wish of your heart?" he asked the next man.

"To save my country, Basileus, " the man replied.

Constantine choked back the emotion that flooded him. "May the All Holy One bring you safely home, soldier. May He be merciful unto you and reward you in this life… and in the next."

So he went, bidding each farewell, and blessing each. He stepped forward to the last man, and the iron control he had imposed on himself melted. "Trevisano! What do you here?"

"The same as everyone else, Majesty. I wish to save the Queen of Cities. The Jewel in the Cross."

Constantine bit down on his emotion. He embraced the young captain silently, unwilling to trust himself to speech until he had composed himself. "We need you, Trevisano. Return safely to us," he whispered, his voice cracking. "Safely…" He stepped back and the gate opened, revealing the black waters of the Marmara. Across the Horn, the red fires of the enemy flickered warning. The men stole out to the boat and hoisted the Ottoman flag. With a sick heart, Constantine watched them slip away into the black night thick with threat.

Unnoticed by the little brigandine, two female figures watched from the Marmara wall above.

Standing hand in hand, Zoe and Eirene bathed them in prayer, beseeching God for His mercy and for His protection of these twelve courageous souls, and for the safe return of them all, but especially the one named Gabriel Trevisano.

Zoe was aware of Constantine's fear that Mehmet would follow up his sea victory with an assault. He didn't, but on the Horn, matters were tense.

Mehmet had built a pontoon bridge and set guns there to hammer the single Blachernae wall where it met the triple Theodosian walls. Every now and again, Ottoman ships pulled out from their anchorage across the water as if to attack the defenders, forcing them to keep vigilant. The booming cannons set Zoe's nerves on edge, and she worried about the wounded who could get no sleep.

"At least there's been no hand-to-hand fighting for days," Justiniani told her as they stood together beneath the olive tree. "We must be thankful for such mercies."

"True, but we can still wish for heaven to muzzle Urban's gun," Zoe replied.

Almost as if Heaven had heard, Urban's great cannon stopped firing the next day. A messenger brought Constantine the news in his council chamber.

"Our spy writes that Urban the Gunmaker is dead," Constantine said, standing at the window and reading the missive by the fading light of day. "Some claim he was distraught over the damage his monstrous machine had done to God's holy city, and in an attack of conscience, sabotaged his gun and blew himself up with it. But some believe it was not he who sabotaged his gun and someone else wrought his doom. The sultan is repairing the damage to the cannon."

Seated beside her father in the council chamber, Zoe watched Constantine thank the messenger and give him a coin.

"May he rot in hell," Constantine said tersely.

He turned his head and looked at the Horn. Blue twilight was falling. The enemy was amassed on the slopes of Pera. The pontoon bridge of logs and barrels Mehmet had built to transport men and cannon bobbed on the waves. He returned to his seat and regarded his advisors. "We have an urgent problem," he said as servants lit candles and tapers around the room. "There will be no fruit on the trees or vegetables in the gardens for weeks. We cannot fish in the Horn. Our livestock is diminishing, and our store of grain is perilously low. Prices are inflated. Those who cannot afford to pay are going hungry. More and more, men are seeking permission to leave their posts and go hunting to feed their families."

Without hesitation, Zoe said, "If they cannot feed themselves, then Augustus, you must feed them at your cost."

Everyone turned to her except Constantine, who looked down at his notes. "Where will the money come from?" he said.

"The churches must be asked for donations of plate," Zoe replied.

"Again?" Constantine demanded, not looking up.

"They know this is no time to count the cost," Zoe replied. "Private houses can also contribute. I am certain my father will give all he can to the effort."

Startled, Lucas jerked up his head. Zoe smiled and offered him a shrug. One by one, Phrantzes, Theo and Demetri promised the same. Zoe's glance, moving around the table, fell on Justiniani. He grinned and gave her a wink. A new knowledge came to her. To her father and Constantine, she was first a daughter and a wife. But Justiniani saw her not merely a woman, but as an equal partner in the war effort. She found it a strangely welcoming feeling.

Constantine's voice broke into her thoughts.

"—you have my thanks," he was saying, looking around at everyone but her. Zoe had the feeling that she had offended him somehow, but she banished the thought. Constantine was under tremendous strain and hadn't been himself lately, for good reason.

"You shall be generously reimbursed when the emergency is behind us," he continued. "Justiniani, you shall oversee a committee to ensure the money is distributed fairly. Let us pray the Venetians come soon and we are not starved into surrender."

A silence fell. Zoe's thoughts went to Trevisano and the men searching for the Venetian fleet. The Virgin be thanked, the absence of news meant they'd managed to get safely past the enemy, Zoe thought. Glancing up, she caught her father exchanging a look with Demetri. The Grand Duke cleared his throat, and all eyes turned to him.

"Meanwhile, Augustus," Lucas said, "there is another urgent matter we must address. We—all of us here—are agreed that the time has come for you to leave."

"Leave?"

"Yes. You must leave Constantinople."

"That is ridiculous."

"Augustus, it's the sensible thing to do," Lucas replied.

"I am the defender of the faith. My place is here. With my people."

"You would be helping your people by leaving, Augustus, "Phrantzes said.

Constantine was taken aback. It was the first time Lucas and Phrantzes had agreed on anything. "How can you say that? How could it benefit my people to see me flee?"

"If you go, you could rouse Europe to its duty and organize a campaign against the Ottomans," Demetri said. "Your brothers and many supporters from the Balkans would flock to your banner."

"Even the valiant George Scanderberg of Albania will surely join you when his treaty with the enemy expires," Phrantzes urged.

"Speculation! Only one thing is certain. If I abandon the city, the defense will unravel."

"It won't unravel. I'll lead them," Justiniani said.

"My people are a fickle lot, Justiniani. They barely follow me, and I am one of them. You, my brave friend, for all your valor and charm, are a foreigner. I cannot leave."

"You need not decide now—" Lucas insisted. "Think about it, I pray you. You may change your mind. All we ask is that you think about it. Will you do that for us?"

Feeling a need for movement, Constantine scraped his chair back and went to the window. He stared at the black night, Halil's words throbbing in his head. The old vizier was right; he had seen what he, Constantine, blinded by confidence, had failed to see. It was all his fault— The Hexamilion Wall. The enmity of Venice and Genoa. The monumental blunder with Mehmet that might doom his civilization and send untold thousands into the hellish abyss of slavery. Now he had the chance to flee. To escape with his life and his freedom and leave his people to pay the penalty for his foolhardy mistakes. He would not do it, by God! He could not do it. It was beyond dishonorable. It was despicable.

He turned back to his friends. Never had they doubted him or blamed him, neither by word nor deed. They put their hopes in him entirely and would follow wherever he led. They were prepared to accept their dread fate, yet they urged him to flee, believing that if he lived, the empire would not die. They deluded themselves, but he had not the heart to strip them of their illusions. Let them hope a while longer. Where was the harm?

"I will consider it."

Zoe had taken no part in the exchange about Constantine fleeing Constantinople. But late that night, alone with him in the Ocean Hall, she added her voice to her father's counsel.

"You must go," Zoe urged as they sat together in the Ocean Hall, she on the reclining couch, and he on the red beaded chair that had become his favorite. "It's the only way to save Constantinople. Europe doesn't realize how desperate the situation is. Only you can persuade them."

"My father and my brother failed to persuade Europe to help us. I would fare no better. If I leave, the city will fall."

"But the city will fall with or without you unless the Venetian fleet comes."

This would be the time to tell her, Constantine thought. But he couldn't bring himself to voice his guilt. He had not even confessed it to Isidore who took his confession; how could he reveal it to her? What would she think of him then? He had lost all whom he had loved, and maybe God's love, too. Now he was losing Zoe. He had felt it most clearly in the council chamber when he saw the look she'd exchanged with Justiniani. Until then, he hadn't realized how deeply he loved them both. How many ways can a heart be broken? The woman he loved and his best friend. The man he admired above all others. He found the thought unbearable. But he had to bear it. When this was behind him, he would deal with it. Not now. Now was not the time.

"Emperor Justinian wished to flee when faced with disaster," he said, "but Theodora urged him to stay and fight. You know what she said. 'If you want to save yourself, O Emperor, it is no problem. We have money; over yonder is the sea, and here are the ships. Yet ask yourself if the time will come, once you are safe, when you would gladly give up security for death.' Would you disagree with your favorite empress, Zoe? Can you assure me she was wrong?"

Zoe's breath caught in her throat. She felt nauseous, and her hand went to her stomach. She needed air. She rose to go to the balcony, but a wave of dizziness assailed her. She stumbled and almost fell. Constantine leapt to his feet. Gently, he helped her sit. Pouring from a flask on a nearby table, he brought her wine. She drained the cup. Despite her uncertainty, she was about to tell him about the babe when Apollo shrieked, "Go-go-go!" Zoe stared at the bird, fluttering on his perch. Sometimes she vowed he was human.

A wan smile curved Constantine's lip. Gathering a handful of left-over raisins from the *apotki* on the table, he went to Apollo. For some inexplicable reason, tears sprang into Zoe's eyes as she watched him feed Apollo. He hopped on his hand when he'd finished, and Constantine brought him out of his cage. "I was thinking of giving him his freedom," he said, stroking Apollo's cheek with a gentle touch.

Zoe drew to his side. "But this is all he knows, Constans." She caressed the bird's sapphire and purple feathers, soft as grape skin. "He cannot survive out there. The world is a jungle to him."

Constantine looked at her then, and their eyes met. In the silence that ensued, past and future melded together, pulsing with memories, uncertainties, hopes, dreams, and fears. Zoe knew that she herself had spoken his answer and that it was his final word. There was no going back and no going forward. All lay in God hands. Panic tore through her, and she bit down hard on the scream in her throat. She had chosen to love an emperor, a man of honor, courage, and integrity. Though abandoned by his brethren in the West, he would not flee, and never would he abandon his people. He would stand in the breach to the end, holding the infidel at bay until they overwhelmed him with their numbers. He would die with his empire, and the empire would be his shroud.

A sensation of intense sickness and desolation swept her. She drew her gaze back to Apollo, resting on her husband's finger, and watched tenderly as Constantine eased the bird back into his cage and gently closed the door. How far away was that rapturous time they had known when they'd sat together hand in hand on the velvet sofa, newlyweds laughing at something the dear bird had said as sunset glowed over the earth. It felt so long ago now, a world away, and it was but six months.

Twenty-Nine

As soon as Urban's cannon had been repaired, the bombardment of the walls resumed with vigor. Four hours after sunset on the seventh of May, Mehmet assaulted the *Mesoteichion* portion of the land walls. Fighting was heavy and lasted nearly three hours, but the enemy was unable to force entry over the ruined walls and stockade. A few days later, Mehmet launched another full-scale attack on the Blachernae and Theodosian walls. That, too, was repelled. Even Mehmet's attempt to force the chain across the Horn met with failure.

Constantine was on the Horn surveying the enemy troops on Pera when footsteps came. He turned.

"Grand Duke Lucas requests your presence, Augustus," Dalmata said, striding up. "He has discovered the enemy digging a tunnel at the Caligarian Gate beneath the wall at Blachernae."

Constantine swept past him, Justiniani at his heels. Lucas was deep in conversation with the Scotsman when he arrived.

"—I recommend digging a counter-tunnel to enter the Ottoman mine and burn the wooden supports," Grant was saying, shouting to be heard over the church bells ringing for Prime.

"How soon can you reach the tunnel?" Constantine interrupted, closing the distance.

"In a day or two, Sire. We ' re better at everything than the enemy. We will smoke them out, and if they dig again, we will flood them.

"Stay vigilant." Grant bowed, and Constantine withdrew. "Mehmet is a wily devil and full of tricks," he told Justiniani as they hastened down the tower steps. "I hate to think what other surprises he has prepared for us."

His words proved prophetic. A few days later, at dawn on the eighteenth of May, the defense on the *Mesoteichion* was horrified to see a great wooden tower on wheels standing outside the Gate of St. Romanus. Constantine could hardly believe the evidence of his own eyes. The moveable wooden turret was as high as the outer wall of the city, with steps for men to climb to an upper platform where a pile of long planks waited to be levelled against the wall.

In the hospital tent, Zoe heard the shouts on the battlements and hastened to St. Romanus to see for herself. She made her way through the crowd of soldiers to Constantine, who stood with Justiniani on the ramparts. She covered her mouth to stifle her gasp. The structure was as large as a Trojan horse.

"—they assembled it during the night," Justiniani was saying. "It's bad enough that they can breach our walls now, but that's not the primary purpose of the siege-machine. We've detected workmen beneath the structure. See there—" He pointed to the edge of the ditch, where the masonry had collapsed.

"They're building a road over the moat!" Zoe exclaimed.

"Yes," Constantine replied. "To bring their siege machine right up to our innermost wall." If they managed that, all would be lost. He turned to Justiniani. "We must stop them."

Despite their best efforts and the hails of arrows they dispatched all day, the enemy had the task almost completed by twilight. As Constantine and his advisors studied the massive structure in the gathering gloom, Zoe came to join them on the ramparts.

"What can we do? Anyone have any ideas?" Constantine demanded, addressing those around him.

"If someone got close enough, they could place kegs of Greek Fire around the base," Zoe offered. "That would bring it down."

"Impossible." Constantine's tone was dismissive, even condescending. Everyone concurred. Zoe was flooded with humiliation. "I will do it! Who will join me?" she challenged.

More laughter. Impossible, someone echoed behind her.

"It is possible," Zoe exclaimed, turning on the unknown person. "All it takes is a man's heart, and that I have! A man's clothing you can loan me."

Chuckles. This time the laughter was not at her expense. Her glance touched on Prince Orhan, who looked as if he would speak, and lingered on

Justiniani rubbing his chin thoughtfully. But they remained silent. Suffused with disappointment, she was about to leave when Justiniani said, "The *Zoste Patricia* is right. It can be done."

"What?" Constantine exclaimed. "How can anyone get near enough to deposit the accelerant?"

"By stealth," Justiniani replied. "If that fails, they'll have to fight their way to it."

"It is suicide—" Constantine protested. "At the very least, it is fraught with peril. We could lose everyone we send."

"It is. We could. That is why I have to lead them," Justiniani grinned. "In Coco's immortal words, that will ensure our success."

"Jest not about that," Constantine said darkly. "We cannot afford to lose you, Justiniani."

"It is our only chance, Majesty."

Zoe dropped her lids, awash in an agony of remorse, guilt, and terror. It was her fault he was doing this. To prove himself to her. For the love of Mary, if something happened to him, how could she bear the guilt? She looked at Constantine with all the hope in her being. Refuse permission, I beg you—

"Very well," Constantine agreed. "As it is the only way."

In the pitch darkness of the night, weighted down with heavy kegs of Greek Fire on their shoulders, Justiniani and his men crept to the enemy tower a hundred yards away.

The air was thick with the chirping of night creatures, and Justiniani caught the faint strains of a love song from the distant enemy camp. A soft breeze stirred, ruffling his hair, and caressing his cheek. It was a fine night. A night made for love, not war, he thought.

He forced himself to concentrate. This was hardly the time for reverie.

Slowly, weighing each perilous step, Justiniani led his little band of three men across terrain riddled with potholes, rocks, and debris, and down the slope to the moat. As they neared the ditch, the night air smelled of wet earth and the ground softened into mud. He waved them in, and they waded into the filthy moat the enemy had filled with debris. Moving slowly through the muddy waters, they felt each step carefully, mindful of the hidden dangers of stones and sharp metal objects that could trip them up or slice their flesh. All the while they kept themselves rigidly erect to protect the barrels of gun powder they carried on their shoulders, and the fuses they wore coiled around their heads like turbans that were ropes threaded with fine wire and drenched in accelerant.

Finally, Justiniani and his men crossed to the other side of the moat. Panting, exhausted, they paused to catch their breath before tackling the steep slope that bounded the moat.

Once on flat ground again, Justiniani assessed his approach.

Here lay the most dangerous part of the mission.

The tower was lit by torches halfway up where the guards sat, and though Justiniani and his men wore black from head to toe and had blackened their faces with coal, a some point they might be seen if they strayed into light. Between the tower and the distant hills stretched the darkened valley of the enemy encampment where soldiers made merry. The music and laughter drifted to him on the wind, along with the loud, rhythmic clapping of hands as the revelers marked the beat. One false step, one inadvertent sound, and they would end up on a spike. With that hideous knowledge, the black silhouettes dancing around the campfires took on sinister shapes, and the wind that bore the sound of their drums began to howl in his ears and their laughter to shriek.

Justiniani braced himself. Picking his way warily, he led his men forward. The tower drew closer, a vast and menacing shadow against the distant hills. Silently they moved toward its four supporting columns, and gingerly deposited the kegs of Greek Fire into position at the base of its feet. From above Justiniani's head, where a few solders sat guard behind a wooden screen, came the clinking of dice and smell of grilled meat. All at once his stomach growled fiercely. He froze. So did his men. For a heart-stopping moment he thought they were lost, but the Turks were either too high above to hear, or too engrossed in their gambling to notice.

Unwinding the coiled fuses from around their heads, Justiniani and his men tied them to the barrels. As they worked, Prince Orhan, one of the volunteers, heard the Turks overhead throwing dice and conversing, their voices clear on the warm air. They told of their families and farms, what they missed about their homes, and their plans when they returned. For an instant guilt stilled his hand. But what choice did he have? These men had to die so they could survive and the world could be a better place. He forced his mind back to his task.

Sweating profusely, their hearts thundering in their chests, the small party completed their work and Justiniani gave the hand signal to depart. Moving slowly, vigilantly, they stole back together across the treacherous, uneven terrain, laying the fuses carefully along the ground as they went. They slipped into the foul moat, stepping carefully to avoid injuring themselves on the unseen dangers below. Holding the fuses high to keep them dry, they drew them gingerly across the expanse of the moat. Once on the other side they pulled the fuses taut above the water line, secured them with heavy rocks, and set them alight. Flames shot along the ropes drenched in Greek Fire and hissed toward the powder kegs.

They ran for their lives.

A hellish chorus of Turkish shouts and alarms rang out as they reached the city walls. They pounded furiously on the gates. They were thrown open. Bolts quickly slammed into place.

Exhausted by their ordeal, panting for breath, Justiniani and his men collapsed on the ground just as a thunderous explosion blasted the night. The wooden turret burst into flames, sending a volcano of red fire skyward that lit the blackness with a fearsome display. On the parapet Constantine watched the conflagration with awe. By St. Barnabas, they did it— They truly did it! He ran down the tower stairs, his Varangians in close pursuit. He thanked Orhan and the other two Greeks but reserved his highest praise for Justiniani.

"You went into the lion's den and slew the fearsome beast like a Samson," he marveled as flashes bright as daylight continued to illuminate the night. "I doubt there is anyone in the world quite like you, Justiniani." He called for wine and gave the flask to him with his own hands.

Justiniani downed a long gulp and wiped his mouth with his arm. "Couldn't have done it alone," he grinned. He glanced at his men who were sprawled on the ground, and his gaze moving back over the watching crowd swept past Maria and fixed on Zoe.

Constantine turned behind him to see what had claimed his friend's rapt attention.

Zoe was smiling at Justiniani, and the glow of admiration was in her eyes. There was something else. Relief. Profound and joyous relief.

On the ramparts, Constantine stared into the distance, his face averted from the one he addressed. "Can you back up your accusation with evidence?"

"No, but—"

"Then it is pure speculation. Isn't it, Maria?" He turned and looked at her, eyes cold, his mouth thin with displeasure.

"It is more than that. I know my sister."

"That is not good enough. You are not to speak of this again unless you have proof. Is that understood?"

"Of course, Augustus."

Constantine watched her leave. The afternoon was oppressively warm, even for May, and fog misted his view of the valley. He leaned on the stone balustrade and bowed his head in an agony of indecision. Never in his life had he felt so uncertain and inadequate. Never had he been so confused. His feelings had little to do with the enemy and everything to do with the two closest to his heart.

Zoe… and Justiniani…

He had suspected something for a while now, and despite his dismissal of Maria's accusations, her suspicions had confirmed his own. How far had they taken it? Should he, or shouldn't he, confront them?

And if he did confront them, what then? If they denied their feelings for one another, would it bring him comfort when he knew it wasn't true? And if they admitted it, what could he do? More importantly, how would it impact the war? Justiniani and his troops were indispensable to their survival; without them, the city would fall.

He shouldn't have married Zoe. He was too old for the havoc that love wrought in the heart, and he had known he couldn't compete with the virile young men vying for her affections. If the marriage with the Georgian princess had gone through, how much better it would have been for him. He would have ships and men now, and though the girl was as young as Zoe, their marriage would have been a dispassionate affair, arranged for reasons of state. Not this. This hell.

He passed a hand over his face. He had to resign himself. He had no choice but to let it lie. All will be decided soon enough, he thought. One way or another. He turned his disconsolate gaze on the enemy.

Despite the setbacks he'd dealt the enemy, Mehmet hadn't abandoned his tunneling operations. Instead, he'd imported miners from Serbia. Christian miners, he thought miserably. They'd had no choice but to resist them with every means possible. In this, the Scotsman Grant had proven his mettle.

Using all the methods at his disposal, he had either flooded their tunnels and drowned the miners or poured Greek Fire and smoked them out. This had netted them a prize: the capture of one of Mehmet's senior officers. Under torture, he had revealed the locations of other tunnels, and Grant had destroyed them one by one. Earlier in the day, they'd won their greatest success. The Scotsman had dug a counter-mine under the Blachernae wall near the Caligarian gate and burned the enemy miners to death. Had it not been for the Turk's information, this last tunnel was one they would never have found, for the entrance had been cunningly concealed.

Constantine knew his victories should hearten him, but he also knew they would not be saved unless they received help. If only God would speed the Venetian fleet their way! He'd prayed fervently, beseeching His favor. He'd fasted on every feast day since the siege began, including the two great feasts in May that marked the founding of Constantinople and its founders, Constantine and Helena. Now it was the twenty-second of May, and still there was no sign of the Venetian fleet. Every morning when he awakened in the darkness before dawn, he went to the balcony and stood with his face turned to the Marmara, eyes and ears straining for the cries of watchmen that would announce their arrival. And after every sunrise, he made his confession to Cardinal Isidore, knowing the day could be his last. Remarkably few defenders had died in the fighting, but many had been wounded, thinning the lines, and all were hungry and weary to exhaustion. Supplies of arms, particularly of gunpowder, were running low, and the food situation was growing desperate. He didn't know how much longer they could hold out.

And still no sign of the Venetian fleet.

Constantine removed his helmet and wiped his brow with a damp cloth. All at once urgent hoof beats sounded, accompanied by the shouts of men. Within moments a messenger appeared on the tower stairs.

The man fell to a knee, a fist to his chest. "Augustus, I come from Admiral Diedo! A ship has been sighted tacking up the Marmara! Ottoman vessels are in pursuit!"

"It has to be the forerunner of the Venetian fleet!" someone cried.

Constantine didn't trust himself to reply. They would know soon enough. Till then he dared not rejoice. He led the way down the steps and galloped southeast to the Marmara walls, followed by Dalmata and his Varangians.

Twenty minutes later he took the tower steps two by two up to the parapet by the Tower of Eugenius.

Zoe received the news in the hospital tent. She hastened to the Marmara. But first she summoned her guards. For some strange reason, she had found herself anxious about her safety of late. On three occasions she'd caught sight of the man with the bird as she travelled through the city, and each time he'd appeared seemingly out of nowhere, almost as if he'd been waiting for her. She knew she was being foolish, but unable to dismiss her fears, she'd spoken to John Dalmata, and he'd increased her escort. She never went far from the palace without them.

When she arrived on the Marmara, Constantine was already there, staring out at the sea. She followed the direction of his gaze. In an achingly familiar scene, a little ship was fighting to shake off her pursuers in the south, tacking to left and right, then shooting ahead and turning unexpectedly. She thought of a dolphin pursued by a school of sharks and watched with acute anxiety, her mind a confused mixture of fear and hope.

After an hour of evasive maneuvers, the little ship approached the walls.

Constantine held his breath and glanced up at the sky. The sun was setting. Soon it would be dark. If only she could keep the enemy at bay a little longer! If only she could survive until dark! Then they could raise the chain and she could slip into the harbor to safety.

Beside him, Cardinal Isidore raised his voice in prayer and was joined by all who heard. From farther away arose the chanting of the monks guarding the sea wall. Constantine threw a glance over his shoulder. Along the hills and slopes of Constantinople, people had fallen to their knees, hands clasped, eyes on heaven. Just so had they watched the four brave Christian ships, thinking they were the forerunner of the Venetian fleet.

He turned back to the Marmara and steeled himself. He had to be strong, had to believe that God was with them now, as He had been that other day. And, as he had done on that other day, his eyes kept stealing to the Dardanelles from whence the Venetian fleet would come. But there was no sign of a fleet. The little ship was alone.

The vessel turned out to be the brigantine that had been gone twenty days searching for the Venetians.

In Constantine's council chamber, Zoe waited for Trevisano to arrive. Silence wrapped the room like a thick, suffocating mantle; no one spoke, and no one moved. Everyone stared ahead at the candles flickering on the table, even Constantine who sat with his hands tightly folded together before him, a muscle quivering at his jaw. Zoe noticed that his hands trembled and watched as he removed them from view.

The thud of boots in the hall made her jump. Her eyes flew to the door, her heart pounding wildly. Gabriel Trevisano and the crew of the brigantine crowded the entry. Trevisano was paler and thinner than Zoe remembered, and his face was pinched and drawn and no longer clean-shaven. In the momentary lull that fell, it seemed to Zoe that all the world caught its breath, and she was overcome with a queer sensation of darkness, as if an ominous, palpating presence had crept into the room to cast a spell over everyone at the council table. She gave an inward shudder.

Constantine had the same presentiment. He barely breathed, yet his heart thundered in his ears and his blood raced so rapidly through his veins that he felt as if he were on fire. Behind him the hourglass measured its grains of time in what seemed a hissing whisper as he waited for Trevisano to speak.

Trevisano moved, and the dreadful illusion shattered. He bowed to Constantine. "Majesty, noble councilors," he began. "I regret to inform you that the tidings we bear are not good. We cruised to and fro through the Aegean. We saw no Venetian ships, nor did we hear any rumors of a fleet. When it became evident that further searching was useless, I asked my comrades what they wished to do."

Constantine felt his knees knocking against one another under the table as he listened in growing horror. He balled his hands into fists and forced himself to breathe.

"One man said it was foolish to return to a city that was probably already in Ottoman hands or would soon fall to them. But the others silenced him, Majesty. They felt it their duty to come back and tell you how matters stood—" he broke off. Softly, he added, "Even if it meant we went to our doom."

Pierced to the core by the valor of the men before him, Constantine's heart overflowed with admiration, affection, and gratitude. But facing the wreckage of his hope to save his people and grappling with the annihilation of his empire that was now a virtual certainty, he fought to comprehend. To comprehend that no one cared. That they stood alone. That the whole of Christendom had deserted them, and all that was left of Roman and Christian civilization in the East would fall to the infidel. Pride in his men, grief for his people, and fear for the future warred for ascendancy in his heart, but above all this rose the knowledge that they had waged the good fight, had suffered, overcome, and endured—and all had been for naught. For naught. Yet even knowing this, these men—the best of the best, the bravest of the brave—had returned to his side in defiance of the fate that awaited—

The vast and devastating knowledge swept him with shattering force. He felt as if a gigantic wave held him down deep under the sea, choking the breath from his body. He fought for control, but the flood of wild panic and sorrow that rampaged through his being could not be restrained.

Bowing his head, covering his face, he wept—for them, for himself. For Rome, Christianity and the East. For everyone.

Zoe scraped her chair back and went to him. Justiniani rose with her. Together they stood on either side of him, each with a hand on his shoulder. As tortured sobs racked his body, Constantine reached up and clutched their hands with his own, throbbing with utter, inconsolable despair.

Thirty

Standing before his tent of red silk and gold, Mehmet stared at the walls of Constantinople and the charred remnants of his tower by the moat, burned by Justiniani and his little band of men.

"If yesterday all thirty-seven prophets had told me such a feat was possible, I would not have believed them," he said to his Grand Vizier, Halil Pasha. "Why have I not such men?"

"Perhaps we can woo him to our side, O Holy One," Halil suggested.

Mehmet's hooded eyes turned to his vizier. "Do you think it can be done?"

"Every man has his price."

"Let us hope that is the case here," Mehmet said uncertainly.

"What do you wish to offer him?"

"Everything. He is worth half my army."

Halil Pasha bowed low and blew a kiss from his lips to the sultan. "I will do as the Shadow of God wishes."

Constantine did not sleep. He stood on the balcony, watching the campfires of the enemy across the Horn. He feared the dreams that would come to him if he slept, nor could he still his unquiet heart long enough to rest. It was midnight, the twenty-third of May. Church bells tolled the hour. On the stroke of twelve, the chanting of the *Mesonyktikon* prayers in honor of the holy Trinity drifted from the monasteries where the Midnight Office was being sung. He looked up at the moon. It beamed down, a luminous orb in the night sky. Soon it would be full.

Prophecy said that the Eastern Roman Empire would not fall while the moon waxed, but the knowledge brought him little comfort. Full moons were quickly followed by black skies. When it waned, peril would come. They had withstood the enemy for fifty-two days now. How much longer could they endure?

He gazed at the sleeping city below. All his life he had wanted to be emperor. He lifted his eyes to the dark heavens. *Dear God, why did you choose me—why?* A sharp pain knocked the breath from his body. *If only I hadn't threatened Mehmet. If only I could awaken from this nightmare—*

Zoe watched him. She had tried to offer what comfort she could, but he had not replied to anything she'd said. As often happened these days, he wasn't even aware that she was there. She stood quietly beside him, sending her silent prayers to heaven—for him. For Rome, and Constantinople. For Christianity, and her unborn child.

At daybreak, Constantine left to oversee Grant's anti-tunneling operations and check on the repairs made during the night, and Zoe hurried to her duties tending the injured. Though deaths had been miraculously few in these nearly seven weeks of siege, Zoe found the day a difficult one. She arrived as the body of a defender was being carried out, followed by his distraught mother and weeping sister. She stepped aside to let them pass. When she looked down at the fairhaired youth, she had to stuff her fist in her mouth to quell the cry that came to her throat.

Thomas.

The day grew more onerous as it wore on. The tent rang with screams and curses as Zoe assisted Barbaro with amputations. Even poppy juice failed to stem the pain of those who suffered. Wounded men lay on straw pallets, moaning piteously and crying out for loved ones. Some, delirious with fever, shouted nonsense; others, too weak to swallow the broth she tried to feed them, threatened her composure with their gratitude. But a man with wide-stretched eyes, clearly out of his senses, yanked her braid loose and called her a witch as she knelt to give him water. Shoving her cup aside, he leapt from bed with the fury of a madman and grabbed her by the throat. Had Justiniani not arrived at that moment to help Barbaro restrain him, he might have killed her.

"Are you alright?" Justiniani said.

She nodded.

He took her elbow. "No, you're not… Here, come with me—" He led her outside to the olive tree and made her sit on a long, flattened stone that served as a bench. He sent for wine.

A few birds reveled in the warm air and sang some notes, but a surge of sudden nausea churned her stomach. The babe in her womb would be born in December. What would the world be like in December?

She slumped over and cradled her face in her hands. Did they have seven months? Seven weeks … seven days—

"Here—" Justiniani said.

She opened her eyes and took the tin cup he held.

"Bad day?" He watched her drink.

Not trusting herself to speak, she nodded.

"I suppose you could say every day is bad. Except that it could be worse," he grinned. Her lips curved. It was a wonderful thing he did, making her smile.

"We have held out fifty-three days… It can't be easy for them."

In a weak voice, Zoe said, "For us, you mean."

"No, for them. Besiegers need food and water for themselves and their animals, even when they eat but once a day. And there's always the threat of disease. Mehmet has to dispose of enormous quantities of human waste and keep those funeral pyres burning. He needs tons of wood daily, over a hundred tons of fodder, and tens of thousands of gallons of water." Looking up at the sun, he mopped his brow and the back of his neck with a cloth. "More soon. It's getting hot. If we can hold out ten more days, I warrant he'll be gone."

Zoe broke into a smile so wide she felt her face would crack. There was an end in sight. Ten more days and they would be saved! Surely, they could hold out ten more days— She had heard Constantine say that were it not for Justiniani, they wouldn't have lasted a week. "Thank you, Justiniani," she said softly, her heart in her eyes. "Thank you for coming to save us."

His whole face spread into a sudden smile. With a nod, he turned and strode off toward the Charisian Gate, whistling.

Zoe's heart was light when she returned to her duties, but the respite proved brief. By Nones, they had lost one soldier, and by Vespers, a third lay dying. With his mother weeping softly at his side, he fought to live, his chest heaving with erratic, labored breaths. Monks were summoned and candles lit. The smell of burning incense filled the tent as the young man received the last rites. The priest raised his voice in a hymn and anointed his brow with oil. With a soft, sweet cadence that made Zoe think of the sighing of the sea, the words of the Office at the Parting of the Soul from the Body issued forth, beseeching the mercy of God and the intercession of the saints. Slowly the young soldier calmed and his breathing eased.

"Blessed is our God," the priest intoned, "always now and ever, and unto the ages of ages..."

Zoe swallowed on the constriction in her throat, her gaze on the silent warrior. He is so young. Too young ...

"On behalf of a man whose soul is departing and cannot speak himself, have mercy on me, O God," the priest chanted, concluding the prayer and speaking as if he were the dying man asking forgiveness for his sins. The monks broke into the great hymn to Mary, the *Theotokos*. As the words of the last prayer of the dying were sung over him, the young man ceased his struggle, and it seemed to Zoe that she bore witness to the flight of his soul.

The priest bent down and gently closed his eyes.

A terrible wail rent the tent. Zoe averted her face. Unable to watch his mother's grief, she left for the solace of the olive tree. Leaning her cheek against its ancient bark, she lifted her eyes to the sky. Gold, silver, rose, and glorious oranges lit the heavens in one of the most beautiful sunsets she had ever witnessed. For some inexplicable reason, her anguish peaked, her composure shattered, and she broke down and sobbed.

Constantine returned from the walls as monks sang the prayers of the midnight office. Even in the torchlight, the strain he labored under was evident to Zoe. His posture spoke of utter exhaustion, and he was hollow-eyed. She gave him greeting and led him to the balcony as Aesop served *apotki.* She had to coax him to eat, but once he did, he devoured the small plate. She realized he had skipped dinner yet again. Ten more days, and then, with God's help, all will be put right, she thought.

She contemplated her husband. Engulfed in darkness, he sat with his elbows on his knees, cradling his head in his hands. I should tell him of the child I carry in my womb, she thought. It was too soon to be certain, but it would surely help him to know that in this cruel and uncertain world, something beautiful was happening for them. She knelt and took his hand into her own. "I have joyous tidings for you, beloved. We are going to have a child."

His hazel eyes flew open. Years fell from his face, and she saw again a glimmer of the shining prince she'd loved.

"A child?" Constantine felt a curious lifting of his being, as if an iron fetter around his chest had shattered, admitting light and air. Grief had been his. Glory he would never know. Triumph might elude him yet. But one abiding truth would endure as long as life should last. He had known love. He caught her hand in his own and pressed a kiss to her palm. "What happiness you bring me, Zoe," he said, flashing the dimples she had missed. She took a seat next to him and leaned her head on his shoulder. Smiling, they sat together, admiring the tranquility of God's creation.

The air was clear as crystal, the breeze tender, and the night haunting in its loveliness. The moon was full and high and beamed over the dome of the Hagia Sophia, sending the smooth waters of the Golden Horn shimmering like black onyx. Just so had the full moon shone for a thousand years, cycling through time, a golden orb adorning the velvet skies as the Queen of Cities adorned the velvet waters.

But even as she gazed, Zoe sensed a change. The moon seemed to falter. The light acquired a glow that deepened into a strange red tint, and a black cloud touched its face. She looked at Constantine for his reaction, and as she did, the monks broke off their song. The sudden silence, so abrupt and unexpected, chilled the air like ice. She turned her gaze skyward and stared mouth agape at the dread sight that met her eyes.

The black cloud had obscured the moon and it was no longer full. A pale silver crescent shone in its place. The Hand of God had darkened the full moon, the emblem of their fair city, and replaced it with that of the infidel, the crescent

She rose to her feet, not realizing she stirred, unaware that beside her Constantine did the same. She summoned no cry, for her throat had closed on the horror beating in her heart. Around her a rush of gasps rose from a thousand throats and melded into a hideous hissing noise as all Constantinople shrank aghast beneath the blood-red crescent moon.

No one slept—not Constantine, not Zoe, not the city. And not Justiniani. He watched the shadow pass across the moon like the wings of some vile and evil creature, and as he watched, he shuddered and hope withered in his breast. Weary and sorely in need of comfort after the monstrous portent God had sent, he sought comfort at the tiny chapel in the wall at the gate of St. Romanus. The darkness was dimly lit by a single candle, and he stood for a moment letting his eyes adjust. Then he made the sign of the cross and knelt before the icon of the Virgin and Child. As he bowed his head in prayer, his glance moving across the altar caught on something half hidden behind a flask of tulips. He frowned. Hesitantly, he reached out and drew it to him.

The scrap of parchment bore his name.

Why would anyone write to him in this curious manner? What could they possibly want? Baffled, he opened the letter and bent his head to read.

On the ramparts, Constantine looked up from the missive in his hand to find Justiniani's gaze on him. "And your answer?" Constantine said.

"You have to ask?" Justiniani replied accusingly.

Constantine gave an audible sigh. "I would not blame you if you accepted, Justiniani. If we lose, a fate worse than death awaits those who survive."

"I do not intend to be taken alive."

Constantine fell silent. He looked gravely at him. Mehmet had offered Justiniani command of his mighty Ottoman army and riches and favor beyond imagining. It was an offer to tempt a saint. But if he accepted, it was the end of Rome.

Justiniani read his thoughts. "I promised to fight for Christianity. A promise is sacred. Once given, it must not be broken."

"No one but you would turn away from such temptation, Justiniani," he said in a choked voice. "It is no less than I expected of you. You are a rare man."

"Like you, Majesty," Justiniani said softly. "We are brothers-in-arms, forged of the same mettle. We cannot but keep our word, no matter what the cost."

To fortify the spirits of the people after the devastating eclipse of the moon, Constantine ordered the walls to be blessed with the holiest icon in Constantinople. As gray dawn broke over the city, a crowd gathered before the Church of St. Savior in Chora where the precious relic was housed. The *Hodegetria,* the image of the Virgin painted by St. Luke, was brought out to the chanting of monks. As church bells tolled, it was set on a wooden pallet.

Constantine and the faithful crossed themselves, for legend had extolled the power of its blessing. Zoe watched a team of men hoist the icon on their shoulders. The haunting refrain of a holy hymn rose in the humid air and mingled with incense and the sound of sacred chant. *Save Thy people, Bless Thine inheritance...*

An acolyte lifted his cross high, and the procession moved forward. Led by bishops and a host of black-garbed priests swinging their censers, the throng of bare-footed laity, men, and women, children and nobles followed the Cross down the steep and narrow street that wound along the city walls. Zoe's glance fell on her two brothers ahead and shifted to Isaac, whose hand she held. As the sons of an enemy magnate, they all stood in great peril, but none more than Isaac. Mehmet had a taste for boys his age, and Isaac had heard tales of his Seraglio. His hand trembled in hers, and his blue eyes were stretched wide with fear. For good reason, Zoe thought. Tightening her grip in reassurance, she bowed her head in fervent prayer and poured her heart into the hymn.

A scream rent the air, followed by shouts and a thunderous crash. A bird passed so close over her head that she felt the brush of its wings. With sudden apprehension she remembered the man with the bird.

"What happened?" people asked one another.

"The *Hodegetria* fell off the platform!" someone replied.

Gasps of horror filled the air, and everyone made the sign of the cross. Zoe's gaze flew to Constantine a short distance away. He was surrounded by his Varangians. She only glimpsed his profile, but it was enough: beneath his high crowned helmet his face had turned the color of chalk.

"You are to blame—you with the bird!" someone shouted. "You dropped your end of the pallet on purpose— I saw you!"

"Liar— It was Heaven's doing!" cried the man. "The Virgin has abandoned us!"

His accuser lunged at him, and a fight broke out. Women shrank back in fear. Men joined the fracas, and guards tried to break it up. Still others rushed to pull the miraculous image out of the mud, but the Virgin couldn't be lifted. A chorus of panicked voices rang out. "She's too heavy!" "She's stuck in the mud!" "But we've lifted her before— Heave-heave—" "I am heaving! We're all heaving—she's not moving!"

As Zoe strained to see what was happening, she suddenly realized that a gulf had opened up between her and Constantine. She scanned the crowd. Her guards had disappeared, and not a single familiar face was in sight—not her family, no one she knew, except Isaac. For some reason she thought of the bird and wondered if the man was near. She gave a shudder and tightened her hold of Isaac's hand.

"Stop! You're hurting me!" he cried, pulling his hand away.

A crash of thunder drew her glance skyward. Dark clouds threatened rain, and it was hot and oppressive. A flash of jagged lightning lit up the street, but there was no wind, not a breath. In the distance the sea wrapped around them, strangely still and silent. A giant raindrop splattered her hand, and in the next moment the skies let loose a deluge. All at once the wind rose fiercely and began to shriek with a high-pitched, unholy whistle. The crowd pressed close and jostled and shoved, seeking shelter. An old woman fell, and someone went to her aid, but then another person fell, and soon others were falling. Something struck Zoe's face with stinging force. *Dear God—it's hailing!* That never happened in Constantinople. People halted and screams rang out. Then they all tried to flee at once.

Suddenly Zoe saw what was causing the panic. A tide of muddy floodwater was surging down the street, coming at them forcefully, knocking people to the ground as it rushed past. A mother picked up her child and struggled to safety on the side, but an old man collapsed beside her. Zoe tried to help him, but he couldn't get a foothold in the mud, and people were fleeing blindly past, trampling him. We have to get out of here! she thought. She looked around for Isaac, but he had disappeared. She screamed his name. No one answered; no one came. She cried out for Constantine and Justiniani, but her cries were drowned in the noise of the crowd. People knocked into her as they ran. *Soon it'll be a stampede, and they'll trample me like they did the old man—*

She turned to run but found herself pinned down, unable to move. Beneath the rushing water her feet were mired in mud. In a panic she cried for help—for someone, anyone, to give her a hand. Then, miracle of miracles! —someone grabbed her hand, and with a fierce tug, yanked her free. She turned to thank her deliverer and froze in horror. It was the man with the bird! Screaming, she fought his iron grip, but he dragged her with him as he plowed through the crowd. All at once, out of nowhere, just when she'd given up hope, someone seized the bird-man's shoulder and whirled him around. The man looked up and the stranger punched him in the face. He fell into the stampeding mob and was lost to sight.

A terrible lament arose around her, whipped by the wind, and more people fell. She fought to stand, but she was growing light-headed, unable to balance, and had trouble breathing. She would have fallen but for strong arms that grabbed her. "Come with me!" a voice cried in her ear.

She looked up into Justiniani's face. Her eyes filled with tears of joy. She leaned into him gratefully, his powerful embrace steadying her, guiding her, keeping her erect.

"You're safe now," Justiniani whispered, tightening his hold.

Thirty-One

Few knew that the eclipse of the moon caused Mehmet the same consternation as it did Constantine. Greatly troubled, he sent for a wise man to interpret the sign.

"It is most favorable, Holy of Holies," the wise man said, "for it foretells that the light of the True Faith will soon illuminate the city."

Mehmet gave a wave of dismissal. Though he was gratified to hear that God blessed his endeavor, he still had doubts. He had expected New Rome to fall to him within days, and here it was, more than seven weeks later, still standing. Time and again, with their God's help, the Greeks had found a way to survive for yet another day, another week, another month. His sailors had suffered humiliating reversals, and his soldiers had not yet won a victory, despite their overwhelming numbers and magnificent war machines. Morale was low. He himself had been, in turns, shocked, dismayed, and dejected by his failure to win the prize his ancestors had lusted for since the inception of their dynasty, one that had seemed ripe for the taking. His great guns had been blasting at their walls for nearly two months, battering them, even demolishing them in places. But each night men, women and small children patched them again, and each day, Greeks and Italians took up their weapons and repelled his assaults, sustained by dreams of rescue and hope of aid from the West.

And now that help was on the way. His spies in Venice had managed to delay the departure of the fleet the kingdom had promised the emperor, but they had failed to prevent it from sailing. Dispatched three weeks ago, it had finally reached the island of Chios. Soon it would be here, maybe in days. What then for him? He would be defeated and driven off in disgrace with his tail between his legs like a beaten dog. His prestige at home and abroad would plummet, and he would be the laughingstock of the world. It was a humiliation too evil to be borne. Better to abandon the siege and leave of his own accord.

So brooded Mehmet. In this mood, he summoned his envoy and dispatched him to Constantine with an offer of terms.

Constantine was on the ramparts observing Grant dismantle the last of the enemy tunnels when a party of riders rode up with a white flag. They drew to a halt before the guards at St. Romanus gate; Constantine heard their voices but couldn't make out what they said. His heart quickened as Lucas came running up the tower steps.

"Augustus," he called out. "The sultan sends an offer!"

Hope lit Constantine's heart. Maybe it was one they could accept. A tall, turbaned Turk was escorted up, his long robes whipping around him in the wind. Constantine stared at him in astonishment. "Aristides?"

"My name is Ismail now," replied Muriel's husband, his former Eparch. He bowed in Oriental fashion, releasing a kiss toward him. "Our holy sultan sends greetings and wishes you to know it is not too late to save yourselves from certain slavery or death. These are his terms. The siege will be lifted if you undertake to pay an annual tribute of a hundred thousand gold bezants. Or, if you prefer, Majesty, the citizens can leave the city with their belongings, and none will be harmed. He is anxious to reach an agreement and urges you to accept his terms."

Constantine regarded Aristides, married to the poisonous woman who had humiliated Zoe. He had defected soon after he was stripped of his position, and here he stood now, on the ramparts he should have been defending. This Christian. This Greek who had sold his faith for a bag of gold and rank in the world of the Ottomans. He felt a stab of despair. Never would he understand such men: Urban the Hungarian, Zaganos the Albanian, Baltoglu the Bulgarian, and the never-ending list of other dishonorable traitors.

"We will discuss the sultan's offer with our advisors," Constantine replied. "Pray await us in the hall… You know the one."

Lucas looked around the council table. “If we agree to the tribute, Mehmet will demand immediate payment.”

“If we pay, we shall be vassals of the Ottomans,” Cardinal Isidore said.

“The argument is moot in any case,” Demetri offered. “We can’t raise the money. There isn’t that much gold in all Constantinople. Mehmet must know that.”

“Then what is his real motive?” Zoe asked.

“He’s testing us, my lady,” Justiniani replied. “He wants to know if we think we’re on the brink of defeat.”

Zoe felt his eyes linger on her. She averted her gaze and addressed Constantine. “Can we at least pretend to agree to his terms? It would buy time.”

“Time for what? For help to come?” Constantine said bitterly. “What about his other offer, to allow us to depart in safety?”

“We cannot surrender the city— They will defile our churches!” Cardinal Isidore exclaimed.

“If we don’t accept his offer, thousands will die and many more will be taken into slavery,” Lucas replied. “Surrender would spare the people a terrible fate.”

“Why am I not surprised you speak of surrender, Notaras?” Phrantzes spat. “I have met the man. I am the only one here who has. I say trust him at your peril.”

“Saladin let the people of Jerusalem leave in peace,” Lucas bristled.

“Mehmet is no Saladin. Saladin didn’t impale people. Saladin wasn’t intent on world domination. What is there to stop such a man from slaughtering us as we leave the city?” Phrantzes turned his dark eyes on Constantine. “I pray you, do not make a pact with the devil, Augustus.”

Constantine heaved an audible sigh. “Then we have no choice. We must fight on. But I will make him a counteroffer. He can have everything I own except Constantinople.”

“Constantinople is all you own,” Zoe said gently. “You have nothing else.”

Constantine quirked a weary smile. “I have a few outposts I cannot protect. As to my offer, I know Mehmet will accept nothing less than the surrender of the capital of Rome.”

Demetri leaned forward. “Then you must agree to leave, Augustus. To stay is certain death.”

As Constantine gazed at Demetri, his face blurred. He rubbed his eyes. He was tired, so very tired. "My place is here."

Zoe opened her mouth to protest and shut it without uttering a word.

Constantine scraped his chair back and rose. "Then we are decided. There will be no tribute, nor will we leave. We put our faith in God, that He, in His great mercy, will save His people."

A few hours later, seated on his golden throne, with Zoe and his nobles around him, Constantine summoned his old Eparch. The former Christian strode up, his sandals slapping the smooth marble. Constantine gave him his answer and bestowed the gift of a golden bezant for his service. The Greek bowed with a ceremonial flourish of the hand to the brow, and it seemed to Zoe that the feather in his turban pointed like a dagger at Constantine's heart.

Suppressing the shiver that ran through her, she averted her gaze.

Zoe passed through the Venetian quarter on her way to St. Acacius. A crowd had gathered in front of a carpenter's shop, and a man was arguing with someone whose back was turned to her, someone familiar.

"Is that Minotto?" Eirene asked.

"Yes," Zoe said, troubled. "I wonder what is wrong?" She trotted Ariadne forward.

"—who are you to order us about?" A Greek was saying, glaring angrily up at Minotto from the cobbles where he sat carving a wooden shield.

Another Greek who was sorting logs threw his Greek friend a snide laugh. "He's a Venetian," he spat, making "Venetian" sound like an epithet.

"What are you so hot about?" Minotto demanded. "All I did was ask him to take these shields to the walls."

The Greek who had started the argument came to his feet. "We resent being ordered about by those who failed us in our most desperate hour. We're not taking them to the walls unless you pay."

"You wish to be paid?" Minotto cried in horror. "At a time like this?"

"We expect to be paid," he said coldly. "Our families are starving. We need money for food. It's all very well for you, isn't it? Your family lives in comfort in Venice with plenty to eat. They're safe, and ours will share our fate."

A Genoese from Pera who had been polishing a shield laid his cloth aside. "Listen, we understand how you feel," he said kindly to calm the angry Greek. "These are hard times for us all—"

The angry Greek turned on him violently. “Shut your mouth, you Genoese dog! Pera could have helped us! Instead, they betrayed us to the enemy. You Genoese are all traitors!’

“He’s right,” another Greek said, backing up his angry friend. “Your women and children are safe at Pera. None will share your fate. Ours are here, with us—” His voice cracked. He threw down the block of wood in his hands and walked away.

Minotto, the Genoese and the angry Greek watched him leave. As the wretched man passed Zoe, she saw tears in his eyes.

“He’s right about one thing,” Minotto said. “You Genoese are all traitors.”

“What in hell are you talking about? We’ve fought side by side with you—” demanded the Genoese from Pera, rising to his feet.

“You told the sultan about our plans to burn his ships,” Minotto cried. “That’s why we’re in these straits!”

“The plan failed because Coco charged before he should have,” the Genoese protested.

“And Coco was a Venetian— Like you!” A Greek exclaimed, coming to the defense of the Genoese. “You Venetians are all the same. All talk, and everything a lie! Where is the fleet your Doge promised? Do you see a fleet, you miserable worm?”

“No one’s paying you to carry those shields to the walls!” Minotto yelled, red-faced. “No one’s got any money. If you cared about your families, you’d take them, and if you don’t, so be it. They’ll end up as slaves and mine are safe in Venice—as you say!” Swiveling on his heel, he strode to his horse.

Zoe closed her eyes on a breath. The strain was tearing the city apart. She trotted up to the Genoese and the Greek standing together, gazing miserably after Minotto.

“I will pay you to take the shields to the walls,” she said gently, opening her purse.

From the balcony Constantine spied Zoe’s lavender figure in the distance. She was with Justiniani on the Blachernae wall, and they were deep in conversation, heads together. All his loneliness and confusion melded into an upsurge of bitter yearning. Sick with the struggle inside him, he fought to control his emotion. Soon all will be settled, one way or the other, he told himself. Turning away from the painful sight, he strode back inside to his study.

"—when did you first notice him following you?" Justiniani was saying to Zoe.

She related the facts as she remembered them.

"We lost him in the crowd, but we will find him again and deal with him," Justiniani said. "Meanwhile I'll arrange for an armed guard." Zoe nodded assent.

That evening, as church bells tolled for the Midnight Office and gauzy curtains fluttered in the breeze, Zoe greeted her father in the Ocean Hall and led him to the sunken study. Moments later, all Constantine's commanders arrived for an audience, as arranged. The strident marching of their boots drew Constantine's attention from the sand table where he stood studying the Western defenses.

Phrantzes cleared his throat. "Forgive us, Augustus, but we come for your decision. The heavens themselves suggest that further resistance is hopeless. There is no time to be lost. Even now your escape is not assured. May we prepare your departure?"

For a long moment Constantine stared down at the model of the walls. Then drawing himself erect, he looked up. "If my city must perish, I will perish with it."

"No!" Cardinal Isidore protested. "It is futile to stay! You must leave, Majesty. To live and fight another day!" "Go while you can," urged Lucas. "All will understand. It has been done before." "You have no choice but to leave. For the good of the empire, Augustus, "Admiral Diedo added, "Escape, Majesty, while you can—" Prince Orhan pleaded. "Yes! Go while you can!" Trevisano exclaimed.

"To stay is certain death." Justiniani said.

Their faces blurred in his vision and their pleas melded into a cackle of noise that ran through the chamber, reverberating against the marble, striking the columns, and rising to a roar in his ears. *Go-go-go, certain death, certain death—*

"If the city is taken, you can wage the struggle to win it back," they cried. "Go to Rome, set up an empire in exile so Byzantium does not vanish from the face of the earth—"

"Enough!" Constantine slammed a fist on the desk. "I will not desert my people! If the Queen of Cities falls to the infidels, it is by God's will. Constantine Dragas Palaeologus will not go down in history as the emperor who ran away—" His head swam, images of the Janissaries assailed him, grotesque, distorted. From behind the marble pillars, they surged at him, thousands upon thousands of them— He staggered and put a hand up to ward them off, but still they came, lunging at him, taking on the faces of children—children from the Hexamilion Wall, torn from their mother's arms, placed into Turkish helmets. Children of Christ fighting for the enemies of the cross. *Was this God's will?*

A pain exploded in his chest, his blood drained to his feet, and his knees buckled beneath him. He felt himself falling, and heard a cry, and knew it was Zoe running to his side.

On Saturday the twenty-sixth day of May, the city awoke to deep fog. Asleep at his desk, Constantine looked up to find the whiteness so thick that the balcony was no longer visible. Wearily he rose and dressed. He rode to the Gate of St. Romanus, his progress slow, for his reluctant mare, unable to see where she stepped, kept offering protest. "It is all right, Athena," Constantine clucked gently. "Trust me. I know every pothole along the way, my friend." At St. Romanus he took the tower steps up to his position, followed by his imperial guards. As he moved through the milky whiteness, he heard soldiers talking. He paused his steps to listen, and his retinue did the same.

"You know what this means, don't you?" whispered one in horror. "God is abandoning us."

"What do you mean?" asked an Italian in halting Greek.

"It's the prophecy. The Divine Presence arrives and leaves in thick fog, so no one may see Him," a Greek explained.

"How do you know He's leaving? He could just as well be arriving, couldn't He?" the Italian offered.

"God has been around for a thousand years, protecting us from harm. People saw the Virgin on the walls during the last siege. Now He is leaving and taking the Holy Mother with Him."

Constantine closed his eyes and forced himself to breathe. To breathe and find words to rally his men. But his mind was blank, empty, numb.

Justiniani's voice broke into the conversation. "God works in mysterious ways. Remember the Divine Wind? He may be planning another miracle that requires His presence in heaven to direct."

A chorus of murmurs met the remark as men digested this new idea. Constantine blessed his friend inwardly for his quick thinking. All at once shouts sounded on the Mesoteichion. "Find out what happened," he ordered Dalmata.

The captain disappeared into the swirling fog and reappeared with Justiniani at his side. In Dalmata's hands were several arrows, each pierced with a missive. He handed one to Constantine.

"They are sent from the Christians in Mehmet's camp," Constantine said quietly when he had read. "This one informs us that Mehmet met with his viziers to decide whether to continue the siege or withdraw—" He passed it to Justiniani and accepted another, pausing to glance in the direction of Mehmet's European divisions from whence the sound of chanted prayers drifted to him through the mist. As always at Terce, they commemorated the descent of the Holy Spirit at Pentecost that was celebrated seven weeks after Easter. Torn by conflicting emotions, the old pain under his heart that had plagued him since Hexamilion came again with a wrenching twist. If anyone had told him two months ago that they would hold out seven weeks against such might, he would have called them mad. Yet here they were. For seven weeks Christians had been killing each other even as Pentecost came and went. Now, Christians forced to fight against their faith had at great personal risk sent these arrows of warning. He swallowed on the constriction in his throat and read another message, thankful for the fog that obscured him from his men.

"And his decision?" Justiniani prompted.

Constantine forced himself to go on. "Mehmet has decided to stay for one last assault. He has declared Monday a day of rest and atonement. Our friends warn us to make ready for the great battle ahead. More than that they do not know. They will try to get another message to us when they learn more."

"That explains why the bombardment of the walls has been so heavy these past two days," Justiniani said. "He's softening them up for his final assault."

Aware that his men were listening, Constantine forced himself to keep his voice steady. "We have won every battle we have fought, day after day, week after week, for seven weeks. With God's help, one more victory will be ours, and we will drive the accursed invaders back to their own land."

Cheers went up in the fog as men applauded his words.

Constantine turned to Justiniani. "How are the repairs coming?"

"By tonight the stockade will be nearly as good as new," Justiniani replied.

"I will supervise the work," Constantine said. "You rest, Justiniani."

Justiniani shook his head. "No, I must be here."

He pushes himself too hard, Constantine thought. Suppressing his sudden unease, he gave a nod.

Justiniani examined the stockade, heartened by the progress they had made. The fog had proved a blessing, providing cover from the enemy as they worked, but now a sea wind was blowing in and the mist was dissipating. It was a relief to him that they were almost done.

He turned to praise the men, women, and children laboring with him when a thunderous boom shook the earth and he was slammed to the ground. A shower of falling rock and debris cascaded over him, burying him face down beneath a crushing weight of tremendous force. Unable to move, barely able to breathe, he tasted dirt in his mouth and felt the world darken and spin. He knew he was losing consciousness and forced himself to inhale, but there was no air. Fierce pain exploded in his shoulder and had the blessed effect of reviving him, if only briefly.

He heard people calling his name, but they seemed a world away. Summoning all his strength, he cried, "Here! I'm here…" Even to himself, his voice was barely audible. He swore and pushed up against the load on his back with all his might, but only a few pebbles fell away. Now the blackness intensified despite the pain flaring down his side. He gritted his teeth against the panic that assailed him. Death had always been close. He had always accepted it. But now, more than anything in the world, he wanted to live. For Zoe. For the life they would have together in Lemnos after the war—

"Here!" he heard someone cry, surprisingly close. There was a sudden flurry of activity and a lightening of pressure. All at once strong hands turned him over and faces stared down at him from a backdrop of the most magnificent, exquisite silver sky he'd ever seen. He blinked, blinded by the splendor of the brightness. Choking on the dust in his throat, he coughed violently as they helped him sit up.

"We found him!" men called to one another. "We found the *Protostrator.* He's alive!"

They helped him to his feet. "My shoulder—" he gasped. The men relinquished their hold. "Can you walk, my lord?" someone asked.

He nodded. Gingerly they assisted him to his feet, but he was weak-kneed and had trouble standing. "Here— Lean on me," said a familiar voice.

Justiniani found himself looking into Trevisano's bright green eyes. His head aching, he draped an arm around the Venetian's neck and sagged gratefully against him. "What happened?"

"A great shot from Mehmet's monster cannon landed near you. See there—" Trevisano jerked his head. Justiniani turned to look in the direction he indicated. The section of wall he had been working on was now a pile of rubble. "Another few inches to the right," Trevisano added, "and you wouldn't have made it."

When news reached Zoe that Justiniani had been injured, she rushed to the hospital from the palace storeroom where she'd been gathering towels and bandages. She found Barbaro tending his injury as he sat on a table behind the privacy screen.

"I heard you were wounded—" Fighting her panic, she averted her eyes from the rippling muscles of his bare chest and the crisp chestnut hair that disappeared into the padded loin cloth beneath his scale armor. "I came to offer my help," she said, fixing her gaze on his bruised shoulder.

"I would embrace the chance to have you nurse me, but it's only a splinter." Justiniani attempted a smile, but an oath escaped his lips as Barbaro dressed the wound.

Zoe ran to pour a cup of willow bark mixed in poppy juice, the draught Constantine hated. "Here, take this. It is bitter but it will help."

He drained the contents. "From you, it tastes like wine," he grinned, thinking how lovely she looked with her cheeks flaming like red poppies.

She bit her lip. She wished he wouldn't flirt. Didn't he know by now that people talked? Had they not told him that she belonged to the emperor? She averted her eyes. He's heard the rumors, a small voice said in her head, but he won't believe them because he doesn't want to, and it's all your fault. You have not been honorable with him.

I haven't encouraged him, Zoe protested inwardly, but the voice would not be silenced. *You haven't discouraged him either. You let him hope when there is no hope.*

She looked up. Barbaro was washing his hands in a basin. He picked up a towel and dried them as Justiniani pulled on his tunica. An aide stepped up to strap on his breast plate.

"Where are you going?" she demanded.

"To my post."

"But you need rest!" Her eyes flew to the surgeon. "Doesn't he, Barbaro?"

Before Barbaro could reply, Justiniani said, "There is no time for such luxuries, my lady. You nurse the injured past dark, and I fight by day and repair the walls by night, like everyone else."

"Will he be all right?" she asked Barbaro as they stood together watching him slowly mount the tower steps.

The surgeon laid his towel aside. Softly, he said, "With God's help."

A clamor arose from the land walls. Zoe and Barbaro ran outside to see Constantine and Lucas galloping up and Trevisano hastening down the tower steps to meet them. "Majesty," Trevisano cried. "A rider comes under flag of truce!"

Silence.

Constantine's heart took up an erratic beat. Here was the final warning decreed by Islam. *Surrender the city. Or die by the sword.* For weeks he had known this moment was coming, but he found himself curiously unprepared now that it was here. He had no illusions about the stakes. This was Armageddon. If Constantinople fell, the last glowing ember of the Roman Empire would be extinguished, and with it, the flame of Christianity in the East. Like Troy, his civilization would vanish from the face of the earth and fade from human memory as if it had never been. His stomach churned and he felt a hand close around his throat.

He braced himself and took the tower steps up to the ramparts.

Two horsemen waited before the walls of Constantinople, their white flag of truce flapping in the wind. Constantine forced his parched lips to speak his reply. "We will not deliver the city. We will defend our homeland to our last breath. May God's will be done!"

"I hate you! I loathe you! I wish you were dead!" Maria screamed.

Zoe regarded her sister. She was of her blood, yet there was no common ground between them. There never had been, Zoe realized suddenly. They shared nothing except the seed of their beginning.

"You took Justiniani from me!" Maria cried.

"I've done naught to hurt you, Maria. If I could hand you Justiniani' s heart, I would do it. But it is not mine to give."

"You led him on! If you had told him the truth everything would be different now. I will never forgive you—never, ever!"

Guilt washed over Zoe in a muddy flood. "I wanted to tell him—many times—but I was afraid, Maria. Afraid for us all. If he knew, he might leave, and if he left, Constantinople would fall. How could I take that chance? How could I do that, Maria?"

"You always have an answer for everything! He can't leave now, can he? He can't leave anymore, but you still haven't told him."

"This is not the time—"

"Oh, yes, it is! It certainly is. I'll make you a promise, dear sister. If you don't tell him, by God, I will!"

"No, Maria—you can't! Think what it could mean!"

Maria thrust her face into Zoe's own, green eyes blazing like a madwoman. "Oh, yes, I *can.* Oh, yes, I *will.* Here's my promise to you, dear sister. By this hour tomorrow he will know!" Her voice was guttural, octaves lower than Zoe had ever heard it, almost demonic.

Maria turned and ran out of the Ocean Hall like a whirling storm, her laughter rippling with hysteria, wild anguished notes torn from an inner hell.

Thirty-Two

On Sunday morning, in the blackness before cock's crow, as soon as Constantine left to check on the defenses, Zoe rode to the Chora. Clad in a drab gray linen tunica that reflected her mood and a veil to conceal her hair that was braided and bound in a net, she dismounted and gave Ariadne's reins over to a guard. Eirene leaned down and squeezed her hand. "Courage," she whispered, her own grief written on her face, for old Theseus had died the previous day. The two women looked at one another for a long moment before Zoe turned away wordlessly and headed for the garden.

She caught sight of Justiniani's tall figure ahead in the torchlight as she passed through the gates. He was leaning against the lemon tree, his white bandages and metal breastplate glinting in the darkness. She checked her steps and braced herself. Inhaling a quick breath, she took the terraced steps down. Justiniani looked up and saw her. With rapid, jaunty strides, he came to her along the winding walk. They met by a wide-rimmed stone fountain that no longer ran.

Zoe's glance went to his arm, hanging helplessly in a sling. She gave a shiver. He had always seemed invincible. Now she was reminded that he, too, was mortal and subject to the whims of fortune, as all men were. Her gaze moved to his face, to the compelling, passionate mouth, the strong, square jaw lightly dusted with growth, and the tawny hair gleaming gold in the torchlight.

"Zoe—" he grinned, taking her hand into his. He knew it was to tell him she loved him that she came, and he was engulfed by a glorious, blissful joy. "What have you to say to me, beloved lady?"

She looked away, unable to bear the sudden leap of joy in his olive eyes. Her knees shaking, she put out a hand to the stone fountain to steady herself before forcing herself to look at his face, bronzed by the sun. The thought came to her that he had never looked more handsome, or more vulnerable. "I am here to tell you something I should have told you long ago. A secret—" she blurted before she lost her courage. "Something I have kept from all the world. Now I know I should not have kept it from you."

"A secret?" he said, smiling that endearing smile that had come to mean so much to her.

She marshaled her strength and met his gaze. "I am married." Swept with anguish, she watched the blood drain from his face.

Justiniani's breath froze in his breast, and he dropped her hand as if he held a hot coal. He took a faltering step backward and stood silently, staring at her slack-jawed, his body quivering, his eyes glittering with anguished bewilderment and disbelief. She almost went to steady him, but she knew her touch was the last thing in the world he wanted.

For Justiniani, it was as if he'd been hurled into a black tomb and the lid slammed shut over him, sealing out all air and light and hope. His stomach heaved; his mouth flooded with bile. *Wed! Zoe was wed!* His hopes and dreams and the future that had sustained him these many months shattered with the finality of glass, leaving only shards to pierce his heart. Beyond that there was the knowledge that he had loved and trusted her, and she had betrayed him. He swallowed forcefully and put a hand out to the fountain's edge. He couldn't retch. Not now. Later, but not now.

"Who?" he demanded in a hollow voice.

"The emperor."

"For the love of God!" He closed his eyes and turned blindly away with a groan. Leaning his full weight on the stone rim, he bowed his head, fighting for breath. After a long moment, face still averted, he said, "Why is it a secret that you are empress?"

"To protect me from the sultan," she whispered. Tears rolled quietly down her cheeks, blinding her vision as she looked at him. The clanging church bells that rang for the liturgy rose to a din in her ears, grating with a harsh, unnerving dissonance.

He turned on her violently. "In Christ's name, why did you not tell me sooner? How could you—"

In his accusing eyes she read every thought that came to him. "I never meant for this to happen. I don't know how it did—I love my husband. I am expecting his child—"

He gave a sharp gasp. "Begone!" he cried in a strangled voice, breathing hard. "Begone..." He sank down on the stone and covered his face in his hands.

"Forgive me," Zoe whispered on a sob. Picking up her skirt, she fled blindly through the garden, past the fountain, the lemon tree and the startled monks gathering for breakfast. Heads turned but she paid them no heed. She reached the church as the first crack of morning streaked the dark sky. She entered the outer narthex, passed through the inner, and fled into the *naos.* As the tearful gaze of the *Theotokos* Mary followed her, and the Christ Pantocrator looked on with pity from the walls and domes and ceilings of the ancient, little church, sobs tore from her breast, and she fell to her knees before the altar where she had been married.

Constantine stood at the Gate of St. Romanus, watching Mehmet ride with his heralds through his camp, stopping every few hundred yards to address his troops. The soldiers cheered, and Mehmet moved on. Constantine didn't hear his words, but the chant of his troops reached his ears: *"There is no God but Allah, and Mohammed is his prophet!"*

He caught Justiniani's voice on the wind and turned to see him striding toward him from his position at the Charisian Gate, his arm in the sling. Constantine had been badly shaken by the report of his injury yesterday evening, and for a chilling moment had feared the worst. Remembering with a shudder how seven ships had fled in the night before the siege began, his relief to learn Justiniani's wound was minor had been profound. For well he knew that the Genoese detachment only stayed for love of their commander. If something should happen to him— He banished the thought. "How is the shoulder today?" he asked, suppressing his unease.

"Well enough," Justiniani replied curtly.

Constantine was taken aback by Justiniani's changed demeanor. His voice no longer held the good-natured jocular tone he'd come to expect. But it was more than that. He was distant, and his normally lively eyes were hollow. Constantine wondered if fear weighed on him but dismissed the idea. Justiniani had never been bothered by battle before. *Perhaps his pain is great.* His gaze went to Justiniani's arm. There was something unsettling about the injury, and Constantine couldn't shake his disquiet. *Why now?* The timing seemed ominous.

"I do not want you in harm's way, my friend. Allow me to relieve you of duty until your shoulder is fully healed."

Justiniani didn't reply immediately. At length he said, without inflexion, "I thank you, Majesty, but it was by God's will that I was born ambidextrous. If I cannot fight with two swords, I will fight with one. But I will not sit out this battle. It is why I came."

Constantine was about to protest when loud voices came to him, bantering with one another. "When we have vanquished the enemy, I will kill you, my Venetian friend."

"Not if I kill you first, you Genoese rogue," chuckled the Venetian.

"But before I do, I will collect the debt you owe me," the Genoese went on, ignoring his reply. "That is, if you're still alive to pay it."

"If I'm not alive, you will collect nothing but flies," the Venetian countered. "And you are welcome to them, my friend!"

Laughter greeted this comment. Constantine smiled, and Justiniani threw a soft glance in the direction of the men. "It seems Venetians and Genoese have finally made peace with one another," Constantine said softly.

"A miracle," Justiniani replied.

"We need only one more," Constantine said.

Justiniani made no reply. After an awkward silence, he said, "With your permission, I will go to the tent and have my bandages changed."

Constantine let his disconsolate gaze follow Justiniani down the steps. He thought it was to Zoe that he went. He could not know that Justiniani had chosen his moment so Zoe would not be there.

Constantine lost no time preparing for the final assault. After services at the Church of the Holy Apostles near the *Mese* on Sunday morning, he met with his prefect and his staff of ministers and magistrates. Satisfied that the necessary munitions had been delivered to the defenders on the walls and supplies of water, sand, and soil stood ready to fight the fires that would erupt during battle, he held council with his commanders on strategy and set out to inspect the defenses. He had just completed the walls along the Golden Horn when he was gripped by an attack of severe vertigo that obliged him to return to the palace. Zoe rushed to his side from the hospital. She found him in a weakened state, propped up on a reclining couch where he was attended by Theo. Taking a goblet of wine from Aesop, Zoe pressed the cup to Constantine's lips.

Constantine drained it. "I must return to the wall," he said feebly. He tried to rise and fell back.

"It is all the fasting you have done," Zoe said gently. You must eat first."

A commotion at the door announced Demetri.

"You are needed, Augustus," he called out urgently, striding up. "The city is coming to blows. I went to report an incident to Justiniani and found him fighting with Grand Duke Lucas! God help us. I fear they may kill each other if you do not come!"

Constantine stared at him in bafflement. They had never fought before. *Why now?* With effort he pushed himself to his feet.

Zoe watched him leave with a mute wretchedness she had not known before, and the gnawing pain she'd felt in the Chora garden washed over her in a muddy flood. She collapsed into a chair and raised a hand to her brow. Justiniani, fighting with her father— *What have I done?* Pouring a cup of wine with a trembling hand, she drank, spilling more than she swallowed.

In the gardens and hedgerows of the city, the roses were in glorious bloom and their perfume scented the breeze. Constantine had forgotten how beautiful it was, summer...

He dismounted at the Gate of St. Charisius and gave Athena over to a guard. Even from where he stood at the base of the wall, he could hear their voices on the ramparts, arguing heatedly. "Grand Duke, you need to move your cannons to our side!" Justiniani was saying. "We shall need every one of them!"

The tower stairs loomed before him like a staircase to Heaven. Bracing himself he mounted as resolutely as he could manage, for he knew all eyes were on him, and in him rested all hope.

"How many times do I have to tell you—they cannot be moved!" Lucas roared. "He clearly intends to attack the harbor! You have plenty of men, and my position is not adequately defended. I need these guns!"

Wearily, Constantine made his way to them. Why, in this hour of their greatest peril, did his most vital commanders have to fly at each another's throats?

"What?" Justiniani cried. "Are you too fool to understand what's at stake here, Lucas? He's going to attack the *Mesoteichion* with everything he's got! It's the part of the walls he's focused on since the siege began. We need those cannons!"

"Who are you calling fool, idiot? Are you too dense to understand what I told you? You're not getting them!"

Justiniani spied Constantine along the parapet and strode up to him, shaking with rage. "Majesty! Surely you see the need to have these cannons on the Mesoteichion! Tell him, I beg you."

With an inward sigh, Constantine addressed his father-in-law. "Lucas, the *Protostrator* is right. We need the cannons moved there. If the Mesoteichion falls, it won't matter about the Golden Horn."

By the flare of torches, Zoe toiled on the repairs to the walls and stockade alongside soldiers, town folk, women, and children. All at once strange lights appeared in a ring around the enemy camp.

Everyone halted their work. "What in God's name is that?" someone demanded.

"Is their camp on fire?" an old man wondered aloud.

Voices seized the thought and passed the cry along the defenses. "The infidels' camp is burning—The Virgin has worked another miracle!" Leaning over the walls, they called down to those below. "The Virgin has saved us! The Ottoman camp is burning— Come and see, come!"

Everyone embraced wildly. Letting go their carts, dropping their shovels, putting down their loads, men, women, and children raced up to the battlements, Zoe with them. She stared ahead in rapt amazement. The ring of fire was spreading in an ever-widening circle that lit the western sky clear to the horizon. Someone picked up a flute. Music broke over the night. People held hands and danced. Joy sang in Zoe's veins, and she laughed as she watched them, her heart soaring like a bird's, lifting her higher and higher—

"It is not fire," someone said.

Everyone turned to see who spoke. An awed murmur went up. "The great Justiniani—"

Zoe shrank into the shadows, knowing he would not wish to see her.

"It looks like a fire, but it's an illusion. The camp is not burning," he said quietly. "The hills of Pera are also ablaze. They are not burning either."

"Is it a sign of our fall?" someone asked in horror. There was no response.

A cold shiver touched Zoe's spine. She sank down on a pile of stones and buried her head in her hands. *What is happening? How can this be? What evil force is playing these tricks on us?*

With a shudder of remembrance, Justiniani's words came back to haunt her: *If Satan doesn't interfere, we will win.*

"If their purpose is to instill fear, they are succeeding," Constantine said to Justiniani as they stood on the ramparts gazing at the enemy camp. They watched the ghostly mirage fade until only the campfires still burned.

"You should get some sleep," Justiniani said.

"You as well. It is almost midnight."

As he spoke, church bells struck the hour and the chant of monks went up, offering the prayers of the midnight office. At the same time, the enemy campfires were extinguished. Silence fell over the dark night. Though Constantine knew Mehmet had declared Monday a day of rest before the final assault, he found the stillness unnerving after weeks of noise and tumult. The sense of unease that had been building since Justiniani's injury thundered in his veins, and he felt a rising panic. He inhaled sharply and looked up at the sky that was crowded with thousands of stars. Once, the magnificent immensity of God's handiwork had brought him solace, but not on this night. Not after what they had witnessed.

Something flickered in the distance, lighting up the hillside that had been a shadow among shadows. He stiffened. "Did you see that?"

"Yes..." Justiniani muttered. Strange lights illuminated the western sky, far beyond the reaches of the Ottoman camp, where no light should be. "That is not Mehmet's doing."

Torches flared, and Constantine turned to find Cardinal Isidore hurrying toward him across the parapet. "These lights are over the Hagia Sophia as well— See!" Turning to the eastern sky, the cardinal crossed himself.

Constantine froze. Lights played over the dome of the city's holiest church—strange lights, inexplicable lights. *That was not Mehmet's doing either.*

"It's a sign," Theo said, striding up, visibly pale.

A murmur arose, and Constantine caught the looks of consternation that passed between the soldiers. He suppressed a shudder. There had been too many prophecies of doom, too many portents of disaster about to befall. The fire that was no fire. Now these bizarre lights. He had to rally his men and give them hope, or the battle would be lost before it was even fought.

"Satan wishes to darken our hearts!" Constantine proclaimed loudly, his voice firm. "We have held out fifty-five days against overwhelming odds— We may be weary and short of men. Our walls may be damaged and in need of repair. But we have denied the invaders a single victory! With God's help, we shall thrash them one last time and seal our victory with another thousand years!"

Men roared approval.

"By your leave, Majesty," Justiniani said with a bow, "I will go to the Church of Holy Wisdom and pray for God's intercession."

All at once an arrow hissed over Constantine's head and landed at Justiniani's feet. Glancing at the message, he handed it to Constantine. "From one of the Christians forced to fight for the enemy."

Constantine bent his head and read. *Expect the great assault at midnight on Tuesday, the twenty-ninth of May. We pray for you. May God be with you and grant you victory.*

On Monday morning, in the darkness before dawn, Zoe opened her eyes to find Constantine gone and his pillow untouched. She drew on her chamber robe and went to the balcony. Not there either. Perhaps he didn't come back to the palace last night? He wasn't there when she'd returned from the hospital at midnight, and she'd been too tired to wait up. Now she dropped into a chair, utterly drained. A cock crowed, announcing daybreak, and she heard Aesop in the hall removing Apollo's cover and saw him set a few breadcrumbs and bits of cheese before the bird.

"Constans, Constans?" Apollo questioned.

"Tomorrow, Apollo," Aesop said in a broken whisper. "Tomorrow, if God is with us."

He disappeared into the bedchamber, and Zoe turned her gaze on the sunrise that was flooding sea and sky with rose. Gulls shrieked, swooping and diving, seeking their breakfast. Each year at this time the world had been drenched in sweetness and beauty. Now, though dawn might promise a fine summer's day, the city exuded a grim unease as it awaited its hour of destiny. Whatever God had in store for them, she had to believe they would prevail. But what if they didn't? *What then—*

She caught her breath at the horror. Last night she'd dreamed that she walked through the palace and all the passageways were empty and all the doors shut. She'd awakened with a sense of disaster looming. But many times in these weeks, disaster had loomed, and each time they had emerged victorious. *Soon we will know. In a few hours. By tomorrow's sunrise. One way or the other.*

Tomorrow we will know.

She summoned Eirene and dressed quickly, anxiously, overwhelmed by a sudden need for her mother. But when she arrived at her quarters in the *Soros,* she found herself at a loss for words. Alone in an empty room, her mother sat at the window, staring out into space. Beside her stood a flask of wine and a goblet drained of its contents. She knelt and took her mother's cold, limp hand into her own. "Mother, soon we will have the last battle."

No response. Her mother didn't look at her. It was as though she was made of wax and didn't hear. "I want you to know that I have always loved you," Zoe said, her voice cracking. No reaction. None. She found her voice one more time. "I am sorry I disappointed you, Mother."

Silence.

With tears in her eyes, Zoe rose to her feet and kissed her brow. "Farewell, Mother. God keep you." As she reached the door, she thought she heard her mother speak and she halted, her hand on the knob.

"Life disappointed me…" her mother said.

Zoe heard the words like a sigh passing through the room, as one would hear a whisper on the wind. When she looked back, her mother sat as she had left her, unmoving, oblivious, staring into space. *Must have been my imagination.* With a last look, she gently shut the door.

At the hospital she buried her grief in the pain of others, but in the early afternoon, learning that her father, Constantine, and Justiniani were together on the walls, she left in search of them. Constantine was nowhere in sight when she arrived at the Gate of St. Romanus, and she was surprised to find the walls almost deserted. The solitary gaunt-faced, hollow-eyed man-at-arms on duty directed her to the Caligarian gate. "He's there, *Zoste Patricia,* with the *megas doukas* and the great Justiniani."

She ran up the tower steps to her father's position at the corner on the Golden Horn. The fair-haired captain of the guard, Dalmata, stepped aside with a sharp salute, and she saw Justiniani from the back, listening to Constantine. She halted her steps abruptly.

"Halil opposed it. If we lose, he is a dead man," Constantine was saying. Even in profile, his pallor was evident.

"I hear Mehmet promised his soldiers three days to freely sack the city," Justiniani replied in a dull, low voice that felt strange to her ears.

"He also promised the booty—" Lucas broke off, suddenly aware of her presence.

"Zoste Patricia, what do you here, dear lady?" Constantine said. "You should be resting." He looked as pale as a phantom, and her heart twisted. He must have been here all night, checking the defenses.

Her father took her hand and lifted it to his lips. "My dear child," he said gently. "I fear we must bid each other farewell. May I ask for your prayers?"

Her father's hand felt as cold and heavy as stone in hers. Gone was the magnificent presence she had known. In the bright light of day, he looked almost frail with his sunken cheeks and diminished frame. But as she gazed, oddly disjointed memories flashed before her. Again, she was a little girl, walking with him hand in hand, and all at once she was greeting him at the royal harbor and he was smiling down at her, resplendent in gold, a twinkle in his eye. She heard Apollo's screech on the wind, and his cry mingled with the moans of the wounded in the tent, and again she saw the lone, hollow-eyed sentry on the wall at Romanus directing her to Caligarius. All these thoughts, jagged and disconnected, came to her as she gazed into her father's sad green eyes, and the old sick terror she had felt as a child abandoned on the wharf returned in a violent flood. She rose on tiptoe and flung her arms around his neck, feeling she would choke on the pain in her heart. "Father, I love you!" she cried, kissing him tearfully, holding him close, her cheek pressed against his.

"God be with you, daughter," her father said at length, disengaging her arms.

She wondered if he had the same sensation she did: that they would never meet again. She felt disoriented and very tired, weak in a spent kind of way and stood awkwardly, unable to move, not knowing what to do. She felt Justiniani's gentle gaze on her and dropped her eyes, not daring to look at him, but in her heart, she blew a silent kiss in his direction. If she had one wish, it would be to freeze this moment and hold it with her forever, so all three men she loved would remain safe at her side through eternity.

Constantine's voice broke into her thoughts. "I must go to my post now," he said, inclining his head to his commanders. *"Zoste Patricia,* will you walk with me?"

She was dimly aware that her father and Justiniani bowed as they left.

"You must leave the city, Zoe," Constantine said under his breath, his hand on his sword as he strode at her side.

Her breath caught. She would rather die than make a new beginning without him. "I will not leave you." She touched her stomach where their child was forming. Forming, as if all was as it should be. "My world is here, with you."

Constantine halted abruptly. Seeing a guard in the distance, he drew her into the privacy of a tower and took her by the shoulders. "Listen to me—you are going, Zoe! This is an order. If you refuse, soldiers will take you to the ship by force. Your father agrees with me on this. Do you understand?"

"I cannot stop you if that is what you are determined to do, but know this— I will never forgive you!"

"Zoe, Zoe—" he cried helplessly, taking both her hands into his own. "Dear heart, I implore you to go—for the sake of our child, if not for yourself. You must think of him."

"God is with you, Constans—you've held out longer than anyone believed possible. You will repel this assault as you've repelled the others. We will be together, to live as man and wife before all the world and raise our son to be emperor after you—"

"Zoe, Zoe—these are dreams!" He tightened his hold of her hands. "We have to face the truth. We do not know God's mind. You must go."

"You will not fail! You will endure! Repel this one assault and it will be his last. He will withdraw. You will triumph—you will—for the sake of our son, you must—"

He tightened his hold. "Look at me, Zoe. Look—" he cried hoarsely. "He needs only one victory. If we lose tonight, it is over— For us, for Constantinople, for Rome— For everyone and everything! You must leave."

"I will not leave you, Constans." The frenzied emotion was gone, and now her tone was calm, resolute, final.

"You always were stubborn," Constantine sighed, releasing her. "Even as a child. But this is not the last word. We will speak again."

Thirty-Three

After Zoe left, Constantine quickened his pace to his position at St. Romanus, his footsteps echoing in the eerie silence. Some in the city declared that the silence meant the enemy was preparing to withdraw, but he knew they didn't believe it themselves. It was pretense; another face of courage, denying the worst, hoping for the best. He had sent many of his soldiers home to bid farewell to those they loved, but for him there was no rest. His place was here, to prepare for what lay ahead. All his guilt, his fears, his doubts, had to be set aside now. If he failed this time, his people would awaken on the morrow to a fate more hideous than death. He owed them all he could give, for they believed in him, and had stood by him, and kept faith with him, even when they thought him wrong to have embraced union.

"*Kalispera,* Basileus," said the guard at the Gate of St. Romanus. Good afternoon.

"Good afternoon. Fine day. Quiet."

"Yes, *Basileus.* Very quiet."

The man was emaciated and black circles ringed his eyes. Constantine gave him a smile to hide his dismay. "Tonight we shall whip their hides, God willing, and it shall be quiet in our city for the next thousand years."

The soldier looked as if he would say something more. Constantine rested a gentle hand on his shoulder to encourage him.

"Thank you for staying with us," the man said, his voice cracking, tears in his eyes.

Constantine gripped his shoulder hard and nodded before passing on. At his position, he leaned against the stone ramparts and turned his back on the Ottoman camp to gaze at the city. His city. God's city. A maze of broken roads, ruined churches, dilapidated palaces. What did he have here that he couldn't give up? What was there to love the way he did?

It was home.

The rays of the late afternoon sun glanced off the golden crosses of the churches and monasteries, dazzling all the way to the sparkling shores, and from the sea wafted a soft breeze, rustling the leaves of the trees. In the silence of the guns a few birds and butterflies had returned, and with the knowledge that the crisis was upon them, his people had forgotten their quarrels and peace had descended on the jewel that was Constantinople. A distant refrain came to him on the wind, a lone voice, singing in the wilderness; a man's voice, rich, glorious, raised in a poignant hymn of repentance that haunted the quiet air. He listened, his weary spirit lifting with the hymn.

O merciful and compassionate God, You, who receive all who repent, Receive me, a sinner, And have mercy, Messiah…

One after another, other voices picked up the refrain, and the chorus rose until Constantine felt as if the entire earth resounded with the old lament that was a Greek translation from the Hebrew bible. Sung by Christians for a thousand years, the penitential hymn seemed to enshrine all creation in its peace as it winged its way to God, and he realized that the prayer offered by that one solitary voice now lived on the lips of every citizen of the city. It was, he thought, the most exquisite music he had ever heard, for it accompanied a sight so incredible and incomparably beautiful that it could only be heaven-sent. From the seven hills of Constantinople, his people were streaming out of homes, churches, monasteries, and palaces, old and young, men and women, priests and nuns, carrying lighted candles, forming processions, and winding their way along the walls to the Hagia Sophia, banners fluttering and holy images, relics and jeweled icons flashing in the sun. His people were coming together as one, pouring down to the holiest of churches.

Together.

A procession drew into view from Blachernae and moved gracefully toward him to the rhythm of the song, the angelic chorus piercingly sweet and rising in volume. As he gazed, the cortege took on a strange glow, and the colorful silks, the city streets, and the people paled in its brightness. He could smell incense as priests swung their burners over the defenses, blessing the walls, and the gates, and the soldiers standing watch above. The scent, borne to him on the breeze, stirred memories in his breast. Again, he saw Zoe standing on the terrace, drenched in the colors of the dawn and heard his people cheer him as he rode through the Golden Gate. Again, he sheltered on his mother's shoulder and felt her kiss on his childish brow as she gave him the secret of life: *Never look back. Keep moving forward. Do your best and have faith in God.* Warmth flooded him and his spirit swelled, filling the emptiness within, fortifying him with courage and renewed hope, banishing shadows and despair.

The procession drew up before the walls of St. Romanus and halted just below the ramparts by the tower steps, pausing to bless his portion of the wall where the danger was greatest and the need most pressing. Some in the crowd carried roses to adorn the Church of Saint Theodosia by the Golden Horn, for Tuesday was the saint's feast day. As they sang, a young girl took a rose from her bouquet and laid it gently on a tower step. One by one, Lucas and Justiniani, Phrantzes and Don Francisco, Theo, Diedo and Demetri came to his side to watch and listen. Bathed in prayer, blessed with serenity, he took the tower stairs down and joined the procession, his friends falling into step at his side. With one voice, Italians, and Greeks, Orthodox and Catholic, unionists and anti-unionists, emperor and peasant raised their eyes to heaven and sang together. *Kyrie eleison ... Christe eleison ... Kyrie eleison...* Lord have mercy... Christ have mercy... Lord have mercy...

The unity that had eluded him since he was anointed emperor found him now, and it seemed to him a living, holy thing, sacred at its essence, as blessed a touch as the hand of God. As he walked with his people, he was overcome with an all-encompassing oneness with them and a pervasive and profound sense of peace.

Constantine wound his way through the empty passages and peristyles of the palace and passed through the great bronze doors. He stepped out into the bright sunshine of the garden where his troops awaited him and took the marble steps down to the Court of the Sundial. Someone brought him Athena. He mounted his mare with the white hooves and trotted her forward to the edge of the great lawn.

His red-cloaked Varangians snapped their spears to attention at the head of his troops. For a long moment his glance roamed over the thousands arrayed before him. They were men of many nations: Greeks, Venetians, Genoese, Cretans. Here and there a Spaniard, a Scotsman, a Pole, or a Slav. All had answered the call and kept the faith, asking nothing in return. His gaze lingered on those who had grown dear to his heart. There were so many… so many good men… Dalmata, Diedo, Prince Orhan, Navarro, Trevisano, Don Francisco…

And Justiniani.

Justiniani, the dearest of them all. He had come when others had turned away. He had stayed when others had fled. Though it was not his fight, he had spared no thought for himself and had striven with every breath and ounce of will to save the Queen of Cities. *Side by side we have loved, and we have fought. We are brothers of the heart, mirror images of one another, bound together by love and war.*

His gaze fell on Prince Orhan and his friend Navarro, standing nearby. They were outsiders who didn't belong to them or to their faith, yet they had done all they could to defend Rome. *One last battle, my friends, and together we will build a bridge to amity and peace that will save untold generations from endless war.*

He tore his eyes away, seeking Zoe. He found her bright, lavender figure in the distance, standing beneath an orange tree. He gripped his reins tightly in his hands and began his address.

"Comrades in arms… The hour is upon us. A great assault is about to begin, and it has fallen to us to save the Queen of Cities. To my Greek subjects, I say this. A man should always be ready to die for his faith, his homeland, his family, or his sovereign. Now, my people, you must prepare to die for all four." He swallowed on the constriction already tightening his throat. "Remember what you fight for. Freedom. Your faith. Our civilization. And our homeland. If you throw down your arms, you and your unborn will be stripped of identity, faith, and heritage. Your loved ones will be torn from you and taken into harems, slavery, and the darkness beyond. Remember you are the heirs of ancient Greece and Rome, the descendants of the greatest people the world has known— My fellow Greeks, let us prove ourselves worthy of our ancestors!"

Men cheered.

He bit down hard on the emotion that flooded him.

"Men of Genoa, men of Venice, men of courage, most valiant heroes whose swords and prowess have many times saved this great city in these weeks of terror and siege, lift high your swords now! To all I say, have no fear in the face of your enemies. Tremble not before their vast numbers. Remember the four ships and the wind from God that saved them. Defend the empire! Be brave, be steadfast—" His voice faltered, and he knew his energy was nearly drained. "We are in God's hands now. May He save this great city that has been refuge to Christian, Jew, and Muslim for over eleven hundred years. May He grant us victory!"

Amid the roaring tide of cheers, Constantine sat on his horse, feeling utterly bereft, trembling to think he may have delivered the funeral oration of the Roman Empire. He was exhausted in heart, mind, and body. Forcing himself to dismount, he turned to the captain of his Varangian Guard.

Dalmata was tall, almost exactly his height, and Constantine met him eye to eye: hazel to blue. Taking his hand, he rested his other on his shoulder. "All these years you have stood by my side, protecting my life with your own, and I have never thanked you, John Dalmata. You have been my right arm, the one I always relied on, come what may. If we prevail the highest honors in the land shall be yours, and anything you ask shall be given you." He took a deep breath as he gazed at the fair-haired, clean-shaven, raw-boned face with the clear, sky-blue gaze. "If ever I have offended you, or spoken harshly to you, I beg your forgiveness now."

Dalmata's face was set; his generous mouth tightly clamped, and a muscle quivered at his jaw. "I have been honored to protect a noble emperor. Never will I leave your side, Majesty, come what may." His voice was steady, without inflection.

Constantine embraced his captain and held him close for a long moment. He turned to the next man, and the next, walking slowly around the court, from person to person, embracing each and asking forgiveness if ever he had given offense. And each soldier followed his example and did the same with others, in the manner of those about to die.

Standing beneath an orange tree on the side of the garden, Zoe watched Constantine. Blinded by tears, her hand on her stomach, she had listened to his speech drifting to her over the heads of his soldiers and knew she would never forget this day of grief in a garden of sunlight.

When his councilors and commanders had left, Constantine summoned his household to the throne room. They filed into the hall, led by Aesop and a weeping Eirene. Constantine went to her and took her hand in his.

"Forgive me if I was ever harsh or unkind to you in any way, Eirene," he said gently.

Eirene burst into fresh tears, and Zoe came to her side and placed an arm around her shoulders.

"I have a request of you now," Constantine went on. "Your mistress refuses to leave, so I ask that you go in her stead and take Apollo with you. A ship awaits you in Prosphorion Harbor. Board as soon as you can. Farewell, Eirene. May God keep you."

Eirene's choked sobs burst forth with renewed violence. Zoe held her, lending her strength.

Constantine moved to embrace Aesop. The old man bowed but did not rise again. Bent at the waist, his shoulders heaving, he held on to Constantine's hand with both of his own as if he would never let him go. Zoe's mouth worked with emotion as she watched, and she tightened her grip of Eirene's shoulders, as if that might help Aesop.

By the time Constantine had begged forgiveness of all his household and taken his leave of the last servant, the hall vibrated with the sounds of grief as it were a single living, breathing, sentient being. Zoe let go of Eirene and stood with eyes closed, holding a handkerchief to her mouth to smother the emotion that threatened, forcing herself to inhale, and it seemed to her that all the air in the world had been consumed, and none left in Constantinople to breathe. She opened her eyes to find Constantine standing before her, his face, pale and pinched. "Meet me at the Gate of St. Romanus at sunset," he said. Somehow, she found the strength to nod.

Surrounded by a retinue of nobles and Varangian Guards, Constantine rode in the procession moving through the city streets toward the Hagia Sophia for the final service of the day. The sun was low in the western sky, and the afternoon was drawing to a close. The time had come for a last prayer of deliverance. A light rain shower fell, and the crowd shielded their lit candles without slowing their pace. For much of the year, self-respecting Greeks had seldom stepped through the doors of the great church to hear the Divine

Liturgy defiled by the Latins. But on this day all bitterness and rancor was set aside, and no one stayed away from the desperate service of intercession except the few soldiers guarding the walls. There was Cardinal Isidore, in his gold embroidered robes, standing side by side with priests and bishops who would never acknowledge his authority. There were the Venetians, Genoese, Catalans, Cretans, and Greeks, standing shoulder to shoulder with those they once distrusted. Nor did the people who came to make their confessions care whether it was an Orthodox or a Catholic priest who heard them.

The golden mosaics around the church glimmered in the low light of a thousand lamps and flickering candles, and beneath them, the priests in their splendid vestments moved in the solemn rhythm of the Liturgy. As the people gazed, it seemed to many that the images of Christ and His saint, and the emperors and empresses of the Eastern Roman Empire wept over them with compassion and love.

Constantine prayed and asked forgiveness and remission of sins from every bishop present before receiving communion from Cardinal Isidore at the altar. The cardinal met his eyes as he gave him the sacrament, and Constantine knew he wondered if he were administering the last rites to the last emperor of the Romans.

After confession and communion, his commanders and their men left to take up their stations on the walls, while Constantine remained in the great church to make his final peace with God. For an hour he lay prostrate before the altar, alone with his Creator, begging forgiveness for his sins and beseeching Him to save his people.

The soldiers on the walls were black silhouettes against the sinking sun as Constantine and Phrantzes rode along the length of the western land walls together, dismounting every so often to speak to the men and make sure everything was in order. By the time they were done, they had reached the Caligarian gate. Climbing up to a tower at the outermost angle of the Blachernae wall, Constantine stood for a time looking both ways, to the right down to the Golden Horn, and to the left, along the Mesoteichion and the western defenses. All around him lay Mehmet's camp, stretching to the horizon on all sides, as far as the eye could see.

"Soon we will know our fate at the hands of God's executioner," Phrantzes said, breaking the silence that had fallen.

Constantine gave him a wan smile. "I have heard him called worse."

"Evil Serpent... Satan's apprentice," Phrantzes murmured, listing the epithets. "But in my opinion Mehmet fulfills a divinely ordained role in this life. He is God's executioner, appointed to punish sinners."

"Then we shall soon know how God regards us," Constantine said softly. "And now I must depart. It is time."

His heart overflowing with affection and anguish, Phrantzes made a motion to kneel before him, but Constantine raised him up. "This reminds me too much of your dream, dear friend."

"The portent— I wrote it down and noted the date, yet it slipped my mind. But you remembered my old forgotten dream," Phrantzes marveled.

"I found it unsettling at the time, George. Now I know why. It was on this day, the twenty-eighth of May, two years ago, that you had the dream. And here we are, taking leave of one another on May 28th, just as it foretold." Constantine drew Phrantzes close and kissed his eyes. "Now it has come to pass, my friend. Soon we shall know to what purpose, whether good or evil."

He left Phrantzes gazing after him on the ramparts and rode to his post at St. Romanus. He took the steps up to the parapet, entered the tower, and climbed to the top. The rain had cleared, and the air smelled fresh and sweet. He went to the ledge. The wind had risen, and a soft lavender sunset was falling over the earth, streaking the sky with gold. A few sea birds circled overhead. He listened to their cries, finding them strangely soothing. He turned his gaze on the enemy camp.

Would they prevail, or would they fall? Several times in these weeks his men had repelled the Ottomans when defeat seemed imminent. This time felt different. He passed a hand over his face. He had tried to live pure, do right by his people and his God. Had he offended Him by agreeing to union with Rome? Surely God, who knew everything, knew his heart, that he'd only appeased the West to save his city. But, in the end, the West had deserted him, and perhaps God, too.

Somewhere a soldier raised his voice in song, and it was same voice singing the same hymn of repentance that had lifted his heart earlier in the day. Once again, it flooded the earth with a glorious tranquility. *Like a blessing,* he thought.

The words drifted to him on the wind, clearly and more forcefully than before, and he glanced over the wall for the singer. He saw him in profile, standing below to the side, and he was flooded with a sense of awe, for the one who sang the old Hebrew hymn of repentance was none other than the Jew, Daniel Navarro.

A Jew was singing the ancient Greek hymn that was a translation from the Hebrew bible.

It made perfect sense, yet it was so unexpected that it seemed to hold almost divine significance. He inhaled a long, deep breath, and the same love and peace that had come to him earlier enfolded him again, but this time it held him closer and touched him more deeply than ever before. He felt his heart lift with the cadence of the song, and he was no longer troubled but comforted somehow, his being lightened, as if God had washed away his ills.

Life, he marveled. One could never anticipate its twists and turns, and where it would lead or how it would unfold, and from whence comfort would come.

"Constans."

He turned to find Zoe shining brightly in her lavender cloak, her apricot gown and bright auburn hair blowing around her, her wide lovely eyes sparkling like a moonlit sea. He stretched out his hand and she went to him.

"Is it not beautiful?" He draped an arm around her shoulders. He'd forgotten how the world felt when it was at peace. He was grateful for the chance to be here, to savor and remember.

"You gave a fine speech," she said, fixing her gaze on a raindrop on the stone, sparkling in the rays of the fading sun.

Tenderly he pushed a stray tendril of hair back from her cheek. "There is so much I want to say to you, Zoe, and so little time. You make me think of the sunrise. Did I ever tell you that?"

She gave a little laugh. "Only a few times." Memories stirred in her heart, and she saw herself seated at her dressing table, Constantine holding her hair in his hands, winding it into long, silken ropes as he gazed at her in the looking glass, the light of love in his eyes. She couldn't believe she had ever felt distanced from him, ever felt him a stranger. "As far back as I can remember, I have loved you, Constans. Never more than now." She bit down on her emotion. "You are in every way a noble emperor."

"An old emperor, Zoe. One who never understood what you saw in me."

Zoe realized that he was speaking in the past tense, and a wave of panic swept her. "You are everything to me, Constans. You always have been and always will be. Whatever happens—"

"Zoe, did you mean what you said, that you'd never forgive me?" he asked gently.

"Maybe a little."

"I will not force you to leave. But I beg you, Zoe, if you love me—truly love me—go. I have this terrible sense that I have seen my last sunrise." He cupped her face in his hands and looked at her.

She took in the great shadows beneath his eyes with a choking pain, and the lines, the weariness, and the sorrow that seemed accentuated in the gathering dusk, but it was still the face she had loved all her life. Her gaze went to his scar, that old reminder of past violence, and a new anguish seared her heart. "I cannot breathe when I think of leaving you, of never seeing you again—"

He swept her into his arms. Crushing her to him, he covered her mouth with his own, silencing her with his lips. The kiss sent longing flowing through her, and she remembered the passion that had been hers and the joy she had known. *So much tenderness. So much love.* She entwined her arms around his neck and tightened her hold of him, heedless of the armor that cut into her flesh. She wished the kiss could last forever and knew it could not, that it would prove as fleeting as happiness had always proved, and because she knew, she held him close with all her might.

After a long moment, he drew back and unwound her arms from around his neck. "Zoe, my love, it would mean everything to me to know that you are safe. That you and my son are safe. It would help me to bear it if the worst were to happen."

Before she could reply, a terrible crash broke the calm of the evening. She jumped. "What is that—Thunder?"

"No. It is the enemy bringing their guns closer to us near the moat. They have been doing that since before sunset, so the watch tells me."

Zoe shuddered. There was no emotion in his voice. He could just as easily be giving her the time of day. "And those?" she asked, indicating the lights flickering in the gloomy distance, moving across the mouth of the Golden Horn, hoping against hope, and wishing and praying he would say it was the Venetian fleet come to save them.

"They are the Ottoman ships."

Zoe closed her eyes and made fists with both hands to keep from screaming. It was truly here—the moment they had all prepared for, the moment they had dreaded. She lifted her gaze and looked at him to impress on her memory his tall, majestic presence, armor glinting in the fading light, purple cloak blowing in the wind, his pale drawn face, the line of brow beneath the helmet with the cross at its crest and his tortured hazel eyes gazing down at her with love. He could have fled, but he had stayed with his people and would fight for them to his last breath. She thought of Hector before the gates of Troy, and of Belisarius and Leonidas, hopelessly outnumbered, yet undaunted, standing tall, ready to sacrifice themselves for their homeland, men of honor who held duty paramount in their hearts—

She reached for his hands and brought them to her lips and kissed his fingertips, and laid his palm against her cheek, as she done so many times before. *O Holy Mother of God, let him be Belisarius, not Leonidas*— For one had survived, and the other had not.

His voice came again. "You must leave Constantinople, Zoe."

"How can I leave, Constans, when everything I love is here? What would my life be worth without you and my family? How can I go when my mother stays, and no one leaves but a few aged of royal blood?"

"Your mother does not carry my child."

She couldn't move, couldn't speak. The noises came again, strange, terrible noises. Darkness was enfolding her, and the ground was moving beneath her feet, as if with a monstrous life of its own. She opened her eyes to find Constantine holding her up, gipping her by the arms so hard that it hurt. "Zoe, Zoe, there is no time to be lost. The cannons are firing. Soon it will be dark, and the battle will begin. Tell me what I need to hear!"

"It's no use, Constans. I won't go—"

"Zoe, the child in your womb is all that survives me!"

"If you die, I want to die with you!"

"Live and keep him safe. Tell him about his father—"

"Stop it! Stop it!" A wave of nausea assaulted her, and she reeled. Constantine tightened his hold and kept her upright. Someone called up to him, "Everyone is at their post. We await only you and Justiniani!"

Zoe turned behind her to look at the tower. *Justiniani*— She hadn't bid him farewell—it couldn't be—it wasn't yet time! Surely, they still had time! "There is never enough time!" she cried.

"Zoe, listen to me. Your father has designated you guardian of his wealth in Europe. Aesop has the papers. He awaits you on the ship—"

Zoe stared at him, mouth agape.

"If the worst befalls—" He went on quickly, urgently, "you are to buy land in Italy—enough to establish a principality. It will be a refuge for Greeks, a Greek state—a copy of Eastern Rome in every way, so the empire does not die."

She listened in disbelief. "I cannot do this. It is impossible—"

"You can do anything, Zoe."

She searched his face. "You planned this knowing I couldn't live with myself if I refused, didn't you?"

His mouth lifted at the corners. "I knew you wouldn't refuse a chance to do great good in this world, Zoe."

She raised her eyes to his, knowing there was no longer a choice, that she had to go. For his sake. In his place.

Summoning his resolve, Constantine spoke the words he had purposely left unsaid. "Justiniani will take you to his ship. You will watch the battle from there. If we win, you will return. If we fall—" He broke off, added softly, "You will know."

A choked sob escaped her throat, and then another. "No!" She pounded her fists against his unforgiving armor. "No! No, no—"

"My love, it is as it must be. It is as God wills." He kissed her again, but gently this time, with finality. He pulled away and looked at her. "I have entrusted you to Justiniani's care, if I—" He inhaled a quick breath. "If the battle does not go as we hope, you and Justiniani have my blessing."

She searched his face. *Did he mean what she thought he meant?* Horror swept her and a stabbing pain that twisted and convulsed inside her. "You don't think—you can't—"

Constantine grabbed her and drew her to him. "Zoe, I know. Maria told me. And it matters not. I love you. I forgive you. Do you understand?"

"Oh, dear God, you believed her? Maria is a liar! She's in love with Justiniani and jealous of me! God forgive her—these lies were her revenge! I love you. I have never loved anyone else. Only you… Perforce from the day I was born—"

Constantine regarded her with moist eyes. "It does my heart good to hear it, Zoe." He took her into his arms tenderly, and she closed her eyes, and all she could think was that he had proposed to her here, on this tower, by these walls. Sobs broke from her lips.

As if he read her mind, he said, "Just so you wept when I asked you to marry me."

So long ago. Another life. She opened her eyes. A faint smile played on his lips. She lifted her hand to the dimple at his cheek. *Could this truly be the last time I see this face I love?* The grief that ripped through her was a wild, writhing beast. Her breath stopped and came again in ferocious braying pants.

"Zoe—Zoe— Do not weep—think of the good you will do in the world—think of our child."

He dug his nails into her arms. Pain rallied her, and she gulped air. "I love you! No one can ever take your place. No one, ever—"

"God keep you, Zoe. You have been the joy of my life. Now go—go before it is too late!" She turned and fled, running down the tower steps, down, down, down—

Justiniani caught her in his arms as he was coming up the stairs. Her eyes fixed on him, wide with shock and disbelief, with denial, with fear. He seemed to freeze for a moment, then he burst into action. "Make haste—there is no time to lose!" He grabbed her hand and dragged her down the steps to the bottom of the walls and across the twilit path to the horses. She could hardly walk; her legs felt as if they would crumble; her head swam; purple darkness and purple shadows were everywhere. Justiniani threw her on his horse and leapt into the saddle behind her. He spurred his mount and together they galloped through the empty streets, along the walls, to the harbor on the Golden Horn. Prayers and chanting burst from the churches and grew ever louder as they approached the Hagia Sophia. She leaned into him, feeling his warmth, and suddenly she was at the Gate of Eugenius, and sharp rocks were stabbing her slippers, and next she was on the gangplank, climbing to the ship, and then she stood on the deck, and nothing was real, and everything that was happening was unfolding in another world, to someone else.

Justiniani looked at her. His gaze roamed her face, her hair, her mouth, and she felt his love burning through her. He cupped her face in his hands and smoothed a tendril of hair. "Now I must go. They cannot lock the inner gates until I am at my post."

Zoe was instantly alert. "Lock the inner gates? What if you must retreat?"

"There is no retreat."

She gave an audible gasp. Her knees felt suddenly weak, and the deck swayed beneath her feet. He grabbed her hands and squeezed them tightly in his own. "I will return." After a hesitation, he said, "I promise."

She lifted her eyes to his, and in them she read all that he felt and could not say. "God keep you, Justiniani—" she whispered.

He took her fingers to his lips, his eyes locked on hers. His face filled her vision, and she felt the sting of tears as he let go of her hand. A flash of wild grief ripped through her. "God keep you!" she cried to his retreating back. She closed her eyes on the wrenching pain and heard the thud of boots dying away in the darkness.

When she opened her eyes, he was gone.

Thirty-Four

The attack came at midnight. The sudden noise was terrifying. Screaming *Allah Akbar* and trilling their battle cries with drums rolling and clarions blaring, the Ottomans surged against the defenders on the wall. Constantine and his men had been waiting silently, and when the watchmen on the towers sounded the alarm, church bells clanged wildly in warning. In the Hagia Sophia every man of fighting age grabbed his weapon and ran to his post; and women, even nuns, hurried to the walls, to bring water to the soldiers, to fetch stones, to carry wooden beams, to do anything they could to help while old men and women too aged to be of service, shouted hymns so Heaven would hear their prayers.

On the walls the defenders unleashed hails of flaming arrows into the enemy ranks as thousands of Ottoman troops assailed their walls. This first wave was Mehmet's irregulars, the *Bashi-bazouks,* many of them Turks, but many others Christian mercenaries—Slavs, Hungarians, Germans, Italians, and even Greeks, armed with scimitars, slings, bows and a few arquebuses. Behind them Mehmet's military police wielded maces to cut down those who lost their nerve and wavered. The enemy attacked along the entire length of wall, but the assault was fiercest in the Lycus Valley around Constantine and Justiniani at the gates of St. Romanus and Charisius where portions of the defenses had collapsed. Raising their ladders, they scaled the walls, one crowding another. Against them the defenders used arquebuses and culverins and hurled stones, killing many at a time. After two hours of fighting, they were repulsed, and Mehmet sounded a retreat.

"They've served their purpose though," Justiniani panted to Demetri on the walls of Charisius as he wiped the sweat from his brow. "They're wearing us out."

"He's softening us up for his Janissaries," Demetri said. "But we won this round. Pray God we win the next."

"We could use some rest," Justiniani murmured wearily.

"No chance," Demetri replied, downing a gulp of water. "We must reform our lines and replace the barrels of earth of the stockade before they come again."

No sooner had they completed the repairs than the second attack began. Cannons boomed, pounding the walls as regiments of Anatolian Turks surged at the Gate of St. Romanus, shrieking war-cries to the frenzied sound of drums and flutes. Unlike the irregulars, these troops were well disciplined and well-armed, eager for the glory of being the first to enter the Christian city. They hurled themselves at the stockades, climbing over one other in their efforts to attach their ladders on the barriers and hack their way over the top.

Archers let loose a hail of fiery arrows, streaking the black sky with fire. The moon was obscured by drifting clouds, and the defenders had difficulty seeing what was happening, but they fired their cannons blindly, tossed stones, poured seething cauldrons of pitch on the enemy, dislodging their ladders and killing hundreds. The enemy that managed to reach the walls were slain in fierce hand to hand combat.

An hour before dawn Urban's cannon scored a direct hit on the stockade, bringing it down for many yards of its length, and three hundred Anatolians rushed through the gap yelling that the city was theirs. But Constantine led his men in a charge, and they closed around the enemy band, slaughtering most of them and forcing the rest to retreat. The attack was called off, and the enemy retired to their lines.

They had been fighting four hours now. Constantine didn't know how much longer they could endure. A runner came up to him as he stood wiping his face during the momentary lull. He looked up expectantly, anxiously.

"They are holding everywhere, Augustus!" the youth said, grinning from ear to ear. "The Grand Duke is not able to send you reinforcements, but he is holding! Prince Orhan and the monks are repelling the landing parties on the Marmara— Diedo and the Cretans are holding fast at Eugenius. Minotto and his Venetians are holding their section on the Marmara against Zaganos Pasha, and Trevisano is holding on the mid-section of the Golden Horn with Navarro. The fighting on the Blachernae corner of the Horn is fierce, but they hold! And the Grand Duke has been using the Kerkoporta to lead sorties against the enemy flank!"

Constantine smiled and reached for a cup of water. Suddenly a hail of arrows, javelins, stones, and bullets rained down on them.

"Janissaries!" Constantine shouted. "Prepare for Janissaries!"

They were marching to the beat of drums and clarions, not rushing as the *Bashi-bazouks* and the Anatolians had done, but keeping their ranks in perfect order. Wave after wave of the fresh, well armored troops climbed up to the stockade. They tore at the barrels of earth set on top, hacked at the beam supports, and placed their ladders where they couldn't be dislodged. And each wave made way without panic for the next.

Constantine was exhausted, and he knew everyone else was, too. They had fought for nearly five hours with no more than a few moments' respite. But they had fought desperately, with every ounce of strength they could summon, for they knew that if they gave way, it would be the end. The end forever, and ever—

And God was answering their prayers! They were winning! If they could repel this one last gasp of Mehmet's army, they would save the Roman Empire of the East—

Behind him church bells rang and prayers rose to heaven from the crowded churches. *Have mercy,O Lord… Have mercy, OGod…*

The fighting along the stockade was hand to hand now. For an hour the Janissaries made no headway. Then they began falling back all along their lines. Mehmet's clarions sounded he order to retreat. There was a welcome lull in the fighting before a second wave attacked. The fighting continued for what seemed an eternity. All at once another blast of Ottoman clarions sounded, and the second wave of Janissaries fell back.

"They're sounding the retreat!" Constantine called to Don Francisco, joy exploding in his breast. "A second retreat—God is with us!"

In the darkness before dawn, as the third wave of Janissaries began to falter, Johannes Grant came running up to Justiniani on the ramparts of Charisius.

"My lord, Lady Zoe's in fearful danger! We've discovered a plot to abduct her from the ship!" he shouted, joining Justiniani's side to battle a Janissary.

Justiniani froze. In that instant, his opponent lunged for the kill, but Grant blunted the man's thrust with a slash to his belly.

"What?" Justiniani cried, recovering. Protecting his arm in the sling, he swung his sword wildly at the next attacker.

"It seems the sultan thinks she's the emperor's wife," Grant yelled cutting down a Janissary who had reached the top of the ladder. "He means to take her whether we win or not."

Justiniani beat back another Ottoman. "How did you learn this?"

"The man who tried to abduct her was sneaking around the Kerkoporta—" Grant panted between blows. "We caught him unlocking the gate for the enemy!"

Justiniani dispatched the enemy he battled and threw a glance at the dense mass of humanity swarming out of the darkness and rushing headlong up the walls at them. He fought his way to the shelter of a tower where the battle was not as intense. Grant followed his lead. "Tell me everything—quickly!"

"We were about to slit his throat—" Grant resumed, "but he offered the information in exchange for his life. They know Lady Zoe is on your ship. They plan to storm it and take her for the sultan's harem, win or lose!"

Justiniani's breath froze in his throat. *Dear God! Why this? Why now?*

"When? When—" he yelled.

"They are on the way there now—" Grant cried. "They're not leaving without her."

Justiniani's mind was in chaos. He couldn't leave his position in the thick of battle, but what choice did he have? His men were the only ones he trusted to send, and they'd never follow anyone else! He had to lead them—there was no other way to save Zoe. Constantine had to be told. He had to unlock the gates!

Forgetting the battle, forgetting everything except Zoe and distracted in his panic, he stepped out of the shadows of the tower into the flaring light of a torch as somewhere on the ground a Janissary aimed an arquebus up at the ramparts.

"Inform the emp—" A sudden shattering explosion drowned out his words. He felt ice in his chest, then a fierce, burning agony. He couldn't breathe, couldn't finish his thought. Grant had gone ashen pale and was staring at his breastplate. He followed the direction of his gaze. On the left side of his body, his armor was pierced, and blood was seeping below his heart. *It couldn't be! Surely—*

He blinked to focus his vision. Something was wrong with his sight. All at once his legs buckled under him and he collapsed. Men gathered around him, and their shouts rose to a din in his ears.

Grabbing his legs, they dragged him to safety behind the tower. Barbaro appeared at the front of the crowd and knelt beside him. Cutting the leather straps, he removed the breastplate and explored the wound with a gentle touch. Justiniani cried out in pain.

"Once we stem the bleeding, you'll mend," Barbaro lied, exchanging a knowing look with Grant as he ripped Justiniani's shirt open.

"Ship—" Justiniani moaned. "Have to go to—ship— Tell the emperor… Get the key to the—gate."

"Aye, my lord," Grant said, rising.

Justiniani watched him disappear, his stomach churning with pain and anxiety. He fought to stem his rising panic as Barbaro worked on his side, but the pain built with ferocious intensity, and he felt himself sliding into oblivion. No! He couldn't black out now—not now. He couldn't. He mustn't— He had to stay focused. He had to speak to Constantine. He had to get to the ship— He had to save Zoe.

At St. Romanus, Constantine heard a voice calling for him urgently. "Majesty! Majesty—"

He turned. Grant was running up the tower steps. "The commander's wounded, Majesty!"

"How bad?" Constantine demanded, shouting to be heard over the din of battle and the blood suddenly pounding in his ears.

"A shot fired at close range pierced his armor. He's—he's—" Grant swallowed. "It's a mortal wound, Majesty. He's asking to be taken to the ship. He's asking for the key to the inner gate."

For an instant, Constantine didn't breathe.

"There's more, Sire. The Lady Zoe— She's in grave danger—" Grant informed him of the plot.

Terror, black and chill such as he'd not known before spread from his gut into his heart and mind. "Take me to Justiniani!" he yelled.

On the ramparts of Charisius Constantine looked at Barbaro kneeling beside Justiniani. Barbaro shook his head and came to his feet, his eyes confirming the worst. Sick at heart, Constantine gave a barely perceptible nod as he knelt in his place.

"Zoe—" Justiniani gasped, grabbing Constantine's collar. "I have to—save Zoe—"

"You cannot leave. Not now, and neither can I. Grant can lead the men. You can trust him. He will get the ship out safely—"

"No—" Justiniani panted. "My men—won't follow—Grant…"

"You cannot go. If you do, your troops will desert their post to follow you and the battle will be lost. We are winning, Justiniani! We are beating them back! The Janissaries are about to retreat for the last time. Grant can go. He knows what to do."

Justiniani tightened his hold of Constantine's cloak and pulled him close. "Don't you see? It has to be me—they only take orders from me—"

"You cannot lead them. You are in no condition. It is a twenty-minute ride to the ship! Think of the pain of riding in your condition—"

Justiniani struggled to an elbow. "If I mean anything to you—" he said, with a surge of strength, "unlock the gate and let me go. I beg you. I implore you. My friend—"

Constantine bowed his head, tears stinging his eyes. How could he deny Justiniani's dying wish? If he sent Grant and something went wrong— If Zoe was taken into Mehmet's harem, how in God's name would he live with himself, even if he won the battle? Mehmet would kill the child or—horror of horrors— He would let him live and raise him as a Muslim, maybe as a Janissary—

Constantine looked up at Grant and the men around him watching him with fear in their eyes. Behind them the furious battle raged on. *If these men go—only these few—maybe no one will notice? It is still dark—*

"Can he make it?" Constantine asked, addressing Barbaro.

"Maybe. If the pain doesn't kill him," Barbaro replied under his breath.

Constantine looked at Justiniani. "God be with you, my friend," he said softly, squeezing his hand, the anguish in his heart almost overcoming his control.

Justiniani relaxed his grip and lay back, spent, exhausted, but finally at peace. Constantine rose to his feet. He withdrew the key from around his neck and pressed it into Barbaro's hand. "Make haste," he whispered.

Barbaro hoisted Justiniani on his back and made his way down the steps to the inner gate, followed by Justiniani's men. And then like a cold touch on his heart, Constantine saw a crack of light streak the horizon. Darkness was lifting.

In the first light of day, as Constantine had feared, someone noticed. "The commander is leaving!" a Genoese cried somewhere along the walls. "The city has fallen!" The cry was picked up. One after another, the Genoese flung aside their weapons and deserted their posts to stream after Justiniani before the gate could be locked again.

A messenger ran up to Constantine as he was leaving Charisius. "The Genoese are abandoning the Kerkoporta! The enemy is pouring in!"

Constantine flew down the tower stairs and vaulted on his horse. Followed by Demetri, Don Francisco and Dalmata, he galloped to the secret gate. He arrived too late. In the few moments he had spent on Charisius, news had spread about Justiniani, and panic with it. The Genoese were fleeing in a stampede, the strong trampling the weak. The Greeks who stood their ground were too few to stem the enemy tide surging through the gate. Constantine dismounted and tried to rally the men, but in vain he urged them to return. No one heard him; no one saw him. Blindly they pushed past, eyes stretched wide in terror. Constantine realized it was useless. But if they could hold the walls of the Mesoteichion, maybe they still had a chance—

Leaping into the saddle, he turned his reins and spurred his horse back to the Lycus Valley, Don Francisco, Demetri, and Dalmata, his ever-faithful captain of the Varangians in hot pursuit.

On his black destrier Justiniani clung to Barbaro as they galloped through the streets of the doomed city with his men at his side. The world spun and his stomach heaved with sickening nausea. The torturous motion of the horse's hooves sent waves of excruciating pain through him, whipping his torn body into frenzied agony. He wanted to die, but he fought to live. He couldn't give in to pain. If he did, Zoe would be lost forever. Bleeding into the saddle he willed himself to hold on until they got to the ship. For only he could save her now.

When Constantine arrived back at the Mesoteichion, the Genoese were gone. "Help me rally our people!" he shouted to Demetri, Francisco and Dalmata.

But here, too, it was in vain. The Greeks and Venetians were too heavily outnumbered by the hordes pouring over the walls. The slaughter had been too great. The Janissaries were charging now. The Greeks resisted tenaciously, but the sheer weight of numbers was forcing them back. He swung around to Charisius. The gates had been forced open and the battle was raging fiercely in the breach. For a few moments the four of them held the approach to the gate where Justiniani had been carried out. But the defense was broken, and the gate jammed with soldiers trying to escape.

Hordes of Janissaries were swarming over the stockades and over the defenses. Constantine glanced up at the walls and froze. A sick nausea swept him. He blinked to focus his gaze. By the crimson glow of the first streak of dawn the Ottoman banner was being raised on the tower of Caligaria. He turned his disbelieving, horrified gaze on the Golden Horn. All along the northern walls his pennants of the Double-headed Eagle and the Lion of St. Mark were being torn down and the vile blood-red banner of the Crescent Moon of the Ottoman Empire hoisted in their stead.

"My city has fallen," Constantine breathed, "and I still live—"

"I'll not be taken alive!" Demetri shouted, following his gaze.

"Nor I," Don Francisco cried, rushing to join him as he hurried toward the breach at St. Romanus.

"Wait for me—I am coming with you!" Constantine yelled. Demetri and Don Francisco halted their steps as Constantine tore his plumes from his helmet and ripped the regalia of office from his body. Dalmata stepped forward to help with the clasp of his imperial cloak and their eyes met: hazel to blue. "Flee while you can, Dalmata," Constantine whispered hoarsely. "Go with God—"

"I'm not leaving you," Dalmata said.

Constantine saw him through the tears in his eyes, the taut features, the jaw set with determination, the head held high with pride. He gave a nod. They would die together.

"Ready?" Demetri demanded again, panic in his voice.

Constantine looked at the open gate, at the teeming chaos of battling men. He looked at his friends, waiting for him. Commending his soul to God, he lifted his sword to his lips and kissed the ruby cross glittering in the hilt. "Ready," he said, squaring his shoulders.

Leaning her head against the bulkhead, Zoe sat in the cargo hold at the stern of the galley. The plank floor was cold and damp, and she hugged herself for warmth. As they had done with ever-increasing urgency in these five hours since the battle began, her fellow passengers sang hymns beseeching God's mercy. Now their voices fell silent as they watched the unfolding horror through the open shutters. For dawn was breaking over Constantinople, and beneath the crimson pouring into the sky, furious flames licked the western walls. Through a haze of smoke and fire, Zoe watched with them, thinking of Constantine on the burning walls, battling to save his people from the hideous new day being born. She felt numbed by a vast disbelief, and her heart was cold and empty. Clashing steel and cannon bursts roared in the air, and above the fray of battle came the shrieks of terrified animals, screams of women and children, shouts of men and the wild clanging of church bells. In the darkness of the hold, Apollo perched quietly in his cage beside Aesop, silent for once. Eirene was nowhere in sight, but Zoe was too distraught to wonder why.

It was sunrise and her city was dying, shriveling into ashes as she gazed, and she could do nothing to help her, save her, comfort her. *Nothing.* She covered her ears with her hands and closed her eyes.

A shattering noise blasted the darkness. Men thundered up the gangplank, and Christian curses mingled with cries of *Allah Akbar!* The deck boards above their heads began to groan violently with the pounding of boots and din of clashing swords. Women screamed and grabbed their children as Zoe and Maria peered through the overhead grating to see what was happening. Someone yelled, "Where is your empress?" and Zoe saw a Turk pin a Greek against the wall with his scimitar. "Go to Hell!" the Greek spat, and the Turk plunged his sword into him. Blood spurted through the grate, and a drop splashed Zoe's upturned face.

"They want *you!*" Maria said in a horrified whisper, turning her shocked gaze on Zoe. But Zoe was already gone from her side. Throwing open chests and lifting the lids of barrels, she cried out, "Where are the weapons? Help me find the weapons!" As men and women searched, more footsteps and steel clanged overhead, and more death came with more blood. The hold throbbed with fear, sobs, and the screams of children. But all they found were barrels filled with water, sand, rope, food, or cooking utensils. Zoe was beginning to lose hope when someone cried out, "Here, in the bow!" Pushed against the hull stood a giant chest filled with hatchets, spears, swords, and axes, and beside it a barrel of Greek Fire. "Who can handle this?" Zoe demanded, holding out a crossbow. "I can!" a youth exclaimed; his answer echoed by two others. "And this?" Zoe removed the lid from the barrel of Greek Fire. "Me!" Aesop cried. "I was a seaman before the Ottomans enslaved me!" She turned her attention on the women who wept and wailed. "Heed me, if you want to live!" she shouted above the fray. "Your men are dying on our walls, and you must do your part if your children are to live!"

Sword blows from above filled the sudden quiet below. "We have the advantage of surprise but only for a moment—" she told the upturned faces. "Make haste— Work quickly—" Pointing to an old man, she ordered him to blow out his lantern. "You, too—" she ordered a woman cowering in a corner. She turned to a boy with a lantern perched on a coil of ropes. "Cover the flame until I give the order to uncover it!"

Scarcely had Zoe completed her instructions than the hatch was thrown open to a great creaking of hinges and an Ottoman thudded down the ladder. Two women with knives slashed at his legs between the rungs. Cursing in the darkness, he stumbled blindly down the steps and was promptly dispatched by Maria's axe. Another Turk followed and someone smashed his skull with a club. His body was dragged away as yet another appeared in the hatch. "Torch!" the man yelled to his comrades. One was thrust into his hands, and he thundered down the stairs, his curved scimitar held high in murderous rage. But Aesop squirted him with Greek Fire, igniting his tunic. Shrieking wildly, he tumbled to the floor. Zoe lopped his head off with her axe as others doused him with sand to put out the flames. The ladder shook as two more Turks raced down. "Light!" Zoe cried. The boy uncovered his lantern. "Crossbows!" she yelled. Several released their arrows, and one after another the enemy on the ladder fell dead. More boots sounded overhead; more cursing, more blows, and ear-shattering clashes of steel. For an interminable moment no one came down the hatch, and the fracas overhead seemed to subside. Then suddenly another pair of boots appeared on the steps, but cautiously this time. Waiting for the man's torso to appear, Aesop raised his crossbow and took aim.

Looking directly up the hatch, Zoe caught a partial view of the man's face. "Hold your fire!" she screamed, coming out of the shadows to the stairs.

"Grant—" she cried in a tone of wonder, "Grant!"

For a frozen moment he halted midway on the stairs, staring down at Zoe. Then he said, "Thank God!" Cupping his hands to his mouth, he shouted to the others, "Go—go—"

A crash as the gangplank was thrust aside. The gateway slammed shut. Grabbing Zoe's hand, Grant ran back up the steps, dragging her with him. The ship jerked forward, and someone staggered toward her out of the gloom. "Barbaro—" Zoe whispered on a breath. Her eyes flew to the man slung over his back. She gave a muffled sob and heard Maria scream. She reached out to Justiniani with trembling hands and sank to the floor. Barbaro laid him in her lap, and she cradled his head gently in her arms.

"Zoe…" Justiniani murmured, eyes soft with love. "You're safe now… Safe…"

"Hush," she said, stroking his hair. "Hush…"

"I kept my promise… to return."

"Hush."

"To see you… again…"

Blood covered his side. She bit her lip hard.

"Zoe— I came… to save God's city—" He winced in agony.

"I know," she said, tears blinding her vision. "Hush…"

"Tell me… you love me…" he whispered.

She held him close and rocked him in her arms. She kissed his damp brow. "Hush," she murmured. "Hush…" Was there no other word in the entire world?

"Tell… me… you… love me…"

Love. Our joy. Our pain. The ship gave a roll; they were moving out into the open seas, abandoning Constantine to his fate, abandoning Constantinople. An explosion of pain ripped through her being.

"Zoe, tell me… before it's too late—" Justiniani gasped in her arms, his pleading eyes fixed on her face.

"I love you," she said, smoothing his tawny gold hair back with a gentle touch. "I love you… I will always love you both… Forever… Forever—"

Epilogue

THE TOWERS ON THE GOLDEN HORN
IN THE EARLY HOURS OF MAY 29, 1453

Along the stretch between Lucas's position on the western corner and the mouth of the Horn, the fighting had been light. Trevisano with the help of Diedo, Navarro, and their Cretan defenders had held the enemy at bay all night. By morning they were tired but not exhausted. Working in shifts they had even found time to eat and refresh themselves. Navarro, returning to duty after a pleasant rest was munching on a mouthful of bread when he surprised a Turk who, unnoticed by the other defenders, had managed to get high enough on the scaling ladder to peek at him over the wall. Bringing down his broadsword, he promptly cleaved the man's skull in two and dispatched the fellow to his maker.

"Now that's what I call a good finish to a good meal!" Navarro laughed, swallowing the last of his bread. "And here's a fine morning to greet us—" he said, his eyes on the sea where a fiery dawn was spreading across the sky, turning the water scarlet.

"Enough prattle," Trevisano puffed. "How about a hand with these confounded infidels?"

Navarro obliged him. Working as a team, they dislodged one of the scaling ladders and sent a dozen of the enemy hurtling to their deaths on the beach below. Trevisano watched them fall until they hit the ground. He looked at his friends in puzzlement. "I didn't hear them scream."

"Nor did I," Diedo yelled over the fierce clanging of church bells pounding the dawn with frantic warning.

"The bells must have drowned them out," Navarro offered.

"No," Trevisano cried over the din. "Something is different! There are no hymns—"

Until now the sound of Christian prayers had been dulled in his ears by the terrible roar of battle raised by the clashing of steel against steel and the sporadic booming of cannons, but he had known they were there, like an undercurrent of chords guiding a minstrel's melody. Now, the air was utterly devoid of human singing, and the cannons, too, had ceased. What did it mean?

He looked at the Hagia Sophia. No bells rang, and instead of hymns and prayerful pleadings, an ominous cacophony of noise emanated from the gigantic church. Great shouts came to him, breaking like thunder over the city. With growing horror, he realized the tumult was composed of a medley of fearful shrieks, anguished cries, and the sounds of human lamentation. He swung around to the western walls.

At first, he saw nothing but dense smoke and glowing fire. But as he stared, the wind stirred a path though the blackness, and the sight that met his eyes chilled his soul. Gone was the double headed eagle of Rome. In its place, from all the towers along the western front—along St. Romanus, Charisius, Caligaria, and Blachernae—there waved the silver crescent of Islam.

Cries reached his ears. *Apolis eheepsis!*

The city has fallen!

Apolis eheepsis!

He felt his life-blood drain from him. His sword loosened in his grip and clattered to the floor. Men followed his gaze. For a moment, no one moved; no one spoke. Trevisano caught his icy breath and swallowed. "There is only one decision left to make," he said hoarsely, almost to himself. "Will it be slavery or death?"

A silence.

Out of the darkness, someone answered. "Death."

"Death—" said another.

"Death!" they echoed until it became a roar.

"Death…" said a soft female voice.

Trevisano spun around. He stared in bafflement at the sight that met him. "Eirene?" he whispered. Blinking to clear his sight, he watched as she came to him from the shadows behind the well. "Eirene!" he whispered, not daring to disbelieve. In one swift motion she was in his arms, and he was kissing her hair, her brow, her cheeks. Holding her out at arm's length, he searched her face. "What do you here? I thought you were on the ship!"

"I wanted to die with you," she said, her loving gaze roaming his hair and eyes. She raised her hand and traced the precious line of his cheek and jaw. She had not expected to survive the night, yet here she was in his arms, touching him, feeling his warmth. She couldn't believe her good fortune. To have this moment with the man she loved was the greatest gift Heaven could bestow. However brief it proved, sweeter it could not be.

Trevisano took her face into his large hands tenderly. "Have you been here all night?"

"Yes…"

"What would you have done if we had won?"

"Leave quietly, as I came."

He drew her hard against him and kissed her. Her consciousness ebbed and her body flamed. Lost in his embrace, she was flooded by exquisite joy. Then, suddenly, shouts sounded, and something slammed against the stone. Trevisano released her in one swift, abrupt movement. Picking up his sword, he raised it high and looked at his men. "What are we waiting for? Let us kill these bastards!"

From their position at the Horaia Gate along three towers of the Golden Horn, Trevisano, Diedo, Navarro and the Cretans mounted a fierce resistance. Shattered to the core by the fall of the holy city, they battled hard, with every ounce of will and strength that remained to exact vengeance. The fight grew more intense with each passing hour as the enemy came to understand there would be no surrender.

Eirene drew water from the well with a bucket, filled tin cups, and passed them to the men to drink. When they were injured, she ripped fabric from her skirt and bound their wounds. Some returned to the fight, but to those who were fatally wounded, she gave comfort before they died. Trevisano and his defenders unleashed volleys of arrows, poured barrels of seething pitch over those who dared scale the walls, and swung their battle axes and swords mercilessly at all who came within reach. They shot Greek Fire with their crossbows and rejoiced in the terror it engendered as it raced through the air, and celebrated the damage once it landed.

Neither did the enemy spare themselves. They attacked with battering rams, scaling ladders, catapults, flaming arrows, and hooks attached to their lances. But they made no headway. Unable to aim straight at the defenders on account of the machicolations that protected them along this stretch of wall, the arrows they shot went straight up, hit the stone, and fell back on their own ranks. Nor did the fires they set with their missiles injure the defenders, for they had plenty of water from the well, and men in greased animal hides put out the flames as quickly as enemy arrows delivered them.

Seated on his horse at a safe distance, Mehmet watched the fight with growing admiration. "These are brave men."

"Indeed," his commander, Hamza Bey, replied.

"What else can we do?" Mehmet demanded.

"The only thing left is Urban's cannon."

Mehmet regarded him. "How long will it take to bring it here?"

"Two days, likely more." After a long pause, his reluctance evident, Hamza Bey added, "But there is no guarantee it can do the job. The cannon can't be fired from aboard ship, and the beach is too narrow to afford our engineers protection from such good marksmen."

Mehmet mulled the information. He looked up at the sky. The sun was dropping in the west. These men had held out for ten hours since the city fell, more than sixteen since the assault commenced. "They cannot endure much longer," he said.

"A day or two at most," Hamza Bey replied. "And only because they are well provisioned and have plenty of water."

"And courage," Mehmet added.

"Indeed, O Holy of Holies. The only thing they lack is sleep."

"Something tells me these men would also find a way around that." He was suddenly overcome with a wish to be done the matter. After all, these men, heroes or not, were of small consequence to him now. He had achieved what he came to do. He had conquered Rome.

"What is your wish, God's Shadow on Earth?"

"Go to them with terms. Better still, I will go."

Hamza Bey looked at him in astonishment.

"I wish to see the faces of these valiant men," Mehmet smiled.

Ottoman drums rolled and clarions blared, sounding a retreat. Trevisano blinked. He rubbed his eyes to clear his vision, unable to believe the evidence of his own eyes. *What did it mean?* Before he could clear his mind long enough to fathom his own question, he made out a group of riders galloping up to the walls in a cloud of dust, bearing a white flag. Without exception, the figures were richly clad in silken robes heavily embroidered with gold and encrusted with so many jewels he had to shield his eyes from the blinding glare in the late afternoon sun. He guessed the leader to be the one on the gleaming black stallion. An enormous emerald flashed in his plumed turban, and another on his scabbard. The group drew to a halt at the base of the walls.

"We come to offer you generous terms of surrender!" one called up to them.

Trevisano moved out from behind the machicolations and stood atop the wall, staring down at the one who spoke, a man with a long, hooked nose and red beard who reminded him of a parrot. A vague recollection stirred in his mind, and the shock of recognition that came was accompanied by a barely audible oath. *Mehmet.*

"And why would you do that?" Trevisano demanded.

"You have fought well. You have won our respect."

"What are your terms?"

"Freedom. And pardon of life."

"A moment, while I consult with my men—" He turned to the others.

"Can we trust them?" Navarro demanded.

"I don't see why not," Diedo said. "We're already dead men."

"But if they let us go, how will we get home?" Navarro asked.

"Leave it to me," Trevisano said, stepping to the edge of the ramparts. "Pardon of life is not enough," he called back.

A shocked murmur went up. Mehmet raised a hand to hush his men. "What else is your wish?"

"To go home. On our two ships that you see behind you—"

Mehmet turned to look.

"Restore them to us and give us your word, sworn before your God, that you will permit us to leave unimpeded in any way." He rested a foot on the rampart and leaned down. "And one thing more. We have a woman with us. She must be included in the pardon."

Trevisano saw Mehmet exchange a smile with the man on his right. They said something he couldn't hear, and everyone laughed.

"And a dog," Eirene whispered urgently at Trevisano's elbow, showing him the furry gray bundle trembling in her arms that she had found nosing for food on her flight to the gate. Trevisano looked at her in disbelief before turning back to Mehmet. "And a dog!" he amended.

Mehmet exchanged a few more words with his companions. More snickers. The Ottomans shook their heads.

"As *Allah* is my witness," Mehmet said, "you have my word—the ships, the woman—and the dog—are included."

"We accept your offer!" Trevisano called down.

Mehmet gave a nod and turned his horse. Eirene drew to Trevisano's side, and one by one his men came out from behind the crenellations and joined him on the ramparts. They watched Mehmet gallop off, his sumptuously clad retinue at his side.

Trevisano took Eirene by the arms and looked into her eyes. "Where shall we be wed, in Chios or in Venice?"

Eirene didn't reply for a moment. She couldn't make out his face; her vision had blurred with the thundering of her heart, and all she could see was the heartrending tenderness of his gaze. "Is this a jest, Gabriel—"

"Eirene, I am asking you to marry me."

"But I have no dowry to bring you! And your family—"

"Nothing is as it was. The old world we knew is gone, Eirene." He tightened his hold of her. "Do you love me?"

"You know I love you, Gabriel."

"Then nothing else matters. We will be married in Chios." He drew her to him and looked at his men. "Our work here is done… The time has come for us to go."

"Time… to go," Navarro echoed, his voice a sigh on the wind.

Trevisano turned his face westward, and his gaze lingered on the defensive walls of St. Romanus and Charisius, now smoldering and in ruins. He made the sign of the cross. "May God have mercy on Emperor Constantine, the last emperor of the Romans. He was a great man."

"He was a great emperor… The finest. Gallant…heroic," Admiral Diedo murmured at his shoulder. "He could have fled, but he chose to stay. He died with his empire, and his empire is his shroud."

"May God grant him blessed repose and eternal memory," Eirene whispered, her voice cracking with emotion.

Trevisano laid a tender kiss on her brow. "History will not forget him, Eirene… He is a legend. He will live forever, and when men speak his name, it will be in blessing."

Author's Note

The Ottoman conquest of Constantinople led to three centuries of warfare in Europe. The Venetian fleet arrived five days after the fall and from 1453, Venice fell into decline. Within thirty years most of her eastern territories were lost to the Ottomans.

Numerous eyewitness accounts of the survivors are extant in diverse languages: Greek, Italian, German, Slav, Serbian and Polish, attesting to the men from different nations who took part that day. Some fought in defense of the city, while others, sympathetic to the Christian defenders, were forced to fight against it. Depending on their perception and on where they were and what they saw unfold, these accounts differ with one another.

Two of the historical figures appearing in this book, Niccolò Barbaro and George Phrantzes, were among those who left behind elegiac poems, diaries, chronicles, and memoirs of their experiences. Unfortunately for history, Captain Alviso Diedo's official report to Venice, containing a detailed account of the operations during the siege, is not extant and may have been destroyed because it cast aspersions on Venice for its actions during the siege.

In crafting this story, I have drawn from Barbaro and Phrantzes and multiple other sources, including the eyewitness report of the Slavonic Diary of Nestor Iskander,[1] possibly a Greek fighting for Sultan Mehmet's involuntary Christian allies. I have read the major authorities on the subject and consulted others. Those that I found most helpful are listed in the select bibliography.

My interest in this period began when I read a scientific paper that examined the mysterious light phenomena observed during the last days of

[1] Nestor Iskander, *The Tale of Constantinople (of Its Origin and Capture by the Turks in the Year 1453)*, ed. Walter K. Hanak, Caratzas, 1998.

Eastern Rome which have baffled experts into the present day.[2] The ancients were familiar with the aurora borealis and had recorded one on a clay tablet as early as the time of King Nebuchadnezzar around the 6th century BC. But what they witnessed on the eve of the fall of Constantinople seemed to them terrifying, not glorious. Certainly, the end times of the ancient Christian city were rife with ominous portents. The prophecies of doom that pre-date the events of 1453 lend another curious and intriguing dimension.

I did not invent the eclipse of the full moon, the 'fire' in the enemy camp, the strange weather phenomena, or the curious lights in the sky in the last days of the Eastern Roman Empire. Eyewitness accounts report the same omens and prophecies and are consistent with one another. Regarding the fall of Constantinople to the Turks, Niccolò Barbaro states: "our Lord God was willing to make this decision in order to fulfill all the ancient prophecies, particularly the first prophecy made by Saint Constantine, who is on horseback on a column by the Church of Hagia Sophia pointing East, to Anatolia, and saying, 'From this direction will come the one who will undo me.'[3]

The philosopher-monk "Gennadios Scholarios" compiled a list of prophecies and added a few of his own observations.[4] It had long been foretold that the world would end with the Second Coming of Christ. According to the Byzantines, this was scheduled to happen in the seven thousandth year after the creation of the world in 5509-8 BC. Gennadius agreed that the world would end in 1492, and he found morbid consolation in the belief that, in 1453, the time remaining was brief. Gennadius further noted that the city of Constantinople was founded in May and ended in May, and that the Christian empire of the Romans had originated with the Emperor Constantine, son of Helena, and came to an end with another Constantine, son of Helena. Between the first and last Constantine, there had been no emperors of the same name whose mother was 'Helena.'

---

[2] Dr. Kevin Pang of NASA's JPL, an American astronomer, has attributed the extraordinary weather phenomena and strange optical effects to a volcanic eruption in the South Pacific, but the date of the blast cannot be definitively traced to 1453.

[3] Niccolò Barbaro, *Diary of the Siege of Constantinople*, trans. by J.R. Jones, Exposition Press, 1969, p. 61.

[4] Gennadios Scholarius, *Oeuvres completes*, edit. Petit *et al.*, IV, pp.511-12.

Nestor Iskander did not believe that the foundation of Constantinople and its loss by an emperor named Constantine was merely a coincidence but the fulfillment of the city's destiny.[5] In his diary of the siege, Barbaro wrote that God decided the city should fall when it did in order to fulfill the ancient prophecies. Cardinal Isidore, who escaped from the city disguised as a beggar, reported it as a fact, not a prophecy, when he wrote, "...just as the city was founded by Constantine born of Helena, so it is now tragically lost by Constantine born of Helena."[6]

As for Phrantzes' prophetic dream of farewell on May 28, two years before the fall of Constantinople, it is documented in his memoirs. He found it so unsettling at the time that he told everyone sleeping by him to remember the date.[7] Two years later, near midnight on May 28, 1453, according to Phrantzes, he rode with Constantine along the length of the land walls to see that everything was in order. On their way back to St. Romanus, the emperor dismounted near the Caligarian Gate and took Phrantzes with him up a tower at the outermost angle of the Blachernae wall, where they could look both ways, to the left along the Mesoteichion, and to the right down to the Golden Horn. They spent an hour or so in conversation. Then Constantine dismissed him, and they never met again. The dream proved prophetic.

To the development of this story, it has been necessary to bring my own interpretations, motivations, and imagination, but I have made every effort to portray a credible scenario of how this drama may have unfolded, and to do so with respect for the honored dead. I plead artistic license for the name "Zoe" given Anna Notaras in this story. Her sisters took vows and changed their names following the fall, and I felt that 'Anna' may have been her newly adopted name in Venice. For the timeline and details of the historic fall of Constantinople, I have relied mainly on the texts of Steven Runciman, Donald Nicol, John Julius Norwich, Sir Edwin Pears, and Cyril Mango.[8] For those who would like to pursue

---

[5] Iskander, cited in Donald M. Nicol, *The Immortal Emperor,* p. 98, where he states: *See* Dujcev, *Medioevo bizantino-slavo,* III, p.423.

[6] Barbaro, p.?

[7] George Sphrantzes, *The Fall of the Byzantine Empire: A Chronicle*, trans. by Marios Philippides, University of Massachusetts Press, Amherst, 1980, p. 61.

[8] Steven Runciman, *The Fall of Constantinople*, Cambridge University Press, 1965. Donald M. Nicol, *The Immortal Emperor*, Cambridge University Press (1992) First paperback edition, 2002. John Julius Norwich, *Byzantium: Decline and Fall,* Alfred

further reading on the subject, I highly recommend Runciman and the fascinating popular account by Roger Crowley, *1453*.[9]

The reader should know that much remains in dispute about exactly what happened on May 29, 1453, when Constantinople fell. Virtually everything except the broad outlines is disputed by one authority or another. Did the Siege of Constantinople begin on March 31 or April 2? Did the Doge and Emperor John of Trebizond reject Constantine's offer of a marriage alliance, or did Constantine refuse them? Did he have ten ships in his naval arsenal or as many as twenty-six? Did he fall at the Golden Gate or at the Gate of St. Romanus? Did he die a hero holding the breach, as Christian accounts report, or a coward running away, as Turkish sources claim? What became of his body: Was it found and given Christian burial as Chedomil Mijatovich asserts, or was it decapitated and the head stuffed with straw and paraded around the Ottoman empire, as Nestor Iskander and other chroniclers recount?[10] More importantly for the purposes of this story, did he die married, or unmarried?

On this last point, I have drawn heavily from Nestor Iskander. He reported that Mehmet instituted a search for Constantine's empress and learned that she was taken to Justiniani's ship and sailed away when Constantinople fell. According to historian Donald Nicol, Constantine's marriage was already suggested by Aeneas Sylvius Piccolomini, the future Pope Pius II, who wrote in July 1453 to Pope Nicholas V about the survival of the emperor's son. This has been enshrined in his *Cosmographia.* It is thought he obtained this information from the Serbians, who in turn obtained it from the Turks.

Modern historians tend to dismiss a third marriage, and neither Phrantzes nor Barbaro mention an empress, but there are reasons why they might not have known, if Constantine, facing desperate odds of survival, had decided to snatch happiness and wed secretly. Some modern scholars have asserted that Constantine was betrothed, if not married, to the grand duke's daughter,

---

A. Knopf, 1996. Sir Edwin Pears, *The Destruction of the Greek Empire,* Haskell House Publishers, 1968. Cyril Mango, *Byzantium: The Empire of New Rome*, Orion Books, 2005.

[9] Roger Crowley, *1453: The Holy War for Constantinople*, Hyperion Press, 2006.

[10] Chedomil Mijatovich, *Constantine Palaeologus: The Last Emperor of the Greeks: 1448-1453,* Argonaut, 1968. Unchanged reprint of the 1892 edition.

Anna Palaeologina aka 'Zoe' in this novel. In the nineteenth century this was a popular view.[11] Donald Nicol disputes it on the basis that Zoe/Anna herself never claimed she had been the betrothed of the emperor, and that Constantine's nephew, Andrew Palaeologus, son of Constantine's brother Thomas, formally ceded his rights to the Byzantine throne in 1494, stating his uncle had died unmarried.

Zoe/Anna's reasons why she may have remained silent are understandable in view of the threat Mehmet continued to pose after the fall. Certainly, she called herself "Palaeologina." She may have been entitled to do so by virtue of her mother's royal blood, but in that case, it is not clear why her sisters did not do the same. As for Andrew Palaeologus, son of Constantine's brother Thomas, he was born in 1453 in the Peloponnese. His father from whom he would have learned of the marriage was not in Constantinople during this time and would not have known if Constantine had wed secretly. Self-interest would have played a role also. In selling his title for monetary gain, he needed to claim clear ownership.

With Cardinal Bessarion's help, Anna/Zoe developed elaborate plans to establish an independent Byzantine city-state in Tuscany in the territory of Siena. In their correspondence with her, the council of Siena always addressed her as the widow of the last emperor of Rome, Constantine XI. The fact that she never objected to this address is highly significant, and in her silence, it is possible to find confirmation. It is also interesting to note that Aeneas Sylvius Piccolomini, later Pope Pius II, who suggested the marriage in his letter of 1453 to Pope Nicholas V, came from Siena. Was he privy to Anna's secret? Another who believed Constantine was married is the seventeenth century *Grand Logothete* Hierax. Some, however, may deem his account fanciful.

Historian Donald Nicol dismisses out of hand all reports of Constantine's third marriage, including the Greek Chronicle of the Sultans, the sixteenth century patriarchal notary Theodosios Zygomalas, and the highly respected sixteenth century "erudite"[12] professor Martin Crusius of Tubingen, who

---

[11] Runciman, p. 227, refers in a footnote to C.N. Sathas, *Monumenta Historiae Hellenicae*, IX, p. vi, that states Anna was at one time betrothed to Constantine.

[12] Two such references are in the correspondence with the authorities in Siena. A document dated at Siena 22 Jul 1472 requesting assistance addresses Anna as: "*Domina...Anna, sposa già dell'Imperadore, figlia del...Principe mess. Luca, Granduca*

researched the matter in depth. The rumors in Italy that Emperor Constantine left a widow—which Nicol himself describes as "persistent at the time"[13] —are also dismissed. He goes on to state that the tale of Constantine's "fictitious wife and children" [14] passed into Greek folklore from the seventeenth century Hierax.

This, and much else about Zoe/Anna Notaras remains unknown. As Norwich points out, there are things it is impossible to determine with certainty. Lesser details subject to dispute are her position in the family, the number of sisters she had, their names and marriages, and where they were residing on May 29 when Constantinople fell. Did Zoe/Anna leave Constantinople before 1453 for Italy or one of the Greek islands? Were her sisters with her, or were they captured by the Turks and taken into the sultan's harem? Did she ransom them, as some historians claim?

For the sake of morale, the nobles chose not to flee or send their families to safety, as the tragic fate of Zoe/Anna's young brothers attest, and it is entirely likely all the Notaras family remained in the city. Legend holds that Justiniani escorted Zoe/Anna to his ship immediately before the last battle. Her mother, a princess of the Palaeologan dynasty, survived the fall and became Mehmet's highest ranking female prisoner, but died on the journey to Mehmet's harem. The passenger list of a Genoese ship that fled Constantinople lists two Notaras family members. Who were these two Notaras passengers? The most credible possibility—and the one I have chosen—is that they were Zoe/Anna and her sister Maria, Helena already residing in Lesbos. If the Notaras girls were not in Constantinople, why did their mother remain behind?

The few details that seem certain are that Zoe/Anna "Palaeologina" Notaras escaped the fate of her city, that she was known as "Anna" in Venice, that she lived another fifty-four years after the fall and never married, and that she won for herself an illustrious reputation as a patron of the arts and the refuge of destitute Greeks. Another fact not in dispute is that she was not

---

Romeorum". Ed. C. N. Sathas, *Documents inédits relatifs à l'histoire de la Grèce au moyen âge*, IX, Paris, 1890, p. xxxiv, quoting Arch. di Rifor. di Siena, Consigli della Campana, traduzione in Italiano.

[13] Donald M. Nicol, *The Byzantine Lady,* Cambridge University Press, Canto Edition, 1996, p. 101: "The misconception must be attributed to the Sienese government, who had probably been misled by the rumors, persistent in Italy at the time, that the last Emperor Constantine left a widow."

[14] Nicol, *Immortal Emperor*, p. 87.

among those taken captive by the sultan. Whether this means she was not in Constantinople when the city fell, as some argue, or that Justiniani took her to his ship and she escaped, as others insist, is not clear. There seems to be confusion about everything.

Zoe/Anna enjoyed an illustrious career in Venice and lived until 1507. In 1499 she founded a printing press in Venice to publish books in the Greek tongue.[15] She labored tirelessly to establish an Orthodox church so her countrymen would have a place to celebrate their own liturgy. As a result of her efforts, the Greek church *San Giorgio dei Greci* was founded after her death, and here can be seen the 14th century Byzantine icon of the *Blessing Christ* that came from Constantinople with "Princess Anna Palaeologina-Notaras."[16]

Aesop and Eirene are fictional characters, but the account of the Cretans who held out in the towers on the Golden Horn is historically accurate. After the fall of the city, but probably before Mehmet's pardon, the Venetian captain Alviso Diedo, who guarded the Golden Horn, supervised the orderly departure of several Venetian ships and saved many hundreds of Christians from the Ottoman yoke. Gabriel Trevisano, who also helped defend the Golden Horn, may have survived with Alviso or with the Cretans, but his fate is unclear. Barbaro's account lists him as one of twenty-nine Italians taken prisoner by Mehmet and ransomed a year later. Other accounts have Mehmet executing all his Italian prisoners.

The idea that "bad things happen to good people" as punishment for their sins was a widely held belief in the Christian East. In this regard, Phrantzes mentioned Constantine's many efforts to win God's favor through fasting in the hope of saving his people from the Turkish yoke. But "God ignored his offerings; I know not why or for what sins."[17]

The history of the Eastern Roman Empire does not constitute part of the curriculum in most Western countries. In John Julius Norwich's view, this "conspiracy of silence" ignores the immeasurable cultural debt that the Western world owes the Eastern Roman Empire for preserving the heritage of Greek and

---

[15] As recently as 1994, a first edition of *Etymologicum Magnum Graecum* published by Anna's fifteenth century printing press sold at auction at Christie's.

[16] In 1991, St. George of the Greeks was elevated to a cathedral.

[17] Sphrantzes, p. 74.

Latin antiquity through the dark ages that descended on Europe following the fall of the city of Rome.[18] Norwich attributes the deletion of the Eastern Roman Empire from Western education to three factors: its ancestral jealousy of Eastern Rome, what the West regarded as the "sinful" religious differences of Orthodoxy, and the sense of guilt that it had failed the city at the end.

The reader may find it interesting to know that Webster's Ninth New Collegiate Dictionary includes among its definitions of the seventeenth century term "byzantine" as "relating to, or characterized by, a devious and usually surreptitious manner of operation." Norwich mentions the "grotesque" connotation that Byzantium enjoys in the West and attributes it largely to the influence of the eighteenth-century historian, Edward Gibbon. In his comprehensive and important study, *The History of the Decline and Fall of the Roman Empire,* Gibbon condemned Byzantium as an empire constituting "without a single exception, the most thoroughly base and despicable form that civilization has yet assumed."[19]

Norwich refutes Gibbon's assertion by pointing out that eighty-eight men and women occupied the imperial throne in the eleven-hundred-year history of the Eastern Roman Empire.[20] Of these, a few, including the first Constantine, possessed true greatness, some were contemptible, and the vast majority was brave, upright, God-fearing men who did their best, with varying degrees of success. In Norwich's opinion, Gibbon's view ignores the deeply religious character of the Eastern Roman Empire, the many emperors who were renowned for their scholarship, the high literacy of its upper and middle classes, and the astonishing phenomenon and sublime creations of Byzantine art.

To these can be added other achievements. The great mechanical engineering feats of the Eastern Roman Empire seemed like magic to visitors from foreign lands, and the recipe for the incendiary weapon "Greek Fire" ensured the empire's survival for eight hundred years after its invention circa 672 AD. Greek Fire, which could burn even underwater, was a closely guarded state secret, lost to the West. No one can assess how great a blow Western culture sustained on that day when the *Queen of Cities* and Eastern

---

[18] Norwich, p. 449.

[19] Edward Gibbons, cited in W.E.H. Lecky, *A History of European Morals*, 1869.

[20] Norwich, p. 449, excluding the seven who usurped it during the Latin occupation.

Roman civilization fell, but it had to be immense. Certainly, any account of the fall of the Eastern Roman Empire must address painful political issues concerning the role played by Western Christianity in bringing down Christianity in the East, such as the bitterness between the Eastern and Western churches, the devastating Fourth Crusade on Eastern Rome, and the demands of the Council of Florence that split Constantinople into unionists and anti-unionists. Even more disastrously, the West did not send timely help, and significant numbers of Christians actively sided with Mehmet. Writing about Mehmet getting his fleet inside the Golden Horn, Barbaro states in a marginal comment, "It was a Christian who showed him what to do."[21] To this day the question of union continues to divide the two churches, and meetings are held annually to discuss Orthodox and Catholic unity.

Those who witnessed the events of that fateful day when Constantine fell record that he stepped hopelessly into the breach at the Gate of St. Romanus, never to be seen again. From there he passes into legend that says, in Arthurian fashion, that Constantine did not die. According to the legend, an angel turned him into marble and placed him in a cave near the Golden Gate, where he sleeps. It claims the immortal marble emperor will awaken one day and go forth to recover his empire from the Ottomans.

Though no one knows what Constantine looked like, everyone is agreed on his character. Nestor Iskander writes that Constantine was "a philanthropist and without malice."[22] Others record that he had courage and principles and was resolute. A deep sense of patriotism and responsibility for his Roman inheritance ran through him. He was direct and honest, not deceitful like some of his brothers, and he seems to have inspired deep loyalty in those who knew him. He was by all accounts a man of action, adept at the art of war.[23]

The nineteenth century Serbian statesman and historian, Chedomil Mijatovich, describes Constantine as kind and brave, a man who dedicated himself to his people with tireless devotion.[24] In all ways, Constantine XI Dragas Palaeologus proved himself an honorable and generous emperor, gallant and heroic to the end. Most historians do not doubt his integrity and courage. As they

---

[21] Barbaro, p. 37.

[22] Iskander, quoted in Crowley, p. 49.

[23] Crowley, p. 49.

[24] Mijatovich, p. 194.

and many contemporaries have noted, the last Emperor of the Romans did honor to the throne that he occupied and to the nation that he ruled.

As outlined earlier, the conflicting views of eyewitnesses and scholars, combined with the passage of time and destruction of documents that occurred during and after the fall of Constantinople, suggest that little about this great drama can be taken for granted. All historians can do is record such facts as are known and indicate the broad areas of speculation.[25]

Among the few undisputed facts are the following: As Mehmet was about to call his final retreat securing Constantine's victory, Justiniani/Giustiniani Longo sustained a mortal wound and demanded to be taken to his ship, and the emperor granted his request. This precipitated the flight of Justiniani's men and the fall of Constantinople. Most historians condemn Justiniani as a coward for fleeing the scene of battle. Mijatovich is more generous. He concludes that Justiniani is denied immortal renown for a moment of weakness brought on by pain and fatigue.[26]

The charge of cowardice, even in a weak moment, is hard to accept given Justiniani's incredible feats of valor throughout the fifty-eight days of siege. It is also incomprehensible. Not only is it out of character, but to reach his ship Justiniani had to endure a four-mile journey on horseback that took at least fifteen minutes riding at a gallop, an unimaginably agonizing endeavor in his condition when even a slight movement would cause intolerable pain. Far from cowardice, only an exceptionally courageous man would willingly submit to such an ordeal. The question is why? Why did he ask to leave when he knew the stakes? What demanded Justiniani's presence on the ship? Constantine also knew what could happen if he allowed Justiniani to leave. Why did he grant permission when so much was at stake?

Certainly, gratitude and indebtedness played a role in Constantine's decision. No one had done more to save the city than Justiniani, the hero of Constantinople. But for his efforts, Constantinople would have fallen far sooner. But this is nowhere near the full story.

Given the accounts of some chroniclers and historians that Justiniani escorted Zoe/Anna Notaras to his ship before the battle, only one explanation makes sense. That Justiniani asked and Constantine consented suggests some

---

[25] Norwich, p. 440.

[26] Mijatovich, p. 216.

extraordinary drama of tremendous urgency was at play involving the human heart. For them both, there was a higher purpose; some unfinished business of the highest order to attend aboard ship that demanded Justiniani's presence. This theory, pieced together from the historical record, cannot be proven given the great divide in time, but it is an explanation that makes sense of all the facts we have and is in keeping with Justiniani's character.

The death of Constantine XI on the walls of Constantinople marked the end of a fabled civilization that bore an uncanny resemblance to our own with its multi-ethnic society distinguished by religious tolerance and achievements in art, architecture, literature, science, technology, astronomy, medicine, and military prowess. In a reminder that history repeats itself, the issues that dominated Constantine's period nearly six hundred years ago are still issues today: women's rights, political and religious polarization, the Christian-Muslim conflict, and now, war in Europe and a divided nation standing at the point of the spear, defending freedom against the forces of autocratic rule.

Ultimately, however, it is lamentable how easily three centuries of warfare between East and West could have been entirely averted. Had Constantinople been victorious, Prince Orhan would have ascended the Ottoman throne. Given his life's experience, it is fair to say he would have been a bridge between East and West, a healer, and a tolerant ruler. There would have been no sieges of Rhodes or Malta, no invasion of Cyprus or Hungary, no battles for Vienna or Lepanto. Our modern world would have been a much kinder place. In the end, this is the true tragedy of the fall of Constantinople.

Sandra Worth
February 27, 2023

Reviews

Please consider sending in a review of this book.
It need not be more than a line or two!
If you enjoyed this book, sign up for Sandra's Newsletter and
get notified about her forthcoming novel
www.sandraworthauthor.com

ABOUT THE AUTHOR

Sandra Worth is the author of six historical novels on the Wars of the Roses chronicling the demise of the Plantagenets and rise of the Tudors, three with the Penguin Publishing Group U.S.A. She is internationally published and her books have won numerous awards. After a ten-year absence filled initially with research trips to Greece and Turkey and later with grave illness in the family, she is back with TOMORROW WE WILL KNOW, her seventh book and first foray into the Europe-Ottoman conflict, a work that took ten years to complete. Sandra holds an honors B.A. in Political Science and Economics from the University of Toronto. She is aware that her degree has little to do with historical fiction, but after a brief stint in finance, she embraced her childhood passion of writing with renewed dedication, because storytelling is so much more fun. For more information, visit sandraworthauthor.com

Made in the USA
Las Vegas, NV
08 April 2023

70360317R00217